"Ms. Hoffmann dishes up a luscious
entertainment spiced with tangy sensuality."
—*Romantic Times*

"Bobby Hutchinson creates
an in-depth story filled with excellent
subplots and outstanding characters."
—*Rendezvous*

Relive the romance...
Two complete novels
by two of your favorite authors!

KATE HOFFMANN

started reading romance when she was an
elementary school music teacher. She started
writing romance when she was an advertising
copywriter. And in 1993, the year her first
Temptation novel was published, she quit
the nine-to-five world and became a full-time
romance writer. Since then, Kate has penned
more than thirty stories for Harlequin, including
writing for Temptation, Duets, continuity series
and anthologies. Her first single-title release,
Reunited, was published in 2002. She lives in
Wisconsin with her three cats and her computer.
When she's not writing, she enjoys gardening,
golfing and genealogy.

BOBBY HUTCHINSON

is a multitalented woman who was born in a
small town in the interior of British Columbia.
Though she is now the successful author of more
than thirty-five novels, her past includes stints
as a retailer, a seamstress and a day-care worker.
Twice married, she now lives alone and is the
devoted mother of three and grandmother of four.
She runs, swims, does yoga, meditates and likes
this quote by Dolly Parton: "Decide who you are,
and then do it on purpose."

KATE HOFFMANN

Where the Nights Are Long

BOBBY HUTCHINSON

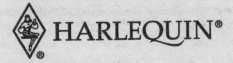 **HARLEQUIN®**

TORONTO • NEW YORK • LONDON
AMSTERDAM • PARIS • SYDNEY • HAMBURG
STOCKHOLM • ATHENS • TOKYO • MILAN • MADRID
PRAGUE • WARSAW • BUDAPEST • AUCKLAND

HARLEQUIN BOOKS

by Request—WHERE THE NIGHTS ARE LONG

Copyright © 2003 by Harlequin Books S.A.

ISBN 0-373-23007-9

The publisher acknowledges the copyright holders of the original works as follows:
DODGING CUPID'S ARROW
Copyright © 1998 by Peggy Hoffmann
NORTHERN KNIGHTS
Copyright © 1987 by Bobby Hutchinson

This edition published by arrangement with Harlequin Books S.A.

Visit us at www.eHarlequin.com

Printed in U.S.A.

CONTENTS

DODGING CUPID'S ARROW

Kate Hoffmann

Prologue

Five years ago

JOE BRENNAN HELD his breath as the rough plank door swung open, its hinges groaning in protest. If the interior of Bachelor Creek Lodge looked anything like the exterior, he vowed he would turn around and head right back to Seattle.

"I should have my head examined," he murmured to himself, his gaze scanning the dilapidated log building. He sidestepped a rotted board on the porch, then squinted into a dust-coated window. A shaft of light illuminated the interior and his gaze followed it up to a huge hole in the roof.

"Look at this," Hawk said, pointing to the log lintel above the front door. Joe and Tanner glanced up. No Wimin Kin Pass was crudely carved into the wood.

"I'm not sure there's a woman on this planet who would willingly set foot inside this place," Joe said.

He never should have let Tanner O'Neill talk him into this harebrained scheme. He and the third in their trio, Kyle Hawkins, had left everything behind—their careers, their homes...fcmales—to move to the wilds of Alaska and start a business.

Tanner's inheritance looked good on paper. A wilderness lodge a mile from the tiny bush town of Muleshoe, land right on the Yukon River with their very own creek running just outside the back door. But the photos didn't do justice to the wreck of a lodge. Had they been more accurate, Joe might have opted to stay home.

In Seattle, he'd had a good job, a partnership in a small law firm with a generous salary. A few weekends a month, he would fly for the Army Reserve, putting a long-held pilot's license to use. He filled the rest of his life with sports and women, two of his favorite pastimes. Life was good and he had been happy.

He knew he'd be giving up more than he could even imagine to move to Alaska. But the plan had been too tempting to resist. Tanner would run the lodge, or what was left of it, and Hawk would serve as a wilderness guide for their clients, once they had them. And Joe would pilot their plane, a De Havilland Otter that the three of them had bought on a shoestring budget. He would ferry clients and supplies from Fairbanks to Muleshoe, landing on the tiny airstrip as he and Hawk and Tanner had done just minutes before.

"Don't be too quick to judge," Tanner warned as he stepped through the door. "Try to think of the potential."

Joe turned to give Hawk a dubious look. "With all this potential, I think we're going to need to buy a bigger plane. Something that might carry a bulldozer." His friend's expression was unreadable but Joe suspected he was harboring some of the same concerns. If the lodge's exterior was any clue, the interior was probably uninhabitable, which left the three of them essentially homeless. Until Tanner's carpentry skills could be proved, they might as well pitch a tent. "Let's see how bad it is," he muttered, crossing the threshold.

Dust motes drifted in the shaft of sunlight that streamed through the hole in the roof. A ragged collection of hand-hewn furniture lay scattered around the room, bits of stuffing littering the floor. A huge moose head stared down at them from above the stone fireplace, as if mocking their high expectations.

"It's not so bad," Tanner said, slowly taking in the disrepair. "Once the roof is patched and we've cleaned up a bit, it will be just fine."

"Fine for raccoons and other wildlife," Joe replied. "We've barely got a roof over our head, O'Neill. And you forget that the nights here are a lot colder than in Seattle."

"Come on, Brennan, where's your sense of adventure?" Tanner teased. "So we'll be roughing it for a while. Suck it up and be a man."

Joe shook his head. "I guess I can always sleep in the cabin of the Otter."

"Or under the stars," Hawk said, distracted by his survey of the hearth. He looked up into the chimney. "Squirrels," was his only comment.

Joe considered his friend's suggestion. For Hawk, sleeping in the wild was no great hardship. In fact, Joe suspected his friend would revel in the rustic living conditions. Hawk would no longer have to leave home to get a wilderness fix as he had done in Seattle, sometimes disappearing for two or three weeks without a word. His buddy was always up for an adventure, the more challenging and spontaneous, the better.

Tanner finished his survey of the interior, then looked at his friends. "I know this isn't what you expected," he said. "And I guess if either of you wants to bail, now's the time to say so." He paused, then hitched his hands on his waist. "But before you make your decision, I want you to know that I'm determined to make this work—with or without you."

Silence hung in the dusty air for a long moment. Then Hawk shrugged. "I'm still in," he said. He looked at Joe and the challenge was evident in his gaze. A good buddy would stick it out, and the three of them were the best of buddies. And at this point, there wasn't much left for Joe in Seattle besides a handful of disappointed women and a storage locker full of his belongings.

Joe raked his fingers through his hair. What the hell was he doing? One look at the tiny bush town of Muleshoe was enough to see that there wasn't much social life in the outback of Alaska. It wasn't as if he couldn't live without women, but he did have certain needs.

"What'll it be, Brennan? In or out?"

Joe turned to Tanner. "I can see us fifty years from now. Three toothless old bachelors reminiscing about the good old days in Seattle. Remembering the last time we laid eyes on a beautiful woman."

"There are beautiful women in Alaska," Tanner said. "They're just spread out over a bigger geographical area. You have to go find 'em."

Joe took a final glance around the lodge, then winced. "I swear I must be crazy. But if you guys are staying, then so am I."

Tanner clapped his hand on Joe's back and laughed. "I knew you couldn't resist. In all the time I've known you, you've never backed away from a challenge."

"This is one time I really wish I was more of a wimp," Joe said, shaking his head. He held out his hand. Tanner placed his palm over it, then Hawk did the same.

"To the boys of Bachelor Creek Lodge," Tanner said.

"Bachelor Creek," Hawk repeated.

"I think we've all gone crazy," Joe said, wondering

why he was always drawn into impossible situations. He suspected it was a character flaw, though he wasn't really sure. But stuck in the Alaskan wilderness, facing a future full of challenges, he knew it wouldn't take long to find out.

1

"ONE OF THESE DAYS, I really should have my head examined."

Joe leaned forward and scraped at the frost-coated windshield of his Super Cub. His gaze caught the air temperature gauge, a nagging reminder of an ever present danger. The outside temperature was forty degrees below zero and his defroster had reached its limit. If he flew much higher, he'd be flying blind. Or the engine would quit from the cold and he wouldn't be flying at all.

He peered through the windshield at the craggy ridges below, so sheer not even snow clung to the rock. Denali. "The High One," as the native Athabascans had named it. Mount McKinley was the highest peak in North America and a magnet for climbers worldwide. And buzzing back and forth between Talkeetna and the mountain were the Denali fliers, those pilots who ferried climbers and gear to "Kahiltna International," the name given to the glacier at the bottom of the climbing route.

Since Joe had arrived in Alaska five years before, he'd heard tale after tale of their exploits—risky landings and daring rescues, true artists behind the controls of their airplanes. He'd grudgingly admired them, until he'd been accepted into the fold. After that, he'd held them in even greater awe.

His initiation had been achieved more by default than daring. He'd been flying a client over "the Hill" on a sight-seeing trip when he'd noticed a spot of color near the edge of the Kahiltna Glacier near Denali's base. He dropped low then circled, his curiosity piqued. What he found had sent a chill through his blood. A Cessna, flipped upside down, the white belly of the plane barely visible against the snow. If he hadn't been looking in that exact spot, he would have missed it, along with countless other pilots flying in the area.

With the approval of his adventure-hungry passenger, he put his own plane down near the crash site, then struggled through the crusty snow to the overturned plane. The two of them had dragged three injured passengers and the unconscious pilot from the Cessna. And later, when more help had been summoned and all had been evacuated to the hospital in Anchorage, he'd been credited with saving the life of one of Denali's favorite fliers, Skip Christiansen, and given honorary membership in the elite fraternity. They'd nicknamed him Eagle Eyes Brennan.

Skip had talked him into this current mess—searching for a stranded Swedish climber who'd attempted a solo winter ascent of Denali. Skip had flown the woman in a week before and now had been charged with coordinating an air search to aid the park rangers. Six planes swept along the climbing route, each one required to descend out of the thinner air for a time after each run for safety's sake.

Had Joe been safe at home in Muleshoe rather than hanging out in a Talkeetna watering hole, trying to charm a beautiful girl into spending the evening with him, he would never have been drawn into the search, flying too high, too cold, breathing bottled oxygen every now and then to keep his head clear.

But Joe Brennan was never one to shrink from a challenge. And flying at the far edge of his talents and near the mechanical limitations of his plane was exactly the adrenaline rush he'd come to crave. Still, that didn't mean that he couldn't question his good sense once he was caught up in another risky venture.

"All right, Brennan," he muttered to himself. "Let's reevaluate your escape plan."

Although Joe was considered a gutsy flyer by his Denali pals, he tempered that characteristic with a good dose of self-preservation. No matter where he flew, over ice or rock, forest or mountain, he always had a contingency plan, a way out if oil pressure dropped or his engine failed.

He spotted a small saddle of clear snow to the north and fixed it in his mind. If worse came to worse, he could put the Cub down there, landing uphill to slow the plane, then turning around to take off downhill. An air current, swirling near the sheer rock face, buffeted the Cub and Joe cursed.

"A solo ascent in the middle of an Alaskan winter," he muttered. "Now, there's a great idea, lady. Why not just jump into a crevasse and get it over with?"

The truth be told, he couldn't begrudge the climber her passion for a new challenge. Since he'd started flying in the bush, he'd accepted one dangerous job after another, always cognizant of his limitations but never afraid to push a little harder. He'd landed on glaciers and sandbars, lakes and landing strips in all conditions, in weather not fit for flying. And he'd loved it all.

He scratched another patch of ice off the windshield. "Come on, sweetheart. Show me where you are. Point the way." He pushed his sunglasses up on his head and scanned the area. Though he was slightly west of the usual route to the summit, he knew that a climber could easily become confused from the altitude or exhaustion.

One misstep was all it took and hypoxia would take over, dulling the senses until frostbite and hypothermia set in. Without a partner to take up the slack, a solo ascent was a ticket to trouble. Before long, a climber would sit down in the snow, unable to move, unable to think. That's when either death or the Denali fliers moved in, snatching half-frozen climbers off the face of the mountain and bringing them back to safety.

Wispy clouds surrounded the plane for a moment and Joe scratched the ice off his side window. "I don't need weather," he muttered at the approaching cloud bank. He dropped lower, beneath the cloud level, heading back down the mountain. The head of the Kahiltna Glacier passed below him now, safe landing and breathable air at eleven thousand feet. Suddenly, a flash of color glittered from an ice face in front of him. He stared at the spot lower on the glacier, squinting to make out a bright blue scrap of nylon.

As he descended on the glacier, the patch of blue became a pack, half-buried in the snow. He looked closer and thought he saw a rope tracing a path into the shadow of a deep crevasse.

Joe snatched up his radio. "Denali Rescue, this is Piper three-six-three-nine Delta Tango. I think I have her. She's well west of the usual route on the lower part of the glacier. It looks like she fell into a crevasse. She was roped, but I don't see her. Over."

The radio crackled and he recognized Skip's voice. "Three-nine Delta, this is seven-four Foxtrot. Good eyes! I'm just off your left wing. I'll go down and search until Park Rescue arrives. Over."

"I found her, Skip, I'm going down."

"Buddy, that's a tricky landing. You catch a ski and you're done, never mind negotiating those crevasses. I took her in, I'll get her out."

"You just back me up. I'm heading down. Three-nine Delta, out."

Joe banked to the east, drawing a lazy circle around the stranded climber. Time after time, he passed over the ice field, flying from bottom to top as he judged the surface, memorizing every bump and hole in the ice. His pulse pounded in his head as he descended, his eyes fixed on a point above him on the mountain. An instant later, he felt the skis shudder and he cut the power. Slowly, the plane climbed the face of the glacier until it would go no further. Then he maneuvered it around until it faced down the slope, ready to take off in the same tracks he'd landed in.

Not two hundred feet below him, he saw the rope. Joe yanked the flap on his hood over his face and adjusted his sunglasses, then pushed against the door with his shoulder. He wasn't sure what he would find, but he hoped for the best.

He grabbed a canister of oxygen that he kept in the plane for high altitude flying, then struggled through the snow, following the rope until the snow disappeared in front of him. Above him, he could hear the drone of Skip's engine as he circled, looking for his own spot to land. He tugged on the rope. "Hey, can you hear me?"

A weak shout came back at him. "Oh, God. I thought I heard a plane. I'm tangled in my ropes. You'll have to pull me out."

Joe sat in the snow and dug his heels into the icy surface, then grabbed the rope and began to haul the
climber up over the edge. To his relief, she wasn't a
large woman and she had enough strength to help him
along. Finally, her parka hood appeared in the snow in
front of him.

By the time he reached her, she'd collapsed. Placing
the mask over her frostbitten face, he ordered her to
breathe. Then he pushed her goggles up on her forehead and watched as her eyes fluttered open. A weak
smile curled the corners of her lips. "Are you real?" she
croaked.

Joe gave the woman his most charming smile, but it
was hidden behind the flap of his down jacket. Even
her frostbitten cheeks and nose didn't obliterate her
pretty face. "Yeah, I'm real. And you're lucky to be
alive."

"I didn't think I'd ever get out of that crevasse," she
murmured with her lilting accent. "I spent the night
there just barely hanging on."

"Can you stand?"

She nodded and he helped her to her feet, holding
the oxygen mask over her face. Wrapping her arm
around his shoulders, he pulled her toward the plane.

"I owe you my life," she said, gasping for breath as
she placed one foot in front of the other.

Joe smiled inwardly, his mind anticipating the reaction he'd get back at the lodge. Both Hawk and Tanner
had marveled at his particular talent with women. To
the amazement of both of his buddies, he always managed to find himself in the company of the most beautiful women Alaska had to offer. And now he'd done it
again, finding a beautiful blonde in a crevasse on the
Kahiltna Glacier.

"No problem," he said. "It's my mission in life to rescue damsels in distress."

She stopped to draw a few deep breaths then looked up at him. "I don't know how I can ever repay you."

Joe grinned. He was a lucky man, in more ways than one. "How about dinner? I mean, after you've had a chance to thaw out. I know this nice little place in Talkeetna that serves great pasta."

PERRIE KINCAID PULLED the collar of her jacket up around her neck and cursed at the cold, unrelenting drizzle. Her eyes scanned the dark street from her spot in the shadow of a deserted building, then came back to the black Mercedes parked next to the loading dock. A bare lightbulb swung slowly in the salt-tanged breeze, sending an eerie wavering light over the battered steel door of the abandoned brick warehouse.

Inside the car, the glow of a cigarette illuminated the profile of the driver. Mad Dog Scanlon. She'd been following Mad Dog's boss so long, Perrie felt as if she and the goon were old friends. She squinted at her watch, then drew a deep breath and cursed again. "Come on, what's taking them so long? It's a simple deal, in and out. All I need is a good look at their faces, just confirmation, and then this story is front-page news."

The smell of salt water surrounded her, drifting inland from the sound with the constant damp that seemed to hang over the city of Seattle in the wintertime. She shifted on her feet and rubbed her hands together, trying to warm her icy fingers. If she had to wait much longer, she might just start to mildew, right along with everything else in this seedy neighborhood.

She should be used to the weather by now. Seattle had been her home ever since she'd left grad school ten years ago. She'd come west, from the University of Chicago, to take a job at the *Seattle Star*. At first she had written obituaries, then moved up to a job in the Lifestyles section. She'd almost been stuck writing fluff for the rest of her career, when the city desk put out a call for a staff writer.

Perrie had begged Milt Freeman, the city editor, to take her on, to give her a chance with hard news, even though she'd been writing gardening and cooking articles for the previous three years. After a week of constant appeals and a case of his favorite scotch, he had finally relented and offered her the job.

Milt had told her afterward that he'd been worn down by her tenacity—not the scotch—the same tenacity that she'd used to become the *Star*'s top investigative reporter. The same stubborn determination she was drawing on this very minute. A good reporter would long for a hot bath and a warm bed right about now. But Perrie considered herself a great reporter, and she was exactly where she wanted to be. Right in the thick of things.

Perrie Kincaid's byline was hot. She had broken four major stories in Seattle in the past two years, and three of them had been picked up by the national wire services. Her peers in the broadcast industry were in awe of her, unable to snatch even the smallest scoops from under her perceptive gaze. And drizzle or none, she was going to break this story, too.

The seemingly abandoned warehouse was actually the nerve center of a major smuggling ring that dealt in stolen luxury autos, cars that had probably been parked in front of one of Seattle's trendy restaurants just hours before. Once stolen, they were loaded into containers and shipped to the Far East, where they were traded for uncut heroin, which was then loaded on the boat for the return trip to Seattle.

The smuggling ring was only a small part of the story. There had been blackmail and attempted murder. But the part that would nab her the Pulitzer was the trail that led right to the floor of the U.S. Congress, to the dishonorable congressman from the great state of Washington, Evan T. Dearborn.

Somewhere inside the warehouse, Dearborn's chief of staff was meeting with Mad Dog's boss, the man in charge of this little operation, Seattle businessman and resident sleazeball, Tony Riordan. For ten years, Riordan had been living on the edge of the law, always involved in something illegal but careful enough not to get caught—and using the profits from his "business" dealings to buy a politician or two. He'd snagged a big one when he'd snagged Dearborn.

Well, Riordan was about to go down, and he was going to take a whole host of his slimy friends with him, including the congressman. The police had been on Riordan's tail for almost as long as Perrie had. Perrie reached into her pocket and fingered her cell phone. Sooner or later she'd have to call in the cops. But not until she had the final piece of the puzzle, hard evidence that would link the congressman's office to Tony Riordan. And not until her story was in black and white for all to see.

The sound of a car door opening brought her attention back to the Mercedes and she watched as Mad Dog stepped out of the car. With nervous hands, she reached for the camera that was slung over her shoulder, praying the shutter hadn't rusted tight in the two hours she'd been standing in the rain. She pulled off the lens cover, then held the camera up to her eye and focused the telephoto lens on the doorway.

A moment later two figures emerged, flanked by a pair of Tony's hulking bodyguards. Perrie smiled to herself as she recognized Tony and the congressman's chief of staff in the viewfinder. Calmly, she refocused and slid her finger to the shutter. But just as she was about to snap her first photo, the sound of a ringing cell phone fractured the quiet of the night.

Startled, Perrie looked over the top of the camera, wondering who would be calling Riordan at two in the morning. But as the phone rang again, she realized that the group on the loading dock was looking in *her* direction. The sound was coming from her coat pocket! In a flash, the two goons on the dock pulled guns and all hell broke loose.

Perrie dropped the camera and fumbled for her cell phone just as the first shot whizzed past her head and careened off the building behind her. She slid deeper into the shadows and flipped open the phone, wincing as another bullet hissed a little too close.

"Perrin? Perrin, is that you?"

Perrie groaned at the sound of her mother's voice. "Mom, I can't talk right now. I'll call you back." She ducked her head as another shot hit the brick wall above her.

"Perrie, this will just take a minute."

"Mom, it's two in the morning!"

"Honey, I know you don't sleep soundly and I figured you were up anyway. I just wanted to let you know that Mrs. Wilke's son is coming home for a visit. He's a dentist, you know, and a bachelor. I think it would be nice if—Perrin? Is that a gunshot I heard?"

Perrie cursed out loud, then slowly worked her way

along the base of the wall. "Mother, I really can't talk now! I'll call you back in a few minutes." She flipped off the phone, then dialed 911, her fingers trembling.

When the operator answered, she quickly gave her name and her location. From where she sat, huddled in the dark, it sounded as if she were in the middle of a war zone. The gunfire was coming from two directions now, and she seemed to be caught right in the line of fire.

Were the cops already on the scene? Or was there another piece to this puzzle she didn't know about? She slid over and risked a look at the melee across the street. Riordan's men were still shooting at her, but someone else was shooting at them. Her missing puzzle piece was heavily armed with semiautomatic weapons, that much she could tell.

"Ma'am, please stay on the line. Is the shooting still going on?"

"Yes, it's still going on!" Perrie shouted. "Can't you hear it?" She held the phone out, giving the operator a taste of her predicament.

"Just remain calm, ma'am."

"I've got to get my camera," she said, realizing it was the first calm and rational thought she'd had since the shooting started.

"Ma'am, stay right where you are. We'll have a car there in about two minutes."

"I need my camera." Perrie slid along the base of the building, back the way she'd come, her eyes fixed on the camera lying near a puddle of water on the rain-slicked pavement. Stretching her arm out, she reached for the strap just inches away from her fingertips. Another gunshot whizzed by and she could almost feel its heat through her jacket sleeve. She winced, then made one desperate lunge for the camera strap.

Her fingers closed around it and she dragged it and herself back to the safety of the shadows. "A picture is worth a thousand words," she muttered as she wiped off the wet lens with her jacket cuff. "Not a thousand of *my* words. A picture would only be worth about a hundred of my words." Her gaze fixed on a dark patch on her sleeve and she sighed as she tried to brush the mud away.

But it wasn't mud on her sleeve. The touch of her own fingers sent a shard of pain up her arm and she blinked in surprise. "Oh, damn," she murmured, rubbing the sticky blood between her fingers. "I've been shot."

A smile curled the corners of her mouth and she giggled to herself, half out of shock and half out of disbelief. "I've been shot." She picked up the cell phone. "I've been shot," she repeated to the emergency operator.

"Ma'am, you say you've been shot?"

"I've always wondered what it would feel like," Perrie explained. "A bullet piercing your own skin. Would it feel hot or cold? Would you know it happened right away or would it take a while?" She closed her eyes and fought back a wave of lightheadedness.

"Ma'am, please don't move. We'll have a car there in thirty seconds. And an ambulance is on the way. Can you tell me where you've been shot? Please, ma'am, stay right where you are."

"I'm not going anywhere," Perrie said as she tipped her head back to rest on the rough brick wall. The rain spattered on her face and she welcomed the cold. It was the only thing that seemed real about this whole incident. "Wild horses couldn't drag me away from this story now," she murmured as the wail of sirens echoed in the distance.

The next half hour passed in a blur of flashing red lights and frantic paramedics. They had hustled her inside an ambulance and bandaged her arm, but she'd refused to be transported to the hospital, choosing instead to watch the scene unfold in the rainy night in front of the warehouse, questioning the detectives who collected the evidence of the shootout.

"Perrie!"

She glanced over her shoulder once to see Milt Freeman approaching, his expression filled with fury. Ignoring his summons, she turned back to the detective and continued her own interrogation.

"Damn it, Kincaid, what the hell happened here?"

"I'm sure you know all about it by now," Perrie called.

The detective looked up as Milt grabbed her arm. She winced in pain and Milt frowned. "Get her to the hospital," the detective advised. "And get her out of my hair. She took a bullet in the arm."

"What?" Milt boomed.

"I'm fine," Perrie insisted, her attention on the detective. "Why don't you let me get a peek at that wallet?"

The detective gave Milt an exasperated look, then walked away, shaking his head.

"This is it," Milt said, drawing her along toward the ambulance. "Two weeks ago, they tampered with the brakes on your car. Last week, they broke into your apartment. And now you're dodging bullets in the middle of a wise-guy war. I want you out of Seattle. Tonight."

"Yeah, right. Where am I going to go?" Perrie asked.

"Alaska," Milt said, pushing her down to sit on the wide bumper of the ambulance.

"Alaska?" Perrie gasped. "I'm not going to Alaska."

"You're going," Milt countered. "And I don't want you to give me any grief about it. You were shot tonight and you're acting like it was just another day at the office."

"It was only a flesh wound," she grumbled, glancing at the bandage around her arm. "The bullet just grazed me." She grinned at her boss. He was not nearly as amused as she was. "Milt, I can't believe I just said that. This is like those guys that used to cover combat zones in Vietnam. I feel like I've finally earned my stripes. I'm not some wimpy Lifestyles writer anymore. I've actually been wounded in the line of duty."

Milt crossed his arms over his chest and leaned back against the rear door of the ambulance, sending Perrie a disapproving glare. "I've called an old friend of mine up in a little town called Muleshoe. Joe Brennan is his name. He runs an air charter service. I go fishing up there in the summer and he always flies me in and out. He owes me a few favors."

Perrie ignored his story and concentrated on her own. Milt was a little upset right now. He'd get over it. "The way I see it, we should run the story now. As far as I'm concerned, we've got all the confirmation we need. So I didn't get a picture. I saw Dearborn's chief of staff there with Riordan. That's the connection."

Milt cursed softly. "All I see here is two dead wise guys and no sign of either Dearborn or Riordan. You've got a big empty hole where you thought you had a solid story."

"I do have a story!" Perrie protested. "And it's here, not in Alaska."

Milt Freeman leveled his gaze on hers. "You're acting like Alaska is Siberia. It *is* one of the fifty states, you
know."

"Yeah, but it used to be Siberia," she shot back. "Before we bought it from the Russians. I'm so close on
this story, Milt, I can smell the ink already. I just need a
few more pieces of the puzzle and we can run with it."

"What you have right now, Perrin Kincaid, is a price
on your head. Someone knows you're onto this story
and they're not about to let you write it."

Perrie stood. "I've got to get back to the office."

"You're going to the hospital and then you're going
to Alaska."

"My files are back at the office. I've got work to do."

"You can turn all your files over to me," Milt said.
"And I'll give them to the police."

"You'll do no such thing!"

"And I sent Ginny over to your house to pack some
clothes for you. After the doctors check you out, I'm
taking you to the airport."

"I'm not going to Alaska," she repeated.

"Whoever shot you tonight will be looking for a second chance. And I've spent too much time turning you
from a Lifestyles hack into a decent reporter to have
you end up dead. You're going to Alaska, Kincaid."

She shook her head stubbornly. "No, I'm not. I'm
staying right here and I'm going to break this story.
Now, what do you think about—"

"The police are going to break this story," he interrupted. "After they figure out who shot you, you can
come back and write it." He reached into his jacket
pocket and held out an envelope. "I had a feeling
something like this was going to happen. There's an
airline ticket to Fairbanks in there. Joe Brennan will fly

you into Muleshoe. I've got a nice safe, cozy cabin for you there. No phones, no bullets, no wise guys. Just peace and quiet. I even asked Joe to stock it with popcorn since you seem to think it's a fair substitute for all of the major food groups. I want you somewhere safe until things cool down around here."

She snatched her notepad from the back pocket of her jeans, wincing as a pain shot down to her fingers, then scribbled an errant thought about the evening's events. "I'm not going, Milt," she said, flipping through her notes. "I have work to do. I won't just sit around all day long waiting for you to call me back here. I can't."

"That's why I've got you a story to cover," he continued. "And this is not a request, Ace—this is an order from your boss."

Perrie glanced up at him and laughed harshly. Milt rarely pulled rank on her. They were more a team than boss and employee. "Oh, yeah, right. What kind of story? Underworld kingpins set up shop in Mulesfoot, Alaska? I don't think so."

"Just last week, three young women from Seattle left their homes and their jobs and traveled to Muleshoe to become mail-order brides. They answered an ad in our paper. I heard your old boss in Lifestyles talking about it. She was planning to send a reporter up to cover their story. I convinced her we should send you."

"What?" Indignant, Perrie jumped up and paced back and forth in front of her boss. "You're sending me back to Lifestyles? God, Milt, I hate writing that dreck." She cursed a blue streak, then shook her head stubbornly. "I'm not going. You can fire me if you want, but I'm staying here to write this story."

Milt leaned closer, fixing Perrie with an intractable

gaze. "You're going to Muleshoe, Perrin Kincaid. You're going to rest and recover from your wound and I will call you when it's safe to come back. This story will still be here, I promise."

"I'm not going," Perrie repeated. "I'm not. And you can't make me."

2

JOE BRENNAN STOOD silently in the waiting area and watched as a line of travelers straggled through the jetway and into the airport. He glanced again at the board, just to make sure he was in the right place, then held the sign up a little higher. He'd written the name Mr. Perry Kincaid on the back of a battered fuel bill that he had yet to pay, but so far, no one had claimed the name.

Maybe the guy had missed his plane. Or maybe Milt Freeman had decided that whatever trouble his reporter was in, it could be best handled in Seattle. All Joe knew was that he owed Milt a few favors and Milt had finally called one in. Though he couldn't show Perry Kincaid much fun in the dead of an Alaskan winter, Hawk might be able to take him ice fishing.

He scanned the waiting area again and his gaze stopped on a young woman who was in the midst of a heated argument with the desk attendant. She wore a short leather jacket and jeans that hugged her backside perfectly. Her auburn hair had been piled haphazardly on top of her head, twisted into an off-center knot that seemed in jeopardy of slipping over her left ear. A bright yellow pencil jutted out of the knot and he watched as she shoved a pen in next to it.

Joe had learned to appreciate a good-looking woman when he could—whether half-frozen on Denali or in

the midst of an argument in the airport. Muleshoe—
and most of Alaska's bush country—was populated
mainly by men, men who fished and hunted and
searched for gold, or men who provided goods and
services to those trying to eke out a living in the Alaskan bush. Muleshoe was not the kind of town that
women found attractive—unless, of course, they were
looking to get married.

Just last week, he'd flown in three women who had
answered an ad in the *Seattle Star*. A group of single
men in Muleshoe had decided that they'd never get
wives unless the women knew they were looking, so
they pooled their money and bought the ad. Erv Saunders asked Joe if he wanted in. For forty dollars, Joe
could buy a chance to read through the letters, study
the photos and pick himself a potential bride.

But Joe had taken a pass. A woman—especially a
desperate woman bent on marriage—would only com-
plicate his life. Besides, in order to get married, a guy
would have to fall in love, and Joe Brennan had never
been in love in his life. For now, he was more than satisfied with an occasional affair, no strings attached.

He studied the woman at the desk, pushing his sunglasses down and the brim of his baseball cap up to get
a better look. His mind slowly formed an image of her
face. But then, before the picture had completely ma-
terialized, she spun around suddenly. The image evaporated, replaced by one more lovely than he'd even anticipated. He fought back a purely instinctive jolt of
desire, an unbidden and electric attraction, then
shoved his sunglasses back up on his nose. He forced
his gaze to fix somewhere over her right shoulder.

Lord, she was pretty, he thought as he risked another glance. Her auburn hair framed delicate fea-

tures—wide eyes, a perfect nose, a lush mouth. He found his eyes drawn back to stare, against his will, and to his surprise, he found her staring back.

She narrowed her eyes and a defiant expression settled on her features. Squaring her shoulders, she started across the distance that separated them. Joe glanced to either side to make sure he hadn't misunderstood the object of her attention. No, she was definitely headed in his direction.

She stopped in front of him, gave him the once-over, then sighed. "All right, here I am," she snapped. "Now what are you supposed to do with me?"

Joe blinked, then slowly lowered the sign he held. "I beg your pardon?"

"You're Brennan, right?" She shifted the bag on her shoulder, then thrust out her hand. He hesitantly took it, holding her slender fingers against his palm. Another jolt of electricity, this time skittering up his arm. "I'm Perrie Kincaid."

He frowned, then shook his head. "You're Perry Kincaid? You're a woman."

She arched an eyebrow and regarded him coolly. "You've definitely been living in Siberia too long."

"I was expecting a man. Perry is a man's name. Like Perry Como. And Milt lead me to believe—"

"It's *i-e*, not *y*," she countered. "And you're not exactly what I expected, either."

His mouth quirked in amusement. Gee, she was a snotty little thing, all full of spit and vinegar. "And what did you expect?"

"Well, being an open-minded feminist, I should have expected Josephine Brennan. But to tell the truth, I expected some potbellied guy with fishing lures stuck in his hat and a cigar butt clenched in his teeth."

"Sorry to disappoint you, Miss Kincaid."

"It's Perrie. Or Kincaid. You can drop the Miss. Makes me sound like a damn debutante." Perrie shook her head and began to pace in front of him. "You know, I should have suspected he'd try something like this. First he confiscates my cell phone. Then he steals my wallet. I don't have a credit card to my name, all my cash is gone. I should have known there was something fishy when he offered to watch my stuff while I went to get a cup of coffee. Then he wouldn't leave the damn airport until my plane left the ground. I tried to get off twice and he was standing there blocking the door of the jetway. Then he tricks you into flying me into some frozen tundra town...Donkeyfoot or Mule-foot or whatever it's called." She smiled and patted the side of her shoulder bag. "But I got him back because I took all my files with me. He's got the key to my desk, but I took the evidence. He's got nothing to give the cops." She stopped, met his gaze and drew a deep breath. "So, what's it going to take, Brennan?"

She talked faster than anyone he'd ever met and it took him a moment to realize that she'd finished. "Take? I don't understand."

She rolled her eyes in exasperation. "Everyone has a price. What's yours? I'll pay you to fly me back to Seattle. Whatever your regular price is, I'll double it. I can't pay you up front, but as soon as we get back I'll pay you in cash. I've got important business back there and I can't waste another minute in igloo country."

Milt had warned him that Perrie Kincaid would try to talk him into taking him back...or her. Damn, this was all he needed! Milt knew exactly how he'd react to the prospect of baby-sitting some hyperactive, run-at-the-mouth woman reporter, especially one with such an attitude. He would have refused, flatly and quickly. But now that she was here, he was stuck with her.

"Do you have luggage?" he asked.

She took his question for acquiescence and smiled in satisfaction. "It will only take a minute for me to pick it up. So, how long will it take to get back to Seattle?"

"Depends on the weather," he replied as he reached for her shoulder bag.

She pulled away from him. "I can carry my own bag, Brennan."

"Suit yourself...Kincaid."

"So...what? Four, five hours?"

"I said, it depends on the weather. There's weather coming in and we're going to have to move if we expect to beat it."

She automatically picked up her pace but he barely had to lengthen his stride to keep up. As they hurried down the concourse, he gave her a sideways glance. For all her beauty, Perrie Kincaid was the most prickly woman he'd ever met.

"I hope you brought something warmer to wear," he commented.

"Why?"

He shrugged. "It can get a little cold in my plane."

"Where is this plane of yours?"

"It's parked at a hangar on the other side of the airport. I've got a truck and we'll drive over as soon as we have your bag. Hopefully we'll get clearance to take off."

"Do we have to ask for clearance, Brennan? Why can't we just go?"

"If the tower advises me to stay on the ground, I stay on the ground. I don't know about you, Kincaid, but I happen to value my life—and my plane."

"Just because I managed to get myself shot does not mean I have a death wish, Brennan. Jeez, Milt is such a worrywart. What else did he tell you? Did he tell you that I was supposed to rest all day and take it easy? Three minutes in some backwoods cabin and I'll be crawling the walls."

Joe stared down at her as they walked, more baffled by this woman with every step. "Milt didn't tell me you'd been shot."

An impatient scowl marred her pretty features. "It was just a small flesh wound. It hardly hurts at all. But Milt seems to think if I stay in Seattle, something more serious is going to happen."

"Milt is probably right."

She stopped cold and groaned, throwing down her bag and planting her hands on her slender waist. "Don't you start on me now, Brennan. I am perfectly capable of taking care of myself. I don't need Milt or you or anyone else telling me how to live my life."

Cursing beneath his breath, Joe grabbed her arm with one hand and her bag with the other and dragged her along with him. "I was simply stating an opinion, Kincaid." She didn't seem like a "Miss" Kincaid to him anymore. And calling her Perrie felt entirely too personal.

"I'm not interested in your opinions," she muttered. "I just want to get home."

She picked up her pace, yanking her arm from his grasp. He took a moment to admire her backside again, the cute wiggle of her hips as she strode down the concourse. He grinned when she stopped and looked back at him impatiently.

"What's the problem?"

He caught up to her. "I don't know why you're so anxious to get home. Milt says you're in danger."

"My boss can be a bit melodramatic."

"Hey, I've got a lot of respect for Milt Freeman. He's a good guy. You should be happy someone like him is looking out for you."

She didn't have a comeback for that. Instead, she sent him an obstinate glare and refused to say another word until they'd recovered her bag and headed for the doors. When they stepped outside, a wickedly cold wind slapped them both in the face and snow swirled around their feet.

"Jeez," she hissed, her teeth chattering. "Is it always so blasted cold here?"

Joe glanced up at the late afternoon sky. The weather was moving in faster than he'd expected. If they didn't get off the ground quickly, he'd be spending the rest of the day and probably a major portion of his evening with Perrie Kincaid. His jaw tightened. To hell with the tower. He'd go whether they gave him the okay or not. "You're in Alaska, Kincaid. What did you expect, palm trees and ocean breezes?"

She gave him that look again, the one that told him she was about to start another harangue. "I expected—"

"The truck's in the lot," Joe said, interrupting her before she had another chance to start talking. He grabbed her arm again and pulled her along. Damn if he wasn't beginning to like Perrie Kincaid better when she had her mouth shut.

They made it to the hangar without further argument, Perrie choosing to sit silently beside him, her eyes fixed on the road. To Joe's relief, the plane was fueled and ready to go when he pulled up. He parked the truck, then ran around the front to open Perrie's door, but she'd already jumped out and was dragging her bag from the back on her own.

Satisfied that she could take care of herself, he tugged his hat down and ran over to Tanner O'Neill, who was standing by the hangar door. "What's the weather look like?" Joe asked. "Are they going to let us go?"

Tanner shouted against the frigid Arctic wind. "If you get off the ground in the next fifteen minutes, you should be all right. You'll be ahead of the storm all the way to Muleshoe. I put the mail sack in back and there's a crate of fresh mushrooms that Burdy ordered for the spaghetti feed at the fire hall Saturday night. There's a load of lumber in the cabin, I've tied it all down. Tell Hawk to unload it and put it in the shed for now."

Joe nodded. He hadn't seen Tanner in more than a week. He and Julia had been married in Muleshoe the weekend before last and had decided on a family honeymoon at Disney World with Julia's nine-year-old son, Sammy. They'd returned and decided to stay in Fairbanks and look for an apartment, where they'd live during the winter months while Sam was in school.

"How is Sam?" Joe asked.

"Sammy loved Florida but misses you and Hawk and the lodge. And Julia is in the middle of tying up all her business affairs in Chicago. By the way, we've made a decision."

"What's that?"

"We're not going to live in Fairbanks during the winter. We've decided to live at the lodge. Sammy will go to school in Muleshoe."

Joe grinned, happy that he'd have his partner at the

lodge full-time, not to mention Sammy and his mom. He'd grown to love the kid and appreciate his mother. Julia made Tanner happier than a man had any right to be. Someday, when Joe was ready to settle down, he hoped to find a woman as sweet and loving as Julia Logan.

But for now, he was left with Perrie Kincaid—a first-rate pain in the backside. She joined them, standing beside Joe, her hair now free of its knot and whipping in her face. "Are we going to be able to get to Seattle?"

Tanner frowned, then opened his mouth, but Joe shot him a warning glare. "Tanner O'Neill, meet Perrie Kincaid," Joe said. "Go stow your luggage in the plane, Kincaid, and hop in. I'll be there in a second."

They both watched her hurry toward the Otter, then Tanner grabbed Joe's arm and pointed at her. "How the hell do you do it, Brennan? You were supposed to pick up some guy from the airport and you end up with a woman. And a beautiful woman to boot."

Joe grinned. "Pure, unadulterated charm."

"If you take her to Seattle, you're going to be flying right into that storm."

Joe chuckled and patted his buddy on the shoulder. "Don't worry. We're not going to Seattle. She just thinks we are. We're on our way to Muleshoe like I promised her boss."

"You're going to put her up at the lodge?" Tanner asked. "Are you sure you want to test the legend again? I let Julia in the door and I ended up marrying her."

Joe shook his head. When Julia Logan had showed up at Bachelor Creek Lodge, Joe had been the first one to move out. Legend claimed that a woman entering Bachelor Creek Lodge was destined to marry one of the occupants and Joe wasn't about to take any chances. The legend had proved true, but Tanner had been the one to be caught. "Perrie Kincaid is staying in one of the guest cabins."

Tanner blinked. "She isn't going to be so happy with that. No indoor plumbing. In the middle of winter."

"Well, she'll have to live with it," Joe replied. "She's not setting foot in the lodge."

Tanner glanced over at Perrie, then back at Joe. "She doesn't look like the type to live with anything she doesn't like."

"I know," Joe grumbled. "But I'll deal with that problem later."

PERRIE HUDDLED DOWN in the copilot's seat, wrapping her arms around herself and stamping her feet. Her breath clouded in front of her and her nose was so cold she was sure it would break off if she rubbed it. "Don't you have any heat in this plane?"

Brennan glanced at her absently, as if surprised that he had a passenger at all. He hadn't said a word since they'd taken off an hour before and seemed quite comfortable with the silence. He closed his hand into a fist and rapped firmly on a spot near the center of the control console. A fan began to whir and, slowly, the cockpit of the Otter warmed to a temperature somewhere above freezing.

"I sure hope the rest of your plane works better than the heater," she muttered.

He grunted in reply, his expression hidden behind his sunglasses and shadowed by the brim of his cap. He seemed intent on the view through the plane's windshield, so Perrie took the opportunity to study him.

She considered herself an excellent judge of character, possessed of the ability to immediately discern a person's true nature and hidden agendas with a simple glance. It had come in handy in her work, allowing her to cut through the bull and get right to the heart of the matter. But Joe Brennan defied an immediate impression.

His physical attributes were simple enough. A long, lean body. Thick, dark hair badly in need of a trim. A handsome face behind the shadowy stubble of a three-day beard. But she'd have to see his eyes to really get a good take on him. And since they'd met, he'd kept his eyes hidden behind his sunglasses.

Perrie turned her gaze to the landscape below them, searching for the first sight of civilization. But all she saw was forest, broken only by spots and strings of white that she guessed were lakes and rivers in the summer. When she couldn't discern their location, she turned her attention back to the pilot.

Why bother to figure out Joe Brennan? It was a waste of energy. After they landed in Seattle and she paid him off, she'd never see him again. What did she care what kind of character lurked behind his shades? As long as he was a capable pilot, she didn't need to know more.

"How much longer until we land in Seattle?" she asked. "I would have thought we could see the coastline by now. Are we going to have enough gas? Or will we have to stop? I could really go for a cup of coffee right about now."

"There's a thermos behind my seat," he said. "And we're not going to Seattle."

Perrie chuckled and peered out the window. "Of course we're—" Her words died in her throat and she slowly turned to him. "What do you mean, we're not going to Seattle? I'm paying you to take me there."

"I'm taking you to Muleshoe, just like I promised Milt Freeman."

She twisted in her seat, snatching at her seat belt with frantic fingers. "We had a deal, Brennan. Turn this plane around and take me to Seattle."

He turned to her and pushed his sunglasses down on his nose. Brilliant blue eyes sparkled with amusement—and challenge. He met her gaze without blinking and she felt a slow shiver work its way down her spine. For a moment, she couldn't breathe for staring at him.

He made a lazy survey of her face and then her body, and she wondered how many times she'd been observed in the same way from behind the reflective lenses. But her instincts suddenly failed her, for all she could read in Joe Brennan's blue eyes was an instant and undisguised sexual curiosity. A curiosity she shared at that very moment.

The realization rocked her senses and an unexpected flood of desire warmed her blood. She forced herself to glance away, certain that his gorgeous eyes were somehow to blame for her momentary lapse. The guy was a first-class charmer, all right, and he was using his charm to renegotiate the terms of their agreement, employing every available weapon, including her newfound weakness for a handsome face and devilish grin. Well, she wasn't going to fall for it. "I—I want to go back to Seattle," she said, trying to cover a tremor in her voice.

His eyebrow quirked up. "You seem to forget who's flying this plane, Kincaid. You go where I go. Unless, of course, you want to jump. I don't have a parachute with me, but that shouldn't matter to a woman like you."

Azure. His eyes were really more azure than sapphire. The same clear blue of the sky outside. She swallowed hard and ignored the heat that rose from her throat to her face. "What is that supposed to mean? A woman like me."

"I know your type. Nothing stands in your way, does it?"

No, Perrie never let anything stand between her and her work. But somehow, coming from him, the comment felt more like an insult. She bristled, her sudden attraction now tempered with defiance. "The hell if I'm going to Donkeyleg," she shot back. With a curse, she grabbed the controls on her side of the plane.

He chuckled, then leaned back in his seat, crossing his arms over his chest and watching her expectantly. "You want to fly her, be my guest. If you can get us back to Seattle, the ride's on me, sweetheart."

She'd never driven a plane before, but it couldn't be all that complicated. She was an intelligent woman, a woman who had once driven in downtown Chicago during a rush-hour snowstorm. At least up here there were no speeding taxis and bothersome pedestrians. There was only up and down and left and right. Though down wasn't a direction she really wanted to explore right at this moment.

Placing her feet on the pedals, she gripped the steering yoke with white-knuckled hands. "You think I can't fly this plane, don't you?" Her words came out through clenched teeth.

"I *know* you can't fly this plane. But I'm willing to give you a chance."

Grinding her teeth, she slowly turned the steering

yoke. The plane responded by making a gentle bank to the right. But as she turned, the plane's nose tipped down slightly. Her eyes went wide.

"You're losing altitude," he commented.

"I know that." She closed her eyes and tried to remember everything she knew about airplanes, then slowly pulled back on the yoke. The plane's nose began to rise again and a self-satisfied smile curled her lips. This wasn't so tough. She glanced at the compass. South. They'd have to head south to get to Seattle. And when they got there, she'd make a try at landing the plane. If she knew one thing about Joe Brennan, he wouldn't let her crash his precious plane over the stupid game they were playing.

"Before you fly into that weather ahead, you better file a new flight plan with Fairbanks. They'll need to know what part of the wilderness to search after we go down."

"We're not going down," she said.

"If you fly us into that storm, Kincaid, I can guarantee we'll go down. The wings will ice up and we won't have enough power to maintain our air speed. We'll slowly lose altitude and we'll probably crash somewhere in the Alaska Range. Maybe if we're lucky, you'll hit Mount McKinley."

"You're enjoying this, aren't you?" she snapped.

"Immensely."

Perrie Kincaid did not accept defeat lightly. The truth be told, she couldn't remember the last time she'd thrown in the towel...except for the Saturday she had tried to fix the toilet in her apartment and it flooded the bathroom and the apartment below. A plumber had been her last resort, and she'd called one only after she'd exhausted all her other alternatives.

The dark clouds looming in front of them would more than likely put an end to her short career as a pilot. If she continued this game of one-upmanship with Joe Brennan, it might even end her life. Hell, she'd go to Donkeyleg with him. But she wouldn't let him win. She'd hop the first bus out of that freeze-dried burg and make her own way back to Seattle.

"All right, we'll do it your way," she said, taking her hands off the controls. "For now," she added beneath her breath.

He grinned, shoved his sunglasses back up, then slowly banked the plane until they were headed northeast again. "I think you'll find Muleshoe infinitely more bearable than crashing into a snow-covered mountainside. We've got a tavern, a general store, a mercantile and our own post office. And there's a spaghetti feed at the fire hall on Saturday night."

"Oh boy," Perrie muttered. "A spaghetti feed. I'll try to contain my excitement."

"Welcome to Muleshoe, Kincaid."

Joe watched Perrie peer through the frosty windshield of his Blazer, which he had parked in the middle of Main Street. She didn't have to look hard to see the town, mostly because the greater part of it lined one street.

The buildings were a ramshackle lot of faded paint and rickety porches, frosted windows and wisps of smoke curling around the chimney pipes. Front yards were cluttered with a variety of snow-covered possessions—old tires, dogsleds, snowshoes, fuel drums, rusted canoes, animal pelts—and anything else worth saving for future use. To the outsider, it might appear a bit shabby, but to Joe, it was home.

"Good grief," she muttered. "It's worse than I imagined."

Joe bit back a snide retort. Right now, he wasn't in the mood to get into another "discussion" with Perrie Kincaid, especially in defense of the place he chose to live. "The lodge is about a mile north of town."

"And where do you live?"

"I live at the lodge," he replied.

Perrie gasped. "I'm staying with you?"

"Actually, you're staying in one of our guest cabins on the property. It's a real nice little place. You'll be warm and cozy. I had Burdy McCormack supply the place with everything you'll need for your stay. If I know Burdy, he's got a fire blazing in the stove and a pot of coffee brewing. He'll be your neighbor. After the Yukon freezes, he comes in from his claim and spends the winter in the cabin next to yours. Burdy makes a run into Muleshoe every day, so if you need something from town or you need a ride in, just flip up the flag on your front porch and he'll stop."

She slowly released a long breath and rubbed her arms. "Don't bother with the cabin, Brennan. Just take me to the nearest public transportation. The bus station will do."

When was she going to give up? He swore he'd never met a more pigheaded, single-minded woman in his life. And why he found her attractive, he'd yet to figure out. "I can't do that," he replied, leaning back in his seat and fixing her with a weary look.

"You might as well." She tipped her chin up in a way that had already become familiar to him. "I'll just walk there on my own. You can't stop me from leaving."

"That would be a little tough, seeing as the nearest bus station is halfway back to Fairbanks."

Perrie closed her eyes, her jaw tightening. *Here it comes,* he thought to himself. She'd been itching for another go-round since their confrontation in the plane and he knew he was about to feel the sting of her tongue. But she slowly schooled her temper and forced a smile. "All right, I'll just stand here on Main Street and stick out my thumb. There's bound to be a truck that comes by headed for civilization. Unless you're going to tell me you don't have roads and trucks up here."

"Oh, we have roads. Trucks, too. But not in the winter. This is the end of the highway, Kincaid, and once you're in Muleshoe after the first big snow, you're pretty much here for the duration. Until the spring thaw, that is."

Perrie arched her eyebrow dubiously. "What about this road? Where does it go?"

"Right now, not much of anywhere. Erv runs the plow. He keeps the road clear out to the airstrip and north to just beyond the lodge. But trying to clear the snow any further is like dusting in a sandstorm. Once you're finished, a new storm just moves in and blocks the roads again."

"Do you mean to tell me that there's no way out of town?"

"Sure there is. In my plane. But you already know I'm not real partial to that idea."

Narrowing her eyes, Perrie cursed beneath her breath. Then she grabbed the door handle and jumped out of the truck. As soon as she hit the ground, her feet slipped out from under her on the hard-packed snow. She steadied herself against the truck then began to pace. "What about food?" she said, stopping to stick her head through the open truck door.

"We bring that in by truck in the fall. Mostly canned and dried. We've got fresh meat frozen over at Kelly's meat locker. Venison, moose, caribou, salmon and a few sides of beef, as well. But if you're looking for fresh fruits and vegetables, you're pretty much out of luck. I bring in what I can, but only when I've got room in the plane."

She paced back and forth a few more times, nervous energy vibrating from her body with each step, then stopped again. "What happens when someone gets sick?"

"If it's an emergency, I fly them out. Or they send up an evac plane from the hospital in Fairbanks. And if the weather is bad, well, then your chances aren't the best. This is a hard life up here, Kincaid. You're pretty much standing on the edge of the frontier. Once you cross the Yukon River, there's not another town for at least two hundred miles."

She clenched her fists and snarled in frustration. Hell, she even looked beautiful when she was angry and about to spit nails. Color rose in her cheeks and her green eyes came alive with light, and he found himself unable to keep from staring.

"How do people get to work?" she snapped.

"Everyone works on the land. They hunt and fish. They get by."

She stopped her pacing in front of him and scrambled back into the truck. Desperation filled her gaze and she reached out and grabbed the lapels of his jacket, then yanked him close. "I have got to get out of here, Brennan. You can take me right now, or I'll start walking. Either way, I'm going back to Seattle."

He pulled off his sunglasses and leaned closer, his mouth hovering over hers, his jaw tight with anger. He could feel her warm breath as it clouded up around his face in the cold. A tiny thread of desire snaked through him and his gaze skipped to her lips. An unbidden urge to cover her mouth with his own teased at his mind. Would her lips be as soft as they looked? How would she taste? And would a kiss finally shut her up?

He gripped the steering wheel with one hand until his fingers went numb. He didn't want to kiss her. What he really wanted to do was shake her until her teeth rattled. "Damn it, Kincaid, don't be a fool. If you try to walk out of here, you'll be dead in a day. The weather can change in the blink of an eye. There's a reason the road is closed. So fools like you won't risk their necks trying to travel. You're here until I fly you out, and the sooner you get that through your stubborn head, the better."

She blinked, then frowned, drawing back slightly to look at him. Her gaze flitted over his angry expression, her eyes wide. Finally, he thought to himself, realization. After all this wasted time bickering with her, she'd decided to listen to reason. Maybe now she'd quit fighting the inevitable. She was here to stay until Milt Freeman told him it was safe to fly her out again.

"You want to kiss me, don't you?" Her husky voice was mixed with an equal measure of surprise and smug satisfaction.

A sharp laugh burst from his throat, but it sounded hollow and forced. He shifted in his seat, but she wouldn't let go of his jacket. What the hell? Was she a mind reader as well as a major pain in the backside? Or was his desire so easy to discern?

It had been a while since he'd had a woman. In fact,

he'd been afraid to admit that he was going through a bit of a slump lately. There had been plenty of possibilities, plenty of romantic dinners, but that was about it. Not prepared to risk betraying another errant impulse to her prying gaze, he turned and looked out the front windshield, slowly slipping his sunglasses back on. "You have a rather high opinion of yourself, don't you, Kincaid?"

She sighed, then released his lapels and pushed away from him impatiently. "It's no big deal. I mean, why try to hide it? You're a healthy guy, living up here in the middle of nowhere. I'm an attractive, educated woman. You can say it, Brennan. I'm certainly not a prude. I'll admit it—I find myself slightly attracted to you, as well. Inexplicable, but an attraction nonetheless."

He reached for the key and started the truck, taking a small measure of satisfaction that the attraction was reciprocated. Still, all his good sense told him that pursuing Perrie Kincaid would be a colossal mistake. The sooner he dumped her at her cabin, the sooner he'd be able to escape from those disturbing green eyes. She was far too perceptive—and outspoken—for his tastes. Even if she was the only decent-looking woman in a fifty-mile radius. "Are you always so blunt?"

"I don't consider it a failing," she said. "In my line of work, it's a necessity. I always say what's on my mind. Why waste time dancing around the issue when you can cut right to the chase? It saves a lot of time and trouble."

"Well, as long as you're here in Muleshoe, you may want to tone it down a bit. You'll make more friends if you don't go blurting out every thought that comes into your head. Especially your rather negative opinions about Muleshoe."

"I'm not planning to stick around long enough to make friends."

"Whatever you say, Kincaid," he muttered, shifting the truck into drive and punching the accelerator. The back end fishtailed until he brought it under control. "I just don't want to be putting you in Kelly's meat locker."

"You'd lock me in a meat locker to keep me here?"

"No, that's where we put our dead folks until we can fly them out to the funeral home in Fairbanks. If you're planning to try to get out on your own, you'll end up there sooner or later."

She wriggled down in her seat and shot him an uneasy look. "I'll keep that in mind, Brennan."

As they drove down Main Street, Joe pointed out the major landmarks—the general store, the tavern, the mercantile, the post office—but she showed little interest. "And that's the brides' house, right over there." He pointed to a little cabin with smoke curling out of the stone chimney. "The bachelors built it last summer when they cooked up their mail-order plan. They figured to bring the brides up in the middle of the winter to test their mettle. If they could survive the snow and cold, then they might just be worth marrying. You might want to stop by and say hello. The three of them are the greatest concentration of the female sex you're likely to see between here and Fairbanks."

"I don't think we'll have a lot in common," she said, giving the cabin no more than a cursory glance.

"You never know."

"I'm supposed to write an article about them. Milt assigned it to me before he banished me from Seattle. I can't imagine why any woman in her right mind would choose to live out here."

"It's not all that bad," he said, wondering why he even bothered to defend it to her. "Some women find it a challenge. Not everyone loves living shoulder to shoulder in a city. All the noise, the pollution...the crime. I wouldn't be surprised if you got to like it a little bit."

"I wouldn't hold my breath if I were you." She leaned her head against the window and observed the scenery in silence.

Joe carefully negotiated the curve out of town, swinging his truck wide around a snowdrift that the wind had kicked up. He sure hoped Milt Freeman knew what he was doing sending Perrie Kincaid to Muleshoe. More than a few women and a good number of men had cracked under the endless boredom and isolation of an Alaskan winter. If the snow and cold didn't get to a person, the endless nights would. Days were short and darkness came early.

He didn't want to be around when Perrie Kincaid started suffering the combined effects of cabin fever and sunshine deprivation. The sooner Milt Freeman and the Seattle police solved her problems, the better off he'd be.

The better off they'd all be.

3

PERRIE LEANED BACK against the rough plank door and listened as Joe Brennan's footsteps crunched in the snow on the way back to his cabin. She was grateful to finally be out of range of those disturbing blue eyes of his. With a groan she let her shoulder bag slip to the floor. A few seconds later, she followed it, sliding her back against the door until she sat down with a thump. "I'm in prison," she murmured as she rubbed her sore arm. "That's what this is. Nothing but a gulag with a lovely dead-animal decor." She sighed. "And a warden cute enough to curl a girl's toes."

She glanced around the cabin at the mounted antlers scattered about the room, then silently cursed Milt Freeman and the scumbag that shot her. If it hadn't been for that one stray bullet, Milt never would have sent her to Siberia. She'd still be in Seattle, working on her story, following leads, tracking down witnesses. Instead, the only thing she had to occupy her mind was a thwarted plan to escape Muleshoe...and the possibility that Joe Brennan might kiss her.

If she had the time to spend, she might find Joe Brennan more than a little intriguing. Perhaps they might enjoy a tumble or two before she headed out of town. After all, Perrie wasn't immune to the charms of a ruggedly handsome man. She'd had a few men in her life—purely on her own terms, of course. But none of them had lasted very long once they'd realized they didn't rank high on her list of priorities.

Besides, she had already counted at least five good reasons why Joe Brennan got under her skin, five good reasons why she couldn't even consider allowing him to kiss her—or tumble her into bed. And the biggest was his refusal to return her to Seattle. How could she possibly respect a man who had no respect at all for the importance of her work?

She scrubbed at her face with her hands. Right now, she didn't want to think about Brennan. Her misguided attraction to him would only serve to distract her from her cause—getting back to Seattle. And he had vowed no assistance on that front. "I'll find another way," she said. "There's got to be another way."

She clambered to her feet and took a slow tour around the cabin, dropping her jacket on the floor along the way. It was nice enough, kind of warm and cozy. The rough plank floors were covered with a colorful assortment of braided rag rugs, making the one large room seem as if it were actually three rooms. A fieldstone fireplace dominated the far wall; an overstuffed sofa and an antique rocker were arranged around it.

At the other end of the cabin, a pair of old iron beds and a scarred dresser served as the sleeping area. The beds were covered by pretty quilts and fluffy pillows. In the corner, a potbellied stove radiated a gentle warmth. Perrie held out her hands for a moment to warm them, then turned to survey the kitchen.

Like the rest of the cabin, it was simple. An electric hot plate, a small refrigerator and knotty pine cabinets that looked as if they'd been homemade. A vase of dried flowers sat in the center of the old oak table. She sighed and rubbed her hands together, then crossed the room to brush aside the drapes of one of the cabin's three windows.

She expected to take a look at the weather. But instead, a face, lined with age and grinning a toothless smile, stared back at her through the glass. She screamed and jumped away, her heart leaping into her throat. The man waved at her, then tapped on the glass and pointed to the door. He wore a fur hat with earflaps flopping at the sides, bouncing up and down until it looked as if he might just take off like some human gooney bird.

Who was this? Surely Muleshoe didn't boast its own Peeping Tom along with all its other civilized features, did it? Placing her hand to her chest, she waited until her pulse slowed, then walked over to the door and opened it a crack.

The face pressed up to the opening, still grinning. "Hey there! You must be the little lady from Seattle."

"I am," she said, wary. "Who are you? And why were you looking in my window?"

"Burdy McCormack's my name." He shoved his hand through the door and she reluctantly shook it before she pulled the door open. Burdy scampered inside with a bandy-legged gait. "Just thought I'd look in on you. Wasn't sure you were here yet."

A cold wind trailed after him and Perrie quickly swung the door shut. His grin faded and he scratched his whiskered chin. "Guess yer not too fond of dogs. Strike is housebroke."

She glanced between him and the door. "I'm sorry, is your dog outside?" She opened the door again and peered out, seeing nothing but snow and trees and a single track of footprints on the front steps. "I'm afraid he's not out here."

"Come on, Strike," Burdy called, waving his arm. "Come on in out of the cold, you sorry mutt. That's a boy. Good dog."

Perrie watched as Burdy McCormack reached down and patted the space near his knee. Space that was not occupied by man nor beast—nor anything real, for that matter. She bit her bottom lip. Good grief, the poor old guy thought he had a dog with him!

For a moment, she considered leaving the door open in case she'd have to make a quick escape. But the cabin was growing colder by the second so she decided the risk was worth staying warm. "That's a nice dog you have. Obedient." She leaned back against the closed door.

Burdy nodded, his grin growing so wide it seemed to envelop his entire weatherworn face. "Took me a long time to train 'im. There weren't no dog along the whole Yukon that could hunt better. But we've both been gettin' old, so we spend most of our time sittin' next to a warm fire." He looked around the cabin. "So, you have everything you need here? Joe asked me to look in on you every now and then."

Perrie rubbed her palms together and studied Burdy McCormack shrewdly. He seemed harmless enough, the type that might be swayed to her cause. A man who showed concern over the comfort of his imaginary dog couldn't be as coldhearted as Joe Brennan had been. "Actually, there is one thing you could help me with. I can't seem to find the bathroom."

Burdy scratched his chin. "That's out back of the cabin in the little house with the moon on the door."

Perrie gasped. "An outhouse? In the middle of winter?" She turned and began to pace the room. "You've got to help me find a way out of here. I can live without television, I can live without junk food, but I cannot live without indoor plumbing. I won't!"

Burdy wagged a gnarled finger at her and shook his head. "Aw, no you don't! Joe warned me about you. Said you'd try to talk me into taking you outta here. That's not gonna happen. I ain't gonna fall for no sweet talk from a pretty lady."

She added another to her list of reasons why kissing Joe Brennan was out of the question. He had a big mouth. Jeez, the whole territory probably knew by now that she'd set herself on escaping Muleshoe. "You don't understand," Perrie said calmly. "I have to get back to Seattle. It's a matter of—of life or death. There's got to be a way out of here."

"There's plenty of ways outta town. More than seven or eight pilots living here, an' each with a nice little bush plane, too."

"Pilots? You mean Brennan doesn't own a monopoly on air travel?"

"Ma'am, this here's Alaska. Cain't git around without a plane."

"Then you have to take me to one of these pilots. I'd be willing to pay you. A lot. You could buy yourself anything. A—a new dog."

The old man chuckled. "Now, why would I want a new dog when I have Strike here? We get along real well and he's hardly no bother. Never barks and don't eat much, either."

"I can see that. He's just about faded away to nothing."

The meaning of her comment didn't seem to register with Burdy. Either the man was totally daft or...or he was totally daft. There was no other way about it. Joe Brennan had left her in the care of a crazy man and his invisible dog.

Burdy shoved his hat back and stared at her with sparkling blue eyes. "Joe wouldn't like it much if I was to help you leave. And I 'spect he's let all the other pilots know that they won't be takin' you out, either. But I s'pose that ain't gonna stop you from tryin'."

"Not a chance," Perrie said. "There's got to be one pilot in this town willing to fly for cash."

Burdy sighed and rubbed his forehead. "Would you like to take a trip into Muleshoe? I was about to get me some dinner down at St. Paddy's and I'd sure love the comp'ny of a pretty girl like yourself."

"You have a church here?"

Burdy chuckled. "St. Paddy's ain't a church. It's the local tavern. It's run by Paddy Doyle. We took to calling it St. Paddy's since most of us spend our Sunday mornings there. He makes a mean Irish breakfast— fried eggs and potato cakes and soda farl and home- made sausage—but he don't allow talking during his church service."

"He's a priest, then?" she asked. A man of the cloth would have to help her. He'd see that she was being held against her will and would prevail upon a local pilot to fly her out.

"Well, he does preside over the town's funerals, but he ain't a priest proper. He just makes us watch church on his big-screen satellite TV."

Perrie's hopes faltered. No priest.

"We all put up with it since the breakfast is so good," Burdy continued, "and 'cause Paddy takes his religion serious. Mass starts at eight and breakfast is served right after."

Perrie found her mouth watering at Burdy's description of breakfast. She hadn't had anything to eat since the previous night. She refused to count airline food as food. And the cup of coffee she'd guzzled at the airport hadn't done much to diminish her hunger. Dinnertime was fast approaching, and with it the need to cook, a skill she'd never quite mastered beyond microwave popcorn.

"Do they serve a good evening meal down at St. Paddy's?"

"Best in town," Burdy replied. "Except for the Saturday feeds down at the fire hall. I do the cookin' then. Spaghetti feed tomorrow night."

"And do the town's pilots eat at Doyle's?"

"Most of 'em."

"Then I think I'll take that ride into town, Burdy. I'm feeling a little hungry and I'm not really up to cooking tonight."

Burdy nodded, his earflaps bouncing. "All right, then. You'll find yourself a warm jacket and some boots in the closet over there. I won't be takin' you out in the cold unless you're properly dressed for it when there's weather rollin' in. And if old Sarah gets it in her head she don't want to go into town, we'll end up walkin'."

"Is Sarah your wife?"

"Nah, she's the lodge's pickup truck. We get on pretty well most times, but she can be an ornery old thing. If she sees you comin' she might get a little jealous and decide she ain't gonna take us into Muleshoe."

Perrie looked up from the floor as she pulled on a pair of oversize rubber boots and shrugged into a down parka. An invisible dog, a jealous truck and an old man more than a few sandwiches shy of a picnic.

Just what else would Muleshoe have to offer in the way of entertainment?

DOYLE'S TAP TAVERN, or St. Paddy's as the locals called it, was already bustling with people when Burdy showed her inside. As she scanned the room, Perrie slowly realized that she was the only woman in the place. It didn't take long for the rest of Paddy's patrons to realize the same thing. Conversation slowly ground to a halt as every eye turned toward her.

Perrie forced a smile and reached for Burdy's arm. "Why are they all looking at me like that?" she murmured.

Burdy straightened and puffed out his chest. "I s'pose they're all wondering how an old coot like me managed to put such a fine-lookin' woman on my arm." He cleared his throat. "This here's Miz Perrie Kincaid. She'll be stayin' here in Muleshoe for a while. She's looking for a pilot to fly her outta here."

Six of the bar's patrons stepped forward, but Burdy held up his gnarled hand and shook his head. "The first guy to offer Miz Kincaid a ride will have to answer to me and Joe Brennan."

The six stepped back, their expressions clouded with disappointment, but their interest barely quelled. Perrie shifted nervously and glanced at Burdy.

"And she ain't here lookin' for a husband, either, so you all can stop your gawkin' and get back to your fun."

"I'm perfectly able to speak for myself," she said as Burdy drew her along toward a table.

He gallantly pulled out the red vinyl chair for her, then helped her out of her parka. "'Course, you'll be expected to dance with them," Burdy said, once he'd seated himself across from her and settled his imaginary dog at his feet.

Her gaze snapped up from the menu to his face. "What?"

"Well now, that's only common courtesy up here. They can't dance with each other, and when there's a woman about, they don't waste much time. I expect you'll get twirled around the floor more times than you'll be able to count. If you're lucky, the brides will stop by and reduce your odds of gettin' dizzy."

Burdy had no more said the words when the front door of Doyle's swung open and three women stepped inside. Perrie wouldn't have known there were women behind the parka hoods and scarves except that the conversation stopped again and every man in the place turned to look. "That's them," he said. "They're a promisin' lot. Better than the first three."

"There were three others?"

"Yep. The boys placed the ad down in Los Angeles. I guess they thought they might get lucky and nab themselves a movie star or one of them supermodels. Those three girls lasted about a week before Joe had to fly them out. They just weren't cut out for the cold. But these three—I got my money on at least two of 'em stayin'."

Perrie watched them slip out of their coats and take their places at a table. They looked like normal, intelligent women to her. All three were attractive in their own different ways and, from what she could see, ranged in age from midtwenties to early thirties. "What about their grooms?" she asked. "Aren't they going to get mad if someone dances with their girls?"

"It don't work that way. The boys that paid in get the chance to go through the letters and choose the girls.

But once they're up here, it's pretty much a free-for-all. The man who woos 'er wins 'er fair and square."

"That doesn't seem fair to me. What about the men who didn't pay?"

"Well, there ain't many single men that didn't get in on it. There's me...and Paddy. He's still pinin' over the wife he lost a few years back. And there's Ralphie Simpson. He's been married and divorced five times so he don't want any part of a woman bent on marriage. And that's it, except for Joe Brennan and Hawk."

"Every unmarried man in town except for you and the other four is looking for a bride?"

"That's about it."

She glanced over the top of her menu at Burdy. "So, what's the story with Brennan? How come he isn't in on the bride deal?"

Burdy scratched his chin as he pondered her question for a long moment. "I don't rightly know. I 'spect he likes bein' a lone wolf. Though there ain't a shortage of ladies lookin' to put an end to that. They all say he's a real charmer, knows exactly how to treat 'em. They're always talking about his eyes, though I can't figure what's so special about 'em."

"His eyes? I don't see anything remarkable about his eyes, either," Perrie lied. "And as for charming...well, he certainly isn't my type."

"You know, he rescued a purdy thing off Denali just a few days back. Plucked her right off the mountain and saved her life. He's a helluva pilot, too."

Perrie's interest was aroused and she leaned forward. "Really? He didn't mention that."

"He don't brag on himself much. But everybody likes him. He's generous to a fault. Last winter, he flew Addie Pruett out when her ma fell ill. She didn't have the money to pay for the flight, so Joe told her she could do his laundry for three months in exchange. And he brings me fresh vegetables for my fire hall feeds without charging me for the freight. I 'spect he don't charge me full price for the produce, either, but I don't have proof of that."

Perrie's journalistic instincts kicked into overdrive. "What did he do in Seattle?"

A shrug was all Burdy had for that question. The old man cocked his head in the direction of the bar. "Why don't you ask him yourself? He's sittin' over there at the end of the bar. He's been watchin' you since we sat down."

She turned to look and found Joe Brennan leaning back against the bar, his pale eyes fixed on her with another disconcerting gaze. For an instant, she thought of looking away, of avoiding his direct stare. But instead, she tipped her chin up and gave him a little wave. His only response was an oh-so-subtle lift of his eyebrow before he turned to talk to the man next to him.

For the first time since she'd met him, he wasn't wearing a cap. His thick dark hair brushed the collar of his flannel shirt and fell in a boyish shock across his forehead, careless and incredibly sexy. His sleeves were rolled up to his elbows and her gaze drifted along smooth, muscular arms and strong, capable hands. She noticed how his jeans hugged narrow hips and long legs when he hooked his heel on the foot rail. No doubt about it. Joe Brennan filled out a pair of jeans better than any man she'd ever met.

"You fancy him?"

She twisted around at Burdy's question. "What? No. Why would you think that?"

Burdy shrugged, a grin quirking the deep grooves

around his mouth. "Haven't met a lady yet that could resist him. And you seem interested."

"I'm a reporter," she snapped. "Learning deep dark secrets about people is what I'm good at." Perrie leaned back in her chair. "And I'll wager you dinner tonight that I can find out what Joe Brennan did in Seattle before he came here."

"I'd take you up on it, but Joe said you don't have any money."

She frowned. Burdy was right. How was she supposed to live here in Muleshoe without a penny to her name? Milt had stolen all her money, had forced her into exile. Did he expect her to starve, as well. "You're right. I don't have any money."

"Not for gamblin'. But Joe said your boss gave him the okay to pay your way around town. Paddy'll run a tab and so will Louise Weller down at the general store."

"Well, if I choose to wager a dinner here or there, Milt Freeman can damn well pay for it," Perrie said. Her chair scraped on the rough wood floor and she stood up. "This will take me about five minutes. You can order the cheeseburger plate and a beer for me while I'm gone."

She fixed her gaze on Joe Brennan's wide, flannel-covered shoulders and headed across the room. But she'd barely gotten five feet before a beefy man with a thick black beard stepped in front of her.

He cleared his throat and she watched a blush creep up his cheeks. "Miz Kincaid. My name's Luther Paulson. I'd be obliged if you'd take a turn around the dance floor with me."

Perrie opened her mouth to refuse, but the poor man looked so nervous that she didn't have the heart. She smiled weakly and nodded. "All right. A dance would be nice. But just one."

"I wouldn't impose myself on you for any more," Luther said, his expression brightening.

True to his word, Luther didn't ask for a second dance. Nor did George Koslowski, Erv Saunders or the other three single men who came along after them to claim just one turn around the dance floor. She'd tried to remember their names, but after the third, they all became one big blur of facial hair and flannel. And the three brides hadn't fared any better, for they were out on the dance floor with her the whole time, chatting amiably with their partners.

She finally pleaded thirst and at least four men jumped to buy her a beer. But she waved them off and made her way to the bar through the crowd of hopefuls that surrounded the dance floor, refusing more invitations along the way.

The stool beside Joe Brennan was empty now, as were almost all the stools, the former occupants now cluttered around the dance floor hoping for a shot at a female partner. She slid in beside him, sending him a sideways glance.

He smiled. "You're a popular lady tonight," he said. He didn't look her way, merely stared into his mug of beer.

"Not so popular," she said. "You didn't ask me to dance."

He chuckled, then took a long swallow of his beer. He set the empty mug on the bar and turned to her. "Those men out there have a reason for dancing with you and it's pretty serious business. I'm not one to stand in their way."

"And I suppose you can't think of one reason you might have to ask me to dance?"

"Oh, I could think of a few," he said. "But then, I've got more than a few reasons *not* to dance with you, Kincaid."

"And what might those be, Brennan?"

"Well, beyond the fact that you'd talk my ear off and try once again to get me to take you back to Seattle, I also might be thinking that it would give you the wrong kind of ideas about me."

Perrie slowly nodded. "You're worried about what I said earlier. About you wanting to kiss me. Well, I won't hold that against you, Brennan. I've been fully informed of your reputation with the ladies." She reached over and grabbed his arm. "Come on, then. If you won't ask me, I'll have to ask you."

He growled softly in protest, but turned and followed her out to the dance floor. Perrie expected more of the same clumsy embarrassment that she'd had from her other partners. But Joe slipped his arm around her waist and pulled her effortlessly into his arms. He moved with the music, as if he'd been dancing all his life, and suddenly she was the one who felt clumsy and uneasy.

Her breath caught in her throat as his hand splayed across her shoulders, then slowly slipped toward the small of her back. His touch sent a tingle down her spine, and for a moment, her knees went soft. "You dance very well," she murmured, fixing her attention on his chest, avoiding his eyes once again.

"Surprised?"

"Maybe," she conceded. "So what's your story, Brennan?"

"My story?"

She looked up at him, now that she'd managed to start breathing again. "Yeah, what brought you up here to live in the Great White North? Burdy says you used to live in Seattle until about five years ago."

"Have you and Burdy been gossiping about me?"

"We were talking about the brides and the subject turned in your direction. He couldn't tell me much more. He says you're a crackerjack pilot, though."

He lifted a dark eyebrow. "I do all right. I haven't lost a passenger yet, although I was sorely tempted earlier today."

"Then you're fearless?"

Joe chuckled. "We have a saying here in Alaska, Kincaid. There are bold pilots and there are old pilots. But there are no old, bold pilots."

Perrie smiled. "I like that. So, who were you before you became a bush pilot, Brennan? And how do you know Milt Freeman?"

He stared over her shoulder for a long moment as if contemplating what he was going to tell her. But then he shrugged. "I had a job like most folks do. I sat behind a desk and pushed papers." He glanced down and met her gaze. "I'm afraid it's a rather boring story for a woman like you, Kincaid."

She narrowed her gaze. "And I'm afraid I don't believe you, Brennan. You forget that I've got a nose for a story and I smell one right now. Milt mentioned that you owed him a favor or two. For what?"

"Let's not talk. I thought you wanted to dance."

His voice was warm, persuasive. A little too persuasive for Perrie's taste. "Did you and Milt meet up here or did you know each other back in Seattle?"

"Were you born a reporter, Kincaid?"

"Actually, I was. From the time I was a little kid, I

wanted my own newspaper. In fact, I used to publish a little neighborhood journal called the *Honey Acres Gazette*. I wrote the stories and drew the pictures and I made ten copies and passed them out to the kids in the neighborhood. I was the one who broke the story about the stray cat living in the culvert under Mrs. Moriarty's driveway."

"You are quite a woman, Kincaid." He chuckled, then pulled her closer. At first, the feel of his long, lean body pressed against hers was too much to take. Her pulse quickened and her mind whirled. But then, as they danced, she realized that she enjoyed the crazy sensations racing through her body.

That's the key, Perrie thought to herself. *Don't fight it, enjoy it...but not too much.* She cleared her throat. "Well, I told you about myself, now why don't you spill your guts, Brennan?"

"I'm not going to answer your questions. If you want to write yourself a story, why don't you write the one Milt gave you? About the brides."

She rolled her eyes. "The brides are easy. I need a challenge and I think I've found one. You're going to be sorry you didn't fly me back to Seattle, Brennan, especially if you're keeping any secrets."

He yanked her closer, his arm tightening around her waist until she could do nothing but allow her body to mold itself against his. Every thought in her head took flight again as her hips rubbed against his, as her hand skimmed along his muscular arm and her fingers folded against his palm. A flood of warmth seeped into her cheeks as her mind wandered to other aspects of Joe Brennan's anatomy.

But her speculation was cut short when Paddy Doyle appeared beside them. "Sorry to interrupt," he said, wiping his hands on his apron, "but Louise Weller just called here looking for you, Joe. She says little Wally was shoveling snow off the roof and he fell. She thinks he may have broken his leg."

Joe loosened his grip and she took the opportunity to step back a bit. As she did, his hands slipped from her body and a sliver of regret shot through her. She fought the temptation to step closer again, to place his hands where they'd once been. Instead, she risked a glance up at Joe, but he seemed unaffected by the break in their physical contact.

His jaw tightened, then he ran his fingers through his hair. "I swear, that boy has broken more bones than he's got in his body. His dad's insurance company's damn near paid for my plane."

Paddy nodded. "She's put a splint on it and said she'll meet you out at the airstrip."

"We've got weather and it's getting dark. I don't know if I'm going to be able to get him out." He turned and walked off the dance floor, his thoughts now occupied with more important matters.

Perrie followed after him, stumbling in the oversize boots. She snatched up her jacket from the chair across from Burdy, then grabbed the cold cheeseburger. "I'm going with you, Brennan."

He spun around, almost as if he'd forgotten she was there. He sighed and shook his head. "Give it up, Kincaid. You're staying right here. You're safe and I intend to keep you that way." He looked at Burdy. "Keep an eye on her, will you?"

Burdy nodded. With that, Joe grabbed his jacket and his cap and stalked out the door. Perrie watched him leave, his words echoing in her head. Her heart skipped and a smile twitched at her lips. It was kind of nice having someone care about her safety, especially a man as sexy and compelling as Joe Brennan. The notion made her feel all warm and gooey inside.

Perrie blinked, her silly fantasies grinding to a halt. Scowling, she shoved her hands into her jean pockets then turned back to the table where Burdy and her dinner waited.

"Get a grip, Kincaid," she muttered to herself. "Going soft in the head for Joe Brennan is not going to get you out of Muleshoe and back to Seattle." She pulled out her chair and sat down, tossing her jacket on the floor.

As she silently munched on the cold cheeseburger, she let her mind wander back to Joe Brennan. An idea slowly formed in her mind, and as it crystalized, a laugh bubbled out of her throat. Why hadn't she thought of it before? It was all so simple.

She knew exactly how to get back to civilization! And as soon as Joe Brennan returned from Fairbanks, she'd put her new plan into action.

"I'M PRETTY SURE it's broke," Burdy said, scampering ahead of Joe on the snow-packed path to Perrie's cabin, his movements quick and nervous.

"What the hell happened? She was fine when I left last night."

"She says she slipped on a patch of ice and fell walkin' to the outhouse in the dark. I shoulda been there. A lady like Miz Kincaid ain't used to the weather here. They don't have ice in Seattle. And them boots I gave her are a couple sizes too big."

Joe frowned, a slow suspicion growing in his mind. "You weren't there when she fell?"

Burdy shook his head. "I'm sorry, Joe. I know you

tol' me to watch her, but a man cain't stay with a gal like that twenty-four hours. It wouldn't be seemly." The old man gave Joe a solemn look. "People might talk."

A smile quirked Joe's lips as an image of Burdy and Perrie, caught in a romantic tryst, flashed in his mind. "I'm not blaming you, Burdy. In fact, I'd be willing to bet that Perrie Kincaid is up to something. She'd do just about anything to get out of Muleshoe."

"You mean to say that little gal broke her wrist on purpose?"

Joe took the front steps of Perrie's cabin two at a time. "No, I don't think her wrist is broken at all. I think she's faking, Burdy, and I'm about to prove it."

Gathering his resolve, he knocked at the front door, then pushed it open. He caught a brief glimpse of Perrie before she scrambled back into bed and pulled the covers up to her chin. Burdy waited on the porch, carrying on a low dialogue with Strike. By the time Joe closed the door behind him, she was beneath the quilts, her right arm clutched to her chest.

She looked so small and frail, tucked into the huge iron bed. Her auburn hair was mussed, falling in disarray around her face. For an instant, he felt a small measure of delight in seeing her again. But then he quickly smothered the feeling as he realized that it would have meant he had actually missed her. Hell, he barely knew her.

He crossed the room in three long strides, composing an expression of deep concern on his face. When Joe reached the bed, he slowly sat down on the edge. Her wince at the movement told him that either Perrie really had hurt herself—or she was a consummate actress. He was willing to wager on the latter.

Reaching out, he gently brushed her hair from her forehead, ignoring the flood of heat that seeped into his fingertips and set his nerves on fire. "What happened?" he asked, his voice soft with feigned worry. "Burdy says you hurt your wrist."

"I—I think it's just sprained. Nothing to worry about. It—it'll be fine in a few days."

Joe hid a smile. So she was trying to turn the tables on him. "But it could be broken." He reached out and took her forearm in his hands. Her wrist was limp and he wove his fingers through hers to test the joint. His mind instantly focused on her hand, so smooth and soft in his. A lady's hand. Long, delicate fingers that might drive him mad with— Joe cleared his throat and blinked hard.

"Do you really think it could be broken?" Her words were soft and breathy and he glanced up to meet her wide green eyes.

The intensity of her gaze rocked him, yet he couldn't draw his eyes from hers. "I'm not sure," he said, leaning closer. "What do you think?"

He could feel her breath soft on his face, quick and shallow, as if his nearness made her uneasy. "It really does hurt," she offered. She added another wince for good measure.

Joe let his gaze drift down to her mouth. Suddenly all thought of catching her in her lie slipped from his mind. He found himself transfixed by her lips and he leaned forward and brushed his mouth against hers.

A tiny moan escaped her and he deepened his kiss, savoring the taste of her. He'd thought a lot about kissing her in the hours since he'd left Muleshoe, many more times than he'd care to admit. But he'd never imagined it would be as good as it was.

Perrie Kincaid knew just how to kiss a man, how to tease and tantalize with barely an effort. Her mouth moved gently under his and tiny sounds rose from her throat, urging him on. Her fingers slowly splayed across his chest and slipped up inside his down jacket until they twined through his hair at the nape of his—

Her fingers. Joe's thoughts came back into sharp focus and his mouth curved beneath the onslaught of hers. "I don't believe it's broken," he murmured, letting his lips slide down to her throat.

"Hmm?"

Slowly, he reached back and grabbed her hands, unwinding her arms from around his neck. Dazed by what had passed between them, she stared at him, uncomprehending. "I said, I don't think your wrist is broken." He held her arm out in front of her and shook it until her hand flopped back and forth. "I'm not a doctor, but I'd say your wrist is just fine. It even looks like that sprain cleared up pretty quick. Maybe it was the kiss."

Slowly her eyes cleared and her confusion was replaced with anger. Anger at him, and at herself for falling into his trap. She sputtered, then cursed softly. "You did that on purpose."

Joe lifted his eyebrow. "What?"

"You know what! You—you kissed me. Distracted me."

"And you kissed me," he countered. "And I do believe you enjoyed it. Enough to forget your little plan to get me to evac you out to the hospital in Fairbanks, Kincaid."

She shoved him aside and crawled out of bed, then began to pace the room. Every few seconds, she shot him a frustrated glare before returning to her pacing.

"I can't believe this," she muttered. "I'm trapped here. There's no way out. No one cares that I've got a huge story to break back home." She stopped and braced her hands on her hips. "Do you have any idea how important this is?"

"Important enough to get killed for?" Joe asked. "No story is that important."

Perrie opened her mouth to reply, then snapped it shut. For a long moment, she was silent. "What do you care?"

Strangely enough, he did care. The more time he spent with Perrie Kincaid, the more he cared what happened to her. But the hell if he was about to tell her that. "Milt Freeman cares. And I owe him a favor. So, whether I want to or not, I have to care."

"What kind of favor?" she challenged.

"He saved my life." Joe wasn't sure why he chose to tell her that, though he wasn't prepared to explain himself further. Maybe he'd hoped that she'd see how determined he was and forget about leaving Muleshoe. But he could see from her expression that he'd only kindled her curiosity.

"And when was that?" she asked.

Joe shook his head. "That is none of your business. Now, if you've recovered sufficiently, I've got work to do. I'd suggest you go into town with Burdy. He's got to get ready for the spaghetti feed and you can shop for groceries. You're going to be here for a while."

Turning on his heel, he headed toward the door, satisfied that he'd finally put an end to all her escape plans. Whether he liked it or not, he was stuck with her.

"Just wait one minute, Captain Charm," she called. "I'd like to discuss the plumbing situation with you."

Joe braced his arm against the doorjamb, refusing to turn back and face her. "And what might that situation be?"

She stalked across the room and placed herself between him and the door. "Where the hell is my bathroom? Burdy has me traipsing through the snow to a damn outhouse."

"You should be satisfied with running water," Joe replied. "Most folks in town still get their water from the town's well house."

"I demand a cabin with indoor facilities."

He gently pushed her aside and opened the cabin door. "You've got hot water. And there's a tub on the back porch. You drag it inside and fill it. Or you can take a sauna with me and Burdy and Hawk every night if that's too much work."

She followed him out onto the porch. "And you consider this civilization?"

"We discuss all manner of subjects during our saunas. Philosophy, literature, politics. You'd be surprised."

"I'm not talking about your conversations. I'm talking about toilets."

Joe turned to face her, meeting her angry gaze. "This is Alaska, Kincaid," he said in an even voice, fighting the urge to soften the hard line of her lips with his mouth. "It's supposed to be rugged. That's part of the experience. I told you it was a tough place, especially for a woman."

He expected her to make another plea for escape. After all, she hadn't chosen to come to Alaska of her own free will. She'd been coerced into coming and he really couldn't blame her for being uncomfortable with the amenities—or lack of them. But Perrie surprised him by bracing her hands on her hips, a stubborn expression suffusing her flushed and angry features.

"Just what are you saying? That I'm not tough enough for Alaska?"

Joe shrugged, disarmed by her mercurial moods. "You're the one who's whining about the plumbing. Now, if there's nothing else, I've got a flight to make." She opened her mouth to protest, but he held up his hand. "No, I'm not taking you with me."

"That's not what I was going to say!" she shouted as he strode down the path. "If you can live without indoor plumbing, I can, too."

"Good," Joe shouted over his shoulder, "because you don't have much choice."

Burdy caught up to him halfway back to the main lodge. He fell into step beside Joe, then gave him a sideways glance. "I don't s'pose yer plannin' to tell her that there's indoor facilities in the lodge?"

"And have her move in with me and Hawk?"

"There's an empty room until Sammy and Julia and Tanner come back for the summer."

Joe stopped and shot Burdy a disbelieving look. "Would *you* want to live with her?"

"Well, she really didn't choose to come up here. You could make her life a little more comfortable," Burdy suggested.

"There's no room in the lodge for guests. Tanner and his new family are coming back in a few days. And you know what happened when Julia set foot inside the lodge. I'm not willing to take any chances."

Burdy chuckled. "I expect that you and Hawk will meet your match before long." He paused and grinned. "Maybe you already have?"

Joe sighed. "Don't you start on me. I've got enough

on my mind trying to run Polar Bear Air. With Tanner involved with his wife and new son, he hasn't been much help here at the lodge. And Hawk is long over-due for one of his disappearing acts."

"Then why don't you jest do as the lady asks and take her back to Seattle? Must be a pretty big debt you owe her boss."

"Why don't you mind your own business," Joe growled.

Burdy shook his head and whistled for Strike. When the imaginary dog reached his side, he leaned down and patted him on the head. "Seems to me yer pro-testin' a little too loudly."

With that, the old man took off toward the lodge, muttering to Strike as he walked.

Joe pulled off his cap and ran his fingers through his hair. Truth was, he'd love to return the woman right back to where she came from, but Joe Brennan didn't welch on his debts. He owed Milt Freeman his life and he wasn't about to let his friend down.

Even if it meant putting up with Perrie Kincaid for another few weeks.

4

PERRIE STOOD on the front porch of the brides' house. She pushed the hood of her parka back, then fumbled out of the oversize mittens Burdy had lent her. She'd been in Alaska for four days and already she was climbing the walls. She could only spend so much time wandering around her cabin and eating breakfast, lunch and dinner at Doyle's. Either she'd eat herself into oblivion or she'd go stark raving mad from cabin fever.

The only choice left was to follow Milt's orders and write his blasted story about the mail-order brides. It would take her about an hour to interview the subjects and another few hours to put the story together. Considering her own feelings about marital commitment, she could at least offer a completely unbiased viewpoint.

There had never been much time in her life for men beyond a few passionate, short-term flings. It wasn't that she didn't want to be part of some man's life. She liked men—well-read men with interesting careers, charming men with clever smiles and deep blue eyes.

An image of Joe Brennan drifted through her thoughts and she pinched her eyes shut and tried to will it away. Yes, Joe Brennan was attractive. And if he wasn't so set on making her life miserable, she might consider him more than just a convenient outlet for her frustration. But when push came to shove, he was probably like all the other men she'd known. He would never be able to put up with her life—the late hours, the broken dates, her single-minded devotion to her work. And he lived in Alaska.

To be honest, after a few months with a man, she usually found herself a little bored. As a reporter, she prided herself on her ability to learn everything about a person in a very short time. Unfortunately, once she learned all she could, there was little else to talk about. A once promising relationship usually fizzled in short order. The only reason she had the slightest interest in Joe Brennan was because she hadn't been able to crack that roguish facade of his and bend him to her will.

Perrie sighed. Whoever said women could "have it all" didn't have a clue as to what it took to be a top-notch investigative reporter. She had resigned herself long ago to never "having it all." She wasn't even sure she wanted it all, considering that "all" just took too much energy to have.

A devoted husband and a loving family were fine for other women, but not for Perrie Kincaid. She had taken another road long ago, made choices that required a near solitary pursuit of her dreams. She couldn't go back and change her mind. She'd come too far. This was all she had—her work—and she was happy with that choice.

She knocked on the door, and a few moments later it swung open and she was greeted by the warm but hesitant smile of a slender blonde, one of the trio from the bar. "You're that woman visiting from Seattle, aren't you?" the woman asked.

Perrie shouldn't be surprised. Talk would travel around a small town like this quickly. She held out her hand. "Hi, I'm Perrie Kincaid from the *Seattle Star*. I've been sent here to interview you and the other mail-order brides. May I come in?" She didn't wait for an invitation, just shook the woman's hand firmly then slipped past her into the cozy warmth of the cabin. Experience had told her that confidence went further than manners when it came to getting a story.

She slowly strolled around the main room of the cabin, making a mental inventory of her surroundings. A few descriptive phrases to set the scene added color to human interest stories. The cabin was much larger than hers, boasting separate bedrooms and a variety of modern conveniences. She nearly moaned out loud when she pushed open the bathroom door and came upon a shower and a toilet.

"My name is Linda Sorenson," the woman said. "I must say, I was startled to find a woman at the door. All our guests have been men."

"I can imagine," Perrie murmured, recalling the scene at Doyle's. "I'm here to write a follow-up to the original story published in our paper." She stopped to stand in front of the fire. When her hands were warmed sufficiently, she turned and faced her subject. "This is a very nice cabin. There are three of you living here?"

Linda smiled, then rearranged the magazines on a scarred coffee table. "The others are out back. Would you like a cup of coffee?"

Perrie couldn't help but put aside her professional demeanor. Linda seemed so friendly, and right now she could use all the allies she could find, since Brennan had most of Muleshoe watching her every move. Maybe the three brides could offer some help in her escape plans. "Sure," she said with a smile, pulling her notepad from her pocket before she slipped out of her jacket. "I'm having trouble adjusting to the cold so anything warm would do." She made a few notes and waited until Linda returned from the kitchen with the coffee, then sat down across from her on the sofa.

Linda smoothed her palms along her legs. "What would you like to know?"

"Why don't you tell me why you decided to come to Alaska?" Perrie asked after taking a sip of her coffee.

Linda took a deep breath then let it out slowly. "It's hard to explain without sounding a little silly. Do you believe in destiny, Miss Kincaid?"

Perrie glanced over the rim of her mug. "Destiny?"

"One day, I was looking through the newspaper. I rarely have time to read the paper. I'm a nurse and my schedule is rather hectic. But I had time that day and I saw the ad for brides. I knew that I had to come to Alaska. I just felt as if something—or someone—was waiting for me here."

Perrie sighed inwardly. It did sound a little silly. "Actually, I'm not a big proponent of destiny. I think a person determines their own future. Fate doesn't have anything to do with it."

"Have you ever been in love, Miss Kincaid?"

Perrie paused, not sure how—or whether—to answer the question. What did her love life have to do with the story she was writing? She was the one asking the questions. Besides, she wasn't sure she wanted a complete stranger to know that Perrie Kincaid, a highly intelligent thirty-three-year-old woman, wasn't even sure what love was.

"Why don't we stick to your story?" she said lightly. "Why are you so sure you want to get married?"

"Because I know I'd be really good at it. I want

someone to share my life with, I want to fall in love and have children and grow old with a good man."

"And you expect to find that man here in Alaska?"

"Why not? He could be here. The odds are good."

Perrie smiled. "But the goods are kind of odd, don't you think? Besides, how do you know your destiny isn't waiting for you in Newfoundland?"

Linda smiled. "Well, if I don't find him here, I'll just have to keep looking."

"There are other things in life besides marriage, aren't there?"

"Sure there are. And I'm not necessarily set on marriage. But I'm never going to give up on finding love."

Perrie considered her words for a long moment. Was she missing something here? She'd never considered love very important at all. In fact, she considered men more trouble than they were worth. Was that because she could put such a crazy emotion in perspective? Or was it because she'd never come close to feeling that emotion?

"So you hope to find love here in Muleshoe? And what will you do if that happens? Are you going to give up your career in Seattle and move up here?"

Linda smiled. "I don't know. That's what's so exciting about this whole thing. I'm not really sure what's going to happen until it does. I'm enjoying the journey as much as the destination."

Perrie stared down at her notepad. All of this sappy stuff was not going to make a story, unless she was writing it for one of those romance magazines. She glanced around the room, then back at Linda. A long silence grew between them, broken suddenly by the sound of the front door opening.

The other two brides stumbled inside, laughing,

their jackets covered with snow. Perrie stood and watched as they tugged off hats and mittens. They both turned to her and regarded her with curiosity until Linda stood and made the introductions.

The tiny brunette, Allison Keifer, spoke first. "I didn't know we were going to be interviewed again. We would have been here earlier but we've been practicing."

"You have to practice finding a husband?" Perrie asked, leaning forward. Maybe there was something to this story.

"No," Mary Ellen Davenport replied, giggling. She was a prettily plump woman with pale brown hair and a sparkling smile. "We're practicing for the Muleshoe Games. They're having a brides' competition next weekend, on Valentine's Day. We compete in all sorts of things—snowshoeing, dogsledding, wood chopping."

"I suppose it's so these men can see what kind of wives we'll make," Allison said. "But we're just going to have fun. And there's a nice prize for the winner. A weekend up at the resort at Cooper Hot Springs. Everything's included, the room, the flight, the—"

"The flight?" Perrie asked. "Someone's going to fly the winner out of Muleshoe?"

Linda nodded. "And after the games, there's a dance at Doyle's. Are you interested? The brides' competition is open to any single woman."

Another plan began to form in Perrie's mind. She could train with the brides and win the event and at the same time get a nice angle on the story. And once she escaped Muleshoe, she'd be able to find her way back to Seattle and finish a story that really mattered.

"Sure," Perrie said. "I think I'd like to enter the games. Tell me more."

"You'll need to practice if you want to win," Mary Ellen said. "There are a few single women from town who are entering. Ringers, I say. They'll be tough to beat. You can practice with us."

"Or you can get one of those dishy bachelors from Bachelor Creek Lodge to help you," Allison teased. "You're staying there, aren't you?"

Perrie nodded.

"Lucky girl."

Perrie arched her eyebrow. "Lucky?"

"That's bachelor central. Three of the dreamiest guys in Alaska and they live up there."

"If you're counting Burdy as a bachelor dreamboat, you've definitely been in the wilderness too long."

"Oh, no. Not that Burdy fellow. I'm talking about Joe Brennan and Kyle Hawkins. And there's another one, but he just got married—Tanner is his name, I think. Linda had a date with Joe Brennan the night we arrived here."

Perrie tried to look indifferent but her interest was piqued. Leaning forward, she asked, "He didn't waste much time, did he?"

"He took Allison out the night after that," Linda countered.

"He asked me out, too," Mary Ellen admitted, "but I had a previous engagement."

"He was really charming, but not the marrying type," Linda commented.

"Charming," Perrie repeated.

"He's just so sweet and attentive," Linda continued. "And funny. And cute, too. He has this way about him.

It's hard to explain, but it makes you want to tear off his clothes and drag him into bed."

"Mel Gibson eyes," Mary Ellen observed.

"A little boy in the body of a man," Allison added. "But definitely scared of commitment. A one-date wonder."

"Then you both went to..." Perrie couldn't finish the question, a strange surge of jealousy stopping her words.

"Of course not!" Linda cried.

"Though I was tempted," Allison added. "Those eyes of his could melt a girl's panties."

Perrie scolded herself silently. What right did she have to be jealous? Or envious? She'd pegged Joe Brennan as a ladies' man from the moment she'd met him. A confirmed bachelor who used his charm and good looks to make women weak in the knees and breathless with adoration. Even she hadn't been immune.

At least she was smart enough to see Brennan for what he was. And clever enough to keep her distance. Though it hadn't been too hard, considering she hadn't seen much of him lately.

Linda laughed. "It took Allison about three days to evaluate every bachelor within a twenty-mile radius. She's got this down to a science."

"I believe in being thorough," Allison said. "After all, I'm the one who has to look at him across the dinner table. I only want the best."

"The only one she can't figure out is Hawk," Linda teased.

Perrie glanced up from her notes. "Kyle Hawkins? Brennan's partner?"

"They call him Hawk. And he's the only man who hasn't said a single word to her," Mary Ellen said. "He reminds me of Gregory Peck in that old movie...I can't remember the name."

"Mary Ellen never remembers the names of movies. And if you ask me, that Hawk is a little too quiet," Linda said. "Maybe he's hiding a tortured soul."

"I haven't met him yet," Perrie admitted. "I'm not sure I want to. Brennan is enough to deal with."

"You're a reporter," Allison said. "Find out all about him and then tell us."

Perrie slowly closed her notepad. "I'll make you a deal," she said with a conspiratorial grin. "You teach me how to chop wood and walk on snowshoes and drive a dogsled, and I'll report back on the mysterious Mr. Hawk."

Mary Ellen giggled. "This is going to be so much fun! Just like that old movie where the three girls go to Rome and find love. The one with the fountain? Only this is Alaska and there are four of us...and no fountain."

"I'm not in this to find a husband," Perrie quickly explained. "All I'm interested in is the trip out of Muleshoe."

JOE PULLED THE FRONT DOOR of the lodge closed and dropped his sunglasses over his eyes against the sundrenched snow. The days were getting longer and the bitter cold that had marked all of January was beginning to release its grip. It would be months until the river broke up and spring came, but they were halfway through winter now and there was an end in sight.

A curse split the silent air and he turned and glanced up at Perrie's cabin. He'd spent the past five days flying supplies into the bush and hadn't had time to check on how she was doing. She and Burdy had become friends and the old guy had taken her into town for meals, but beyond that, Perrie Kincaid had been keeping herself busy with her own activities.

To tell the truth, she wasn't nearly as much trouble as he first thought she'd be. She'd obviously come to the conclusion that there was no way she'd be able to get out of Muleshoe and had decided to make the best of her free time. He casually strolled up the path toward the cabins, a satisfied smile curling his lips. He had won this little battle between the two of them and he couldn't wait to gloat.

As the cabin came into view, he caught sight of Perrie, lying in the snow, her feet up in the air. A stab of concern pierced his mind and he wondered if she'd really injured herself this time. But then he noticed she was wearing snowshoes.

"Hey!" he called. "Are you all right?"

Perrie turned over on her side and regarded him with thinly veiled hostility. Her hair was caked in snow and her face was wet. She looked as if she had taken a header into a snowbank. "Go away!" she cried. "Leave me alone!"

Joe stood over her and couldn't help but laugh. She looked so darn cute, all covered with snow and ready to explode with anger. "What the hell are you doing?" he asked, holding out his hand to yank her to her feet. He turned her around and brushed the snow off her backside. It wasn't until he'd pulled his hand away that he realized how intimate the contact actually had been.

"I'm practicing," Perrie said, twisting away from him and finishing the job herself.

"Falling into the snow?"

"No, Mr. Smarty Britches, snowshoeing. It's just that

these things are so big, and I'm supposed to try to move as fast as I can, but my feet get all tangled up. It's like running in swim flippers."

"Why do you have to move fast?" He paused, then held up his hand to stop her reply. "Let me guess. I assume you aren't planning to run a footrace with a stampeding moose, so I'm going to have to surmise that you've decided to walk to Fairbanks?"

She tried to move away from him, but one of her snowshoes caught the edge of the other and she began to lose her balance again. He reached out and grabbed her elbow, but as soon as she righted herself, she pushed him away. "I'm going to enter the Muleshoe Games next weekend. And I'm going to win that trip to Cooper Hot Springs. And once I do, I'll be out of Muleshoe for good."

Joe laughed, the sound echoing through the silent woods. "You're going to win the brides' competition? You're not even a bride-to-be."

Perrie bristled. "I'm a single woman. And I'm a reasonably fit individual. I work out...sometimes. You don't think I can win?"

"Not a chance, Kincaid."

Perrie bent down and fumbled with the leather straps on the snowshoes. She lost her balance again and tumbled back into the snow, but this time he didn't help her up. She wrestled with the snowshoes until she'd managed to pull both of them off, then scrambled to her feet. "You just watch me," she said, her chin tipped up defiantly. "I've been practicing splitting wood and I'm getting pretty damn good at it. I've actually hit the log twice with the ax and I've only been practicing for an hour."

She stalked around the side of the cabin and returned with an ax and a log as if to prove her point. He watched her push the log into a snowdrift before she hefted the ax up on her shoulder.

"Be careful with that," he warned. "Should you be doing that with your sore arm?"

"My arm is fine. Besides, I know what I'm doing."

"You should set that up on top of a harder surface before you—"

"I don't need any advice from you!" Perrie snapped, raising the ax.

Joe watched as she brought the ax over her head. But he could see that her aim was seriously off. Instead, she swung to the right of the wood and buried the ax in the snowdrift, continuing down until the blade hit rock beneath the snow.

"Eeeoow!" she cried, snatching her hands back, stung by the impact. She jumped up and down and rubbed her palms together, her eyes watering with the pain. Finally, unable to handle the ache, she sat down in the snow.

"I told you—"

"Oh, zip it!"

Joe grinned and sat down across from her, then reached out and pulled off her mittens, then his gloves. Slowly, he rubbed her fingers between his hands, working his way up through her palms to her wrists. "There's a rock border all around this porch."

"Thanks for warning me."

"It feels worse in the cold."

Her fingers were warm against his, tiny and delicate. Her nails were trimmed short and unpolished. He wouldn't have expected a perfect manicure from a woman as practical as Perrie, especially since she didn't wear a lot of makeup, either.

She had a natural beauty all her own. Her ivory skin, now touched with pink from the cold, was perfectly smooth. Impossibly long lashes framed her clear green eyes. And her mouth, that wide mouth with those lush lips. He'd found his attention drawn to her mouth again and again, remembering the kiss they'd shared.

His gaze lingered on her mouth for a long moment. "Is that better?" he murmured.

She didn't answer and he looked up into her eyes to catch her staring at him. He wasn't sure what came over him, but the next thing he knew, he bent forward and covered her lips with his. She fell back into the snow and Joe stretched his body over hers, groaning at the feel of her soft form beneath his.

He rolled her over in the snow, pulling her on top of him and holding her face between his palms, afraid that she might break their kiss before he was ready. But she seemed to have no intention of pulling away.

Gently, he explored her mouth with his tongue, tasting and teasing. For an instant, rational thought returned and he wondered just what he was doing rolling around in the snow with a woman who wanted nothing more than to make him look like a fool.

But the truth be told, Joe liked the way she kissed. She didn't go all soft and breathless in his arms, but instead she kissed him as if she were truly enjoying the experience. He'd never known a woman who had tempted him so sorely, yet managed to drive him crazy at the same time. She was a challenge, and Joe never walked away from a challenge.

He pulled her beneath him once more, his lips never leaving hers, an intimate contact that he didn't want to break. His mind swam with images of her and he couldn't help but draw back and look down at her.

Her eyes were closed and her lips moist, parted slightly. The cold had turned her cheeks pink and snowflakes still dusted her auburn hair. Her lashes fluttered, but before she could look at him, he brought his mouth down on hers again. A soft sigh escaped her lips and she wriggled beneath him, arching up against him.

In all of his life, he'd never met a woman he couldn't charm—until Perrie Kincaid. Clever compliments and boyish grins just didn't work on her. She preferred the direct approach, like a spontaneous kiss in the snow— a kiss that was growing more passionate as time passed.

He tried to refocus on the feel of her mouth against his, but strange thoughts pressed at his mind. Why was he so attracted to her? He'd always preferred women who were sweet and biddable, not sharp-tongued and prickly. More likely, the challenge was in simply trying to get the upper hand with Perrie in their ongoing battle of wills. She was the last woman he should involve himself with...the last woman he should want.

Perrie must have read his mind, for at that moment, she pulled back and looked up into his eyes, her brow furrowed in confusion. Slowly she regained her sense of reality and her gaze cleared. She cursed softly, then pushed him off her. "What do you think you're doing?" she demanded.

Joe braced his hands behind him. "The same thing you were doing."

"Well, stop it!" Perrie brushed the snow off her jeans and jacket, then jumped to her feet.

"Are you sure you want me to stop?" Joe asked.

"I certainly don't want you kissing me anymore!"

Joe leaned back on his elbows and grinned at her. It

wasn't hard to see that the kiss affected her as much as it did him. "Why? Afraid you were enjoying it?"

With a growl of frustration, she snatched up a handful of snow and threw it at his face, then turned on her heel and headed to the front steps of her cabin. "I didn't enjoy it. How could I enjoy it? I'd rather...stick my tongue on a frozen doorknob than kiss you again."

Joe stood up and brushed the snow from his clothes. "Well, Kincaid, I'm sure you and the doorknob would have plenty in common."

She narrowed her eyes and glared at him, her gaze colder than the snow creeping down the back of his jacket. "Just stay away from me."

"You'll never win the competition. You're a city girl, Kincaid. You can't handle the wilderness. You're not cut out for it."

"What? You don't think I'm tough enough? Hey, I took a bullet in the arm to get a story. I'm a lot tougher than you think."

"All right," Joe conceded. "Though I consider a bullet in the arm for some damn newspaper article more stupid than tough."

"I'll win, if only to prove to you that I can."

"And if you do by chance win, I'll let you go to Cooper."

She braced her hands on her waist and kicked snow at him. "You'll *let* me go to Cooper?"

"Hey, I'm responsible for your safety, Kincaid. And I take my responsibilities seriously. But if you win, you can go to Cooper. I won't stand in your way."

"Damn right you won't stand in my way. I'll run right over you, Brennan. My footprints will be all over your chest."

Joe laughed. "Are you threatening me, Kincaid?"

"Just stay out of my way," she warned. She turned and hustled up the porch steps, but tripped along the way. With a vivid curse, she clambered to her feet and finally made it inside, slamming the door to punctuate her anger.

Joe sat in the snow for a long time, chuckling and shaking his head. If there was one thing he liked about Perrie Kincaid, it was that she always managed to surprise him. He'd never met a woman who could kiss him like a wanton one minute, then threaten to do him grave bodily harm the next.

PERRIE LAY IN BED, staring at the ceiling. Afraid to move, almost afraid to breathe, she clenched her teeth and prepared to push herself up. This was all Joe's fault. If it wasn't for his taunting the day before, she wouldn't have spent three hours yesterday working on her wood splitting.

She had tumbled into bed at sundown, crawling under the quilts to warm herself. Burdy arrived an hour later to take her to supper, but she could only call to him. Now, after a good night's sleep, she expected to feel refreshed. Instead, she felt as if she'd been run over by a cement truck, then rolled around in the hopper for good measure. If she hadn't been able to see her arms in front of her, she would have sworn they'd been pulled from their sockets and tied in a bow behind her back.

"Up," she muttered to herself. "Up, up, up."

Gritting her teeth, she rolled over and managed to rise to a sitting position, the pain streaking through her limbs. A hot bath would do much to relieve her aches and pains, but she wasn't sure she had the energy to drag the tub inside and fill it.

Her feet hit the cold floor just as a knock sounded on the front door. Wincing, Perrie stood up. Maybe she could sweet-talk Burdy into filling the bathtub for her. The crazy old guy seemed intent on making her stay as comfortable as possible. "Hang on, Burdy. I'm coming."

But Burdy McCormack wasn't the only one waiting on the other side of the door. A stranger stood on the porch, his long dark hair fluttering in the wind. She suspected the man that watched her with an indifferent expression was the notorious Hawk.

"Joe tells us you're goin' to enter the Muleshoe Games," Burdy said, hopping from foot to foot excitedly. "And then you're goin' to write about it in yer paper."

She winced, then rubbed her forearms. "I thought I'd give the games a try," she said, surprised by Burdy's interest. "As long as I'm stuck here. Besides, it would be a good angle for the story."

Burdy held out a folded sweatshirt and a cap, both with the Bachelor Creek Lodge logo emblazoned on them. "Well, you got yourself a sponsor, Miss Kincaid. Me and Hawk are goin' to train you, get you ready for the games."

Perrie smiled and shook her head. "I don't think Joe would approve."

"Well, we won't tell him, then," Burdy said. "Besides, I think it would be good publicity for the lodge. It's not every day we can git our names in a big city paper. We will git our names in the paper, won't we?"

Perrie contemplated Burdy's offer for a long moment. Though she could practice wood splitting and snowshoeing on her own, she had serious doubts that she'd be able to hop on a dogsled the day of the games and win the race. "If you and Hawk help me train, then I guess I could mention the lodge and my trainers as many times as I can in my article."

Burdy's head bobbed up and down and he laughed, the sound like a cackling chicken. "That's a deal, then. You git yerself dressed and meet us at the dog pens. Hawk is goin' to teach you how to mush."

Perrie wanted to beg off, to plead for a day's rest. But she had only one more week to train, and she couldn't pass up the opportunity to get behind the controls of a dogsled. Besides, Hawk did not seem like the type of man to tolerate any wimpy excuses about sore muscles and aching backs. "I'll be right out," Perrie said.

Hawk held up a pair of fur boots he'd been holding behind his back. "Mukluks," he said, as if that were all the explanation needed.

Perrie hesitantly reached out and took the gift from him. Stumbling around in the oversize boots Burdy had given her had been as exhausting as the wood splitting. And she suspected that it hadn't helped with her snowshoeing, either. "Thank you," she said softly, sending Hawk a grateful smile. "I really need these."

He didn't say more, just turned around and strode down the front steps. Burdy nodded, then ran after Hawk, leaving Perrie to wonder at their true motivations. Joe had made it clear that he didn't encourage her participation. But she had every right to enter the brides' competition—and every intention of winning first prize.

It was no small feat to get herself dressed, but she managed. As she tugged on the mukluks, she sighed in delight. Made of leather and fur, they were incredibly soft and warm and they fitted her feet perfectly. She imagined that her snowshoeing would improve immediately.

Fifteen minutes later, she found Burdy and Hawk at the dog pens. They stood near the sled, a simple invention made of bent wood tied with leather thongs. Burdy hustled toward her, then patted her on the shoulder. "You listen to Hawk, now. He'll teach you all you need to know."

"You're not staying?" Perrie asked.

"I got to go check my traplines," he replied.

"But, I—"

"Don't be scared of him," Burdy said in a quiet voice. "He don't bite." With that, the old man hurried off, his cheery whistle breaking the still silence of the woods.

Perrie turned to Hawk and forced a smile. "So, where do we start?"

Hawk cocked his head and she followed him over to the dog pens. He opened the door, wading through the pack of jumping and barking dogs. "Come on," he ordered.

Gingerly, she stepped inside the pen. She'd never been a big fan of animals, especially in numbers greater than one. Her childhood hadn't included any pets except for a goldfish or two and an ant farm.

Hawk pointed to a huge white husky. "Loki," he said. "Lead dog."

"He's very...cute," Perrie commented, giving him a sideways glance. "So, how long have you known Joe Brennan?"

Hawk ignored her question. "Grab his collar and bring him to the sled."

Perrie's eyes widened. She could picture herself grabbing at the huge dog, only to have the husky eat her arm for lunch. The other dogs bumped and jostled her for attention, but Loki stood apart from the pack, watching her suspiciously. "Don't be a wimp," she murmured to herself.

Slowly, she approached, holding out her hand. "Hi, Loki," she said in a soft voice. "You're a pretty doggy. And a nice doggy, too. You're not going to—"

"Come, Loki!" Hawk's sharp command startled her and she jumped back as the dog moved toward her. But rather than attack her, the husky bounded to the door of the pen, and stood at Hawk's side.

Chagrined, Perrie followed the dog, then took his collar and led him out of the pen. She watched as Hawk demonstrated the process of putting on the dog's harness and hitching that harness to the towline. He pointed to the next dog, and this time, emboldened, she stepped inside the pen and grabbed the second husky.

"Come," she said firmly. The dog fell into step beside her and patiently allowed her to put him into the harness. She clipped him onto the towline and repeated the procedure over and over. Hawk watched her silently, allowing her to make her own mistakes. By the time the last dog had been harnessed, she felt confident in her abilities.

She brushed the snow off her jeans and straightened, waiting for Hawk to compliment her, but he stood silently, arms crossed over his chest. Perrie cleared her throat. "Why are you helping me with this?"

Again, she felt as if she were talking to a brick wall—a very handsome brick wall with penetrating gray eyes and a profile that had been sculpted by a master.

"Are you doing this to bust Brennan's chops?" Perrie asked. "Because if you are, I'm behind you one hundred percent."

Hawk bent down and showed her how to operate the snow hook, then guided her onto the runners of the sled. He stood behind her, their bodies nearly touching, his arms trapping her on the sled. She expected at least a minor reaction to his closeness. After all, he was an incredibly handsome man.

But she felt nothing, not even a tiny measure of what she experienced when Joe Brennan touched her. She bit back a silent curse. What was it about Brennan? Of all the men she'd known, he had the capacity to make her heart race and her breath disappear. And he also had the capacity to kindle her temper as no one had ever done before.

"Mush, Loki. Mush, boys. Hup, hup." The thirteen huskies darted forward until the towline snapped taut. The sled jerked forward, and suddenly, they were skimming across the snow. Her thoughts of Joe forgotten, Perrie laughed out loud, holding tight to the sled for fear that she might fly off.

"Gee, Loki! Gee!"

The lead dog veered off to the left and she felt Hawk shift behind her, balancing the sled during the turn. She added her own weight to the turn, then smiled as the sled smoothly straightened and continued down the trail.

"Haw, Loki! Haw, boys!"

This time the sled turned to the right. Perrie cataloged the commands, carefully studying the way Hawk maneuvered the sled. They made their way down to the Yukon on a narrow trail and then circled back to the lodge. When Hawk called "Ho!" to the dogs, bringing them to a stop, she felt a sliver of disappointment.

He stepped off the back of the sled and Perrie moved to do the same, but he shook his head. "Try it on your own."

She blinked. "Really?"

He nodded.

Perrie drew a deep breath and pulled up the snow hook. "Mush!" she called. "Mush!" This time the dogs took off at an easy lope.

At first, Perrie was tentative, afraid to urge the dogs any faster. But after she'd called them through a series of curves in the trail, she shouted an enthusiastic "Hup, hup," and they responded with a burst of speed. Without Hawk's weight on the sled, it seemed to fly across the snow, and she had to take the turns very carefully to avoid losing control.

All around her, the woods were silent, only the squeaking of the sled runners and the shuffle of the dogs' paws to break the crystalline stillness. She completed the circuit from the river to the lodge three times, until Hawk waved her to a stop. Breathless, she hopped from the sled. "That was wonderful!" she cried. "I can't believe it was so easy."

"It isn't always easy. There are open creeks and fallen trees and moose that want to share the trail." Hawk moved to the front of the sled and began to unhitch the dogs.

Without a second thought, Perrie hurried to do the same. "I'm not sure that Brennan would approve of this," she ventured.

Hawk raised an eyebrow but didn't look at her. "Why is that?"

"Since I got to Muleshoe, Brennan has decided that

I'm somehow too feebleminded to know what's good for me. He thinks he's protecting me by ordering me around. But he's driving me crazy."

"You confuse him," Hawk said.

Perrie opened her mouth to question his comment, but he turned away before she could speak.

"Now we feed the dogs," he said.

She trailed after him. "Wait a minute. What do you mean, I confuse him?"

"Just what I said." He handed her a pair of five-gallon buckets. "Go up to your cabin and fill these with water."

"*He* confuses *me*," Perrie said. "One minute he's yelling at me and the next he's throwing me down in the snow and—" She stopped short, aware of the flush of heat that slowly crept up her cold cheeks. "I—I just don't know what he wants from me. I can make my own decisions. If I want to return to Seattle, I should be able to—without asking his permission. Right?"

Hawk studied her for a long moment and she thought he might agree with her, or even explain the complexities of Brennan's behavior. "Water," he finally said, nodding to the buckets.

With a resigned sigh, Perrie trudged up to her cabin to fill the buckets. If Kyle Hawkins and Joe Brennan were such good buddies, just why was Hawk helping her?

Maybe he didn't approve of the way Joe was treating her, either. He seemed like a reasonable man, though it was hard to tell. He said only enough to get his point across and no more. But he was a good and patient teacher. The only thing she couldn't discern was whose side he was on.

One by one, she carried six buckets of water back to

the dog pens. When she was finished, Hawk showed her how to mix the food for the dogs. In addition to regular dog food, she added bits of cooked moose liver and dried fish to the huge bowls, then stood outside the pens and watched as Loki and his pals greedily lapped up the feast.

"We'll train again tomorrow," Hawk said, staring down at the dogs.

"Why are you doing this?"

Hawk shrugged. "Nothing better to do," he said, turning to walk toward the lodge.

Perrie hurried after him, falling into step beside him, struggling to keep up with his long-legged stride. "If you really want to get to Brennan, you'd help me find a way to get back to Seattle. You must know another pilot who'd take me back. I'd be willing to pay you."

"Have the dogs hitched by noon," Hawk said, lengthening his steps until he was well ahead of her.

Perrie stopped and watched his retreat, cursing softly. It was clear Hawk was standing firmly on Joe Brennan's side. And he wasn't going to be any help at all in her quest to return to Seattle.

5

JOE PACED THE PORCH of the lodge, glancing through the woods at Perrie's cabin every few steps. He stopped and stared across the snow, then resumed his pacing.

"Just what are you up to, Kincaid?" he muttered.

If he hadn't known better, he'd have suspected she'd already achieved her escape from Muleshoe. Over the past few days, he'd barely caught sight of her. In fact, whenever he was around, she seemed to disappear. When Joe had asked Burdy what they'd been up to in the last few days, the old trapper had been oddly close-mouthed.

Whatever they'd been doing, it had kept Perrie out of his hair and off his case. He wasn't sure whether she was still training to enter the brides' competition in the Muleshoe Games. And to his knowledge, she hadn't made another attempt to engage a pilot. Perhaps she'd finally resigned herself to the fact that she'd be staying here in the wilderness until Milt Freeman said it was all right to go home.

The thought of Perrie leaving Muleshoe caused an unwelcome pang of regret. To be honest, he enjoyed her company. Even though they spent most of their time arguing, he found her to be a challenge. Unlike the other women he'd known, Perrie hadn't instantly fallen victim to his charms. He had a sneaking suspicion that turning on the charm did more to turn her off than anything else.

She was smart—not just intelligent, but clever, with a biting wit and the ability to see right through his motives. He liked sparring with her because she wasn't afraid to stand up to him. She kept him constantly off balance for he was never quite sure what she'd do or say to prove her point...and Perrie *always* proved her point.

He had found one chink in her armor, though. She liked to kiss him. And he sure as hell liked kissing her. His mind flashed back to the kiss they'd shared in the snow in front of her cabin, the feel of her body stretched beneath the length of his, the taste of her lips and the silken feel of her hair between his fingers.

If she hadn't put a stop to their roll in the snow, he wasn't sure where it would have led. All he knew was that Perrie Kincaid had a way of testing the limits of his control. Had she wanted, she could have teased him right into dragging her into her cabin and making love to her.

But she hadn't wanted. She'd taken him far enough to prove who was really in control and then she'd slammed on the brakes. But had it all been a game with her? Or had she experienced the same reckless desire that he had? There was something in the way she kissed him...

Normally, he maintained such rigid control around women, taking care to keep his emotions in check. But whenever he came within ten feet of Perrie, it was as if his oil pressure suddenly dropped and he lost all altitude. No matter what he did to compensate, he couldn't seem to keep himself level with the horizon.

If he didn't know better, he might think he was falling in love with her. But then, how the hell would he know? He'd never been in love before. And he wasn't sure that he'd even know love if it kicked him in the behind. Still, he knew what love *wasn't* and it wasn't supposed to be easy.

That was the problem. In all his relationships with women, everything had always been so easy. From the time he was old enough to notice the opposite sex, they were noticing him with undisguised appreciation. He'd cultivated his talent for charming women quite early in life and it had served him well. But it always seemed so simple...too simple. And anything that easy wasn't worth having, was it?

No, the only things worth having were the things he'd had to fight for, the things that offered up a challenge. Joe had never backed away from a challenge in his life. Hell, that's how he'd ended up in Alaska, why he'd jumped at the chance to fly search and rescue, why he continued to find himself drawn toward Perrie Kincaid.

He looked up to find himself standing at the door of her cabin. Frowning, he glanced back at the lodge. He had stepped outside to retrieve his logbook from the front seat of the Blazer, but somehow he'd ended up here. Cursing softly, he turned around, but then an idea struck him and he decided to knock.

"Hawk?" she called, her voice muffled by the door.

Jealousy tweaked his temper. Since when had Hawk been visiting her cabin? He hadn't even known they'd met. Hawk hadn't mentioned it. Besides, what could the two of them possibly have in common? Perrie never stopped talking and Hawk never seemed to start.

"Burdy?" she called after he didn't answer.

"It's Joe," he finally said.

"What do you want?"

By the sound of her voice, Joe could tell he was the last person she wanted to see. She slowly opened the door and stood looking up at him, tugging her bulky cardigan more tightly around her as if it might offer some type of protection. Frigid air and a spindrift of snow swirled around her feet and he noticed that she'd found some new footwear, a pair of handmade mukluks.

"New boots?"

She looked down. "Hawk gave them to me," she said.

Another surge of jealousy rushed through him, but he bit back a defensive reply and forced a smile. "Then you met Hawk?" he asked.

"A few days ago. What do you want?"

He felt her impatience growing and he scrambled for a reason for his visit, certain she was about to slam the door in his face. "I was wondering if you'd like to take a little trip."

Joe cursed inwardly. That wasn't what he'd intended to say at all! What the hell was he doing, inviting her to accompany him on a supply flight? Jeez, they'd actually have to be in each other's company, trapped inside the plane, for at least a few hours.

Perrie studied him suspiciously, then frowned. "What kind of trip?"

"I'm flying up to Van Hatten Creek, about sixty or seventy miles northwest of here, to deliver supplies. And I thought you might like to come along. But you don't have to if you don't want to." He almost hoped she'd refuse. "I have to warn you that if you go along, you're going to have to promise that you won't sneak off and try to get yourself back to Fairbanks."

"Today?" she asked.

"No, next month," Joe said sarcastically. "What? You have other plans?"

He watched as she considered his invitation for a long moment. What possible alternative did she have? It wasn't as if there were that much to do in Muleshoe. Unless she and Hawk had plans...with each other. He fought back the last rush of jealousy he'd tolerate and forced another smile. He would have thought a trip out of Muleshoe would be too tempting to pass up. After all, wasn't that what she'd been angling for since she arrived?

"All right," she replied. "I guess I'll come along."

He didn't expect to feel happy about her reply, yet he did. In fact, he was looking forward to spending the day with Perrie. Perhaps they'd be able to forget the animosity that hung between them and institute a truce of sorts. Maybe then she wouldn't have to run to Hawk for companionship.

"And if you're thinking about sneaking back to Seattle, you might as well know that the nearest settlement to the Gebhardts' cabin is about thirty-five miles away over pretty rough terrain. And John Gebhardt doesn't own a plane. And there are no roads, either. So, you still want to go?"

"I'm not thinking about sneaking off," she snapped, her eyes narrowing in anger. "Why do I get the distinct impression that you don't trust me, Brennan?"

He grinned, breaking the tension between them. "Gee, Kincaid, no wonder you're such an ace reporter. Here I thought I was fooling you. Now, get your jacket and mittens. And put a few more layers of clothing on. We're leaving in five minutes. I'll wait in the truck."

He turned and strode down the front steps of the porch, leaving her to stare after him. He could almost read her thoughts. What was he up to? she was wondering. Joe Brennan wasn't the type to do something nice for Perrie Kincaid, especially since she'd been such a pain from the instant they'd met.

Perhaps he *was* hoping for a truce of sorts. But it would have to be an uneasy truce to begin with. If she thought for an instant he was letting down his guard, she'd be sorely mistaken. He wasn't about to go soft on his promise to Milt Freeman.

By the time he'd pulled the Blazer out of the shed and turned it around, she had made her way up to the lodge. She hopped inside the truck and slammed the door, then turned to Joe. To his utter surprise, she smiled at him. Not a cool, calculating smile, but a sweet and genuine smile, a smile that warmed his blood and made him forget his resolve.

"Thanks," she murmured. "I was starting to go crazy inside that cabin."

Without a reply, Joe put the Blazer in gear and maneuvered it up the narrow drive to the main road. He felt her gaze on him many times during their drive into Muleshoe and out to the airstrip, but he kept his eyes fixed on the road.

When they arrived at the airstrip, he drove right up to the Super Cub, then turned off the ignition. He watched as she searched down the row of planes for the familiar Otter that she'd arrived in, before her gaze returned to the Polar Bear Air logo on the tail of the Cub. Apprehension colored her expression, and for a moment she almost looked afraid. The Super Cub was a small plane, with room for only two, maybe three passengers, but it was the best plane for bush flying because it was able to take off and land virtually anywhere—gravel bars, frozen rivers, even on the side of a mountain.

"Nice plane," she murmured.

"You'll like the Cub. It's a great little plane."

"I think *little* would be the operative word here. Why are the wings fluttering like that?"

"They're made out of cloth," Joe replied.

"Cloth," she repeated.

He hopped out of the truck and ran around to her side. For a moment, he thought she might lock herself inside the Blazer and refuse to get into the plane. Obviously, there was a limit to her stubborn pride and her constant need to best him. That limit was sitting next to the truck, the stiff wind fluttering the fabric wings, the passenger cabin no larger than a carnival ride.

"You'll love it, I promise. It's a bluebird day, Kincaid. A day perfect for flying."

Perrie bit her bottom lip, then forced a smile as he helped her out of the truck and into the cramped rear seat of the plane. He slipped into the pilot's spot in front of her, and in moments the engine burst to life, the propeller a spinning blur in front of them.

They bumped down the snow-covered airstrip, gaining speed, the plane shuddering and shaking until it felt as if it would fly apart at the seams. Then, in an instant, they were airborne and the Cub rose like a bird on the wind, almost silently, save for the soft whine of the engine. He heard Perrie slowly release the breath she held and then a small sigh escaped her lips.

He turned and looked over his shoulder at her. "Are you all right?"

Her eyes were wide as she peered out the window, then looked at him. "This is incredible," she cried. "It's not like we're in a plane. I feel like a bird, like I'm flying under my own power. It's...it's so exhilarating."

Joe smiled and banked sharply to the north. "It's the only way to see Alaska, Kincaid."

"I knew it was wild, but until you see it from the sky, you don't realize how desolate it all is. It's almost frightening."

"Makes you feel kind of small, doesn't it? As if all the problems in your life are pretty insignificant."

"Yes," she said softly. "It does."

They flew for a long time in silence, then Joe banked the plane to the right and pointed out the window. "That's Van Hatten Creek," he said. "And you can see the Gebhardts' cabin in the little clearing to the south. You'll like the Gebhardts."

"We're going to land?" Perrie asked.

"Yeah. Whenever I deliver supplies, I stop and have lunch with John and Ann and their kids. Stuck out in the bush like this, they enjoy the company. And Ann's a helluva cook."

"But where are we going to land?" Perrie asked.

Joe glanced back to see her worriedly looking out the window for a break in the thick wooded terrain. "Right down there," he said. "Between the cabin and the creek."

"What? There's not enough room to land a plane down there. I thought we were going to throw the supplies out the window. I didn't know we'd be risking our lives on this trip."

"Sweetheart, I could put this plane down on the roof of their cabin if I had a mind to. You just watch. Like a walk in the park."

"This is no time to prove a point, Brennan. Just put the plane down where you normally do. And try not to kill us in the process."

He glanced back to see her fumbling with her seat belt. "Don't you trust me, Kincaid?"

"Not as far as I can spit," she replied.

Joe chuckled, then banked the plane to the left and began a sharp descent over the treetops. He heard Perrie cry out in alarm as they dropped out of the sky, the skis almost skimming the spruce forest below. And then, a tiny screech as they touched down. And finally, a long moan that stopped as soon as the plane did.

He unbuckled his seat belt and twisted around, only to see the color gradually return to Perrie's pale face. "What'd I tell you, Kincaid. Like a walk in the park."

PERRIE STUMBLED OUT of the plane on wobbly knees, grateful there was solid ground beneath her feet. She couldn't believe how they'd simply dropped out of the sky onto a tiny patch of snow. The plane had barely touched the ground before it skidded to a stop just yards from a thick stand of spruce. She'd been told that Joe Brennan was a great pilot, and now she'd seen proof.

She took a few steps then stumbled. He reached out to steady her, his hands lingering on her waist for a long moment. And then, to her surprise, he stole a quick kiss, his lips touching hers, sweet and fleeting. "Are you all right?" he asked, cupping her cheek in his hand.

Perrie nodded, flustered by Joe's sudden show of affection. The kiss seemed so natural, so easy that she momentarily forgot that he took such pleasure in making her miserable. Kissing him made her feel just the opposite, all shivery and flushed at the same time. "I—I'm glad we're on the ground," she murmured.

When she finally regained her composure, she turned to see a family hurrying toward the plane, the two small children, dressed in hooded fur parkas and tiny mukluks, stumbling through the snow to get to Joe. Joe scooped them both up in his arms and twirled them around before setting them back down.

"Did you bring us a treat?" the smallest child cried.

"Don't I always bring you a treat, Carrie?"

The little girl nodded, then grabbed Joe by the hand to lead him back to the plane. While he unloaded the supplies from the Cub, the parents of the two children approached Perrie. They were both dressed in larger versions of the fur parkas that their children wore.

"I'm Ann Gebhardt," the woman said, holding out her mittened hand. "And this is my husband, John. And those are our two kids. Carrie, who's four, and Jack, who's three. Welcome to our home."

Joe stepped up beside her, a wooden crate balanced under each arm. "Ann, John, this is Perrie Kincaid." He paused. "She's a...friend who's visiting from Seattle."

Though she should have found his description of her awkward, she actually had to smile. Did Joe really consider her a friend? She'd assumed he thought of her as a thorn in his side, a thorn he enjoyed kissing every now and then, but a thorn nonetheless. But maybe they were becoming friends. The notion wasn't that distasteful—especially if it meant they'd be kissing each other on a regular basis.

Ann slipped her arm through Perrie's and led her toward the cabin. "For once, Joe brought *me* a treat. I don't think I've had an adult conversation with another woman for two or three months."

Perrie looked at her, shocked by the revelation. "I can't believe that."

"The last time we left the cabin was at Thanksgiving to visit friends who live thirty miles from here in Woodchopper. The winters are always a little lonely. But once summer comes, we do some traveling."

They slowly climbed the front steps of the cabin. Perrie glanced back to look at Joe, but he just grinned and gave her a wave, then turned back to the two children, who had tumbled into the snow at his feet. "I'd like to hear more about your life here," Perrie said.

"What could you possibly find interesting about my life?"

She laughed. "I'm a reporter. I find everyone's life interesting." In truth, she couldn't help but admire a woman who chose to live in the midst of the wilderness, a woman who faced true challenges every day.

Ann opened the front door of the cabin and showed Perrie inside. The tiny home was snug and cozy, a cheery fire blazing on the hearth and the smell of fresh-baked bread thick in the air. "This is my life," Ann said, tugging off her parka and fur mittens and hanging them on a hook beside the door. "It's hard to believe I once lived in a co-op in Manhattan and worked at one of the city's largest brokerage houses."

"You left New York City to come here? That must have been quite a change."

Ann took Perrie's jacket and pulled out a chair at the table near the fire. A few moments later, she placed a steaming mug of coffee in front of her, then turned to tend a cast-iron pot hung over the fire. "I came up here on a vacation six summers ago, and when it came time to go home, I couldn't. I just couldn't bring myself to go back to the rat race, so I chucked it all and moved here.

I had plenty of money saved, enough to live on for years. I worked a few odd jobs and then I met John. He was teaching botany at Columbia and was here for the summer on a grant to study plant life near the Arctic Circle. After a month, he asked if I would marry him, and then we decided to stay here in Alaska so he could continue his work. And here we are, with two kids, living in the bush and loving every minute of it."

As Perrie sipped her coffee, she learned more about the Gebhardt family's life in the wilderness. After only a half hour, she felt as though she and Ann had been friends for years. Perhaps that's what living so far from civilization did—it made instant friends of perfect strangers.

She admired the woman's tenacity and strength, her incredible ability to make do with whatever the land offered and to be completely satisfied with her life. Perrie had always considered herself quite resourceful, but compared to Ann Gebhardt, Perrie Kincaid was a soft and spoiled city girl who couldn't survive a week without telephones, grocery stores and electricity. Maybe Joe was right. Maybe she didn't have what it took to live in the Alaskan wilderness.

They continued to talk as Ann set the table, until John and Joe burst in the front door, the children scampering around their feet. Joe had brought the family three crates of supplies and a small box of books for John's research. The family approached the delivery as if it were Christmas, delighting in each item as it was unpacked from the crates.

Once everyone had shrugged out of their parkas, they all sat down to eat a hearty meal of caribou stew and bread, fresh and warm from the oven. For dessert, Ann served a dried-apple tart with thick cream she poured from a can. It was the best meal Perrie had ever eaten, tasty and satisfying, more so because she knew how much work had gone into every ingredient.

The conversation during dinner was lighthearted. The Gebhardts were interested in any bit of news from the civilized world, and Joe recounted everything that was happening in Muleshoe, including the latest on the mail-order brides and the upcoming Muleshoe Games. Time after time, their gazes met across the table and she made no attempt to look away.

Ann and John listened to his stories closely, laughing at the silly asides that Joe added to each story, and Perrie found herself completely enamored of her companion. He was so warm and witty that he could melt the heart of even the most jaded listener.

When he finally ran out of news, he and John grabbed the two children and settled in front of the fire for a game of Chutes and Ladders. Ann brought Perrie another cup of coffee and sat down across from her.

"Well, I've told you everything you wanted to know about living in the bush. Now it's time to tell me all about you and Joe. It's so nice to see that he's finally found someone."

"Found someone?" Perrie paused, then smiled in embarrassment. "You think that Brennan and I are... Oh, no. We're just friends. I mean, we're not even friends. Most of the time we pretty much hate each other."

Ann laughed. "I can't believe that. The way he looks at you. And the way you look at him. It's obvious how you two feel about each other."

"I—we—I mean, we're really just friends. We barely know each other."

"He's smitten. I've known Joe Brennan for a long

time, and in that time, he's known a lot of women. But I've never seen him look at anyone the way he looks at you."

"How many women?" Perrie asked, her curiosity finally getting the best of her. "Just a ballpark figure."

"Well, I dated him for a few months," Ann admitted. "Until I met John. But there was never really anything between us."

"You dated Joe?" Perrie said, her voice filled with disbelief. She shook her head. "Are there any women left in Alaska that he hasn't dated?"

"He's a real charmer, our Joe. But that doesn't matter, now that he's found you."

"He didn't find me," Perrie said. "I was sort of dropped on his doorstep. He doesn't even like me."

"Oh, he definitely likes you. He may not realize it yet," Ann said. "But he will. Just you wait and see."

"I'm not going to be around long enough for that. As soon as I can, I'm heading back to Seattle. Back to civilization."

"That's what I said every day of my vacation six years ago. But this place just grabbed hold of me and wouldn't let go. To think that I almost went to Paris for two weeks instead of coming here. Sometimes little decisions have the ability to change the entire course of our lives. It must have been destiny." The last was said with a wistful smile as she turned her gaze to the two children playing in front of the fireplace.

They continued to talk of inconsequential things, but Perrie's thoughts returned again and again to Ann's odd assessment of Joe. Perrie had seen nothing in his behavior to indicate that he cared in the least for her. Sure, he'd kissed her a few times. But to hear Ann tell it, Joe Brennan had probably kissed half the female population of Alaska.

No, there was definitely nothing going on between them. Perrie Kincaid was an expert at reading the motives of those around her and she'd picked up nothing from Joe Brennan except hostility and disdain, punctuated by a few crazy moments of intense passion.

A few minutes later, Joe returned to the table with his empty coffee mug. "I'm afraid it's time for us to go. Perrie and I have one more stop before we head back to Muleshoe."

"So soon?" Ann cried. "It seems like you just got here."

Perrie stood and Joe helped her into her jacket. When she was all bundled up against the cold, she gave Ann a hug, then stepped back. Suddenly, she realized that she'd probably never see this woman again, and after they'd become such instant friends. Ann would live her life in the bush and Perrie would return to Seattle.

She wasn't sure what to say. "Have a nice life" seemed so trite, and "See you soon" sounded like a lie. In the end, she simply said goodbye and walked out the front door to the plane, turning back once to see Ann waving at her from the porch.

Joe helped her back into the plane and she continued to stare at the family. "They're really living life, aren't they?" Perrie murmured as he took his place in the seat in front of her.

"Yes," Joe said, "they really are."

"She's very brave. I don't think I could ever live out here."

"I bet you could," Joe replied. "In fact, I think you could do pretty much anything you set your mind to, Perrie. You just have to have a good reason to do it."

"What would I do out here? I mean, there are no newspapers to write for, no politicians to expose, no readers who want to know the truth."

"You don't even know what you're capable of until you try."

Joe started the engine on the plane and Perrie girded herself for a white-knuckle takeoff. Maybe Joe was right. Maybe she'd been so occupied with her career in Seattle that she'd never even considered any other options.

But why should she? She loved her job. And she was perfectly satisfied with her personal life. What more could she possibly want? She had no answer for that question, but she sensed that somehow Ann Gebhardt, a woman who lived in the middle of nowhere and existed on nothing, had much more than Perrie would ever have.

PERRIE STARED OUT the window of the Super Cub as it skimmed over a vast, flat landscape—endless white from horizon to horizon. It looked so different from the mountains and forests that surrounded Muleshoe. She glanced at her watch and realized they'd been in the air nearly a half hour, easily enough time to get back to the airstrip at Muleshoe.

She sat up and tapped Joe on the shoulder. "Where are we?" she asked.

"That's the southern edge of the Yukon Flats below us," Joe replied. "We're not far from Fort Yukon and the Arctic Circle. I thought we'd take a little side trip. I have something special I want to show you."

"We're that far north?" Perrie asked. "What are we doing up here?"

Joe looked over his shoulder and smiled. "You'll see," he said.

A few moments later, Perrie felt the plane begin to descend. "What's wrong?" she asked, trying to keep the panic from her voice.

"Nothing. We're going to land."

She stared down at the desolate wilderness below. Unlike the small area they'd landed in at the Geb-hardts', there were plenty of wide open spaces to put down here. But there wasn't a cabin in sight. "There's nothing down there."

"There's a lot here," Joe replied, peering out the win-dow, searching for something in the snow below. "You just have to look a little more closely."

He finally set the plane down on a wide, treeless ex-panse of snow, landing so smoothly the only thing that told her she was on the ground was the hiss of snow beneath the plane's skis. He shut the engine down, then helped her out of the plane, tossing a pair of down sleeping bags at her feet.

"We're spending the night here?" Perrie asked.

He threw a thick blanket over the engine to keep it warm. "Only if you get really lucky," he teased. "Come on."

They walked away from the plane, his eyes scanning the area, still searching. Then he stopped and unrolled the two sleeping bags. Wrapping one around her shoulders, he pointed to the ground. Once she was set-tled, he sat down beside her in the snow and handed her a pair of binoculars.

"Are you going to tell me what we're looking for?"

"Just be quiet and watch," he said.

They sat, silently, for more than a half hour. Though the sun was bright and the air calm, she still felt the cold seeping into her bones. She was about to ask him when they would leave when he slowly raised his arm and pointed to the horizon. "There," he murmured.

She held up the binoculars and stared out over the snow. A movement in her field of vision caught her attention and she carefully focused. Her breath caught in her throat as a huge gray wolf appeared out of the snow.

"I saw him for the first time about three years ago," Joe explained. "I was flying some supplies up to Fort Yukon in the Otter and had some engine trouble, so I had to put the plane down. I was working on the engine when all of a sudden I looked up and there he was, watching me."

"Weren't you afraid?"

"Wolves aren't aggressive. They're afraid of man and would never attack unless they're provoked. Or sick. I think he was just a little lonely, wandering around out here on his own. He was a lone wolf, a male without a family. Probably kicked out of his pack by the alpha male."

Perrie glanced over at him. "Burdy called you a lone wolf once."

Joe smiled. "I guess I am. But not as alone as Romeo was. He was completely alone."

"Romeo?"

"That's what I named him. Every time I flew up here I'd check on him. Sometimes I wouldn't see him for months, and then, there he'd be. He's harder to spot in the winter since he has to wander farther for food. But I think he's starting to recognize the sound of my plane."

"Really?" Perrie asked.

Joe laughed. "No. I'd just like to think we're friends."

"You do have a lot in common."

"Maybe." He paused, scanning the area with his binoculars again. "At least we did, until he found Juliet. Look, there she is."

Perrie trained her binoculars to the left of Romeo. Standing near the huge gray wolf was a smaller black wolf. "His mate?"

"Yeah. Romeo finally decided to settle down a couple years back. I guess he got tired of playing the field."

"Maybe you should have given him some advice," Perrie teased. "The way I hear it, you've got quite a way with the ladies."

"Don't believe everything you hear," Joe said.

"If I were writing a story on your love life, Brennan, I'd have more than enough confirmation to go to print." Perrie studied the wolves for a long moment, then put the binoculars in her lap and looked at Joe. "What about you?" she asked. "Do you ever think about finding a Juliet?"

"Wolves mate for life. I'm not sure I'm the type to be with one woman forever."

"Me, neither," Perrie said. "I mean, with one man. I suppose some people are happy with that. But I've never met a man that I could imagine spending the rest of my life with."

"Maybe you just haven't met your Romeo," he said softly, looking down at her.

"And maybe you haven't met your Juliet," she countered.

His gaze locked with hers, and for a moment, she thought he might kiss her. But then he turned away. "Look," he said. "There's the rest of the family."

Three other wolves appeared behind Juliet, about the same size as their mother but lankier.

"They had five pups last summer," Joe explained, "but they lost two of them sometime in the fall. I'm not sure what happened."

"That's sad," she said.

"That's life in the wilderness," he replied. He glanced at her again. Then, without hesitation, he leaned over and touched his mouth to hers. His lips were incredibly warm, sending a pulse of heat through her body that seemed to drive away the cold.

His tongue teased at hers, and for an instant, she thought about drawing away. But her common sense had fled and she was left with only instinct and the overwhelming need to have more. Unlike their first, challenging kiss or the frantic meeting of mouths that they'd experienced in the snow, this kiss was different. It was slow and delicious, filled with a longing that she didn't know existed between them.

She didn't want him to stop this time. Instead, she wanted to pull him down on top of her and find out how Joe Brennan really felt about her. And how she felt about him. As if he read her thoughts, he gently pushed her back into the soft down sleeping bag, his lips never leaving hers.

Everything that had stood between them—the arguments, the mistrust, the fight for control—simply dissolved, swept away by the stark solitude of the wilderness. They were completely alone, a brilliant blue sky above and nothing but untamed country all around them.

She felt wild, primal, uninhibited, like the wolves they'd watched, driven by instinct and pure need. She wanted to touch him, to feel his skin beneath her fingertips, to run her hands through his hair. Impatiently, she slipped off her mittens then clutched at the front of his down jacket, pulling him closer.

He groaned softly, his breath hot against her mouth. "We're doing it again," he murmured. "You're making me crazy, Kincaid."

"I know," Perrie said, breathless. "We should stop. But I don't want to stop."

"No, we shouldn't stop," Joe said, tugging off his gloves. "Not this time." He pushed her hat off to furrow his hands into her hair. Tipping her head, he kissed her again, deeper and longer, his mouth plundering hers until her head spun with uncontrolled desire.

She shuddered, the passion radiating through her in waves. Joe pulled his sleeping bag over them both, creating a warm cocoon. Slowly, he tugged at the zipper of her jacket, then slipped his fingers beneath the layers of sweaters she wore. When he finally met warm skin, she heard him suck in his breath and hold it.

"This is not the place to do this," Joe said. "It's ten below zero."

"It's warm enough," Perrie said.

Joe pushed himself up, then looked at her, playfully running his finger along her bottom lip. "But there are much warmer places to be, sweetheart. We don't have to risk frostbite to be with each other."

Perrie closed her eyes. "You know, we'd be risking a lot more than frostbite if we let this happen again." Her common sense had returned in full force and she sat up and tugged her jacket closed. "This is ridiculous, Brennan. We can't keep doing this."

"Why not?" Joe asked.

Perrie opened her mouth to reply, then realized she

didn't have a good reason. There had to be a reason. "Because we can't."

Joe nuzzled her neck. "That's not a good reason, Kincaid. If you ask me, we do it pretty well."

"That is not the point," she scolded, pushing him away.

"What is the point?"

"I don't know." The truth was, she *did* know, but she was too embarrassed to put her feelings into words. She liked Joe Brennan and she liked it when he kissed and touched her. And she thought about him a lot more than she wanted to. The problem was, she didn't want to be like all the other women who had lost their hearts to a quick smile and handsome face. "I—I don't know," she repeated softly.

"Well, until you do, I'm going to keep kissing you, whenever and wherever I want."

Perrie zipped her jacket then began to search for her mittens and her hat. "I think we'd better go now."

Joe grabbed her hand and pulled her back down. A long, lingering kiss shook her resolve and she found herself slipping back into the languid pool of desire she had just left behind.

"Whenever and wherever," Joe murmured, nibbling at her lower lip. With a teasing grin, he kissed the end of her cold nose, then scrambled to his feet. He offered her a hand up and she took it, expecting him to draw her back into his arms.

But he didn't. Instead, he grabbed the sleeping bags from the ground and tucked them beneath his arm. "Come on, Kincaid. Let's get you back home where you'll be warm and safe."

6

THE STORY SEEMED to tumble out of her head, word after word, sentence after sentence, as if the entire text had been there all along. The wolves and the Gebhardts, two families living in the midst of the wilderness, bent on survival. Perrie had stayed up all night putting her thoughts onto paper, rewriting each phrase until it was as perfect as it could possibly be.

She wasn't sure what had made her pick up pencil and paper. She had barely stepped inside the door of her cabin after saying a quick and uneasy goodbye to Joe, before she sat down and began to write. And until she began, she hadn't realized that her day with Joe had affected her so deeply.

Joe had called her name as she ran back to the cabin, but she'd been intent on putting some distance between them. Whenever they were together, all her resolve went right down the drain. Either they fought like a pair of pit bulls or they jumped on each other like a couple of hormone-charged teenagers. Until she figured out exactly how she wanted to handle Joe Brennan, she was going to stay away from him. So she wrote.

The day had faded, and rather than switch on a light, she brought an old kerosene lamp to the table. The soft glow seemed to enfold her in a world of her own making, a world without modern conveniences...deadlines and sources...story meetings and proofreaders. For the first time in many years, she wrote from her heart, not from her head. And she rediscovered the true joy of crafting a beautiful sentence, of taking a reader to a place they'd never been.

She had worked all night, catching only snatches of sleep before another turn of phrase would invade her dreams and she'd need to get up and jot it down. Then she would sleep again, and sometimes, mingled with the images of the wolves, she'd see Joe and he would become part of her story, personifying the wolf who had roamed the frigid winters alone.

She had tried to put their encounter in the wilderness out of her head. But it returned again and again. At first, throwing herself back into her work had been an antidote, the perfect way to put his kisses out of her head. But later, she enjoyed the memories, lingering over them as she wrote, reliving the feel of his hands on her body, his mouth over hers.

The day had dawned bright and clear, and when Perrie awoke she saw the story scattered beside her over the quilt. Slowly, she reread what she'd written, making a few more edits. Then she got up and carefully recopied the text onto clean paper. Though she'd brought her laptop along with her, this story didn't want to be written on a computer. This story was more like a letter—a letter from the wilderness.

Although this wasn't the type of story she usually wrote, she was still proud of how it came out. And she was anxious to find out if Milt thought there was any merit in the writing. Not that he'd run the story, but perhaps he'd enjoy her insights on Alaska.

"A fax machine," she murmured, tugging a bulky knit sweater over her head. "They've got to have a fax

machine up at the lodge." Perrie retrieved her mukluks from near the door and pulled them on, then
grabbed her jacket and the sheaf of paper that was her
story.

The air was crisp and biting and her breath clouded
in front of her face as she trudged up to the lodge. The
low log building had stirred her curiosity more than
once since she'd arrived, but she'd tried to avoid it,
knowing that Joe lived inside. She preferred the privacy of her own cabin.

As she stepped up onto the wide porch, she noticed
an old carving above the door. No Wimin Kin Pass.
Perrie smiled. Obviously the bachelors who lived inside felt it necessary to protect themselves from pred-
atory females. Below the large block letters, she read
another phrase. "Except for Julia," she murmured.

Perrie stepped back, wondering who Julia was and
why she was admitted entrance to the lodge. "Well, if
Julia can go inside, I certainly can," Perrie said.

She hesitated for a moment and tried to come up
with an offhand greeting for Joe. After what had
passed between them yesterday, she wanted to make it
clear that she would not tolerate any more spontaneous kissing...or touching. She'd be polite and friendly.
And when she felt that familiar surge of desire that
raced through her whenever he came near...well then,
she'd just turn around and walk away.

Her resolve firmly in place, Perrie rapped on the
front door and waited for a reply. But when no one
came to answer, she knocked again. After the third try,
she decided to venture inside.

The interior of the lodge was a complete surprise.
She expected something as rough as the exterior. But
instead, she entered a huge room that combined a cozy

country feel with rugged log walls and a stone fireplace. Brightly colored woven blankets draped the chairs and sofa, and scattered about the room were interesting little pieces of Alaskan art—a carving here, a handwoven basket there. Rag rugs covered the plank floors and a fire snapped and popped in the fireplace. Compared to her bare-bones cabin, the lodge was backwoods luxury.

"Hello?" she called. "Is anybody home?"

Her call was answered by a high-pitched voice and a flurry of footsteps. A small boy, pale-haired and wide-eyed, appeared from the rear of the other side of the great room. "I'm here!" he cried.

When he saw her, he stopped short then adjusted his glasses on his upturned nose. "Who are you?" he asked.

"I'm Perrie. Who are you?"

"I'm Sam. I live here. Are you looking for my dad?"

Perrie frowned. "That depends on who your dad is," she said. Joe hadn't said a word about having a son, and Hawk didn't seem like the fatherly type. One of the brides had mentioned that the third partner in the lodge had recently married, but he hadn't been married long enough to have a child so old. "I'm looking for Joe."

Sam sauntered up to her side and studied her unabashedly. "Joe isn't my dad, he's my uncle. Well, he's not really my uncle, he's more like a big brother. Or maybe my best friend. My dad's name is Tanner. He's really my stepdad. We flew in from Fairbanks this morning." His eyes twinkled. "Boy, are my arms tired." A giggle burst from his lips and Perrie couldn't help but smile. His laughter was infectious. "That's a joke," he said.

"I know," Perrie replied, joining in his delight.

"What is going on in here?" A slender blonde appeared next to Sam, a dish towel clutched in her hands. "I can hear you all the way in the kitchen!" She stopped when she saw Perrie, then regarded her with a curious gaze.

"I'm sorry," Perrie said. "I knocked, but there was no answer. I'm looking for Joe."

A smile touched the woman's lips. "Are you Joe's Perrie?"

Perrie returned her smile hesitantly. "No. I mean, yes. I'm Perrie...but I'm not..." Her words trailed off. Trying to explain exactly what she was to Joe Brennan was becoming more complicated every day.

"I was just going to walk up to your cabin and meet you!" the woman cried. "I'm Julia Lo—I mean, Julia O'Neill. I've only been married a month. It's strange getting used to the new name." She paused. "So, how has your stay been? Have you been comfortable? I hope Joe has been taking good care of you. He's not usually in charge of hospitality, but Tanner and I have been at loose ends this last month, with the wedding and the move and—" Julia paused again. "Would you care for some breakfast? I've made some muffins."

"Is Joe here?" Perrie asked.

"He's down at the airstrip with my husband. They're unloading all our things. Sam and I just closed up our apartment in Chicago. We're going to be living here now. Is there something I can help you with?"

"I was wondering if the lodge has a fax machine," Perrie asked.

"We sure do. Tanner just put one in last month. It really helps with the reservations and trip details. It's in the kitchen." Julia motioned Perrie to follow her and they walked through a large dining room filled with old tables and a hodgepodge of antique and handmade chairs. Beyond a swinging door was a huge kitchen, as rustic and cozy as the rest of the lodge.

"The fax machine is over there by the phone," Julia said. "Why don't you send your papers and then we'll sit down and visit?"

Like Ann, Julia seemed anxious for female company. Perrie suspected that adjusting to life in Muleshoe was difficult, especially coming from a city like Chicago. Yet Julia seemed incredibly happy and excited, the same as Ann had been. They had their husbands and their families and a life full of challenges.

Perrie had her job. That had always been enough, more challenge than she could handle at times. But when compared to carving out a life in Alaska, Perrie's twenty-four-hour-a-day job as an investigative reporter seemed to lose a bit of its luster.

Sure, people in Seattle knew her name and they waited to read her stories. And she waited, impatiently, for someone to do something wrong. That summed up her whole career. She preyed on the indiscretions of others, exposing their foibles to the entire city of Seattle and delighting in their punishment. Without criminal intent and old-fashioned greed, she wouldn't have a job.

When she looked at it like that, she suddenly saw her career unfold in front of her. What would she be doing in a year...five years...ten years? Would she still be watching and waiting, hoping that some prominent person might take a step on the wrong side of the law? Would she still eat, breathe and sleep her work? Or would she find a new road to take, the way Ann and Julia had?

"Perrie? Do you know how to operate this machine?"

Startled from her musings, Perrie turned and nodded to Julia. "Yes. I—I was just trying to remember the number."

Page by page, her story went through the phone lines from Muleshoe, Alaska, all the way to Seattle. Within a few hours, Milt would read it. She could already hear his tirade as he wondered where her brides story was. In another few days, she'd take part in the Muleshoe Games and she'd finish the story she'd been assigned. And then she'd go home to her comfortable apartment and her exciting career.

"Would you like to sit down and have a cup of coffee?" Julia asked.

Perrie stared down as the last pages slipped into the machine. "I—I can't. I really have some things to take care of." The truth be told, now that she'd avoided Joe's company, she wanted to get out of the lodge before he returned. She wasn't at all sure that she had enough resolve to keep from wanting him as much as she had the last time they were together.

"I can't believe you're comfortable up at that cabin," Julia said. "We have an extra room here in the lodge. You're welcome to stay down here."

"My cabin is fine," Perrie replied.

"But traipsing to the outhouse and hauling in that tub to take a bath..."

"It's all part of the wilderness experience."

"Well, I certainly couldn't put up with it," Julia said.

Perrie frowned. "But you live here."

"And we have a bathroom," Julia said.

A gasp broke from Perrie's throat. "A bathroom? An

indoor bathroom? You don't have to walk to the out-house in the middle of the night?"

"Of course not," Julia said. "That's why I couldn't understand why you'd choose to live in one of the cab-ins when you could have stayed down here."

"I could have stayed here in the lodge?"

"I did when I first came here," Julia said. "Although I'm not surprised that Joe put you out in one of the cab-ins, considering the legend."

"What legend?"

"There's a carving above the door. The prospectors that lived here during the gold rush believed that any woman who crossed the threshold of the lodge would marry one of the inhabitants."

"And I've been hiking to the outhouse in subzero weather and bathing in the sink because Joe Brennan thinks I might decide I want to marry him?"

Julia considered Perrie's words for a moment, then nodded as if the logic were quite acceptable. "Yes, I suppose so."

"Julia, where do you want these boxes?" The sound of Joe's voice echoed through the lodge and Perrie's temper bubbled. The kitchen door swung open and he stood in the doorway, boxes piled so high they blocked his face.

"You can put them down here," Julia said, glancing nervously between Perrie and Joe.

Joe lowered the stack to the floor, then straightened, coming face-to-face with Perrie. He blinked in surprise, then gave her an uneasy smile. "'Morning," he mur-mured. She expected to be uncomfortable with him, es-pecially after what they'd shared the day before. But she'd also thought they'd left all the anger behind them, that they'd become friends. She'd been sadly mistaken.

"You put Perrie out in a cabin?" Julia asked. "Without heat and indoor plumbing? You made her cook her own meals and make her own bed? Is this any way to treat a guest here?"

Joe scowled at Julia. "She's not really a guest."

"Aren't we being paid by her newspaper? Isn't it true that our rate includes all meals?"

"Well, yes. But this is a different situation."

Julia slowly approached Joe until they stood toe to toe. "Here's the situation. I want you to go up to Miss Kincaid's cabin, gather her belongings and bring them back here to the lodge. And then I want you to make our guest as comfortable as possible."

Perrie stiffened her spine and forced a smile. "That's really not necessary. I'm perfectly happy staying in the cabin." With that, she sent Joe a murderous look—a look that said there would be no more long, deep kisses between them. And the last thing she wanted to do was sleep under the same roof as Joe Brennan.

She stalked out of the room, cursing softly with each step. Her thoughts, a jumble of anger and frustration, detoured to an image of Joe Brennan, naked, asleep amid rumpled sheets...finely muscled chest...long, sinewy arms.

"Stop it," she scolded out loud. "You should be thinking about how you're going to get back to Seattle, not wondering what Joe Brennan looks like in bed."

JOE WATCHED as Perrie stormed out of the kitchen. He shook his head and wagged his finger at Julia. "You enjoy making me squirm, don't you?"

Julia grinned, then stepped over to him and gave

him a kiss on the cheek. "I'm going to turn you into a sensitive male if it takes me the rest of my life."

Joe growled. "I should have known you women would stick together."

"There are precious few of us here at the lodge, Brennan," Julia said, wiping her lipstick from Joe's cheek. "I'll do everything I can to even the odds a bit."

Joe picked up a box and hefted it onto the counter. "Don't even think about it. Just because Perrie Kincaid stepped over that threshold does not mean I'm going to marry her. We don't even like each other."

That wasn't entirely true, Joe thought to himself. He liked Perrie more than he wanted to admit. But right now, he would venture that she didn't have a particularly high opinion of him.

"She seems like a lovely woman," Julia said. "I already like her."

Hawk and Tanner strode into the kitchen at that very moment, with Sam hard on their heels. "Hey, I just saw Perrie Kincaid on the porch," Tanner said. "Did she come inside?"

Joe cursed and sent Tanner a poisonous glare. "Don't you start with me. Your wife has already covered that subject quite thoroughly. No, I won't be marrying Perrie Kincaid. Hell, if she's going to marry anyone here, it will be Hawk. She can't seem to stop talking about him." Just the thought brought a nagging jealousy, but it was about time Joe found out what really was going on between the two of them.

Tanner and Julia both turned an inquisitive gaze in Hawk's direction. "Well," Julia said, "what do you have to say for yourself?"

"I gave her mukluks," Hawk replied. "I'm helping her get ready for the Muleshoe Games."

Joe's jaw dropped. "You're helping her?"

Hawk nodded.

"Do you know why she wants to win the brides' competition? So she can get herself up to Cooper and find a pilot to fly her back to Seattle, where someone will probably take another shot at her. She's here in Muleshoe for her own safety."

"You sound awfully concerned for the lady," Tanner commented.

"For a lady he doesn't even like," Julia added as she wandered over to the fax machine. "Perrie left her papers here. Why don't you take them up to the cabin? And while you're there, you can apologize for your inhospitable attitude. Invite her to have dinner with us. And tell her she can stay in the spare room."

"I wouldn't have to apologize if you hadn't made her mad," Joe said, snatching the sheaf of papers from Julia's hand.

"Just kiss her," Sam suggested. "That's what Tanner does when my mom gets mad."

Joe ruffled Sam's hair as he passed. "I'll keep that in mind. I daresay I trust your advice a whole lot more than I trust your mom's."

He made the trip up to Perrie's cabin slowly, not because he loathed the thought of apologizing to her, but because as he walked, he read the story that she'd left behind. With every step, he was drawn more deeply into her words, the stunning visual images she created out of a simple turn of phrase. He'd always known she was a writer, but he never expected she possessed such talent. He thought she wrote about criminals and politicians and greedy businessmen. Not about wolves and the wilderness and the bonds of family.

He finished her story as he stood on the front porch

of her cabin, and when he read the last word, he sat down on the top step and read it all over again. He sat there a long time, thinking about Perrie and the wolves, about loneliness and love. And he realized that he had been wasting his time.

Sooner or later, Perrie Kincaid would go back to Seattle and she'd be gone from his life for good. There was a time when he had wished for that day. But now, he wanted her to stay. Something had drawn them together yesterday at the Flats and he needed to know what it was—because it wasn't just simple lust.

He wanted Perrie Kincaid more than he'd ever wanted a woman before. But he didn't want her in his bed—at least that wasn't the only place he wanted her. He wanted her beside him when he watched the wolves the next time, and he wanted her across the breakfast table tomorrow morning. He wanted to show her the northern lights and the beauty of an Alaskan summer. He wanted her to be there when the ice broke on the Yukon and when it froze again in the winter.

Most of all, he wanted time. Time to figure out why he wanted more time. Time to find out if this fascination he had with her was transitory, or whether he'd be cursed with it for the rest of his life. Time to come to the conclusion that he and Perrie Kincaid weren't meant to fall in love and get married.

The door behind him opened and he turned to find Perrie watching him. Her arms were crossed over her chest and she still looked angry. "How long are you going to sit out here?"

He held up the story. "You left this at the lodge."

She took it from him and rolled it up. "I'm not moving to the lodge."

"I didn't expect you would." He paused. "It's a

wonderful story, Kincaid. As I was reading it, I could see it all over again. You have an incredible talent. Why do you waste it writing about criminals?"

She walked to the porch rail and looked out at a stand of spruce. "What I do is important," she said evenly. "It makes a difference. This is a silly story about wolves. It doesn't make a difference to anyone."

"It makes a difference to me, Perrie. It makes me feel something inside. When I read it, it moved me."

Perrie turned and stared at him blankly, as if she didn't understand what he was trying to say, then shook her head. "It's nothing," she said firmly, folding the papers up and shoving them in the back pocket of her jeans. She took a deep breath and pushed away from the porch railing. "Where's Burdy?"

"He's probably in his cabin."

"I need some breakfast. I want to go into Muleshoe."

Joe stood up and moved toward her. "I could take you," he offered. When she backed away, he stopped and held up his hand.

"I'd rather go with Burdy," she said.

"Listen, I know you're angry. And I'm sorry. I should have asked you to stay in the lodge. It's much more comfortable and—"

"It doesn't make a difference," Perrie replied in a cool voice. "I wouldn't have stayed there anyway. The cabin is just fine."

"No, it's not. It's—"

"What do you want from me?" she snapped. "Do you need absolution for being a jerk? Do you think complimenting my writing is going to smooth everything out?"

"I thought that—"

"I don't belong here," she said in a weary voice. "I

belong back in Seattle. And you're the one who's keeping me here."

"I know how important your work is to you, but I made a promise to Milt and I'm going to keep it."

"A promise to make me miserable?"

"A promise to keep you safe."

"But why you?"

Joe had never told another soul what Milt Freeman had done for him. But now it was time to tell Perrie. Maybe then she'd understand why it was so important for her to stay in Muleshoe.

"Right after I got out of law school, I worked for the public defender's office in Seattle. I was so full of myself, thinking I'd stand up for the rights of the common man and make the world a better place. But that wasn't the way it turned out. Mostly, I represented criminals. But I did my job very well.

"One day, I had the pleasure of representing a young punk named Tony Riordan. He was your basic wise-guy wannabe who'd been running a small extortion business shaking down some of Seattle's immigrant shopkeepers. I represented him, I lost the case, and he went to jail for six months."

Perrie's jaw dropped. "You knew Tony Riordan?"

"Intimately. After the trial, Mr. Riordan took it upon himself to send a few of his associates to my house to express his displeasure at the verdict. But before I got home that day, a reporter named Milt Freeman called me and warned me. He'd heard from one of his sources that Tony wanted a little payback."

"So Milt saved your life?"

"Or at least my pretty profile," Joe said with a laugh. "The point is, Tony Riordan was dangerous back then and he had nothing to lose. He's got a lot more to lose now, Perrie, and you're the one who's threatening to take it away."

"I can take care of myself," Perrie said stubbornly, crossing her arms over her chest.

Joe cursed softly. "Is it so hard to believe that someone cares about you?" Her mouth tensed into a thin line and Joe knew that he'd finally driven his point home. "Milt cares about you. And I care about you."

A cynical smile curled her lips and her chin tipped up defiantly. "I guess you'll do anything to keep me here, won't you." She started down the front steps. "I've got to find Burdy."

"Come on, Perrie," he chided, following after her. "You can't stay mad at me forever."

She turned, grinning at him as she swaggered backward. "Just watch me, Brennan."

"Why can't you think of this as a learning experience?" he called. "I bet you'll never walk into your bathroom again without appreciating the beauty of indoor plumbing. Or turn up the heat without remembering the wood you hauled to feed the stove in the cabin."

"Keep talking, Brennan. Sooner or later you might just convince yourself that you're doing a good thing by keeping me here."

He stopped and watched her walk toward Burdy's, admiring the quick sway of her hips, the focused energy of her stride. Chuckling to himself, he started back toward the lodge.

It was getting harder and harder to stay angry at Perrie Kincaid. To tell the truth, the more he knew of her, the more he liked her. She was stubborn and opinionated and she knew her own mind. She didn't let anybody push her around. He admired that about her.

Beyond that, he thought she was just about the prettiest woman he'd ever known. He'd never really looked at her as anything but a pain in the backside, tough as nails and prickly as a hawthorn tree. But then, out of the clear blue, he had come to realize just how incredibly alluring she was.

Joe shook his head. That was one opinion he'd have to keep to himself. It wouldn't do to have everyone in the lodge and all of Muleshoe know that he was attracted to Perrie Kincaid.

PERRIE SLID ONTO a bar stool and grabbed a menu. Paddy Doyle lumbered over and wiped his hands on his apron. "Miz Kincaid. How are you this sunny morning?"

"I'm fine, Mr. Doyle. I think I'll have a lumberjack breakfast...with an extra order of bacon...cheese on the hash browns...and a double milk."

Paddy raised his eyebrow. "You sure you want all that for breakfast? You usually just have a doughnut and coffee."

"I'm in training," Perrie said.

Paddy scribbled her order on a scrap of paper, then walked it back to the kitchen. He returned a few moments later with a large glass of milk. "I heard you're entering the brides' competition," he said. "All the bachelors around town are lookin' forward to seeing how you fare. See if you're decent marriage material."

Perrie smiled. "The rules say any single woman can enter. But this single woman isn't interested in marriage. Just in the first prize."

"I also heard that you spent some time inside the Bachelor Creek Lodge this morning."

Perrie blinked in surprise. She'd visited the lodge

less than an hour ago and already Muleshoe's version of Walter Cronkite was on the story. "My first and last visit."

"I wouldn't be too certain of that. A lady sets foot in the lodge and she's bound to be married." Paddy laughed. "Not one of them boys paid a cent into the bride scheme and now they're falling like tall timber. First Tanner. Now Joe. Hawk will be next."

"I'm not marrying Joe Brennan," Perrie insisted.

"I bet Joe was plenty mad when he found out you got inside the lodge. He's been dodging marriage since I met him five years ago. You know, he's dated pretty near every available woman in east Alaska."

"I know that, Mr. Doyle. Everyone knows that. Seems Joe's social life is front-page news around Muleshoe."

"Would be, if we had a newspaper." Paddy rubbed his chin. Bracing his foot on an empty beer barrel, he leaned up against the bar. "You work in the newspaper business, right?"

"When I'm not withering away in the wilds of Alaska," she said, sipping at her milk.

"I need some advice." Paddy reached back and untied his apron. "Come with me. I want to show you something."

Her curiosity piqued, she followed him through the bar to a rear door, then up a dusty narrow stairway to the second story of the building. Paddy came to another door and threw it open.

"This stuff has been up here forever," he said. "I was thinkin' about putting in a nice dance hall up here, for parties and weddings and such."

"What is this?" Perrie asked.

"This is what's left of the *Muleshoe Monitor*," Paddy

explained. "Paper started when this was a boomtown during the gold rush days. Lasted until the thirties and then the old guy that ran it moved to Fairbanks."

"This is incredible," Perrie said, moving to stand near the line of old wood cabinets on the wall. The galleys from the final edition of the *Monitor* still lay on the table, covered with years and years of dust. She brushed off the masthead to get a better look. "When I was in junior high, I worked for my town newspaper. They had all the old block type left and they used it for signs and posters. I would sit and cast headlines. Local Girl Wins Pulitzer, Kincaid Awarded Nobel Peace Prize. Things like that. Now it's all done on computer."

"I want to sell this stuff," Paddy said. "What do you think it's worth?"

Perrie picked up a composing stick. "This is... probably not worth much. I'm not really sure. To someone like me, it's fascinating. When I was a kid, I dreamed about having my own paper."

"Back when Muleshoe was a boomtown, in '98, we had enough folks living here to support a paper. Nearly two thousand. And with all the money bein' made, there was plenty of news. The guy that ran the place passed on in 1951 and no one ever came back to claim his property. That press has been sittin' there ever since, collecting dust. Probably take half the men in this town to move the thing. Or I guess we could break it apart."

"Oh, no!" Perrie cried. "You can't do that."

Paddy shrugged. "Not much else to be done. Come on, Miz Kincaid. Let's go see if your breakfast is done. You hear of any market for this old junk, you let me know, all right?"

She nodded and Paddy headed for the door. But Perrie lingered for a moment longer. The scent of ink still permeated the room, even after nearly fifty years. She closed her eyes and her thoughts drifted back to the little print shop she'd loved when she was a kid. It was because of that place that she'd become a reporter.

For an instant, she wished Joe was with her. She wanted to share this with him, the same way he'd shared the wolves with her, telling him about the first time she'd realized she wanted to be a newspaperwoman. And then she remembered how things had been left between them.

They were like a pair of magnets, at times attracted and at other times repelled by each other. She could understand the latter. But where did the attraction come from? Sure, he was handsome, but she'd never been hung up on physical attributes. She assumed he was intelligent, although she had never carried on a scholarly conversation with him. He was definitely charming, the type of man that most women found irresistible.

Maybe it was something else, something less obvious. Though he was friendly enough, he always seemed to stop short of any shared intimacy. Most men she'd known could talk for hours about themselves, but she hadn't managed to get a single iota of personal information out of Brennan beyond his revelation about his debt to Milt Freeman. When she questioned him, he just brushed her curiosity off with a clever quip or a teasing remark.

Perrie would hazard a guess that there hadn't been a woman on the planet who had managed to get inside Joe Brennan's head—or inside his heart. She wouldn't be the first—and she didn't want to be.

THE WOODS WERE DARK and silent when she returned home, the soft crunch of her boots echoing off the tall trees and disappearing into the night. Perrie had spent the entire day away from Bachelor Creek Lodge, simply to avoid seeing Joe again. Breakfast at Doyle's, lunch with the brides and practice for the games after that. She even spent an hour before dinner above Doyle's, reexamining what was left of the *Muleshoe Monitor*.

She wasn't really angry with Joe. But she wasn't ready to forgive him yet, either. One step toward a truce usually resulted in another step backward. Why couldn't they just get along? She was stuck here in Alaska for who knows how much longer, forced to see him every day, whether she wanted to or not. The least he could do was leave her in peace.

But did she truly want that? More and more, she found herself looking forward to their time together. And even worse, she enjoyed the bantering, the arguments, the ongoing battle for control. Joe Brennan was the first man she'd ever met who didn't let her walk all over him.

She'd always been a single-minded person, a woman who made her opinions known. Men had been attracted to her in part because of her notoriety, her position as a successful reporter. But Joe was not part of her world; he lived outside the orbit of the *Seattle Star*. He didn't care that she was Perrie Kincaid, award-winning journalist. He knew her as Perrie Kincaid, pain in the butt, unhappy guest, woman with a single mission—to get out of Muleshoe, Alaska, at any cost.

But lately, she hadn't been as obsessed with escape as she had been when she'd arrived. During her training session this afternoon with the brides, she'd all but forgotten her reason for entering the games. Through all the snowshoeing and wood splitting and dogsledding, her thoughts were on Joe—on how she'd prove to him that she could handle the rigors of life in the wilderness.

Something had changed between them, a change so subtle she'd barely noticed it. Since their day with Romeo and Juliet, she'd begun to look at Joe Brennan as more than just a minor roadblock in her plans to write the Riordan story. He had wormed his way into her life, teasing and cajoling, challenging her at every turn. In her mind—and her heart—he'd become an incredibly sexy, attractive, intriguing man.

Perrie slowly pushed open the front door of her cabin, trying to push the tangle of thoughts aside, as well. Why couldn't she make sense of this? She'd always had such command over her feelings. But Joe Brennan defied every attempt she made to define her feelings, to restrain her fascination...to keep herself from falling head over heels for him.

As she stepped inside and closed the door against the cold, she noticed a small white envelope on the floor in front of her. Her heart skipped a beat. Could it be from Joe? But when she saw the childish scrawl on the outside, she scolded herself for such a ridiculous reaction.

With a tiny smile, she tugged a handmade Valentine from the envelope, realizing for the first time that Valentine's Day was coming up very soon. She'd never paid much attention to the holiday. Once she'd been transferred out of Lifestyles, she'd been spared the syrupy articles about hearts and flowers, sentiment and romance.

"Roses are red, violets are blue," Perrie read, "I'm happy to have a new friend like you. Sam." She traced her finger over the ragged letters of the little boy's name, a flood of affection filling her heart. She couldn't recall ever receiving a valentine before, beyond the little cards exchanged in grade school. No boy, or man, had ever taken the time to express his fondness for her in such a sweet way.

She leaned back against the door and closed her eyes. Now was not the time for regrets. She'd never had any real romance in her life. But she'd had professional success beyond her wildest dreams. Her work was so exhausting she'd never noticed the empty apartment she came home to night after night. Why did it suddenly seem that it wasn't enough? Why did she feel as if she deserved more?

Perrie slammed her fists back against the door, only to have the sound echo back at her. She jumped away from the door and another knock sounded from the other side of the rough planks.

"Perrie, I know you're in there. I've been waiting for you to get back. Open the door."

She reached for the knob, then pulled her hand back. Drawing a long breath, she cleared her mind of all her silly romantic notions about Joe Brennan, as if he would somehow be able to read her thoughts once she opened the door. But she didn't anticipate the tiny thrill that shot through her when she came face-to-face with the man once again.

He smiled at her, the soft spill of light from the inside of the cabin illuminating the handsome planes and angles of his face. "Hi."

She couldn't help but return his smile. He had an uncanny way of soothing the tension between them, of charming away all the animosity with a teasing word or devilish grin. "Hi," she replied. It was all she could say with the breath left in her lungs.

What was wrong with her? She felt like a lovesick teenager. How could she have gone from complete frustration to heart-pounding attraction in the course of a single day? What had changed?

"Are we still mad at each other?" he asked.

Perrie sighed. Was it even possible to stay angry with Joe Brennan? She thought not. "No. I'll probably curse you up one side and down the other the next time I have to hike to the outhouse in the middle of the night, but for now, I'm feeling generous."

He reached out and grabbed her hand. "Good. Because I have something special I want to show you." He tugged her back outside the cabin, then pulled the door shut behind her.

"Where are we going?"

"Not far," he said.

He pulled a flashlight from the pocket of his jacket and they headed down a path that took them deeper into the woods. The tracks from the dogsled had packed the snow, and even in the dark, she knew they were headed toward the river.

They walked side by side, silent but for the sound of their boots against the snow. He held her hand, her bulky mitten firmly in his grasp, and when she slipped, he circled her shoulder with his arm, pulling her close.

It all seemed so natural between them, this casual touching, as if they'd crossed some invisible line in their relationship that allowed them to acknowledge their regard for each other. She liked the way it felt, his hands on her, yet with no sexual overtones.

"Are we almost there?"

"Almost," he said. "Stop right here."

She looked around but saw only what she'd seen for the last few minutes. Thick forest nearly obliterating the stars above. Snow on either side of the path, illuminated by the weak glow from his flashlight. "What is it?"

He stepped behind her and covered her eyes with one hand. He placed his other hand at her waist to steady her, then nudged her forward. "Just a few more yards," he said. "Don't be afraid. I won't let you fall."

"I—I'm not afraid," Perrie said softly.

When she'd taken the required number of steps, he stopped her, then slowly pulled his hand away. It took a moment for her vision to focus and then her breath caught in her throat.

They stood on the edge of the forest, overlooking the wide, frozen expanse of the Yukon. And there, in the northern sky, hung a kaleidoscope of swirling color, so strange and unearthly that she was afraid to breathe. Red, purple and blue washed the black horizon in brilliance, like a giant spirit rising up into the sky in a jeweled coat.

"I knew you'd want to see this," he said.

"I—I don't know what to say."

He wrapped his arms around her waist and pulled her back against his long, lean body. His chin rested on the top of her head. "You don't have to say anything. I wanted to be the one to show you."

"It's incredible."

"I've never seen an aurora this nice in the middle of winter. They usually occur in the fall and spring. But every so often, on a dark night in winter, the sky comes alive with light. You can almost feel it in the air."

"Do you know why they happen?" Perrie asked.

"Protons and electrons from sunspots start floating around in space," Joe explained, leaning over her shoulder until she could feel his warm breath on her face. "They get drawn into our atmosphere near the magnetic poles and they light up and dance and put on a show."

"Why didn't I notice it on the way home?"

"The headlights on the truck, the trees on either side of the road. Or maybe you just weren't looking."

Perrie turned around in his arms and stared up at him. She couldn't see his face in the darkness, but she wanted to believe he was looking down at her. "Thank you for bringing me here."

"I wanted to show it to you. I only wish you could see it from the air, because it's even more glorious. Maybe someday..." His voice drifted off when he realized, as she did, that there wouldn't be any "some-days" between them. "I thought you might write another story."

"I will," Perrie said.

They stood there for a long time, facing each other, Perrie imagining the strong features of his face, his chiseled jaw, which felt so good beneath her hands, and his mouth, as potent as aged brandy. She wanted him to kiss her, here and now, while they stood under this magical light. She wanted to wrap her arms around his neck and draw him close until all their thoughts became actions, words transformed into sweet taste and touch.

The intensity of her feelings took her by surprise. How could she have spent so many days with this man, yet never realized how she felt? A few days ago, she wanted nothing more than to put him out of her life. And now all she could think of was being near him.

She wanted him to kiss her, and hold her, and make love to her until the sun drove the colorful lights from the sky. The revelation sent a shiver through her and she trembled.

"You're cold," he said. "We should go back."

"All right," she said. As they retraced their path through the woods, Perrie's mind scrambled for a way to make this night last a little longer. She could grab Joe and kiss him, the same way she'd grabbed him that very first day in the truck, daring him to reveal his true feelings for her.

But she didn't want to force the issue. If Joe Brennan wanted her as much as she wanted him, then she would have to be patient. For the first time in her life, she didn't want the control. She needed Joe to take the first step.

But there had to be a way to encourage that, a way to show him how she felt. Perrie cleared her throat. "This was very thoughtful of you...Joe." His name didn't come naturally to her lips. She'd grown so used to calling him Brennan that "Joe" almost seemed like an intimacy reserved for lovers.

"You know there's nothing that says we can't be friends," he said, his attention still fixed on the path in front of them.

"What kind of friends?" Perrie asked.

"The kind that doesn't fight all the time?"

They reached the front porch of her cabin and he held tight to her hand as they climbed the slippery steps. "I'm sorry I've been so hard on you," she said. "I understand that you take your responsibility seriously." She opened the door and stepped inside, deliberately leaving the door wide in an unspoken invitation. To her relief, he followed her inside.

"And I can live with that," Perrie continued, shrugging out of her jacket. "If you can understand how important my job is to me. It's my whole life."

He took a step forward, then gazed down into her eyes. Gently, he drew his fingers along her cheek, and with a start, she realized that he'd removed his gloves. The contact sent a current of desire racing through her.

"There's more to your life than that, Perrie," he murmured.

She opened her mouth to contradict him, but the words that came out were not what she intended to say. "I want you to kiss me," she blurted. A flush of heat rising on her cheeks betrayed her mortification and she looked away, unable to meet his gaze.

He took her chin between his thumb and finger and forced her eyes back to his. "I want to kiss you."

But he didn't bend closer, didn't bring his lips down on hers. Instead, he slowly let his hands drift down from her face, running his fingers along her shoulders until his caress reached her breasts.

Perrie closed her eyes as he cupped the soft flesh in his palms, his warmth seeping through the layers of clothes until she could almost imagine his skin touching hers. She held her breath and he lingered there for a long time, teasing at her nipples until they were hard against his touch. When she opened her eyes again, he was staring down at her, his blue eyes glazed with unmistakable desire.

Slowly, the caress dropped lower, her skin tingling with every delicious inch. Her belly, her hips, her backside. And then he slipped his hands beneath the layers of sweaters she wore and began to work his way back up to where he began.

Still he didn't kiss her, though he moved close, his lips hovering over hers. His soft, uneven breathing was all that touched her mouth. His quiet words drifted into her consciousness. She tried to understand their meaning, then realized that they were as disjointed as her own murmured pleas.

Without his kiss, every sensation he created with his hands was more powerful, more deeply experienced, touching the very center of her soul. She wanted to tear her clothes off, and his, as well. And like the clothes they wore to protect against the cold, they'd been trapped under layers and layers of misunderstanding. She wanted to strip all that away, to find the real man beneath, alive with desire and vulnerable to her touch.

She reached out and unzipped his parka, then drew her hand along the front of his shirt. But when she moved to unfasten the top button, he stopped her, taking hold of her hand and bringing it to his lips.

He kissed her palm and each of her fingertips, then allowed her hand to drop to her side. "I'd better go," he murmured with a smile of regret.

"You—you don't have to go," Perrie said.

"Yes, I do. We just became friends, sweetheart. We can't become lovers in the same night." With that, he turned and opened the door, then walked out into the frozen night.

Perrie stood in the doorway, shivering in the cold, watching him make his way up to the lodge. When the frigid air finally cleared her senses, she began to realize what had passed between them. He wanted her as much as she wanted him. And the next time they were together, they would become lovers.

Perrie wrapped her arms around herself, a shudder of anticipation coursing through her limbs. For the first time since she'd arrived in Alaska, she didn't want to leave. She wanted to stay here at the lodge and learn what she already believed—that Joe Brennan would be an incredible lover.

"HOW DO YOU KNOW if you're in love?"

Perrie looked around the room at each of the brides. First Linda, who considered her question with great seriousness. Then Mary Ellen, whose dreamy look predicted a romantic, movie-inspired answer. And then Allison, whose idea of love probably changed as often as the weather.

The brides' cabin reflected the full glory of tomorrow's holiday. Bouquets of hothouse flowers decorated nearly every surface, and Perrie had learned that one of the bush pilots had made a special run to an Anchorage florist to fill all the orders from the town's bachelors.

Boxes of candy littered the coffee table, and other gifts and tokens of affection were scattered about the room. The brides were scheduled to go back home at the end of the month, and the competition for permanent companionship was heating up. After the Muleshoe Games, Perrie predicted that there would be a number of proposals made to each of the girls, though she wasn't sure whether they'd accept.

"I don't know if there's any way to explain it," Linda said. "I guess you just know when you know."

"Bells will go off inside your head," Mary Ellen said. "You'll feel all tingly and shaky and you'll see stars. Angels will sing."

Allison groaned. "That only happens in the movies, silly. The way I see it, it's possible to love almost any man, if you really want to."

"You mean if he's handsome enough, he doesn't wipe his nose on his sleeve, and he has enough money to keep you happy?" Linda asked.

Allison grinned. "That sums it up quite nicely."

"But there must be more," Perrie said. "I can't believe so many people in this world have fallen in love and they haven't written these things down somewhere."

"Is this for the story," Linda asked, "or are you interested for personal reasons?"

"For the story," Perrie lied, but she could tell Linda saw right through her. "All right. I may need the information in order to evaluate my growing feelings toward an...acquaintance."

"Hawk or Joe?" Allison asked. "And if you say Burdy, I'm going to scream."

"It's Joe. Although both Hawk and Burdy have been perfect gentlemen, sweet and accommodating, I seem to find myself attracted to the resident scoundrel. The man has dated every single woman in Alaska, he delights in making my life miserable, and he has absolutely no concern for my career." Perrie paused to reconsider what she was about to say. "And I think that—against all common sense—I might be in love with him."

They had spent nearly every minute together since

their night with the northern lights. By day, he would take her to all his special places in and around Muleshoe. And in the evenings, they would sit in front of the fireplace in her cabin and talk. She would work on her stories and he would read them.

And later, as night closed in around them, they would kiss and touch. Although she'd been certain that they would become lovers, Joe had been careful not to push them forward too fast. Just when it seemed there would be nothing else to do but make love, Joe would smile sweetly and kiss her good-night, leaving her to wonder why he insisted on waiting.

Mary Ellen clapped her hands in delight, snapping her back to reality. "Oh, that's so sweet! It's like destiny, isn't it? Like that old film with Cary Grant and that French actress. Only they met on a tropical island and this is Alaska. And he wasn't a pilot. But it was so romantic."

"Does he feel the same way about you?" Linda asked.

"I don't know," Perrie replied. "To be honest, I'm not real familiar with all of this. I mean, I've never been in love before. And I don't think any man has ever been in love with me. I've had relationships, but they've never made me feel this way."

"Joe Brennan is definitely a good catch," Allison said. "He's got a successful business, he's handsome, and I bet he kisses like a dream."

Perrie sighed. "Yeah, like a dream."

"What makes you think you're in love with him?" Linda asked.

"At first, I wasn't sure. But then, after I thought about it, I realized it was something really silly. That's why I wanted to ask you."

"It's his eyes, isn't it?" Allison asked. "He's got those incredible blue eyes."

"I bet it's because he's a pilot," Mary Ellen ventured. "Pilots are so dashing and brave."

"It's because he likes the way I write."

The three women stared at Perrie, a trio of confused expressions directed her way.

"I—I wrote this story about a family of wolves that he took me to see. And I combined it with a story about a family living in the bush. I didn't think it was anything special, but Joe thought it was. And now he takes me to all these special places and he asks me to write stories about them. And then we...read them together."

"That's it?" Allison asked.

"No, not completely. I've always worked hard at my job, but no matter what I accomplished, it never seemed to be enough. There was always this vague ambition that I had to satisfy, another goal just out of my reach. But when Joe says that he likes my stories, that's enough. That's all I really need. Suddenly a Pulitzer doesn't seem to matter anymore."

"He respects you," Linda said. "And he's proud of you. That's a wonderful thing."

Perrie smiled. "It is, isn't it? It's so strange, but I feel as long as he believes in me, that's enough." She ran her fingers through her hair and groaned. "At least, I think it is. How am I supposed to know? I've been away from my work for so long, I can't be sure. Maybe I don't love him at all. Maybe I'm just bored and he's a convenient distraction."

"You don't have to decide right away," Linda said. "You've got time."

"But I don't!" Perrie cried. "Sooner or later, I have to

go home. I have a career to think about, and if I stay away much longer, I won't want to go back. What if I stay and then I find out I'm really not in love? Or what if I go back home and realize that I am?"

Mary Ellen reached over and patted Perrie's hand. "There, there, don't get so upset. I think you should follow your heart. When the time comes to decide, you'll know."

"She's right," Linda said. "Listen to your heart. Don't analyze this like one of your newspaper stories. Don't try to look for all the facts and figures. Just let it happen the way it happens."

Perrie nodded, then stood up. "All right, that's what I'll do. I'll listen to my heart." She walked over and grabbed her parka, then pulled it on. "I *can* listen to my heart. By the way, are there any new developments on the romance front for you three?"

"I've been seeing Luther Paulson," Linda said. "He's a really sweet man. So gentle and caring."

"George Koslowski has invited me to his place to watch movies tonight," Mary Ellen said. "He's got *Roman Holiday* on tape. Any man who loves Audrey Hepburn can't be all bad."

"And I've decided to pursue Paddy Doyle," Allison finished. "He's still a young man and he's got a successful business. He's handsome in a burly sort of way. And he's been widowed for two years. That's long enough."

Perrie nodded distractedly, her thoughts still on Joe Brennan. "That's nice," she murmured as she walked to the door. "I'll see you all at the games tomorrow."

She needed to be alone with her thoughts. As she walked down the main street of Muleshoe, she contemplated everything that the brides had said, and all that she'd told them. Now that she'd actually put words to her feelings, they didn't seem so confusing.

She was in love with Joe Brennan. And that was all she needed to know for now.

THE SUN GLEAMED off the snow, the reflection so bright that Joe had to shade his eyes to see beyond the lodge. In the distance, Perrie methodically split wood in front of the shed. Hawk had provided her with plenty of logs and a newly sharpened ax and she worked at the task with a single-minded intensity.

He had to admire her tenacity, even if he didn't approve of her purpose. Though she'd come a long way with her wilderness skills, he hadn't the heart to tell her that she probably couldn't win. Besides the three brides, there were four other single women who had lived in the area for years who coveted a weekend at the Hot Springs, all with finely honed talents.

Even if Perrie did manage to emerge victorious, he was still determined to protect her safety. The organizers of the Muleshoe Games had approached him about providing the air travel to Cooper and he'd accepted. Perrie was in for a surprise if she thought she'd make a clean getaway. If she went to Cooper, he'd go along. And he'd make sure that once they got there, she wouldn't want to leave the room.

Over the past few days, they'd connected in a way so unexpected that he wasn't sure what he was feeling. Every minute they spent together had brought them closer and closer. And now, he could barely imagine a day without her.

They had become friends, and soon they would become lovers. Every night, he had wanted to stay with her, to continue their sensual explorations. But as soon as he touched her in such intimate ways, he knew he was lost. The only way to halt the inevitable was to leave.

She wouldn't be like the others. When it finally happened between them, it would be something very special. And it would happen. Cold showers and pure thoughts could take him only so far. Sooner or later, his resolve would crumble and he'd give way to the desire that seemed to fill him every time he looked into her eyes.

Joe took another sip of his coffee, then tossed the rest over the porch railing and headed into the lodge. Julia was busy dusting the great room and she smiled as he walked through to the kitchen.

He filled his empty mug from the freshly brewed pot, glancing at the mess that Sammy had spread across the kitchen table. The little boy was so wrapped up in his own activities that he barely noticed Joe's presence.

"What are you up to, buddy?"

Sam chewed on his lower lip as he carefully wielded scissors on a large piece of construction paper. "I'm makin' a valentine for my mom."

Joe frowned. "Aren't you starting a little early?"

"Valentine's Day is tomorrow. I already made one for Perrie a few days ago. I put it under her door."

"Valentine's Day is tomorrow?"

"I bet you didn't get Perrie a present, did you?" Sam asked.

"I guess I didn't think of it."

"She's your girlfriend, isn't she?"

Joe considered the boy's question for a moment, then nodded. "Yeah, I guess she is. At least, I want her to be."

"Then you better show her how much you like her."

Joe sighed. It was already too late to get her a gift. Flowers weren't an option in the dead of winter, and with all the bachelors in town angling for the brides' good graces, he suspected that Weller's General Store would be sold out of anything resembling a romantic gift.

He needed something to show Perrie that he no longer thought of her as just a guest or an acquaintance or a constant intrusion in his life. That he'd found a place for her in his heart. That he cared for her more than any other woman he'd known.

"Maybe you could make me a valentine for Perrie?"

Sam sent him a sideways glance, then shook his head. "That wouldn't be right. You need to make it yourself. My mom says that if you make a gift yourself, that means it's from the heart."

Joe sat down next to Sam and picked up a paper doily. "Where do I start?"

Sam handed him scissors and a piece of construction paper. "Make a heart. Just fold it in half and cut it out. Then paste it on a doily. Girls like doilies."

"How do you know?"

Sam held one up and studied it. "It looks like ruffles and lace. Girls like that stuff. And they like glitter and these little round sparklies."

"Sequins?"

Sam nodded and pointed to the bottle of glue. "Paste 'em on with that."

Joe watched Sam put together his valentine and then began to work on his own. He hadn't touched paper and glue since he left grade school. The glue seemed to stick to everything, and before too long, he had sequins stuck to his palms and glitter under his fingernails.

"What are you going to write on it?" Sam asked, carefully observing Joe's progress.

"I thought I'd sign my name."

Sam slowly shook his head. "You gotta write something sweet and mushy. Or make up a poem. Girls like poetry."

"I'm not good at poetry."

"Then you have to tell her how beautiful she is. Say her skin is like rose petals or her lips taste like cherry soda."

Joe blinked in surprise. "That's pretty good. Can I use that?"

"You should think of something on your own. What do you want to say to her?"

Joe wanted to tell her how beautiful she was, how much he loved to be with her. He wanted to ask her to spend the night with him. But he couldn't put that on a valentine. "How about if I ask her to go to the dance at Doyle's?"

"That's good," Sam replied. "Girls like dancing."

"I'm going to have to remember these tips. Girls like doilies, sequins, poetry and dancing." Joe finished the valentine, then took a few moments to compose his message before he stepped to the kitchen sink to wash the glitter off his hands.

"Are you gonna give it to her now?"

"I thought I would. She's out practicing her wood splitting."

Sammy picked up his valentine and held it out in front of him. "Just remember," he said distractedly, "if she tries to kiss you, run away as fast as you can."

Joe wasn't about to follow that bit of Sam's advice. If Perrie did decide to kiss him, he'd probably drag her into the cabin and begin where they had left off the night before. He grabbed his valentine from the table and tucked it inside his jacket, then ruffled Sam's hair as he walked past. "Thanks for the help, buddy."

Joe found Perrie back at her cabin. She sat on the porch, her attention centered on adjusting the straps on her snowshoes. "How's the training going?"

She glanced up and he thought he detected a blush rise on her already rosy cheeks. Her smile warmed his blood and he bent down and kissed her mouth. Strange how kissing her felt so natural, how he barely had to think before he pressed his lips to hers.

"I can't seem to get this strap right."

"Here, let me see." He took the snowshoe from her and carefully readjusted the strap. "How's that?"

"Why are you doing this? I thought you'd be the last person to help me."

"If you're going to compete, you should do your best."

"Do you really mean that?"

"Yes," Joe said, knowing the truth in his words. "I'd like to see you leave all those wimpy brides in the dust."

Her green eyes sparkled with surprise. "I'm getting really good at the wood splitting. I'm still a little shaky on the snowshoes, but I think, with Hawk's dog team, I've got the mushing competition sewn up."

"Did you know there's a dance at Doyle's after the games are over?"

She sent him a curious glance, the corners of her mouth quirking up. "I heard something about that."

Joe withdrew the valentine from his jacket and held it out to her. He didn't know what to say. To tell the truth, he felt a little silly handing her a handmade card. But all his reservations dissolved at the tender smile she gave him. He said a silent thank-you for Sam's advice, then sat down beside her on the steps.

"You made this yourself?"

"With some advice from Sam. He told me not to let you kiss me."

Perrie laughed. "You're taking your cues from a nine-year-old?"

Joe bumped against her shoulder playfully. "So, will you go to the dance with me, Kincaid?"

"Only if you kiss me again," Perrie teased.

He leaned closer, their noses nearly touching. "I think that could be arranged."

He kissed her then, a soft, simple kiss. He didn't know such an innocent act could bring such a powerful reaction. Desire flooded his senses and every thought dissolved in his mind until all he was conscious of was the feel of her lips on his. Her mouth was so sweet; he had become addicted to the taste, needing more and more.

Then she drew back, her gaze fixed on his mouth. "I'll go to the party at Doyle's with you," she murmured.

"Good," Joe said. He pushed to his feet, then brushed the snow from the back of his jeans. "I guess I'll see you after the competition."

"We aren't going to see each other tonight?"

He reached out and cupped her cheek in his palm. "Sweetheart, I think you better get some rest tonight."

"All right," Perrie said. "It's a date. I'll see you tomorrow."

Joe shoved his hands in the back pockets of his jeans and nodded. "Yeah, a date. I'll come down tomorrow morning and get you. We'll ride into Muleshoe together."

"That would be nice," Perrie said.

He whistled a cheery tune as he walked back down the path to the lodge. He'd never really set much store in romance. But he had to admit that a handmade valentine had touched Perrie's heart. His mind flashed an image of her reaction and he smiled to himself.

He was through with waiting. The next time he touched Perrie Kincaid, he wouldn't stop until every desire, every secret fantasy they shared had been completely satisfied.

8

EVERY PERSON IN MULESHOE, from the smallest child to the town's oldest citizen, one-hundred-year-old prospector Ed Bert Jarvis, gathered on Main Street to watch the games. In the middle of a long winter, any social activity was hailed as an "event." And this year's event was even more special.

Ed Bert, born in the year of Muleshoe's "boom," served as the grand marshal of the parade, a ragtag collection of decorated pickup trucks, dogsleds, snowmobiles and a pair of bicycles. They were accompanied by the town band, which consisted of Wally Weller on trumpet, his wife, Louise, on saxophone, and son, Wally Jr., on drums.

Perrie had never seen anything like it. Though the temperature still hovered around zero, no one seemed to notice. Fur parkas and mukluks were standard uniform for half the population, while the more stylish half chose down jackets and Sorel boots. No one stayed home.

She'd convinced Paddy Doyle to cover the event as a stringer for the *Seattle Star*. The barkeeper wandered around with his camera, hoping to find a few good shots to accompany Perrie's article on the mail-order brides and boasting about the press pass that she'd clipped to his collar.

The brides' competition had been scheduled for

midafternoon, the final event after the general competition for the townsfolk. Contests of strength and speed were interspersed with a bed race, an ice-carving contest and an event that involved stuffing as many pickled eggs into a competitor's mouth as humanly possible.

To Perrie's surprise, the three brides from Seattle hadn't offered much competition in the snowshoe race. They had all dropped to the rear of the pack and watched excitedly as Perrie and four other women raced ahead. The four other competitors, all longtime Alaskan residents, hadn't entered to find a husband. Like Perrie, they were after the first prize.

Perrie managed to finish third behind a pair of sisters, trappers who ran their own mitten-sewing business from a cabin ten miles from town. They were stout women without Perrie's quickness. But then, they spent most of the winter walking around in snowshoes.

To Perrie's surprise, Joe met her at the finish line, offering words of encouragement as he helped her unstrap her snowshoes. Hawk joined them, and as the trio headed over to hitch up the dogs, both men gave her more advice on proper race strategy.

The dogsled competition was Perrie's best chance at a win. Hawk had informed her that his dogs were the fastest and best trained of all the teams. To add a measure of safety, the women didn't race together. Instead they covered a course of nearly a mile that wove in and out of town and were timed from start to finish.

Perrie nervously waited at the starting line, trying to keep the dogs from bolting in the excitement. Joe stood at the head of the team, hanging tight to Loki's collar. He sent Perrie a confident smile and a wink as she listened to Hawk's simple instructions.

"Don't let the team get away from you," he said. "You're always in control. Anticipate the turns and make sure the dogs are ready. Then balance yourself."

Perrie glanced over at the woman who held the fastest time so far, a tall, slender competitor in her early forties whose brother had once raced in the Iditarod. "She was fast," Perrie murmured.

"She was smart," Hawk countered as he stepped away from the sled. "But you're faster."

Joe let go of Loki's collar and joined Hawk on the sidelines. "Go get 'em, Kincaid."

Perrie took a deep breath and waited for the starter's gun. At the sound, she yanked out the snow hook and urged the dogs on, running behind the sled for the first twenty yards. In her nervousness, she nearly tripped and fell, but she gathered her composure and hopped on the back of the sled just in time to make the first turn off Main Street.

"Mush, boys," she called, her voice gaining confidence as the sled gained speed. "Come on, boys, mush!"

The race seemed to pass in a blur, the wind cold on her face and her breath coming in short gasps. The dogs responded well, as if their pride were at stake along with Perrie's. Loki anticipated each command and Perrie's turns were smooth and easy. When she reached the final straightaway, Perrie urged them on and she nearly flew down the snow-packed street.

She crossed the finish line to a rousing cheer from the crowd, then instantly forgot the command to stop the sled. Panicked, she shouted to the dogs as they ran right through a small crowd of onlookers beyond the finish line. Now that she'd given them a chance to run, they didn't want to stop.

She saw Joe's face pass by and wondered if the dogs would continue running until they got back to the lodge. Finally a voice boomed over the crowd. "Ho, Loki, ho!" Hawk called.

"Ho, Loki," Perrie cried. "Ho, damn it, ho!"

The dogs slowed, then stopped, and she tumbled off the back of the sled into the snow. A few moments later, Joe knelt down beside her, laughing and brushing the snow off her face.

"Are you all right?"

"I feel like an idiot," Perrie muttered, sitting up. "I couldn't remember how to stop them."

"Well, lucky for you, they don't take off points for style. You gave the crowd a decent laugh."

Perrie groaned and lay back down in the snow. "How badly did I do?"

Joe bent down over her and grinned. "You've got the best time so far. And the Seattle brides are the only ones left to race. Come on, get up. You need some rest before the wood-splitting competition if you're gonna win this thing. Hawk will tend to the dogs. I'll buy you a hot cocoa and we'll discuss your strategy."

She let him pull her to her feet and he slipped his arm around her waist as they trudged back toward the crowd. Several of the town's single men came up to her to congratulate her on her time and inquire if she planned to attend the dance at Doyle's. She smiled and nodded, too exhausted to speak.

"I suspect your dance card will be full tonight," Joe said in a tone that barely hid his irritation.

"Jealous?" she asked, wincing at a cramp in her foot.

"Of those guys?"

"You hold a rather high opinion of your charms, Brennan."

He pulled her closer. "I happen to know that my charms don't work on you. I'm just saying that if you do manage to win this competition, I can guarantee that you'll have more than a few proposals to consider before the evening's done—both decent and indecent."

"And what kind of proposal are you planning to make?"

He stopped and looked down at her, his eyebrow cocked up in surprise. "That depends," he said slowly, "on what kind of proposal you'll accept."

Perrie knew where this bantering was leading and she wasn't sure what to reply. Ever since Joe had first touched her that night in her cabin, she'd thought of nothing else but what might happen the next time they were together. Would they make love? Or would something push them apart again, some doubt or misunderstanding?

And if they made love, what then? Would she wave goodbye and return to Seattle, filing Joe in among all the failed relationships and forgotten lovers in her past?

Perrie forced a smile and turned her attention to the crowd. What other choice did she have? It was clear that she couldn't stay in Alaska. She had a successful career waiting for her in Seattle. Besides, she'd been told over and over again that Joe Brennan was not the type to seek a permanent relationship. And neither was she. Even if she wanted to love him, she wouldn't let herself.

Whatever had begun between them would have to end on the day she left Muleshoe. They could continue this little dance of theirs, maybe even make love, but sooner or later she would say goodbye. And knowing Joe Brennan, he'd move on to the next available woman.

The thought of Joe with another woman brought her own twinges of jealousy, but she pushed them aside. Falling in love with him would be nothing but disastrous. And allowing herself any regrets about what they might or might not do would only add to the mess. She could make love to Joe Brennan and then leave him. She could and she would.

"Do you think I can win the wood-splitting competition?" Perrie asked, anxious to put their conversation back on a more benign track.

"Sweetheart, I think you could do just about anything you set your mind to."

Perrie bit back a curse. Every time she thought she'd figured Joe Brennan out, he would say something that made her lose all her resolve. How the hell was she supposed to keep herself from loving him when he called her sweetheart and told her he loved her writing and touched her until her blood felt like liquid fire?

They drank hot chocolate and waited as the rest of the brides finished the dogsled race. As Joe predicted, she came out the winner and currently led in the point total. But it was plain to see that three other competitors had a distinct advantage over her in the ax-wielding department—mainly due to biceps the size of tree trunks.

When the wood-splitting competition was ready to begin, Joe accompanied her to her spot, then gave her a quick peck on the cheek, causing a major reaction with the crowd.

"We can see you got yer bride all picked out, Brennan!" someone shouted. "That legend is at work again!"

Perrie could only force a smile as a flush of embarrassment warmed her face. But Joe merely laughed and waved at them, taking the teasing with his usual good nature.

"Don't hurry," he said. "Just do your best."

"I'm never going to win. Look at those women! They could bench-press a Buick."

"Yeah, but you're much prettier, sweetheart. In fact, if they had a 'pretty' competition, you'd win hands down." With that, he turned and left her to stand in front of the crowd with the other seven single women. A tiny smile touched her lips and she picked up the ax and hefted it up to her shoulder.

She'd have three minutes to split as much wood as she could. And the rest of the day to savor the fact that Joe thought she was pretty.

The whistle sounded and she carefully set a log on end and raised the ax. Her aim was true and the wood cracked. A few more raps with the ax and one log became two and she repeated the process. Three minutes seemed like three hours, and before long, she could barely lift the ax, much less hit the log. Her arms burned and her back ached, and finally, when she thought she might just fall over from the pain, the whistle sounded again.

The crowd erupted in cheers and she collapsed on top of the woodpile. She watched as the judges worked their way down the line, counting the number of logs split. When they reached her, she rolled off the pile of logs and rubbed her sore arms.

In the end, one of the Alaskan Amazons won the wood-chopping contest. She wearily pushed to her feet and began to scan the crowd for Joe, when the judges returned to her spot and placed a huge medallion around her neck. At first, she wasn't sure what it all meant, and Joe added to her confusion when he grabbed her and spun her around.

"You won, Kincaid!"

"I placed fourth," Perrie gasped, grabbing hold of his arms.

"No, you won. The whole thing. You had the most points."

Perrie gasped. "I won?"

Ed Bert Jarvis shuffled over and pushed an envelope under her nose. "Here's yer prize, missy. Congratulations."

Perrie squirmed out of Joe's arms and snatched the envelope from the old prospector's hand. "I won the trip to Cooper?"

"You did."

Perrie screamed and waved the envelope at Joe. "I won, I won. I'm going to Cooper!" She threw her arms around his neck and hugged him hard. Then she looked up at him. His blue eyes darkened slightly before he brought his mouth down on hers.

He kissed her long and hard and deep. The crowd screamed its approval, but this time Perrie wasn't embarrassed at all. She tipped her head back and laughed. She'd conquered the wilderness and she'd proved to Joe Brennan that she could handle anything

Alaska tossed her way. She was going to Cooper. In no time, she'd be back in Seattle.

The only problem was that she didn't want to leave Alaska. There was one more thing she needed to conquer...and he was kissing her at this very moment.

DOYLE'S WAS PACKED when they arrived. Music blared from the jukebox, mixing with the chatter of the crowd. Joe held tight to her hand as he led her through the press of people. He hadn't let go of her hand since he'd kissed her in front of the entire town. Odd, how they'd suddenly become an item. Everyone now looked at them differently, as if they belonged together.

Did people believe they were already lovers? Did they think he might actually be in love with her? Or did they all think that she was just another one of Joe Brennan's conquests? She shouldn't care what anyone thought, but she did.

As they made their way through the room, she had to stop time and time again while the townsfolk congratulated her on her win. Finally, when she met up with the brides, Joe disentangled their fingers and continued walking toward the bar.

"He looks positively besotted," Allison said, envy filling her voice. "I don't know how you do it. You weren't even looking for a man when you came here and you end up snagging the cutest bachelor in town."

"I haven't snagged him," Perrie said, uncomfortable with the notion. It wasn't as if she wanted to marry him...although the thought might have crossed her mind once or twice.

Didn't every woman think about marriage, about a

husband and children at least once in her life? So what was it about Joe that summoned such ridiculous thoughts? She'd dated men much more suitable—stable, trustworthy men with good careers and monogamous personalities.

Boring men, she thought to herself. Safe men. That was one characteristic that she could never apply to Joe Brennan. He was the most dangerous man she'd ever met. Maybe that's what she found so alluring, the danger that he might just break her heart. She'd been throwing herself in harm's way her entire career, and now she'd moved the danger from her professional life to her personal life.

"Well, you sure proved you fit in up here," Linda said, giving her a hug. "I can't believe you won the dogsled race. I fell off three times. And Mary Ellen didn't even get on. The sled ran off without her."

"I had good training," Perrie said, glancing over at Joe and Hawk as they leaned against the bar. She distractedly listened to the brides' conversation, adding a comment here and there to appear interested. But all she was really thinking about was how long it would take before she and Joe were alone.

She caught his eye and gave him a little wave. With a grin, Joe turned to take a bottle from the bar, then made his way back to her. When he finally stood by her side, he wove his fingers through hers. The contact made her heart skip and start again.

"Come on," he said, leaning close. "There's an empty table over there."

He nodded to the brides, then led her away. When they reached a table in a dark corner, he pulled out her chair with unexpected gallantry, then produced a bottle of champagne from behind his back. Two wineglasses appeared from his jacket pockets and he placed them on the center of the table.

"Champagne?" she asked as she tugged off her jacket.

"We're celebrating," he said, sitting down across from her and tossing his own jacket across the back of a chair. He worked at the cork for a moment, then it popped off, champagne bubbling out of the bottle. "It's not Cristal, but it's the best Paddy has to offer."

He poured her a glass and then filled his halfway. "To the most determined woman I've ever met," he said, touching his glass to hers.

She smiled, then sipped at the champagne as she scanned the crowd. Everywhere she looked, she found men staring back. At first she smiled, but then she started to feel a bit uneasy. She took a gulp of champagne. "Why are they all looking at me?"

Joe leaned back in his chair. "They're wondering if they should come over and ask you to dance."

"But they asked me to dance the night I arrived here. What are they afraid of?"

"Now they think you're with me."

The bubbles from her champagne went down the wrong way and she coughed. "Am—am I with you, Brennan?" she asked, her eyes watering.

"You could call me Joe," he teased. "I think we know each other well enough, don't you, Perrie?"

"Am I with you, Joe?"

He gazed into her eyes for a long time, his devilish smile sending her back for another gulp of champagne. "Yeah, you are." He laughed. "You were amazing today, Perrie. I really didn't think you could do it, but you did."

"I guess you underestimated me," Perrie said, tipping her chin up stubbornly.

"I have a nasty habit of doing that," he replied. "In more ways than one." Joe reached over and took her empty glass from her hand. "Would you like to dance?"

Perrie nodded, wondering what he meant by his comment. How had he underestimated her? Was he still afraid that she'd plan an escape while she was in Cooper? Cooper Hot Springs was only a short distance from Fairbanks. Surely she could find a pilot to fly her to the airport. One phone call to her mother and a promise to appear at Sunday dinner would secure her a plane ticket.

Although, if her mother knew she'd met a man in Alaska, the plane ticket would not be forthcoming. Her mother's fondest wish was for a son-in-law. A doctor or dentist. She'd probably even settle for a pilot, as long as he was capable of fathering her grandchildren.

The dance floor was crowded, but Joe found them a small spot and pulled her close. A country-and-western tune wailed in the background and he pressed his body along hers and began to move with the music.

He really was a good dancer. The first time she'd danced with him she'd been surprised. But now, he held her differently, more intimately, and dancing with Joe took on a whole new meaning.

She wanted to seduce him, to tease and taunt him with her body, to lead him where she wanted him to go. The glass of champagne she'd guzzled emboldened her and she wrapped her arms around his neck and pressed her hips into his.

Perrie had never tried to deliberately seduce a man. She wasn't even certain she knew how. But instinct overcame insecurity and she simply moved with the music, nuzzling her face into the soft flannel of his shirt.

A soft groan rumbled in his throat and she felt his heartbeat, strong and sure, as she let her hand drift over the hard contours of his chest. They made a slow circle around the dance floor, yet she didn't notice any of the other dancers. The music and the noise and the people seemed to recede into the distance and all she could hear was Joe's gentle breathing against her ear.

Her fingers clutched at the front of his shirt and she pressed her forehead into his chest. Why was there always flannel between them? Why couldn't she have met Joe on some tropical island where the men barely wore clothes? Then she'd be free to touch him in all the ways she wanted.

The music stopped, but they kept on dancing, ignoring the silence between the songs. Somewhere during the long string of records, their dance became more intimate, a prelude to something new and exciting. She wished them to a different place where only silence would accompany their movements, but the jukebox still played and the people still shouted.

Perrie risked a glance up at him and their gazes locked. The passion in his eyes caused her heart to lurch. He pulled her hips tight against his, and his desire, hard and hot, branded her flesh through the fabric of her jeans. His meaning was clear. He wanted her as much as she wanted him, and nothing would stand in their way.

"So what's going to happen tonight, Perrie?"

"I don't know. But whatever it is, it's not going to happen here."

He grinned. "Then I think we'd better leave."

Before she could say another word, he left her on the dance floor, weaving his way to their table. An instant later, he was back with their jackets. He helped her slip into hers, then took her hand and led her to the door.

As soon as they got outside, he grabbed her around the waist and pressed her up against the brick wall near the door. His mouth ravaged hers, his hands desperately searching for soft, warm flesh beneath her sweater. He pulled her leg up against his hip and rocked against her until she could imagine him above her and inside of her.

"I want to love you, Perrie," he murmured, biting the tender skin in the curve of her neck.

She furrowed her fingers through his hair and pulled his head back. "Then take me home," she challenged.

WITH A CURSE, Joe frantically rummaged through the junk in his bedside table at the lodge. Why hadn't he planned ahead? The instant he'd opened the front door of Perrie's cabin, he knew he'd forgotten something. And now, the first time he was making love to a woman he truly loved, he hadn't come prepared.

He froze, stunned by his thoughts. No, it couldn't be. The words just slipped into his head by mistake. But he'd never, ever used those words before. "I love Perrie Kincaid," he said slowly, testing each syllable as it formed on his lips.

Saying it out loud was all it took to realize that he spoke the truth. He loved Perrie Kincaid. And tonight, for the first time in his life, he'd truly make love to a woman. He would hold her in his arms and he'd never have to leave. He'd never wonder when—or how badly—the whole thing would end. He loved Perrie Kincaid.

A soft knock sounded on his bedroom door and Tanner called his name from the other side. When he replied, his buddy pushed the door open a crack. "You're back early," he said with a smile. "I thought you and Perrie would be out all night celebrating."

"We are," he replied, shoving the bedside drawer shut. "She's waiting for me up at her cabin. What are you doing back so soon?"

"Sammy was exhausted. And these days Julia is feeling a little tired, as well."

"Is she all right?" Joe asked. "She's not sick, is she?"

"She's pregnant," Tanner said.

Joe gasped and his jaw dropped. "You and Julia..."

"No, Burdy and Julia," Tanner teased. "Of course me and Julia. We've wanted to tell you since we got back, but you've been impossible to pin down. You've been spending so much time with Perrie."

Joe rose from the bed and walked to the door, then pulled Tanner into his arms and pounded his back. "I'm so happy for you," he murmured. "You and Julia deserve all the best. And so does Sammy. Jeez, Tanner, you're going to be a father. Hell, you're already a father. You and Sammy are great together."

"And what about you?" Tanner asked. "It wasn't hard to see what was going on with you and Perrie."

He turned away to pace the room. "I was just thinking about that." Joe paused, but the words were no longer difficult to say. "I love her. I've never felt like

this before, and believe me, I'm as surprised as anyone. But she is the best thing that ever happened to
me. She's obstinate and impertinent and opinionated.
And she never backs away from an argument or a
challenge."

"These are her good qualities?"

"Yeah," Joe said with a laugh. "And she's sweet
and caring and she's got a talent for writing that I've
never seen before. She's so smart. I can talk to Perrie
about anything. And she can see right into my head
and know what I'm thinking. I can't fool her." Joe
sighed. "She's not easy, but that only makes me want
her more."

"What are you going to do?"

"I haven't gotten that far yet."

"Well, you'd better think quick. There was a phone
call for Perrie earlier this evening. Her boss called. I
guess it's all right for her to go back to Seattle."

Joe closed his eyes and cursed, raking his fingers
through his hair. "Great. I finally realize I love her
and she's going to go home the minute she hears."

"Is she? Are you sure about that?"

"That's all she's wanted from the day she got here,"
Joe said. "You don't know Perrie. Even if she did love
me, she'd never admit it. That stubborn pride of hers
wouldn't allow it."

"You're going to have to give her the phone message. And you're going to have to tell her how you
feel."

"Which first? The trick is in the timing," Joe said.
"Will she love me or will she leave me?"

Tanner chuckled. "I guess that's up to you. You
give her a good enough reason to stay and she will."
That said, Tanner stepped out of the room and closed

the door behind him, leaving Joe alone with his thoughts.

How could he be so sure of his own feelings and not have a clue about Perrie's? She was attracted to him, but was it only physical? Would she take what she wanted and then walk away? Such poetic justice, to finally fall in love and then be forced to take a taste of his own medicine.

Joe grabbed the box from the bedside table and shoved it in his jacket pocket. He wasn't going to get any answers sitting alone in his bedroom. All the answers he wanted were waiting with Perrie.

He strode through the lodge and out the front door, his thoughts focused on only one thing. He'd tell Perrie how he felt and then he'd tell her about Milt's call...and then he'd wait for her reaction. He wouldn't have to wait long. Perrie wasn't one to keep her feelings to herself.

The distance between the lodge and her cabin was covered in record time. When he opened the front door, he expected her to be waiting for him where he'd left her, standing near the door. But then he realized how long he'd been gone.

Her jacket was tossed on the floor, followed by her mittens and hat. His gaze traced the path of mukluks, sweater and jeans to the bed. Slowly, he crossed the room to find Perrie, dressed in her T-shirt, curled up beneath the covers of the bed, sound asleep.

Joe knelt down beside the bed and studied her face. Her cheeks were still pink from the cold and her hair tumbled around her face. Long lashes, dark against her skin, fluttered faintly, as if she were struggling to escape the bonds of sleep. He leaned over and kissed her. His gaze stopped on her arm and he fought back a flood of anger at the person who had come so close to taking her life. He ran his fingers along the ragged red mark.

She opened her eyes and smiled at him sleepily. "I'm sorry. You were gone so long. And I was so tired."

"I should go and let you sleep. You've had a busy day."

She reached out and placed her palm on his cheek. "I want you to stay." She wriggled over on the bed and patted her hand beside her, a silent invitation to join her.

Joe pulled off his jacket and tossed it on the floor beside her clothes, then kicked off his boots. The bed gave beneath him as he crawled in beside her. He bent over her, his head braced on his elbow, and slowly traced the shape of her mouth with his thumb. A tiny smile touched her lips and then she kissed his fingers.

Desire flooded his senses, overwhelming in its intensity, and he pulled her beneath him, settling his hips against hers, his hands braced on either side of her head. She was warm and vulnerable, and with every kiss, he could feel her need growing to match his.

Every touch, every sigh were perfection, and he realized that loving her had become more than just words. He loved her with his mouth and his hands, and everywhere he touched, she came alive beneath him. He wanted to know every intimate inch of her body, he wanted to be able to understand her sighs and moans, the fleeting expressions that crossed her face.

The quilt tangled around them, and he muttered impatiently, unable to free her or himself. Finally, he pulled it from between them and she smiled. "I'm not cold anymore," she murmured, her eyes half-closed. "Are you?"

They lay side by side, foreheads pressed together. "Sweetheart, I'm warm. Very warm."

She toyed with the buttons of his flannel shirt. "Then help me take this off."

He growled and sat up, tearing off his shirt and the thermal underwear beneath. The touch of her hand sent a shiver racing through him. He watched as she smoothed her palm over his bare chest, her fingers like silk, teasing at the line of hair that ran from his collarbone to the button of his jeans. When her touch wandered below his waist, his jaw tensed and he pinned her hand behind her.

She was all soft flesh and gentle curves, and his palm pushed beneath her T-shirt. Her shoulders, her breasts, her belly, her hips. Before the night was through, he would memorize every inch of her. And if she ever left him, he would be able to close his eyes and remember each detail. But he wouldn't let her leave. He would make love to her and, in their passion, they would form an unbreakable bond.

Somehow, she managed to wriggle out of her T-shirt, and Joe's breath froze in his throat when he saw that she wore nothing beneath. He closed his eyes and nuzzled her neck, then slowly worked his way down, biting, nibbling, until his mouth closed over a taut nipple.

She murmured his name and twisted beneath him, furrowing her fingers through his hair. He felt such absolute power, yet at the same time such startling vulnerability. He could make her moan with pleasure and she could break his heart.

He kneaded her flat belly, moving lower and lower until his fingers found the silky scrap of her panties. Her breath was quick and shallow, every soft sound a frantic plea for more. He slipped his hand beneath the lace and touched her, and she cried out again and arched her back.

"You feel so good," he whispered. "So good."

"So good," she repeated. Perrie drew a ragged breath. "Oh, what are you doing to me?"

"Do you want me to stop, sweetheart?"

"No, no, don't stop. Touch me there. Just like that. Touch me there."

She pulsed with need, growing wetter beneath his fingers with every caress. He wanted to carry her to the edge and then catch her as she fell into sweet oblivion. He felt her tense and he knew she was near.

"Let go, Perrie," he murmured. "Let go. Let me love you."

Her breath suddenly stopped and he watched her face as a glorious expression of pleasure suffused her beauty. And then she shuddered and groaned and twisted beneath his hand. Wave after wave of ecstasy rocked her body and he held her close, whispering her name.

When she finally drifted back to reality, she released a weak breath and closed her eyes. He listened as her breathing slowed and her expression relaxed. He stared down at her lovely face, the color high, a sheen of perspiration dotting her forehead.

For a long time, he studied her, committing each feature to memory, burning an image of her into his brain. He closed his eyes and he could still see her, the face of an angel and the body of a goddess.

When he looked at her again, he saw that she was

asleep. Joe touched his lips to her forehead, then pulled her body into his, nestling her backside against the nagging ache of his arousal. Wrapping his arms around her, he smiled. He held heaven in his arms and he wasn't going to let her go.

Tomorrow there would be time to say all that needed to be said, to tell her his feelings. To tell her about the phone call from Milt. But for now, none of that mattered. They'd finally found a place where pride gave way to passion, a place they might enjoy for a very long time to come.

9

SHE WOKE UP IN HIS ARMS, and for the first time in her life, Perrie felt utter contentment. The room had gone cold, the fire in the stove having burned to ash before sunrise. She snuggled beneath the quilts and listened to his breathing, deep and even and warm against the back of her neck. Seattle seemed so very far away... miles and miles and nearly a lifetime.

Here, with him, she felt safe and secure. Joe cared about her, he believed in her. And suddenly, she didn't have to work so hard to believe in herself. The pressure that weighed on her day-to-day life had disappeared. There were no thoughts of stories and deadlines and awards. Instead, her mind spun with images of exquisite tenderness and unfettered passion.

They hadn't made love last night, but they'd shared an incredibly intimate experience. She had given herself to him, stripped of all her inhibitions, vulnerable to his touch. And rather than feeling regret or embarrassment, Perrie felt sheer exhilaration. The world spun faster today, the sun shone brighter. Their lives together began when he took her to the edge and then caught her as she fell. And in his arms, she would be happier than she ever dared dream.

Like a cream-fed cat, she smiled and stretched. But his leg was thrown across her hips, the denim rough against her skin, and she couldn't move more than a few inches either way.

Perrie closed her eyes. For now, sleep was her only option, for she didn't want to wake him...not yet. She looked down at his arms, wrapped around her shoulders, strong and capable, and those hands that had worked such magic on her body. She wove her fingers through his and brought his hand to her mouth, kissing it softly. Who was this man who stirred such a deep desire in her? She barely knew him, yet she felt as if she'd known him her entire life.

Had destiny brought them together? She'd never believed in fate or karma, preferring logic and reason over all explanations. But something more powerful was at work here. If not for Tony Riordan and a stray bullet, she might have lived her entire life never knowing Joe Brennan. She might never have set foot in Alaska. And she might never have come to love a man the way she loved Joe.

The thought that they might never have met was unfathomable, and she drew a deep breath and banished it from her mind. She wasn't sure what the day would bring, but she had to believe that Joe felt the same way about her. And if he did, then her life would never be the same again.

A soft moan rumbled in her ear and Joe shifted and stretched behind her. She held her breath, but she could tell that he was awake, and she slowly turned around in his arms. He gazed down at her with half-hooded eyes and gave her a sleepy grin.

"You're still here," he murmured.

Perrie reached up and brushed a lock of hair from his forehead. "I could say the same of you."

He nuzzled her neck. "I can't think of any place I'd rather be. How about you?"

"I could think of lots of places, but I'd want you there with me."

"Where?" Joe asked.

"A big hotel with a big bed. And room service to cook us breakfast. Palm trees and sunshine and a beach towel for two."

He frowned. "Do you really hate the cold that much?"

"No," Perrie said. "I just hate all the clothes. And bundling up every time I need to go to the outhouse." She ran a playful finger down his bare chest. "And I like you much better without flannel and long underwear."

Joe smiled and kissed her on the tip of her nose. "So, when are you going to take your trip to Cooper?"

His question surprised Perrie. She'd forgotten all about her trip. And now that he brought it up, she wasn't sure what she was going to do with the prize. She had no intention of going back to Seattle before Milt called her. And Cooper was a long way from Muleshoe...and Joe. She couldn't imagine spending two hours, much less two days, away from him.

"I—I hadn't thought about it. Why do you ask?"

"I just thought you'd be anxious for a change of scenery. You've been stuck in Muleshoe for two weeks. And you worked so hard to win the trip."

Was he so eager for her to leave? She'd told him from the start that she'd use every option available to get back to Seattle. Did he still expect her to make a run for it? Was he hoping she would? "I suppose I should go soon. I'm not sure when Milt is going to call."

An odd look crossed his face, but it was gone before

she had a chance to figure out what it meant. "Why don't you go today?" he suggested.

Perrie blinked in confusion. "Today? But isn't that a little soon? I mean, I'm not even sure if I can. There are reservations and the pilot and—"

He snuggled up to her and sighed. "Don't worry about the pilot. I'm the pilot," Joe said. "As for reservations, the resort doesn't see too many visitors this time of year. We'll probably have the place all to ourselves. It will be very romantic."

Perrie sat up in bed, pulling the sheet up around her chin. "You're the one who's supposed to fly me to Cooper? Since when?"

He stared up at her, his arm thrown across his forehead. "I've always been the one. I donated my services to the organizers of the games as soon as I found out you were entering the brides' competition. I wasn't about to take any chances."

Reality came crashing down around her and her dreamy state evaporated in an instant. How could she have been so foolish? She'd forgotten what had brought them together in the first place. Joe had a job to do, a favor to return. Was all this just part of the job? Had she somehow mistaken obligation for true emotion?

Perrie closed her eyes and calmed her scattered thoughts. This wasn't real, this life she and Joe had been sharing. She'd been swept away by silly schoolgirl fantasies of happily-ever-afters. Real was Seattle and her job.

"You wanted to make sure I didn't go back," she said, her voice deceptively even.

"At first...maybe. But you're not going back to Seattle. So we can turn this into a nice romantic weekend."

"Then you trust me?"

"Of course I trust you. Perrie, I only want you to be safe. You understand that you're better off in Alaska with me, right?"

She didn't know what to say. She felt as if she were lost in the wilderness without a compass. All these feelings were so new and unfamiliar, she had no landmarks to keep her on course. Her whole life, she'd always been in control. But now she'd turned that control over to someone else, and it left her dazed and vulnerable.

Damn it, if she wanted to go home, she could. He had no right to stop her! After all, she was a grown woman, able to make all the choices in her life, including whether she wanted to risk that life to get a story or whether she wanted to take a chance with Joe Brennan. And he shouldn't have a thing to say about it.

Perrie calmly marshaled her composure. "All right," she said. "Let's go to Cooper. Today."

"We'll leave after lunch," Joe said, tugging her back down into the bed.

"No," Perrie replied. "I think we should leave now." She grabbed her T-shirt and yanked it over her tangled hair, then crawled out of bed. "I should pack. And you should go up to the lodge and get your things."

Joe grabbed her hand and pulled her down to sit on the edge of the bed. "What's the hurry? Come back to bed, sweetheart."

She stood up. "No, I think we should leave now."

With a groan, Joe rolled out of bed. Perrie tried to ignore the way his muscles bunched and rippled as he held his arms above his head and stretched. He raked his hands through his hair, then bent down and snatched up his shirt from the floor. "All right. I'll go throw some things in a bag and come back and get you in fifteen minutes."

He slipped his feet into his boots and shrugged into his jacket before he grabbed her again and kissed her. "We're going to have a wonderful time," he murmured.

She watched him leave the cabin, then sat back down on the edge of the bed. Perrie pressed the heels of her hands to her temples. What was she doing? She had been in Muleshoe for two weeks. Long enough to forget all about why she was here in the first place. A story that had seemed so important suddenly didn't make any difference at all—and all because of one man. A man she barely knew.

And what had happened to her journalistic instincts? Why couldn't she read Joe Brennan's motives and feelings the way she was able to read so many others? He had to know that Cooper represented her only opportunity to escape, to get back to Seattle. He had to know she'd try. And when she did, would he stop her, or would he let her go?

Maybe this was just an easy way to end things between them. Over the past week they'd been nearly inseparable. Sooner or later, Perrie had expected some declaration of his feelings, but he hadn't said a word. Maybe he didn't have feelings for her. Or perhaps she was just another in a long line of women who blew in and out of his life like spindrift.

Perrie drew a deep breath. She would formulate a plan. They would go to Cooper and she would find a way to leave. And if he let her go, then she'd know he didn't care. And if he made her stay, then she would demand to know why. He would have to reveal his true feelings for her—or admit that he was only doing a job.

A shiver ran down her spine. It all came to this. All this love she felt for him was riding on the answer to an impossibly simple question: Would he stop her?

Suddenly, she didn't want to ask the question. If she stayed in Cooper, she'd never need to know the answer. Perhaps it was unwise to force the issue, especially so soon. But then, the choice was bound to come up, for Milt would be calling her back to Seattle any day.

Somehow, it seemed easier this way. If he didn't want her, at least she wouldn't have to see it on his face. She'd walk out of his life without looking back. She would give them both a graceful exit.

Perrie stood up and rubbed the goose bumps from her arms. This was the right thing to do. She'd never been one to delay the inevitable. The sooner she knew, the sooner she could get on with the rest of her life.

The only problem was, she wanted the rest of her life to start now. And she wanted it to include Joe Brennan.

"I THINK WE SHOULD HAVE separate rooms."

Joe stopped short and looked at Perrie, not sure that he heard her right. They'd just arrived at the resort after an hour-long flight and Perrie had picked the last possible moment to drop her little bombshell. He knew something was bothering her for she'd been distant and uneasy since they'd left Muleshoe.

He thought she'd be happy that he had come along. After all, they'd spent so much time together in the past few days; he'd never considered that she might want to spend some time away from him. And after last night... What better place for them to be alone together but a beautiful resort in the middle of winter?

Sleigh rides, good food, dancing and the hot springs...indoor plumbing. He couldn't think of a more romantic place within a day's flight of Muleshoe.

But the trip *had* been hers, Joe mused, and he had essentially invited himself along. Maybe he was pushing too fast. Last night had been a huge step for them and he wouldn't be surprised if she harbored a few regrets. "Sure," he said. "Separate rooms are fine."

Perrie forced a grateful smile. "I mean, it's just that...well, we haven't really...and if we decide we don't want to, then—"

He reached out to stroke her cheek but drew his hand back before he touched her. "Perrie, it's all right."

"People might talk," she murmured, hoisting her shoulder bag up and starting toward the door.

Joe stared after her, shaking his head. If she really believed he bought that explanation, then he had some Alaskan swampland to sell her. It was obvious that she didn't want him along. When she won the prize, she assumed that she'd be going to Cooper Hot Springs with another pilot, one who wouldn't be watching her every minute of the day and night.

As he walked through the front door of the resort, realization hit him square in the face and he stopped, frozen in his tracks. She was planning to leave. Damn it, after all they'd been through, all that had happened between them, she was still determined to get back to Seattle.

Joe closed his eyes and tipped his head back, fighting the anger that bubbled up inside of him. Fine, he thought to himself. The hell if he was going to make her stay. Milt Freeman said it was safe for her to come back, so why not let her go? If Perrie could so easily throw away what they'd shared, then maybe it wasn't as special as he thought. She was just biding her time with him, waiting for the chance to get back to her real life.

Joe stepped up beside Perrie and filled out a registration card, signing his name with a frustrated flourish. Then he grabbed both of their keys and headed down the hall.

She caught up with him and touched his arm. "You understand, don't you?"

"Sure," Joe said. "This is your trip, not mine. In fact, if you want, I can fly back to Muleshoe right now."

His words seemed to take her by surprise, and for a second, he thought she might just accept his offer. "No, I'm glad you're here. Why don't we get unpacked and then we can get some lunch?"

Joe unlocked Perrie's room door and helped her carry her bags inside, tossing them on the bed. If she was determined to leave, he might as well make it easy for her. "Actually, I could use a shower," he said. "Why don't we meet in an hour? After we have lunch, we can try the hot springs."

Perrie nodded, then walked him to the door. "So I'll see you in an hour."

Joe stared down at her, wondering if this was the last time he'd ever look into her beautiful green eyes. Would she leave as soon as he was out of sight? He wanted to pull her into his arms and kiss her, to tell her that he was in love with her. But a strong instinct for self-preservation prevented him from saying anything. Time would tell if she really loved him.

He bent down and kissed her cheek. "All right, I'll see you later."

When he reached the privacy of his own room, Joe dropped his duffel on the floor and cursed softly. Leaning back against the door, he raked his hands through his hair. "The first woman I ever love and she doesn't love me," he muttered. "Serves you right, Brennan."

As he stood against the door, he heard a sound outside in the hall. He turned and peered through the peephole in the door. Perrie looked both ways, then headed down the hall. A cynical laugh escaped his throat and Joe opened the door to follow her.

A few minutes later, he stood in the shadows in a corner of the resort's lounge, his attention fixed on the transaction being negotiated at the bar. His jaw tensed and his heart hardened. He should have known she'd try. He should have known.

He watched as she spoke to the bartender before she moved down the row of chairs to a man who sat alone at the end of the bar. They talked for three or four minutes, Perrie glancing around the room every few seconds, as if she knew she was being watched. Then she shook his hand and hurried out of the bar, passing so close to Joe that he could nearly touch her, yet never noticing his presence.

Joe watched until she was long gone before he stepped from the shadows. In a few strides, he crossed the room and slid onto the stool next to Perrie's gentleman friend. He turned and glanced at the guy, who nursed a half glass of beer. "The woman. The pretty one with the red hair. What did she want?"

The guy scoffed. "What business is it of yours, buddy?"

Joe stared at him long and hard, wondering if he should grab him by the collar now or wait a few more seconds. He slowly stood and leaned over the guy. "It's my business, all right? Answer my question."

The guy shrugged, his cocky attitude cooled by Joe's thinly veiled temper. "She wants me to fly her to Seattle."

"Is she paying you?"

"She gave me a credit card number for starters. Said there would be an extra five hundred for me in Seattle if I was willing to wait for the cash."

"What's your name?" Joe asked.

"Andrews. Dave Andrews."

"I've heard of you. So, Andrews, if I check you and your plane out, am I going to be happy?"

"Hey, buddy, I'm a good pilot. And I keep my plane in top shape. You can ask any of the guys around here."

"When does she want you to fly her out?"

"Late this afternoon."

Joe reached in his pocket for his wallet, then withdrew two fifty-dollar bills. "Call her room and tell her you can't fly her out until tomorrow morning. She's in room 37."

"Who the hell are you?"

"The name's Brennan. Joe Brennan."

Andrews blinked in surprise. "Polar Bear Air? Aren't you the guy who found that climber on Denali a few weeks back?"

"Yeah, that's me."

Andrews smiled and clapped him on the shoulder. "I heard all about that. Good eyes. But if you want this lady to go back to Seattle tomorrow morning, why don't you just fly her yourself?"

"I'm not sure that she's going to leave," Joe replied.

"I'm hoping she'll decide to stay. So if she doesn't meet you, I don't want you coming to look for her, all right?"

"But how am I gonna get paid?"

"I'll pay you."

Andrews considered the request for a moment, then nodded. "All right." He took a long swig of his beer. "What is this woman to you? Wife? Girlfriend?"

"I'm not sure yet. But I'm about to find out." Joe pushed away from the bar, then turned back. "One more thing. If she does leave with you, and she changes her mind, I want you to bring her back here. I don't care where you are, just turn around and fly her back. All right?"

"Man, you must have it real bad for this girl."

The man had a talent for stating the obvious. "You'll do it?" Joe asked.

Andrews nodded. "Yeah, if she wants to come back, I'll bring her."

"I'd appreciate that. Now call her and tell her the flight's been delayed."

Andrews nodded and asked the bartender for a phone. Satisfied that he'd covered all his bases, Joe turned and walked out of the lounge. But instead of returning to his room, he headed out the front doors of the lobby into the frigid cold.

This was a dangerous game he was playing, risking his heart on a woman he'd come to love. If he had any shred of common sense left, he'd walk away, save himself the pain and regret he was certain to feel. But his heart overruled his brain. He couldn't give up on them, not yet. He had to believe that somewhere in Perrie's heart she cared for him, maybe even loved him. And that given time, she'd recognize her feelings.

But did he have enough time? Or would the clock

suddenly run out, leaving him with nothing but memories of a woman he'd loved and lost?

PERRIE STOOD NERVOUSLY in the hallway outside her room, watching as Joe pushed the room key into the lock. She knew this moment was coming, but she was completely unprepared to handle it.

She and Joe had spent a wonderful day together, swimming in the hot springs, enjoying a long, leisurely dinner and taking a sleigh ride through the snow-kissed woods. For brief snatches of time, she forgot all about her plan to leave him and, instead, found herself captivated by his charm and gentle humor.

All this would have been avoided, had her pilot kept to their original plans. She would have left Joe waiting in his room before dinner, while she flew away to the safety of Seattle. Now she would have to wait until daybreak to make her escape.

Joe pushed the door open, then stepped aside. Perrie slowly walked past him, silently rehearsing the excuse she would give. She turned, but to her surprise, he was standing right there, so close she could feel the heat from his body.

In the blink of an eye, he pulled her against him and captured her mouth with his. He kissed her long and hard and she let him, knowing that it would be the last thing they shared.

He pressed his forehead against hers and looked down into her eyes. "You are so beautiful, Perrie. There are times when I can't keep from touching you." With gentle fingers, he brushed the hair from her temple, then touched his warm lips to the spot. But he didn't kiss her again. It was as if he were waiting for her to say something.

Drawing up her courage, Perrie smiled brightly and stepped out of his embrace. "I—I'm really tired," she said, inwardly cringing at the trite excuse. "I think I'd like to turn in early." She swallowed hard. "Alone."

He showed no reaction to her words. In her heart, she wanted him to brush away her excuse and carry her into the room to make wild, passionate love to her against all her protests. But Joe simply shrugged and smiled.

"I'm tired, too," he said, his gaze fixed on her face.

He stared at her a long time, as if he were memorizing her features. And then he blinked and shook his head. "Good night, sweetheart." He kissed her once more, a sweet and quiet kiss that nearly melted her icy resolve. She felt his fingers caress her cheek and then he was gone.

The sound of his room door closing drove a dagger into her heart and her breath caught in her chest at the pain. "Goodbye, Joe Brennan," she whispered, her throat tight with welling emotion.

The silence of her own room closed in around her. Perrie lay down on the bed and covered her eyes with her arms, willing away the doubt that assailed her mind. This was for the best. Even if they did love each other now, they would soon grow apart. To be together, one of them would have to give up their dream, and a sacrifice like that would soon cause regrets and recriminations.

Joe Brennan was a bush pilot in Alaska and Perrie Kincaid was a reporter in Seattle. Nothing they could do or say would change that fact. For them, love had been impossible from the beginning.

Perrie curled up on her side and stared at the bedside clock, counting the seconds for each minute that passed. Her eyes slowly closed, and soon she found herself floating between conscious thought and sleep.

Images of Joe drifted through her mind, but she didn't try to push them aside. She could almost feel his lips trace a path from her cheek to her mouth. She imagined the two of them at her door, imagined a different end to their time together. Her breath felt warm against his cheek and she listened, trying to make out the words she spoke. She pinched her eyes shut and focused her thoughts. And then, she heard herself.

I want you. I need you. I love you.

"I want you," Perrie murmured, opening her eyes. "I need you." She pushed up from the bed. "And I love you."

A force more powerful than all her resolve pulled her toward the door. She opened it and stepped out into the hall, her gaze fixed on the room across from hers. Perrie reached out and touched the smooth wood, then, closing her eyes, she rapped hard.

The door swung open and he stood there, bare-chested, the light from his room gleaming off his smooth skin. "Perrie? Are you all right?"

"I—I want you," she murmured. "I need you. I—I—"

She tried to retreat but her feet were frozen to the floor. When she couldn't move, she closed her eyes instead, hoping that this was all part of her dream and would disappear in time. But then she felt his mouth on hers, the warmth of his lips, and she knew that she'd stumbled into something real.

He buried his face in the curve of her neck, and bent down, scooping her into his arms. This felt so right, so perfect, and no matter how Perrie tried, she couldn't make herself regret her decision. She and Joe belonged together, at least for this one night.

Joe kicked the door shut and leaned back against it. "I wanted you to come. I hoped you would." His mouth found hers again and he held her, enraptured, in a soul-shattering kiss.

He crossed the room, then gently placed her back on her feet. He gazed down into her eyes and she saw the desire there, dark and dangerous. If she touched him now, there would be nothing to stop them. And she didn't want to stop.

Slowly, she reached out and placed her palm on his chest. His heart beat strong beneath her fingers, quickening slightly as her hand drifted down to the waistband of his jeans, to the smooth ripple of his flat belly and then no further.

"Touch me," he said, his fingers furrowing through the hair at her nape.

She could hear the need in his voice, the urgency, and in that moment, she realized the power she had over him. He could no more resist than she could. They were both lost to this passion that raged between them. And whether it was born of love or lust, it didn't make any difference—it had to be satisfied.

Perrie splayed her fingers over the front of his jeans, tracing the hard ridge of his erection beneath the taut denim. He sucked in a sharp breath and moaned softly, a wordless plea for more. Emboldened, she stroked him, teasing him until he pushed her hand away.

As quickly as she had gained it, she lost her power and he took control. He tugged at her sweater and with a soft oath yanked it over her head. As if a floodgate had been opened, they began to tear at each other's clothes, tossing away the barriers between them with each piece of clothing.

When they were both naked from the waist up, he suddenly stopped. He stared down at her and with a sure hand cupped her breast in his palm. Then, with exquisite patience, he slid down along her body, his lips and hands branding a path as he moved from her shoulder to her breast, to her waist, to her backside.

Desire built inside her with every tender caress and she could think of nothing more than total surrender. And when he knelt in front of her, he finished the job he had begun, undressing her with great patience and restraint, his mouth exploring every inch of newly exposed flesh...her toes, her ankles, the curve of her calf and the soft skin of her inner thigh.

Perrie braced her hands on his shoulders, his muscles bunching and shifting beneath her fingers as he moved. And when she stood naked before him, she felt her pulse quicken and her breath disappear. There was no way to go back now, no thought of escape. For this moment, she belonged to Joe, utterly and entirely, without fear or regret.

He advanced again, across her belly, nibbling and kissing, moving lower and lower until his tongue penetrated the moist core of her desire. Her knees buckled and she cried out his name as wave after wave of pure sensation raced through her body. He eased her back on the bed, drawing his hand along the length of her, from neck to hip, the heat from his fingers marking her skin.

There was no other man for her, now or ever. After this night, she would never again feel this surge of passion or the power of his touch. She would grow old knowing that only one man had seen to the very depths of her soul, had driven all inhibition from her body, and had possessed her in the most intimate way.

With Joe, she had become a woman, not just in name, but in the very heart of her being. Beneath his touch, she came alive, transformed by the pleasure they took in each other. She arched against him, his hair soft between her fingers as his tongue continued to work its magic. Coherent thought slipped from her mind and all that remained was pure pleasure.

With each stroke, the tension in her core grew until she twisted beneath him, aching for her release. Again and again, he brought her close, but then drew her back from the edge with delicious care. Frustrated, she tugged at his hair, pulling him back, impatient with this game he played. "Enough," she said.

A lazy smile curled his mouth and he watched her through half-hooded eyes. "What do you want? Tell me."

"I want you," Perrie said. "Inside of me."

He stood and skimmed his jeans and boxer shorts down over his hips, kicking them off with bare feet. Then he turned and rummaged through his duffel until he found a small foil package.

Biting her lower lip, she held out her hand and he placed the condom in her palm. Raising herself up to sit on the edge of the bed, she gazed at him, taking in the ripe beauty of his body, taut muscle and hard desire, a silken shaft of steel. With trembling fingers, she sheathed him, and then together, they tumbled back onto the soft bed.

He settled his hips between her legs and she closed her eyes and lost herself in the feel of their bodies, skin against skin. Smooth muscle met soft flesh, hard desire probed moist heat, and two bodies slowly became one.

Nothing had prepared her for the power of their coupling. As he drove inside of her, she lost all sense of reality and, instead, spun on a vortex of overwhelming pleasure. The blood burned in her veins and soft, incoherent cries escaped her throat with each thrust. Nerves tingled deep inside of her, and as he moved faster, the tension grew.

She wrapped her legs around his waist, and all at once she felt herself soar toward her release. Her muscles tensed and she stopped breathing, and then it came, surging through her and pooling at the place where they were joined. He cried out at the same time and she dug her nails into his back as he gave himself over to her.

She lost all sense of time. Seconds were marked by heartbeats and minutes by soft gasps for breath. As they drifted back to reality, her thoughts cleared and she felt a warm sense of contentment. This was her reality now. She had loved a man as she had loved no other. Later, in the dark of night, she could think about all that she was going to lose. But for now, she and Joe were together.

She waited for him to say something, but he didn't. He just pulled her into the curve of his body and wrapped his arms around her, so tight that she wondered how he'd ever let her go.

It was as if he were waiting for her to speak, to tell him what she felt. Perrie closed her eyes and slowed her breathing, pretending to sleep in the hopes that she might stave off any passionate declarations. But that was not to be, for a long while later, in the silence of the night, Joe drew her closer.

"I love you, Perrie," he murmured, his warm lips

pressed against her shoulder. "And I know you love me."

Hours later, long after Joe had drifted into sleep, Perrie still lay awake. Though morning approached, the room was dark. She slipped out of bed and gathered her clothes, then silently dressed. No matter how hard she tried, she couldn't draw her gaze away from him. He looked so sweet, so vulnerable, the sheets twisted through his limbs, his hair mussed.

But this was all a dream. That's what she had to keep reminding herself. For the past two weeks, she'd lived someone else's life, a woman she barely knew. With a man she barely knew. She couldn't change the rest of her life just because she had let herself get lost in a fantasy for a short time.

With all the courage she possessed, Perrie took one last look at Joe, then turned and walked to the door. Everything would be all right. She would be able to put this all behind her once she got back to Seattle.

10

WHEN JOE WOKE UP the next morning, she was gone. He had almost expected her to stay. But then, what had passed between them probably had meant even less to her than he had imagined. Like a fool, he had waited around at the resort until noon, hoping that she would return. But by then she was halfway to Seattle, and he knew the odds were not in his favor.

He'd seen the last of Perrie Kincaid. In a few days she'd be happily back in the midst of Seattle's underworld, chasing wise guys and dodging bullets. Hell, how could he blame her? Muleshoe must have seemed as dull as dust in comparison. Spaghetti feeds, dogsled races, endless cold and snow. There were times when the place drove him a little crazy, too.

He had packed his bags and left for the small airstrip on the west side of Cooper shortly after noon. As soon as he'd gotten up in the air, he'd turned the plane toward Muleshoe. But he'd known there would be no relief at home, for everywhere he'd turned he would see Perrie—in her cabin, with the dogs, trudging through the woods on a pair of old snowshoes. And later, when he finally put an end to this day, when he lay in bed alone, he would see her in different ways, naked in his arms, her body flushed with passion, her eyes filled with need.

The fire snapped, sending a shower of sparks over

the hearth and bringing Joe back to the present. He slouched down on the sofa and turned his attention to his flight log. Now that he was back at the lodge, the reminders seemed almost overwhelming. Nothing he did could put her out of his head.

He had been a fool to fall in love with her. In all the time he'd lived in Alaska, he'd never once allowed himself to need a woman. And then Perrie was dropped on his doorstep, and within days he'd fallen, and fallen hard. Yet through it all, he'd ignored one basic fact. She never wanted to be in Alaska. Perrie Kincaid belonged in Seattle.

Odd how the cards fell. Until five years ago, Joe had lived in the same city, had driven on the same streets and dined at the same restaurants. And then he had decided to change his life, to look for new adventures in the Alaskan wilderness. Only to fall in love with a woman from a life he'd left behind.

"Hey, what are you doing back here? I thought you and Perrie were spending the weekend at the Hot Springs."

Joe twisted on the sofa and saw Tanner standing in the middle of the great room, a power drill in his hand. "Well, things don't always go as planned."

Tanner crossed the room and sat down on the end of the coffee table. "Is she gone?"

Joe nodded.

"You told her about her boss's call?"

A cynical chuckle was all he could manage. "I didn't have to. She left on her own. Hired a pilot within an hour of our arrival at Cooper and then took off the next morning. No goodbyes, no 'see you soon,' nothing."

Tanner sighed and rubbed his palms on his knees. "Hey, buddy, I'm sorry."

The flight log snapped shut and Joe straightened. "Well, don't be. I should have known better. I mean, it's not like she chose to come up here. She was forced into it."

"And she didn't choose to fall in love with you?"

"She wasn't in love with me," Joe replied, shaking his head. "If she were, she would have stayed."

"Not necessarily. Julia didn't."

"Julia's different. She's not as...difficult."

Tanner laughed. "You don't know the half of it, Brennan."

"There just wasn't much chance for Perrie and me. I should have realized that, but I got caught up in something neither one of us really thought out."

"So, you're just going to let it go?"

Joe considered Tanner's question for a long moment, then nodded once. "Yep." He got up from the sofa and gathered the papers he'd spread around him on the cushions. "I've got to make a run up to Fort Yukon. I think I'll spend the night there."

"What if she calls?" Tanner asked.

"She won't call." Joe grabbed his jacket from the back of the sofa, tucked the flight log under his arm and headed for the door.

When he reached the solitude of the outdoors, he drew a deep breath and looked up at the sky. But against his will, his gaze was drawn to Perrie's cabin. A vision of her flashed in his mind and he pushed it aside with a soft oath. He needed to get back up in the air. Once he was flying, he could clear his thoughts.

But something pulled him toward her cabin and he slowly trudged up the hill, knowing that he'd only revive more memories. He stopped once at the bottom of the steps, then continued to the door and walked inside.

The cabin was just as she'd left it. Julia hadn't known that Perrie wasn't returning, so she hadn't called Edna to clean it. He crossed to the kitchen and picked up a coffee mug, running his fingers over the handle as if he might still feel the warmth of her hand, but it was as cold as the air that filled the room.

He set the cup down, then wandered over to the bed. The pillow still smelled of her shampoo, sweet and fruity. He could almost feel her hair between his fingers, silken strands of fiery auburn. And they'd slept in this bed just two nights ago and— Joe cursed softly. Was it necessary to torture himself? There were plenty of regrets to go around. He didn't have to dredge them up.

"I have to get out of here," he muttered, throwing the pillow back on the bed.

He strode from the cabin and headed toward the shed. As requested, Burdy had loaded five crates of building supplies into the back of the pickup, supplies that had been delivered from Fairbanks by another bush pilot. Joe had planned to fly them up to Fort Yukon after he and Perrie returned from Cooper Hot Springs. But now he could make his delivery early and have an excuse to get away from the lodge.

Hell, maybe he'd just keep flying, hopping from airstrip to airstrip until he managed to purge Perrie Kincaid from his head. He'd go south or east. Maybe he'd find a warm place, an island somewhere, with beautiful women and endless bottles of rum. Or he could fly to a city and lose himself in the midst of crowds of people and concrete buildings.

Joe jumped in the truck and started the engine, then

carefully wove through the trees on the narrow, snow-packed drive. He sped through Muleshoe and headed out of town for the airstrip, ignoring the flood of memories that came with each familiar landmark in town.

The Super Cub was still warm from his trip back from Cooper. He loaded the crates, then glanced at his watch. He had plenty of time to make Fort Yukon before dark.

He steered the Cub out onto the runway and increased the throttle. The plane took off in an instant, lifting up into the air before he'd covered half the airstrip. Joe closed his eyes as he climbed into the sky, the whine of the plane's ascent like a balm to his nerves.

He banked north, the wilderness spreading out in front of him. He could lose himself in Alaska as easily as he could lose himself anywhere else. And if he flew far enough and high enough and long enough, maybe then he'd forget her.

PERRIE STARED at her computer screen, watching the cursor blink until her eyes began to cross. She shook her head and rubbed her eyes with her fingertips. Maybe she should have stayed at home instead of coming in to the office. She'd left Alaska at sunrise and it was now nearly eight in the evening. But she'd been away for so long. The sooner she got back into her daily routine, the sooner she could put the last two weeks behind her.

Besides, she had to finish the brides story. It hung over her like a dark cloud, filled with flashes of memory and rumblings of regret. She couldn't think of her time in Muleshoe without thinking of him—and all they'd shared. And the brides story was part of that.

Him. Maybe if she didn't call him by name, he

wouldn't seem so real. Perhaps she could learn to look at Joe Brennan as nothing more than a brief passage in her life, a vague remembrance, part of a story she'd soon put to bed.

But no matter how hard she tried, Joe refused to become anything less than a living, breathing man who intruded on her thoughts again and again. The memories were so vivid and so alive that she could still feel his skin beneath her palms, still taste his mouth against hers, still hear his soft moans in her—

"Kincaid! You're back."

Blinking hard, Perrie snapped herself out of the daydream, almost thankful for the distraction. She straightened in her chair, mentally steeling herself for one of Milt Freeman's rants. Her editor would not be happy to see her, but he'd have to deal with it. There was no way she'd let him send her back to Alaska. She was here and she planned to stay.

Perrie turned to smile at him, but to her surprise, he seemed genuinely happy to see her. Where was the man who demanded that she be banished to the wilderness? Where was the man so set on protecting her? "I *am* back, Milt."

He patted her on the shoulder. "Ah, Kincaid. I've missed you. I thought you'd be back sooner."

"Well, I would have. But I was stuck in Muleshoe, thanks to you. I tried to leave. Unfortunately, your pal Joe Brennan made sure there was no way out of town."

"Good man, that Brennan. I knew I could trust him with the job."

"He got the job done, all right," she said.

"When I called the other day, Joe's partner said you two were out. So, you and Brennan got along?"

"Yeah, we got along." The last person she wanted to

blather on about was Brennan. It was bad enough that her thoughts were filled with him. She didn't need Milt bringing his name up in conversation every— Perrie frowned. "You called the lodge?"

"Yeah. Evening before last. The FBI arrested Riordan and Dearborn. Case against them is solid. I thought you'd be here yesterday so we could get your piece in the Monday morning edition. I had to have Landers write the initial story. By the way, where is all your research? I went through your—"

"They got Riordan and Dearborn? But how could they? I took all my evidence with me."

"They're the FBI, Kincaid. They specialize in catching crooks and they had all kinds of evidence of their own. They've been on to Dearborn longer than you have. And once you were safely out of the way, they could finally do their job."

Perrie frowned. "If you hadn't sent me to Muleshoe, I would have broken that story. I was..." She paused. "You called the lodge on Saturday evening?"

"Isn't that what I said?"

"What exactly did you tell them?"

"I said it was all right for you to come back. O'Neill said he'd let Brennan or you know right away. I figured you'd have Brennan fly you out the minute you heard. So where the hell were you? And when can I have your story?"

Perrie's mind raced. Joe must have known it was all right for her to go home to Seattle. After they'd returned from the Muleshoe Games, he had stopped at the lodge. Had Tanner given him the message then? And if he had, why hadn't Joe passed it along to her?

A single thought raced through her mind. Had he *wanted* her to stay? Perrie buried her face in her hands and rubbed her tired eyes again, trying to make some sense of the situation.

Since she'd left Alaska, something had been niggling at her brain, but she hadn't been able to put it into words. Now it suddenly became clear. He hadn't told her that she could leave. And when she had left, he hadn't even tried to stop her. In fact, he'd almost opened the door and let her go. He'd known it was all right for her to return; he'd known since they'd slept together the night before.

"He just wanted to have sex!" she cried, not realizing until too late that she'd spoken out loud.

"Who wanted to have sex?"

Perrie shook her head and waved distractedly at Milt. Brennan had kept the news from her deliberately. She frowned. But then, she'd been the one to show up at his door. Had she stayed in her own room, they never would have made love that night at the resort.

Love. The word rang in Perrie's head. He had said the words while she had pretended to be asleep. *I love you, Perrie, and I know you love me.* At the time, she'd brushed them off, thinking that they were empty of meaning outside the bedroom.

But what if Brennan was speaking from his heart? What if he truly loved her? "But if he loved me, why did he let me leave?" she said.

"Kincaid, what the hell are you mumbling about?"

Perrie glanced up at Milt, then shook her head and groaned. "I'm so confused. And I think I may have made a big mistake."

"On the Riordan story?"

"Oh, to hell with the Riordan story, Milt. I'm talking about me and Joe. I just walked out on him. When, all the while, he believed I would want to stay."

"Stay where?"

"In Alaska."

Milt stared at her, head cocked, as if she'd completely lost her mind. Then he patted her on the shoulder again. "By the way, I showed your wolf story around. Great piece of work. In fact, one of the syndicates got hold of it and called me. Wanted to pay big bucks for more. I told him you didn't live in Alaska and there wouldn't be more."

"I could live in Alaska," Perrie said, the notion not nearly as ridiculous as it once seemed.

"No, you couldn't," Milt replied. "You work in Seattle."

"I wouldn't have to work in Seattle. I could work in Muleshoe. I could call that syndicator and sell my stories to him. I have a lot more. And I could string for the Fairbanks or Anchorage paper. Or I could start my own paper. There's this old newspaper office above Paddy Doyle's tavern. I mean, I'd have to upgrade the equipment, get a computer, maybe even a new press. And there's not much circulation. But Joe makes flights into the bush all the time. I bet those families would be glad to get some local news. And running a weekly would be—"

"Kincaid! Stop! You're talking like a crazy woman. You can't live in Alaska."

A slow smile grew on Perrie's lips. "Yes, I can. I can live wherever I want."

"But what about your career?"

"I'm a writer, Milt. I can write anywhere, including Muleshoe, Alaska."

"I think you're overtired, Kincaid. Jet-lagged. Maybe you've been in the wilderness too long. It's my fault. I made a mistake sending you there. Go home. Get some rest. You can write the Riordan story tomorrow."

Perrie reached down beneath the desk and grabbed the strap of her shoulder bag, then yanked it out. "No, Milt," she said, placing the bag in his arms. "You can write the Riordan story. Here are all my notes and research and evidence."

"The story is yours, Kincaid. You have to write it."

She stood up. "No, I don't. Right now, I have to go back to Alaska. I have to find out if Joe Brennan really loves me."

"Joe Brennan loves you? My Joe Brennan?"

Perrie laughed. "He *was* your Joe Brennan, but now he's *my* Joe Brennan." She grabbed the phone from the corner of the desk. "I have to call him and tell him I'm coming." She snatched her hand away. "No, maybe I should just fly up there and talk to him." She shook her head. "I'll call Julia. I'll let her know I'm coming. She can pick me up at the airstrip."

Perrie rummaged through the bag Milt held, searching for her day planner before she realized she didn't have the number for the lodge. "I need the phone number. Get me the phone number, Milt. Never mind, I'll get it."

She sprang out of her chair and hurried toward Milt's office. His phone file was on his desk and she riffled through it until she found the card for the Bachelor Creek Lodge. Grabbing Milt's chair, she pulled it up to the desk and sat down, then dialed the phone.

Her heart pounded in her chest and she prayed that Joe wouldn't answer. When she finally spoke to him again, she wanted to be standing face-to-face. She wanted to be able to look into his eyes and see the truth there.

The phone was answered on the first ring. "Joe?" said a feminine voice.

"Julia?"

"Who is this?"

Perrie cleared her throat. "It's Perrie Kincaid."

"Oh, Perrie. Thank goodness you called. Has Joe contacted you?"

Perrie frowned. "No, he hasn't. Isn't he there?"

A long silence met her question. Then Julia finally spoke. "Perrie, I have some bad news. Joe was ferrying supplies to a town near the Arctic Circle and he never showed up. He filed a flight plan and he radioed ahead so they were expecting him before dark. He took the Cub. At first we thought he might have flown down to see you."

"Me?"

"Tanner said he seemed pretty upset after you left. We thought he might have flown down to Seattle to straighten things out."

"He—he isn't here," Perrie said. "He didn't call."

"Hawk says that Joe would never deliberately deviate from his flight plan. That's why we're worried."

"He's a good pilot," Perrie murmured. "The best. He'd never..." Her heart turned to ice and her breath froze in her chest as the true meaning of Julia's words sank in. Joe's plane had gone down in the wilderness and they didn't know where he was.

She brought her fingers to her mouth to stop a cry of fear, then blinked back the sudden flood of tears pressing at the corners of her eyes.

"I'm flying up there," Perrie said, her voice surprisingly calm. "I'll get a flight out as soon as I can. I may have to fly into Anchorage and then on to Fairbanks, but I'll get there by morning. I promise."

"Perrie, you don't have to—"

"I want to be there, Julia. I belong in Muleshoe."

"All right. Call the lodge before you leave Fairbanks and I'll send Hawk out to the airstrip to pick you up."

"I'll be there as soon as I can. And, Julia?"

"Yes?"

"If they find him before I get there, would you tell him that I love him? And that everything will work out?"

THE TINY AIRSTRIP at Muleshoe appeared in the distance just as the sun was rising. Perrie stared out the window of the bush plane, shielding her eyes against the glare, hoping she might see the red wings of Joe's Super Cub. But as the pilot descended, her heart fell, as well. There was no sign of the plane.

She said a silent prayer, hoping that Joe had turned up at another airstrip, hoping that he was safe in some other bush town. She'd been in the air all night, flying from Seattle to Anchorage to Fairbanks. And then she had struggled to find a bush pilot in the early hours of the morning.

They'd left Fairbanks before dawn, and as they came into Muleshoe, she realized that she hadn't slept in more than two days, since the last night she and Joe had spent together at her cabin. Her thoughts skipped back to that night, and then to the night after, when they'd made love.

She couldn't allow herself to believe that they would never see each other again. Joe had to be alive and safe. He flew in the wilderness all the time and he had bragged that he could put the Cub down anywhere he pleased. If he'd had trouble, perhaps he'd safely landed the plane and was just waiting to be found.

"Looks like there's someone down there," the pilot shouted, pointing to the far end of the runway.

Perrie squinted against the rising sun and saw the Blazer parked near the row of planes. As the pilot circled the landing strip, she caught sight of Hawk, staring up into the sky. She had talked to him by phone right before she'd left Fairbanks and there had been no news of Joe. Now, two hours later, she wondered if anything had changed.

The plane landed on the smooth snow and slid to a stop. Perrie shoved the door open and hopped out, then ran across the snow toward Hawk. She threw herself into his arms and he hugged her tight, picking her up off the ground. Then he set her down and stepped back. "I'm glad you came."

"Has there been any news?"

Hawk shook his head. "They're sending out search planes right now. We'll find him."

"What about his radio? Hasn't he tried to contact anyone?"

"Maybe his radio is out."

"But how could the radio just go out, unless—" Perrie stopped short, not wanting to complete the thought. Unless the plane was damaged. Unless Joe had crashed somewhere in the wilderness.

"There are lots of reasons he could have lost radio contact," Hawk assured her. "If he put down in a valley, the mountains might block the signal."

"You know the route he was flying, don't you? So the search teams can find him more quickly?"

"He was flying up to Fort Yukon. He never—"

"Fort Yukon?" Perrie asked. "He was going to Fort Yukon?"

"He was taking supplies up there. He has survival

gear in the plane. Sleeping bags and dried food. So if he had to put her down, he would be able to wait for us to find him."

A sudden thought came to Perrie's mind when Hawk mentioned sleeping bags. "I think I might know where he is," she said. "What if he put the plane down for a reason, then couldn't take off again?"

"Why would he put the plane down?"

"Maybe he stopped to see Romeo and Juliet," Perrie replied.

"The play?"

"No, the wolves," she cried. "You know, the family of wolves that he watches up at the Yukon Flats. He took me to see them."

"Joe visits a family of wolves?" Hawk seemed completely taken aback by the revelation. "Can you remember where you landed up there?"

"We were at the Gebhardts' cabin."

"On Van Hatten Creek?"

Perrie nodded. "And then we flew west, I think. I didn't notice at first, but then the landscape looked so different from Muleshoe. There was a huge mountain out the left window and I remember the sun was shining off the snow. There were no trees on it."

"That was probably Snowy Peak."

"Then I think we turned north again, out of the sun. There were lots of trees below and mountains. But then the landscape kind of cleared and there was a wide area that was just snow. It was really flat, like a river covered in white. And that's where Joe put the plane down. He said we were on the southern edge of the wildlife refuge."

"Was there another peak? You should have seen it to the east. Bear Mountain."

Perrie bit her lower lip and tried to remember, but once they'd landed, she had lost her sense of direction. Her attention had been focused on the wolves and on Joe, not on the surrounding mountains. "I don't know," she said in a shaky voice. "Maybe there was. I'd know the landscape if I saw it. I remember that peak."

The pilot from the bush plane walked over toward them, Perrie's bags in his arms. "Here are your things, ma'am."

Perrie grabbed his arm. "How much fuel do you have left in your plane?"

"Enough to get me back to Fairbanks."

"Enough to fly up to Fort Yukon?"

Hawk picked up on her idea. "Never mind about the fuel. We can fill the plane up here. I need you to fly me up to Yukon Flats."

"Me, too!" Perrie cried. "I'm coming along."

The pilot shook his head. "But I've got to get back to—"

"This is a search and rescue," Hawk explained.

The pilot's expression immediately turned from indifference to concern. "Who are we looking for?"

"Joe Brennan."

"Polar Bear Air? I know Brennan."

"We think he might have put the plane down on purpose somewhere up on the flats yesterday."

The pilot grabbed Perrie's bags and tossed them inside the Blazer. "Then let's refuel and get up in the air. Maybe we can find him before he has to spend another night in the cold."

Hawk nodded, then grabbed Perrie's hand and gave it a squeeze. "We'll find him."

The next fifteen minutes passed in a flurry of activity. Hawk helped the pilot refuel, then he called the lodge on the plane's radio just as they were taking off to let Tanner know their plans. They were up in the air before Perrie had a chance to grow impatient.

"He went to see Romeo," she murmured. "I know he did."

She stared out the window from her place behind the pilot's seat, trying to remember the landscape that she'd watched so closely that day. When they reached the spot above the Gebhardts' cabin, she sat up straighter, hoping that Joe's plane might be sitting out front. But Perrie saw nothing there except snow and a thin curl of smoke from the chimney.

The pilot veered west and Snowy Peak appeared in her window. "This is right," she called. "We took off in this direction. We were just about even with the peak when Joe turned north again."

The pilot waited until the plane drew closer to the mountain, then banked to the right. Below them, the landscape looked unfamiliar and Perrie's heart twisted. "This isn't right," she said. "I don't recognize this."

"Just wait," Hawk called from the copilot's seat. "I think Joe might have followed the Little Black River north. Before too long it meets Paddle Creek and there's a wide flat area right near the edge of the refuge."

She took a deep breath and pressed her palm to her heart, trying to calm the rapid pounding in her chest. She felt the crunch of paper beneath her jacket, then reached inside and withdrew the valentine Joe had made for her. Throughout her trip back to Muleshoe, it had rested near her heart, a reminder of what they had shared. She stared at it now, as if willing some mystical power from the paper and lace.

She wasn't sure how long she looked at it, rubbing her fingers over Joe's casual scrawl, remembering the day he'd given it to her.

"Well, I'll be damned."

Perrie looked up to see Hawk staring out his window, a pair of binoculars pressed to his eyes. "What? Do you see something?"

Hawk slowly lowered the binoculars then turned and smiled at Perrie. "You were right. He's down there. And the plane looks like it's in one piece."

Perrie scrambled to the window on the other side of the plane. In the distance she could see a splash of red against the white snow. "Is he all right? Can you see him?"

Hawk looked down again and nodded. "He sees us. He's waving."

Perrie leaned back in her seat and closed her eyes. A surge of relief, followed by apprehension rushed over her and suddenly she wasn't sure of what she'd planned. What if she'd been mistaken? What if Joe didn't love her the way she thought he did?

"I'm going to put her down," the pilot called.

"Are—are you sure?" Perrie asked. "I—I mean, someone else could rescue him. You've already done so much."

Hawk turned and looked at her. "He'll be happy to see you."

His words were so direct and so confident that Perrie couldn't help but believe him. She smiled, then mouthed a silent "thank you" to the man who had become such a good friend.

The pilot circled once, but Perrie was afraid to look

down. Her entire life, her happiness were riding on this landing. On the hope that she was right about Joe and that he truly did love her. The hope that he wanted her to come back to him, that there was a place in his life for her.

Moments later the plane was on the ground, and they slid across the snow until the pilot pulled back on the throttle and they came to a stop. Through the window, Perrie watched as Joe ran toward the plane, but she was frozen in her seat, unable to move.

Hawk hopped out and ran toward him, then grabbed Joe around the neck and gave him a hug. They talked for a minute, their heads bent, and then Hawk looked back to the plane. Perrie said one more prayer, pushed the door open and stepped outside.

But as she left the shadow of the plane's wing, Joe turned and started back toward the Super Cub. She stepped into the sunshine and Hawk called to Joe. He turned back, a grin on his face. And then he saw her.

Perrie held her breath, her fingers clutching at the valentine in her hands. His grin gradually faded to an expression of confusion and then disbelief. He pushed his cap off and ran his hand through his hair, then shook his head.

Their gazes locked, and, finally, after what seemed to Perrie like an eternity, he slowly started toward her. With each step his smile grew, along with the relief she felt. He stopped, then laughed out loud and held out his arms. Perrie gave a little cry and raced toward him.

She threw herself into his embrace, so hard that they both nearly fell back into the snow. His fingers furrowed through her hair and he brought his mouth down on hers, kissing her wildly, frantically, joyously.

"I thought I'd never see you again," he murmured against her lips. "What are you doing here?"

"I had to come back," Perrie replied, trailing a line of kisses along his jaw. "I had to tell you."

"To tell me why you left?"

"No, I had to tell you why I have to stay." She looked up into the brilliant blue of his eyes. "I love you, Joe Brennan."

He stared at her a long moment, then glanced up at the sky and smiled. "You had better love me, Kincaid," he said, looking back down at her. "Because I sure as hell love you."

With a shout of delight, Perrie wrapped her arms around his neck and kissed him hard. "Do you know how scared I was? When I called the lodge and they told me your plane was missing, I didn't know what to do."

"I stopped to see Romeo and Juliet," Joe said. "I stayed a little too long and when I tried to take off, I couldn't get any power. Ice in the fuel line. By the time I figured that out, it was too dark to see to fix it. I just got it cleared when I saw your plane."

Perrie held his face between her palms. "Why didn't you use the radio and call someone?"

"I did. I radioed Fort Yukon but I couldn't raise anyone on that end. So I radioed the lodge and left my location with Sammy. I explained that he was supposed to have Tanner call Fort Yukon for me and tell them I'd be there in the morning."

"Sammy didn't say a thing."

"Hawk told me that after Fort Yukon reported me late, Julia sent Sam off with Burdy, knowing that he'd be upset if he knew I was missing. They didn't explain the situation to him. And Sam just forgot to mention that he'd talked to me."

"I was so worried. I thought I'd lost you."

"Why did you leave me, Perrie? Why did you just walk away?"

She pressed her forehead into his chest, unable to meet his gaze. "Because I was stupid and scared and I didn't believe that you really loved me. I just thought you were doing your job, doing what Milt wanted you to do."

Joe chuckled and tipped her chin up. "Milt never mentioned anything about falling in love with you."

"I meant sleeping with me."

"He didn't mention that, either. I thought of that all on my own."

Perrie felt a warm blush creep up her cheeks. "We are good together."

"Yes, Kincaid, we do make quite a pair," he teased. "And since you agree, I suppose there's only one thing left to do."

Perrie gave him a coy look, as anxious as he was to return to the lodge and a nice warm bed. She felt as if she could sleep, and make love to him, for the next week. "And what's that, Brennan?"

"You'll have to marry me."

She gasped, his words taking her breath away. When it finally returned, she cleared her throat. "Marry you?"

"Just say yes, sweetheart. We'll figure out where we're going to live and what we're going to do later. Right now, all I need to know is that you'll spend the rest of your life with me."

With a shout of delight, she launched herself into his arms again, this time knocking them both down into the snow. They rolled over and over each other, kissing and laughing until Joe pinned her arms over her head and lay on top of her.

"So will you?" he asked.

"Yes, yes, yes. But only if we can live in Muleshoe," Perrie replied.

Joe blinked in surprise. "Really. You want to live in Alaska?"

Perrie nodded and Joe pressed her face between his palms and kissed her, long and deep. Then he looked up and smiled, his gaze fixed on the far horizon. "We're being watched," he said, rolling off her.

Perrie turned onto her stomach and braced her elbows in the snow. Across the wide expanse of flat land, she saw a movement, a flash of gray against a background of white. Romeo came into view and, a few seconds later, Juliet appeared.

Joe put his arm around Perrie's waist, then leaned over and kissed her on the temple. "Do you think they approve?" he asked.

"Every lone wolf deserves a mate," Perrie said. "And now you've found yours."

With a low growl, Joe pulled her into his arms, and, in that moment, Perrie knew she'd found her place in the wilderness. She'd found her soul mate. And together, they'd make a life for each other.

NORTHERN KNIGHTS

Bobby Hutchinson

CHAPTER ONE

THE PHONE RANG shrilly, and Quinn glanced at the old-fashioned face of the watch on his arm. It was seven-fifteen in the morning, and he'd just flipped his eggs on the plate with his bacon. His toast was hot and the first steaming cup of the day's gallon of coffee gave forth its rich aroma.

Where the hell was Maisie? It was Tuesday, Quinn reflected, and she ought to be at work by now. What did the RCMP hire a clerk typist for if not to answer the phone?

Quinn swallowed a mouthful of breakfast, and then paused with a loaded fork poised between mouth and plate.

The ringing continued unabated.

"Maisie," he roared at the top of his lungs. There was no answer, and the phone rang again.

That was the trouble with living across the hall from the damned office, he raged silently. When would the RCMP realize that even its bachelor members needed a separate residence, living quarters completely away from the office, the jail, the job?

The relentless summons went on and on, and with a muffled curse, he snatched up the extension.

"Dawson Police Office Quinn here," he growled, running the words together.

"Whitehorse RCMP, Staff Sergeant Billings speaking.'' After four years of frequent phone calls between Dawson and Whitehorse, Staff Billings still announced himself in the same strictly regulation manner, and followed with predictable heavy-handed humor. ''Haven't the mosquitoes and blackflies packed you away yet, Quinn?''

God, at seven in the morning!

''Afraid they don't get up this early, Staff. Busy up here, we're a major Yukon tourist center now, not a quiet residential area like Whitehorse.''

It was a moldy joke, but Billings's dry chuckle rustled over the three-hundred-odd miles separating the towns.

''Well, Quinn, that's why I'm calling so early. You'll be happy to know you're getting another constable up there to lighten the load. Constable Johnstone, Chris Johnstone, should be arriving by police plane about ten this morning. You won't have the paper on the transfer yet, I only heard yesterday myself.''

Quinn's mouth twisted cynically under his mustache.

''Constable Chris Johnstone, huh? Is this another one of those boys with fancy degrees and wet palms that Depot's turning out like sausages these days, Staff? I hope Mrs. Johnstone's little boy Chris has more going for him than that last young whelp they shipped up here.''

Billings's martyred sigh echoed over the crackling connection. The sergeant felt that years of dealing with Michael Quinn by rights should have qualified him for hardship allowance. He anticipated an explosion in another minute or so, and he decided to delay the inevitable as long as possible.

"Well, it's not like it used to be in the old days when you and I went through Depot, Quinn," he said placatingly. "You've got to keep an open mind with young recruits, y'know. Young Kramer wasn't emotionally suited to the territories. It's a different world up here in Rory Borealis land."

Quinn rolled his eyes to the fly-flecked ceiling and gave a silent groan. Who the hell was writing Staff's lines these days, anyhow?

"Can Chris handle himself physically? Is he a good big brawny lad, this Johnstone?" he queried hopefully.

The connection was getting worse. There was dead silence for a moment, and Quinn hollered impatiently, "Hello? Hello? You there, Staff Billings?"

At last, the familiar scratchy voice sounded in Quinn's ear.

"This is going to be a new experience for you and for Constable Johnstone. Eh, I should add it's Ms Constable Johnstone. Chris is, eh, of the female gender."

Quinn slowly removed the receiver from his ear and stared down at it as if it had bitten him.

"A woman? A female constable? They're sending me a woman constable?" he queried dazedly.

From the earpiece came the faint dry crackle of traitor Billings, being a determined optimist as he plotted a hasty exit.

"Now, don't get excited, Quinn. Let's just play this by ear, no nasty preconceptions. Remember, the force has to learn to change with the times, and us along with it, even here in the outposts of civilization. Women have been members of the force for more than ten years already. Plane will be there at ten. Keep a stiff upper lip, upward and on and all that. Goodbye, Quinn.''

Stunned, Quinn replaced the receiver. He slumped at the battered wooden table under the window, staring out at the blue and gold world he'd been mindlessly enjoying just moments before.

It was June fourteenth in Dawson city, Yukon Territory. It was late spring, a season that Quinn gloried in, a heady season in the far north where dusk falls at midnight and the sun is bright and hot again by 3:00 a.m....the season when residents are able to recognize one another by their facial features instead of the color of their parkas. The season when tourists pour into town, visitors with lunatic notions of life north of the sixtieth parallel, many of whom would need not so gentle reminders that law and order were alive and well in Dawson, enforced by none other than Corporal Quinn of the RCMP. And, if Quinn was lucky, by a tough and brawny young recruit fresh out of training and eager to learn.

A tough and brawny young male recruit.

Now, Staffing was about to make a mockery of what Quinn had worked four long years to establish. What the hell did they think a woman could do with drunken prospectors determined to kill one another with broken beer bottles, especially if a crazed eccentric was on the scene, eager to help by shooting them down with his loaded shotgun?

The woman couldn't stay, and that was that. He'd put her on the next plane out, and deal with Staffing later.

Ten, Billings had said. Quinn sighed deeply and sloshed more thick, bitter coffee into his cup.

For a day that had started full of good feelings and

sunshine before the phone call, this one was going downhill like a runaway freight train.

IT WAS ACTUALLY 10:40 before the Twin Otter with its distinctive blue and yellow stripe and RCMP crest on the side finally whined and bumped to a stop on the tiny airfield two miles outside of town.

Chris smiled down at the admiring young man who'd piloted her and stepped lithely to the tarmac a second before he could gallantly take her arm.

"Thanks, Sarge. I really enjoyed the flight," she complimented him, and he beamed.

"My pleasure, Constable, believe me," he assured her.

She stood beside the plane and looked around curiously, filling her lungs with the smell of fresh, unadulterated northern air.

Mmmm.

Her lungs were going to like it here, at any rate. She was going to like it here, she corrected herself firmly, despite the misgivings she'd had about coming north and being a uniformed policewoman once again.

The undercover work she'd been doing for Commercial Crime section these past few months was undoubtedly far more exotic than anything she'd be called on to do here in sleepy little Dawson City, of course. And she couldn't help feeling just a tiny bit let down about being back in uniform again, because working undercover had been the very thing she'd longed to do in the force; it had been a romantic job, full of the high adventure and the excitement she'd always wanted in her career.

She and her partners had infiltrated the largest car

theft ring on the Niagara peninsula, a complex organization run by the notorious Andollini family, and had brought its members to trial.

If that trial had taken some of the shine off the assignment, well, Chris supposed, that was only natural.

She suppressed a shudder even now, standing here in the warm sunshine, remembering the three long weeks of sordid and endless detail, the strain of being a witness for the crown against vicious and angry underworld figures who felt she'd tricked them.

She had, of course. It was the job she'd been trained to do. But facing Louis and Frank Andollini, the kingpins of the operation, day after day in court, enduring their malevolent stares and not so veiled threats, was a sobering and exhausting experience, one she'd just as soon forget.

She'd felt disappointment and righteous anger when the third brother, Angelo, managed to get off, despite the fact that he was as guilty as the others.

"I'll get you, bitch," he'd snarled at her evilly after the trial.

The RCMP had taken his threat seriously, which was exactly why Chris had come to be here in Dawson.

"You've done a commendable job, Constable, but we feel it would be risky to leave you undercover at this point," her commanding officer had told her. "You've attracted heat. Because we were unable to convict Angelo Andollini, we feel you may be in danger until all this blows over. Therefore, we're putting you back in uniform and sending you somewhere quiet for a spell."

Somewhere quiet immediately suggested interior

B.C. to Chris, some tiny town close enough to the sunny Okanagan that she could visit her parents once in a while.

Then she was shipped off peremptorily for northern familiarization training, and her hopes of being posted to interior B.C. evaporated.

When the RCMP decided to put one of its members on ice, the organization did a thorough job. She soon learned that she wouldn't even be able to write to her family directly, nor they to her. All communications were to be funneled through Ottawa while she was here, and phone calls were definitely out.

Well, she'd simply make the best of it. She started walking briskly toward the patrol car she could see parked near the buildings.

A figure in navy trousers and an open-necked short-sleeve service-issue shirt—undoubtedly the formidable Corporal Michael Quinn she'd heard so much about in the past few weeks—was lounging on the vehicle, one arm bent across the hood. When he saw her coming, he straightened and came striding across the landing field, silhouetted against the brilliant morning light.

Chris couldn't see his face or features as she walked eagerly toward him, but she wanted to make a good impression, so she pressed her shoulders back and lifted her head, smiling bravely to hide the sudden nervous queasiness in her stomach.

It was exciting, but it was scary as well, meeting this man she'd partner for however long they left her in Dawson. He was something of a legend, Corporal Quinn, one of the old guard in the RCMP, the type who still maintained the law with an iron fist in a velvet glove.

Was there a warm and welcoming man behind the myths?

He drew nearer, and her head tilted still farther back and up, trying to see what he looked like.

Heavens, he was tall. And broad. The closer he came, the bigger he seemed to be.

Intimidating, a man this big. Chris felt her throat close, and she gulped faintly.

Then her training took over. She drew up smartly, gave her widest grin and held out a hand to the scowling giant with the tumbled dark hair spilling from under his hat. He was now only an arm's length away, six foot four at least of overwhelming manhood, positively dwarfing her five and a half feet.

"How do you do, Corporal," she said smartly. "I'm Constable Chris Johnstone."

The intense heat of the sun was the last thing she'd expected of the Arctic, and she felt a drop of moisture trickle between her breasts, and then another.

Darn! There came several drops down her temples as well, just when she most wanted to appear cool and collected.

Chris wasn't used to being back in uniform yet, and the service-order khaki shirt, and the blue patrol jacket with navy-blue tailored trousers, were stifling. She could feel her short crop of thick curls turning into tightly coiled wire under the brimmed regulation hat.

And her hand hung on and on between them like an appendage neither of them knew what to do with.

She finally withdrew it, and a wave of heat that had nothing to do with the sun rolled up to her scalp.

What kind of corporal had she drawn in this lottery, anyhow? Didn't he know about handshakes?

A deep bass voice rumbled from the man in front of her, the words spaced at one-second intervals.

"Constable Johnstone, I don't know what the hell they're thinking of down at HQ, but I'm telling you right off the bat this is no place for a woman."

The testiness of his tone and the blatant chauvinism set Chris's temper flaring in an instant.

"I'm a police officer first and foremost, and yes, I happen to be female. Just what's wrong with that, Corporal?"

Quinn's eyes took inventory before he could stop them, looking up and down the slender, curvaceous lines of the woman standing stiffly in front of him. Tilted forward at a cocky angle toward her small nose, her hat covered her forehead and most of her hair. The eyes spitting sparks at him were wide and deeply set, the same arresting shade of cobalt blue he'd seen in chunks of silver ore, and the black curling lashes surrounding them were outrageously long. She was pretty, no argument there.

But it wasn't her eyes or the ridiculously innocent heart-shaped face that made him swallow.

It was the rest of her. Even the no-nonsense female version of the police uniform couldn't begin to hide the lushness of her, the swelling breasts thrusting out at the tunic, the long legs and gracefully rounded hips sheathed in tailored police trousers.

There wasn't a single thing wrong with her that he could see. She was cute, and small, and stacked, and spirited too.

Which was perfect in a lady, except that this lady was supposed to be his constable, his partner, his trusted right-hand man. Who the hell needed a partner who made embarrassing things start happening in his groin?

The young pilot had appeared beside them with her suitcases.

"Shall I put these in the cruiser, Corporal?" he inquired diffidently. He glanced regretfully at Chris. "I'm due to head straight back to Whitehorse within the hour."

Quinn glowered at him, and the boy flinched. What he ought to tell the kid to do was load Johnstone and her luggage both back in the plane this instant and send them straight back to headquarters where they belonged.

Except while he'd been waiting here, he'd also been thinking about that.

He'd finally had to admit that he had no reason the force would recognize as valid for sending her back on the same flight she'd arrived on. But he'd think of something, by God. He just needed a bit more time, that was all.

"Stow them in the trunk of the cruiser over there, it's not locked," he finally snarled, and then turned again to his new constable.

Her face was flushed, and she was still glaring up at him, chin tilted and eyes narrowed for battle. He noticed she had a sprinkling of freckles across her nose and cheeks, and something about those innocent brown flecks against the cream of her skin made him soften inside.

What the hell, it wasn't her fault. Somebody at Staffing had screwed up, and they'd just have to straighten it out. In the meantime, he could at least be civil to the kid.

"I'm Quinn," he belatedly remembered to say to

her, gesturing to the dusty blue and white patrol car parked on the edge of the tarmac. "Might as well get going. C'mon, Ms Constable," he remarked in an attempt at jocularity.

Chris felt rooted to the spot with fury at the insulting label. Ms Constable indeed.

He strode around the car and opened the passenger door for her, not waiting for her to get in before he walked around and slid behind the wheel. He had the motor running before she'd made a move. Well, his manners stank, she already knew that, she fumed.

"My name is Johnstone, Constable Johnstone, and I'd prefer you call me that." Chris's anger made her voice tremble slightly.

He just nodded amiably, as if he were humoring her, and there was little to do except climb in beside him and rebelliously slam the door as hard as she could.

He paid no attention.

The wheels screeched as he turned the car around and aimed it down the narrow road, and she braced her shiny boots firmly on the floorboards to keep herself in place while hurriedly fastening her seat belt. The way he drove, a seat belt was a blessing.

She noticed that the windshield of the cruiser was badly cracked in several places, making it tricky to get a clear view of the road. The upholstery was torn as well. In fact, the car was a disgrace, and the narrow, potholed road they were bouncing along was worse. She could only hope Quinn knew their path by heart. They were winding close beside a wide, fast-flowing river, and he didn't believe in slowing down for curves.

Once Quinn motioned toward the river with a desultory gesture, making Chris gulp audibly. She wished to heaven he'd keep both hands on the wheel.

"That's the Yukon. Used to be the major highway to Dawson and the goldfield," he commented, and then lapsed into preoccupied silence again.

He'd taken his hat off and dropped it between them on the seat, and now she could see the ebony tangle of thick wavy hair springing up where his hat had flattened it, curling down much too far over the tops of his ears and down his neck. Obviously he ignored the strict RCMP dictum of short back and sides. The weather-beaten dusky skin above the audacious bush-whacker's mustache looked slightly raw and freshly shaved, and his shirt was clean but rumpled. He looked tough, and she searched for a word to describe him. Untamed? Savage?

He was both less and more than those.

Dangerous?

She finally stared at him openly because he didn't seem to notice her watching him at all. He was frowning, engrossed in either his thoughts or the alarmingly rough road they were bouncing along.

His was a proud and intimidating profile: bushy eyebrows shielding narrowed obsidian eyes, a high-arched nose balanced by a stubborn, strong chin. Handsome. Rugged.

Even up close he looked larger than life. Every part of him was massive: his head, his neck, his chest, his hands and arms. Chris knew he had to be at least forty, but his shirt fitted easily, no straining of buttons over a paunch, and the side arm in its holster rested on flat stomach and narrow hips. He seemed all hard muscle, and she suddenly had a clear vision of him, wearing the red serge of the early North-West

Mounted Police, seated on a wild-eyed lunging black horse, leading a cavalry charge, saber in one hand and reins in the other.

With, of course, a troop of men behind him.

Men. Not women.

Women were undoubtedly safe at home where they belonged, weeping and waiting and yearning over their heroes.

Corporal Quinn, she concluded succinctly, swinging her gaze away from him and back to the broken windshield, *you are a mastodon, an all but extinct relic of an earlier age. It's time someone took you in hand, my friend, and brought you up-to-date on what's going on out there in the real world.*

The problem was, Chris wasn't at all sure she wanted the job. It would undoubtedly mean conflict, and she hated to admit it, but she was tired, mentally and physically exhausted from the past months of constantly playing a part and of often being in physical danger.

She couldn't even get used to the fact that she was free to be herself again. At the moment, it was hard to remember who that self was.

She still wasn't sure how she felt about being this far north, either.

"They call that stretch of road down there the Top of the World highway when it gets a little closer to Inuvik," the pilot had told her, pointing down at the narrow and deserted ribbon of land below them.

Dawson felt enough like the top of the world to Chris, never mind going any farther north.

And now here was Corporal Quinn, making ugly chauvinist noises. Maybe she didn't want to stay in

Dawson any more than he wanted her to, she pondered uncertainly.

Still, usually she welcomed a challenge, and working with him would be a challenge, all right.

"Dawson."

Quinn's terse announcement came as they rounded a corner, and when the first buildings of the town appeared he jutted his chin at the collection of ramshackle wooden structures.

"Here we are. This is Front Street, Dawson City. That's the police office. Single man's quarters and cells are in the back of the building." He nodded toward a nondescript two-story wooden building on what proved to be the main street.

"I'll drive around a bit, give you an idea what the town looks like, seeing as you won't be staying long."

Chris had been curiously peering at the old wooden buildings they were passing, many of them propped up on what looked to be new wooden pilings, others tilting at odd angles to the ground.

She whipped around, and she narrowed her eyes at Quinn's profile as his laconic words penetrated.

"Exactly what do you mean by that? I've been transferred here, Corporal. Most transfers last a good six months or a year. Unless I give you very good reason, there's absolutely no grounds for refusing to work with me."

He shook his head stubbornly, still squinting out the windshield.

"No point even unpacking your bags. I'll have the whole mess straightened out in a couple of days. There's no way I'd let a lady like you do town patrol alone here on a wild Saturday night, and I've already got a clerk typist in the office for the paperwork and the radio, so it would be a waste of my time and yours to let you stay.''

Flabbergasted, Chris stared at him. He probably actually thought that oh-so-reasonable tone of voice would convince her, she thought in amazement.

His tone roughened. ''I've told them at Staffing a million times I need a tough young buck up here who can handle himself in a fight. Obviously, you're fresh out of training, full of that bull they've dreamed up about female members being able to do a man's work. Nothing against women, or you personally, you understand...''

Lord a-mighty, she thought. *Why would I ever take a statement like that personally?*

''...but whatever they told you, Training Depot isn't the real world,'' he was explaining ever so kindly. ''In many ways Dawson is still a frontier town, and I'm too busy wrestling it into some sort of order to have time or energy to baby-sit my constable. So back you go.'' As if the entire matter was settled, he asked politely, ''Hand me those dark glasses in the glove compartment, would you?''

She popped open the catch, retrieved the glasses and slapped them into his outstretched hand, trying in vain to use the calming meditative techniques she always used in times of extreme stress. They totally eluded her now, and her voice trembled with fury.

''I've been out of training for five whole years now, Corporal. I spent the first two in fishing villages along the B.C. coast, and the next three working undercover for Commercial Crime. I haven't needed a baby-sitter since I was eight, and nothing against you personally, but maybe this town could benefit from a mentality that believes wrestling isn't the ideal method of law enforcement.''

Quinn didn't respond, or give her any indication that he'd even heard her. He purposefully fitted the sunglasses over his eyes and hooked them behind his ears, steering casually, first with one hand then the other.

''Please drive me back to the police office, Corporal,'' Chris asked when his glasses were firmly in place at last and her voice was under some semblance of control. ''I'd like to unpack and get settled in. My transfer says I start work tomorrow morning.'' Her tone was now cool and unruffled, and she felt smugly proud of herself, but inside she was still seething. ''I've been transferred here, and I'm staying.''

Quinn could smell the disconcerting light freshness of her scent in the car, and behind the dark lenses his peripheral vision showed him the absolute determination on her face.

He grinned wryly. He had to admit that she had guts. The little speech she'd just made about her past service was impressive, if it were true. Ms Constable must be older than she seemed if she'd already been in five years. Fishing villages were rough going; he knew because he'd been there.

She didn't bully easily, and he liked that, but she still had to go, no question about it. No point in arguing with her over it, though. From past experience, he knew women never argued fairly. Besides, having her riding beside him made him uncomfortable. She was just too womanly to be a police officer.

He turned a tight, neat U at the end of the street and drove rapidly back to the office without another word, pulling up in front as if he were a teenager with a hot rod, squealing the brakes, burning rubber and making her flinch. Chris's father and brother had taught her respect for good machinery, and she had a hunch Quinn had missed that particular life skill.

She tried to take her own bags out of the trunk of the car, but he lifted them firmly out of her hands and walked ahead of her down the wooden sidewalk and in the front door, bracing it with his foot so that she could enter.

"Maisie, this is Constable Johnstone," Quinn announced tersely, heading straight on through the room and out another door.

Chris hesitated, then smiled brightly and nodded to the plump, fiftyish woman with the startling henna-colored topknot of hair, who was staring at her, large glasses perched on the very end of a tiny nose.

"How do you do?" Chris said politely, and Maisie looked slowly up and down Chris's uniform, then just as slowly let her ample body sink back and down into the chair as if she were overwhelmed. In slow motion, she shoved the glasses up and peered through them at Chris's face.

"You're his new constable?" she said in a bemused tone, and Chris nodded.

"Well, did you ever! All I can say is it's about time. It's about damn time we had some women policemen up here," Maisie pronounced fervently, and then grinned widely, a grin that stretched her generous red lipsticked mouth to its impressive limit. "Honey, this is gonna be a treat, a real treat. I'm pleased as punch to meet you. I'm Maisie Webster."

Chris hastily shook the pudgy manicured hand Maisie offered, mumbled something about being glad too, and hurried through the door through which Quinn had disappeared.

The door led to a long hallway, past a room that was probably Quinn's office on the left, a cell block with two cells, and finally, at the far right back corner of the building, the single person's quarters, consisting of a large bare room with a narrow cot, a battered chest of drawers and a small table and chair, plus an adjoining bathroom.

Mustard-colored linoleum covered the floor, and the walls were painted an odious shade of green. Tall, narrow windows with pull-down blinds looked out on a fenced backyard and an expanse of brown grass, empty except for an umbrella-style clothes rack where men's navy-blue briefs and several police shirts hung limply, drying in the sunshine.

Quinn had dumped her suitcases on the bed, and as soon as Chris entered the room he hurried toward the door, where he paused for a moment, ducking under the doorjamb so as not to knock his head.

"My quarters are over on the other side. Through the connecting door in the hall, there's sort of one big room for both kitchen and living area. You're welcome to use it. There's not much in the fridge because I eat out except for breakfast, but have whatever you can find. Maisie can fill you in on where the cafés are. See you tomorrow morning, Ms Constable."

With that terse message he was gone, leaving Chris exasperated with the Ms Constable bit, but smugly pleased that at least he'd said no more about her leaving on the next plane.

He might as well forget that idea anyway, she determined, grimly unlocking her bags and beginning to haul out armfuls of tailored police shirts and distinctly frothy underwear, because she was staying—and that was that.

She unpacked rapidly, changed into faded jeans and a light blue cotton shirt, explored the backyard and the kitchen-living area Quinn had mentioned and was absolutely unimpressed by both. Then she ventured into the office.

Until she found a grocery store, Chris decided that she'd have to settle for café fare, and she was getting hungrier by the instant. Quinn's fridge had been an icy plain with islands of eggs, bacon and beer, and little else.

"Hi, honey, you get all settled in back there? Maybe we could do a face-lift sometime on that room of yours. It sure needs it," Maisie said by way of a greeting, and the husky rough voice with its overtones of real concern suddenly made Chris feel warm and welcomed for the first time that day. It also made her feel weepy, and she swallowed hard.

"It's awfully...green, isn't it?" Chris managed, and Maisie shook her head ruefully.

"I swear men are all color-blind, his nibs the corporal included. We sent a requisition through for a new paint job for the quarters just last year, and would you believe that was the color Quinn chose for all the bedrooms? I tried to tell him tactfully that shade of green makes anybody's complexion look like they've got malaria, but the corporal don't listen too good once his mind is set."

Isn't that the truth, Chris agreed silently. Aloud, she diplomatically changed the subject. Quinn was her superior officer, and it wouldn't be right to encourage gossip about him. Yet.

"Can you tell me if there's a restaurant within

walking distance, Maisie, a place where I could maybe get a salad?''

"Honey..."

Would Maisie call her Constable Honey when she was on duty? Chris found herself wondering giddily. She stifled a giggle at the thought, sobering quickly when she remembered Quinn's patronizing "Ms Constable."

"You're in walking distance of the whole damn town from here, honey. Dawson only has about a thousand permanent residents. Mind you, in the summer there's lots more people visiting. It gets downright crowded sometimes. We're the only place in Canada with a legal gambling saloon, that's Diamond Tooth Gertie's place, y'know, and the tourists love the folklore about the gold rush days. Whole damn town's getting restored—we got grants from the government to do it. And of course, there's the fact that Robert Service wrote most of his poems here. You'll see his cabin back against the hill, can't miss it.''

There was pride in Maisie's voice when she spoke of her town's heritage, and after Chris had received vague directions to Nancy's Café and set out briskly in search of lunch, she realized quickly that Dawson itself was steeped in that same pride in history.

The town was small, and Chris was already aware of its isolation from the rest of Canada—she'd learned before she arrived that only two buses arrived each week from Whitehorse, and in the summer the trip took six hours. Only two small passenger planes serviced the area, on a similar biweekly schedule, and in winter the schedules were nonexistent.

As she strolled along the dusty wooden sidewalks—Front Street seemed the only paved street in town; the rest were gravel—Chris had an overwhelming sensation of entering a colorful time warp, as if the town were full of the residue of yesterday, the excitement and fervor of the gold rush not a hazy memory but instead a living reality, happening just out of earshot on the next block, or the next...

Not that the town was either quiet or deserted. Dawson had the river at its front and a fair-sized mountain backing it, and within these confines it was absolutely bustling with energy. There were cars, trucks and campers on the streets, people going in and out of stores, work crews swarming over ancient wooden structures that seemed on the verge of collapsing.

Stopping curiously beside one of these log derelicts, Chris found herself being openly admired and whistled at by the young men in work shirts and jeans struggling to raise the building enough to put the same wooden pilings underneath that she'd noticed when she first arrived.

"Why are you doing that?" she asked the nearest youth impulsively.

Suddenly bashful now that he was being spoken to, he blurted, "Because of the permafrost, ma'am," and moved toward the security of his buddies. Wickedly, Chris followed him, enjoying the switch from the pursued to the pursuer.

"What about the permafrost, what does it do?" she demanded, and one of the other men, a darkly handsome youth with a full beard, took time to explain.

"These old buildings were all constructed right on the ground, see, and up here there's always permafrost. So each spring when the thaw comes, the buildings sink into the mud and that's why they've all gone crooked like this. If we don't get them up on skids, pretty soon they'll all tumble down and part of Dawson's history will be lost.''

There it was again, this peculiar fascination with history that Maisie also had. Thoughtfully, Chris thanked him and walked on, mesmerized by the strange names painted on wooden signs adorning the business area.

There was Klondike Kate's, Purveyors of Clean Rooms and Fine Foods. There was a square block of a tiny building that claimed to be the Old Shanty Art Gallery, and farther along, a long flat structure with Red Feather Saloon, Wines Liquors and Cigars painted on its side. Finally, there was a new building still under construction, with a modest wooden sign that said Nancy's.

And parked conspicuously in front of the door was the RCMP cruiser.

Chris felt slightly nervous all of a sudden and slowed her brisk pace. Now what should she do? Another meeting with Corporal Quinn wasn't exactly her idea of a pleasant way to spend her lunch hour on what remained of her afternoon off, and he'd made it plain he didn't want her company, either. On the other hand, Maisie had definitely recommended this particular café as having what she termed "good, edible grub.''

To heck with it. Squaring her shoulders, Chris marched up to the door and in to beard the ogre in his den.

Some strange sixth sense had drawn Quinn's gaze away from his companions and out the wide front window in time to see his new constable swinging down the street. She had a distinctive walk, a proud, almost cocky strut to her, and he admired Chris lasciviously as she neared the door. She'd changed out of uniform, and the snug jeans she now wore overwhelmingly confirmed his earlier conclusions about her figure.

She had a tiny waist and neatly rounded hips, and the hair that had been hidden under her hat was free, a waving cap of shiny dark brown curls cut close to her well-shaped head.

Jim Murphy was sitting beside Quinn, facing the door of the café, and he let out a low, appreciative whistle under his breath when Chris walked in.

"Now where'd she come from?" he murmured, and Parker Jameson twisted around to see, then raised one hoary eyebrow and allowed a wistful smile to twist his mouth somewhere under his copious white beard.

Their reactions, reminiscent of his own when he'd first seen Chris, made Quinn vaguely uneasy and stirred an unexpected spark of...what? Anger?

His fist curled in disgust around the thick coffee mug in his hand.

Female members.

The force was going to hell in a hand basket, sending women up here on northern service.

What did the new regulations suggest doing, for instance, when your friends made these lewd noises about your partner? And he was afraid this was only the beginning, if she stayed around.

From across the small room, Chris identified what she thought was probably antagonism in Quinn's black gaze as he stared at her, and she shriveled inside, wishing frantically she'd never come in.

Forcing the cheery grin she'd pasted on to extend

to her eyes, she squeezed around other patrons and headed straight for him.

"Afternoon, Corporal," she said as cheerfully as she could manage, meeting his eyes bravely. "Maisie sent me over here for lunch."

Chris was aware that Quinn's companions, a scruffy-looking younger man with sleepy eyes and an old gent with a kind face, sporting a wild white beard and mustache, gaped up at her for long seconds and then in unison turned their eyes to Quinn.

"Gentlemen," he said quietly in that deep, almost rumbling voice with its sardonic undertone, his dark eyes challenging hers, "this is the latest addition to the Dawson RCMP detachment. Meet my new partner, Ms Constable."

The taunting moniker was drawled slowly, condescendingly, and if Chris had been one step closer, she knew she'd have been sorely tempted to pour his brimming mug of steaming coffee slowly into his lap and gleefully take the consequences.

Instead, she said firmly, "Chris Johnstone, Constable Johnstone. How do you do?" and went on smiling although it felt as if it were going to kill her. Then she sat down firmly in the vacant chair close beside Quinn, just because she was absolutely certain he didn't want her there.

CHAPTER TWO

THAT EVENING, Chris still couldn't say with certainty exactly what she'd eaten for lunch.

She did remember Quinn introducing his companions, a young soft-spoken taxidriver named Jim Murphy, and a colorful-looking older man called Captain Parker Jameson, who told her pleasantly that he'd been running a summer cruise boat on the Yukon River for years.

"Ever been north before, Ms Constable?" Jim asked her diffidently.

"Johnstone, Constable Johnstone," she enunciated precisely, but Jim simply nodded and looked confused, and with a sinking in her stomach, Chris decided there wasn't much use arguing about it. Quinn had won this round.

To her chagrin, and his amusement, she'd probably be Ms Constable for as long as she stayed in Dawson.

"I've never been this far north before, no," she answered Jim, then sipped the coffee the waitress had poured as soon as she sat down. She was doing her best to ignore the disquieting awareness sitting close to Quinn unexpectedly aroused in her.

"I've spent the past couple of years in Canadian cities. Coming up here is a real change for me."

"Think you'll stay?" the taxidriver asked wistfully. Chris gave Quinn a telling glance, then said with all the certainty she could inject into her voice, "Absolutely. I've been transferred here, and of course I'm staying. I'm going to love it." She hoped she wasn't gritting her teeth as she said it.

Quinn didn't argue or refute her words as she half expected him to. He simply raised his heavy dark eyebrows questioningly as if he were surprised at her vehemence, and took a huge bite out of the roast beef sandwich in front of him.

"That's what they all say the first few days. People who come here all insist they're staying," commented Parker from behind his yellowing beard. "Most newcomers love the North the first week, get bored the second week, and run like hell for the outside by the third."

"Why's that?" Chris asked, and Parker said succinctly, "Isolation, permafrost, mosquitoes, blackflies, nights that last all winter, daylight that goes on all summer. Makes people weird if they stay. You'll see."

Sitting in her biliously green room hours after that conversation, freshly showered, wearing the floor-length cotton T-shirt she slept in, Chris wondered if Parker was right. By the watch on her arm, it was already eleven-thirty at night, but the sun was almost as warm and as bright as it had been at noon, and the people walking up and down the street and the cars passing on the road outside sounded exactly the same as they had earlier that day.

It was Chris's first experience with the perpetual arctic daylight, and she determinedly told herself she found it exhilarating—well, maybe a tiny bit disquieting, she admitted reluctantly. How did you sleep, for instance, when your brain insisted it was noon instead of midnight?

She'd been briefed in the northern familiarization course about the difficulties in adjusting to these long periods of summer daylight and the correspondingly long arctic night.

"Most of us are conditioned to fairly equal periods of daylight and darkness, and our internal clocks are regulated to being awake and asleep correspondingly," the lecturer had warned. "You'll find it difficult to adjust at first, and you'll have to discipline yourself to going to bed in bright sunlight, or getting up and doing a normal day's work in total darkness."

Sunshine certainly didn't make her feel sleepy. And to make matters worse, this room was anything but inviting or relaxing.

Chris mentally reviewed her day. She'd spent the afternoon exploring the town thoroughly, scouting out the various stores, even taking a stroll through the new recreational center built, incongruously, right behind Diamond Tooth Gertie's Saloon.

It was a different sort of town from the small Okanagan communities she'd grown up in, different, too, from the coastal fishing villages she'd been posted to for short periods after Depot.

Dawson had more of a sense of history, and less of an air of permanence. The combination of north and gold had left an indelible imprint, and she'd lost track of time as she explored.

Finally, when her stomach had warned it must be suppertime, she'd bought two huge bags of groceries from the friendly, and extremely nosy, woman in the market. Then she'd returned home, stowing the supplies in the bare cupboards in the kitchen, reviewing several possible menus in her mind and then finally eating several cartons of yogurt and a cheese-filled bun quickly at the table under the window.

It wasn't that Chris didn't know how to cook; in fact, she actually enjoyed it. The simple fact was that cooking for one person had never appealed to her, and there'd been no sign of Quinn all afternoon.

She told herself she was vastly relieved by his absence. He'd given her absolutely no reason to invite him to share a meal, that was certain.

It was just…lonely in the strange detachment building by herself.

Chris plunked her bottom on the hard, narrow mattress, rested her chin in her cupped hands and surveyed the few pitiful changes she'd been able to make in her private living area that afternoon. Things would get better when her trunk arrived later in the week, she silently assured herself, but at the moment the room was starkly uninviting.

Several bottles of perfume and a brightly floral cosmetic bag looked marooned on the scarred dresser top, and her clock radio sat alone on the small table beside the bed. Her uniforms and personal clothing were carefully hung in the closet, her shiny boots and shoes neatly arranged on the floor underneath, hats on the shelf above, exactly the way she'd been taught to arrange her belongings during training.

There was one comforting personal comment, however.

On the table beside the bed stood the framed picture of her family, taken when she was home on leave last spring.

The portrait made a break in the otherwise unalleviated green of the wall. Paul and Rosemary Johnstone stood under an azure-blue sky by a turquoise lake, both wearing ponytails and nondescript wrinkled shorts and shirts, looking comically androgynous and unlike anybody's parents.

They were flanked by Chris and her sister and brother, all three taller than their parents, all with smart short haircuts, all dressed in stylish casual clothing. The photo gave the impression of three young yuppies with their arms around two aging hippies. Which, Chris mused fondly, was absolutely accurate. Except her parents had been hippies before the term was in general use.

The photographers had captured Chris's parents' typical expressions of confused surprise, and the picture made Chris grin in delight each time she looked at it.

Candlelight parents in a chromium age, her brother Shane had lovingly dubbed the older Johnstones, and all at once Chris felt a crippling wave of homesickness for the whole crazy Johnstone clan, for her brother Shane, for her sister Ariel, for her parents.

She'd love to phone them tonight, to tell them her impressions of her new posting. The force's ban on direct communication with them somehow doubled her feeling of alienation here.

Stop being childish, Johnstone, she lectured herself sternly. *You chose your life, you know that.*

Dawson might be a very long way from the sunny Okanagan area of south-central British Columbia where she'd grown up, but her career in the RCMP was light-years removed from the gentle, idealistic childhood her parents had provided, light-years also from what they'd envisioned their younger daughter doing with her life.

The sound of gravel spraying and tires burning rubber out front suddenly distracted her.

A car door slammed. A key sounded in the front office door.

Quinn was home. Her heart gave a thump, and for some crazy reason began to beat faster than before.

Chris quickly drew her legs up on the bed and pulled the sheet up to her neck, wondering irritably why Quinn's presence should make her react in such a juvenile way. He certainly wasn't going to barge into her room and order her to bed, she chided herself. And even if he did, her nightwear was anything but provocative.

She'd lived in close quarters with dozens of men during training, and it hadn't affected her this way. She'd damned well better get over it.

She and Quinn would be living in different areas of the same house for the coming months, working intimately at the task of policing a small town, and she'd just have to get used to him. This was ridiculous.

She heard footsteps coming along the hallway. He was singing under his breath, but she couldn't catch the words. His deep baritone thrummed through the dusty air like a droning bee, and in her imagination Chris followed his confident, striding progress through the house into the kitchen. She listened to the fridge door slamming, then a clumping upstairs to what must be his bedroom, then the sound of heavy footsteps moving back and forth over her head, back down the stairs and through the door into the hallway.

Between one note and the next, the singing stopped abruptly, and Chris knew as clearly as if she'd seen him do so that he'd glanced over at her closed door and suddenly remembered she was in there, perhaps sleeping.

She stifled a giggle as the footsteps became noticeably quieter, and she could envision the huge man tiptoeing down the hall. What a strange combination he was, absolutely maddening in some ways, touchingly thoughtful in others.

A moment later, the cruiser roared into life and the protesting sound of the accelerating motor made her shudder.

If he was no gentler with women than he was with machines, Quinn would be an absolutely terrible lover, but somehow Chris didn't think he would be. There was a nebulous air about him of sensuality and restraint and passion held in check....

Appalled at the turn her thoughts had taken, Chris flopped down on the unyielding foam pillow in disgust. The last thing she ought to be wondering about was Quinn's prowess as a lover, for pete's sake. She should be thinking instead of what nasty surprises he was dreaming up to make her first day at Dawson detachment both miserable and memorable.

She should be going to sleep.

Shutting her eyes firmly against the distracting light still pouring around the sides of the window blinds, she consciously regulated her breathing and counted backward from ten to one, seeing the numbers in three dimensions marching across the mental screen in front of her closed eyelids, envisioning herself going deeper and deeper into a restful state of mind.

The meditation process was as familiar as breathing for Chris. She'd practiced it every night for as long as she could remember.

She imagined herself driving competently in the

cruiser toward an emergency call, handling it easily and with confidence.

She imagined Quinn shaking her hand in congratulations for a job well done.

She imagined herself working beside him in various situations, the two of them meshing as an efficient team.

She imagined herself receiving commendation and a promotion.

Joy filled her as it always did when she meditated. She imagined cool, soothing darkness, a peaceful sky ablaze with moon and stars, and her mind hovered now on the very brink of consciousness.

Just before she slipped over the edge, her capricious imagination placed her inside that darkness, inside strong male arms that were encircling her, almost crushing her against a broad chest.

He adored her, this dream lover. He was filled with both sensual excitement and a profound peace. His mouth came down slowly, far too slowly, to meet her eager lips, and she strained to see his face, knowing all the while it would be shadowed, mysteriously anonymous.

But tonight she could see him.

Tonight she saw Quinn's compelling eyes, Quinn's strong face, Quinn's hard lips beneath the flowing mustache, and a sense of destiny fulfilled came over her.

She tumbled into sleep then, and when she awoke it was still daylight, morning daylight by the hands on her clock, and she'd forgotten the dream.

HE WAS ALREADY in the kitchen when she walked in, looking trim in her immaculate uniform shirt and trousers.

"Morning," he greeted her, his voice a pleasing rumble. He twisted his head around and nodded at her. He was standing over a black iron frying pan at the electric range, and the smell of smoking grease and frying bacon filled the room.

His hair was still damp from a recent shower, standing in whorls and eddies around his skull, and his cheeks and chin around the mustache faintly showed the marks of recent shaving.

"Good morning," Chris replied uncertainly. Should she get a pan of her own and cook eggs beside him, or eat the dry cereal she'd bought and forget a hot breakfast?

"How many eggs?" Quinn sounded totally matter-of-fact.

He was scooping crisp bacon out of the pan onto a paper towel, and then neatly cracking eggs and dropping them into the hot grease.

"Umm, two please. Shall I make some toast?"

"Yeah, a stack of it, toaster's over there."

She moved past him, taking note of his gray short-sleeved T-shirt, the blue braces with the yellow stripes bisecting his wide shoulders, the navy-blue police pants and black Kodiak boots.

Dress code, strictly haphazard, she noted, pleased. He looked incredibly virile and a bit vulnerable this way, and there was something disturbingly intimate about standing a few feet away from a man dressed like that, casually making toast as if they shared such duties every morning of their lives.

"Sleep okay? Any problems with the sun being on all night?" he queried, and then frowned, his heavy eyebrows beetling together, centering all his attention on the delicate process of rescuing the eggs unbroken from the pan and onto the platter beside the bacon.

"A bit at first, but then it was fine. Want me to set the table?"

Quinn glanced over at her and nodded. She was as shiny as a polished nugget this morning, and he liked the fact that she didn't seem to wear any makeup. It made her skin seem translucent over the high cheekbones, like a child's face in the morning. Her hair was cut short for a woman and molded to her head in tight, still-wet curls, like the hair on Greek statues he'd seen in books.

He'd always liked long hair before.

He'd never noticed a constable's hairdo before.

"The cutlery is in the drawer under the counter."

"Where are the place mats?"

That threw him. He frowned for a second, heavy eyebrows almost meeting over the prominent bridge of his nose.

"Guess we're fresh out of place mats."

"A tablecloth, then?"

He shook his head. "Old bachelors like me aren't too fussy about the niceties."

She surprised him, demanding forthrightly, "How old are you, Quinn? Thirty-eight, thirty-nine?"

He grinned at her, a nice, friendly open grin, revealing surprisingly white, even teeth, and it made such a difference in his face that she had to stare for a second. He looked engagingly boyish, with just a hint of wickedness in his black gleaming eyes when he smiled.

Hastily, she found the plates and the knives and forks and turned to the table.

"Flattery won't help, Constable. I'm an ancient forty-two. What about you?"

He could easily check her file if he wanted to know, but she was glad he'd asked instead.

"Twenty-nine. Thirty next April."

Quinn came up behind her, plopped the platter of food on the table and went back to the stove for the huge enamel coffeepot.

"You don't look it. I figured you for twenty-two or -three at the most."

"I'm reasonably well preserved," Chris said sarcastically. "But definitely past the first blush of youth."

Now his gaze was surprisingly bold, and she felt a flush come and go as she took her place at the small table.

"Oh," he drawled, "I wouldn't say that. You might have a couple or so good years left in you yet before they pension you off, you never know. Where's the ketchup?"

He ate like a healthy, hungry man, the ever present sun bathing them both in its warmth as it poured through the windows.

Chris chewed and swallowed the tasty meal, aware every moment of the trousered knees sometimes accidentally bumping her own beneath the table, the small homely noises they each made chewing toast.

"How long have you been stationed here, Quinn?" she asked when he poured them each seconds of the tar-black, awful brew he actually thought was coffee.

"Five years this coming August." The sunlight was picking out stray red and gold strands in that brown hair of hers. She had tiny ears, he noted, delicately folded and flat to her head, and whoever cut her hair had cleverly left them exposed. How the hell could ears look sensual like that?

"Five years is a long time to stay at one posting. I thought the force made a point of moving members every couple of years at most."

That little sardonic twist to his mouth was already becoming familiar to her, Chris noted.

"They move you if you're heading up the ladder. If you're a major pain in the butt, they find somewhere like Dawson and plant you there until they can pension you off."

Chris had heard the various rumors about him. She suddenly wanted to know the truth, the real reasons for his rebellion, if that's what it was.

"Is that what you want, Quinn?" she demanded forthrightly. "Is that what you want from life, just to mark time here until pension?" She frowned at him, and her earnest innocence evoked a surge of anger.

"What you want from life and what you get are usually two vastly different things, especially in this noble organization we work for," he snapped. "Haven't you learned that yet?"

Quinn felt uncomfortable, the way he always did when he found someone trying to get inside his head. Why in blazes didn't the goddamn phone ring off the hook this morning as it always had before? He didn't need meaningful conversations with anybody, he liked keeping his own counsel, but for some reason he couldn't deflect her questions the way he'd always done with other people. She had a sneaky way of tunneling under the surface.

This time, she leveled a look on him from those silver-blue eyes that could have felled Dangerous Dan McGrew without a bullet.

"I've learned that life isn't always fair, Quinn, but I do think you get what you work for and what you deserve."

Finally, finally, the phone rang.

"I'll get that, you clean up in here," he ordered, and ignoring the extension on the counter, he hurried through to the office.

Chris studied the littered table, the counter with open egg cartons and lids from jam and ketchup, the grease-spattered stove. There were also dishes stacked in the sink from yesterday, she noticed. Maybe longer ago than just yesterday, she decided when she took a second look.

She'd grown up with a shrewd brother, and a nasty suspicion about Quinn's generosity in cooking for her began to taint her mind.

When he stuck his head in the door a moment later and formally and rapidly gave her the orders for the day, those suspicions were confirmed.

"When you're done here, Constable, I want you to put in your expense accounts and get Maisie to show you the office procedure. You'll have to read all the open files, learn how we do things up here. Maisie's only in three mornings a week, so there's a backlog of reports needing typing. You can tackle those. Anything urgent comes up, buzz me on the radio and I'll handle it." He was shrugging into a khaki shirt, strapping on his holster with rapid efficiency.

Poised halfway to the sink with an armload of dirty dishes, Chris suddenly saw the writing on the wall in brilliant red ink. He was going to relegate the office chores to her, block her from doing any real police work, assign her to the duties all members hated but which were usually shared evenly in the running of a small-town detachment.

"Corporal, I don't want—" she began to protest angrily.

Her outraged protest met with a hasty wave. "We'll discuss it later, Constable. Gotta go, there's a brawl going on over at the saloon."

A brawl? At seven-forty-five in the morning?

The door slammed behind him.

"MAISIE, WHO NORMALLY DOES the janitor work around here, cleans up the living quarters, washes the vehicles, dungs out the cells?"

Maisie was doing her imitation of typing. Chris had studied the procedure for the past few days and was still unsure how Maisie managed to look and sound as if she were typing forty words a minute when she actually turned out about ten. Now, the redhead frowned in concentration, carefully marked the spot on the report she was ostensibly doing, and shoved her glasses back up her nose.

"Constable, honey…" Chris winced. The salutation that had started out sounding amusing was now driving her nuts, but it wasn't Maisie's fault, really. A week of being a glorified janitor, a highly paid housemaid and a reluctant office worker had eroded every scrap of good nature and patience, to say nothing of humor, that Chris had ever possessed.

"The corporal always hired Slocum Charlie for jobs like that before. Mind you, when the last young constable was here—the one before you, that poor boy who had that breakdown and left after the first three weeks—well, he did those chores just like you are now. Between you and me, I think it's like a little test Corporal Quinn gives you young people, to find out if you've got the right stuff. Say, did you see that movie, *The Right Stuff*?''

Chris shook her head absently, and Maisie launched into a detailed explanation of the film's plot, but Chris wasn't listening.

So Quinn had successfully broken the last constable posted here, had he? Ruefully, Chris mused that if the kid had lasted three weeks doing the same crazy-making, boring, unfulfilling tasks she'd been assigned, he deserved a breakdown.

Damn, damn Corporal Quinn! He was as evasive as any seasoned criminal she'd ever heard on the witness stand, and far more elusive. During the past week she'd done everything but barge into his bedroom in the middle of the night, in an effort to reason with him over what her duties should include. But he'd made damned certain he was urgently needed somewhere else every single time.

Short of kidnapping him and tying him up until he'd listen to reason.... Well, she told herself determinedly, there had to be a way to outsmart him, and she'd eventually find it.

In the meantime, there were still files she hadn't read. At least by the time she got back to active duty, she'd probably know more about the caseload here than Quinn himself. She'd bet he'd never so much as glanced in some of these old file cabinets.

The whole system needed updating badly, and she might as well get at it. At least that task would take up the better part of still another endless afternoon in the office.

''Maisie, where are the keys to this file drawer?''

''Now, that's a good question. I've never had any

reason to go in there. I never even knew it was locked. Maybe he keeps them on that key ring in his desk drawer, honey, in his office, but I don't know if you should—"

Chris was already through the connecting door, yanking open the drawers of Quinn's littered desk.

She found the keys eventually, stuck inside a leather case at the back of the bottom drawer. His desk was a disgusting mess, Chris concluded angrily. Quinn was the one who ought to be spending more time in the office. He was obviously months behind on some of his paperwork.

Using the key, she opened the file drawer, tugged out an armload of the yellowed folders, and set to work.

She was still hard at it an hour later when Maisie finished for the day.

"You know, honey, you ought to get out of here and have some fun. Come on over to Diamond Tooth Gertie's one of these evenings, get to know some of the young people around. I'm getting worried about you, never seen anybody up here with cabin fever in the summertime, but seems to me you might have a touch. I never saw you out anywhere having a beer."

"I don't drink, Maisie." Chris was beginning to believe she was the only person in all Dawson that didn't. There seemed to be parties going on in the eternal daylight that simply moved from place to place, and yet from what she could tell, there weren't a lot of enforcement problems because of them.

"Not at all? Then what the heck do you do in your spare time?" Maisie sounded flabbergasted. "Heck, honey, I'm a single career gal just like you, and I'd go bonkers if I didn't party it up a little. What is there to do besides have a drink, go to a party?"

"Well, I read a lot, I jog along the road, I walk around town." Chris was still astonished by the fact that nothing in town ever seemed to close or open at regular hours, that at any hour of the day or night, people were riding bikes or gardening or studiously sunbathing. Dawson residents worshiped the endless sunlight with far more fervor than winter tourists in Miami.

"Sounds to me like you need to meet some other young folks, learn to have a good time," Maisie said sternly. "When winter comes, that's when you read around here, not in the summer," she lectured.

Chris rested her aching head on a hand and thought maybe Maisie had a point. She did keep to herself a lot, that was true. It was probably a habit she had acquired from working undercover, from being alone and on guard all the time.

Here, she'd talked casually to various people, learning strange and interesting facts about the town and the gold rush, but so far she hadn't made any friends.

She glanced up from the file she was reading and smiled warmly at Maisie.

"I will go out one of these nights. See you tomorrow."

Maisie sadly shook her head.

"There you go, that's exactly what I'm on about. Tomorrow, honey, is Saturday, and I don't work. It's Friday today. See, you don't even know the weekend when it hits you. I'm getting my hair done at the beauty parlor, and then Norman's taking me for a drink and some dancing at Gertie's. Why don't you come along with us?''

Chris shook her head. She'd met and liked Maisie's current beau, Norman Bickle, a shy little salesman half a head shorter than Maisie and fifty pounds lighter, but she certainly didn't feel like tagging along on their date.

"Thanks, Maisie, but I'm not in the right mood. Besides, I have to answer the phones for the corporal tonight. See you Monday, and enjoy yourself."

Alone once more with the empty office and the files, Chris suddenly shoved the stack petulantly across the desk and slumped in her hard-backed chair.

Was this what she'd gone through police training for, just to sit around a stale office all day and read outdated files? Maybe she should take Maisie's advice tonight and go see what Friday night offered in a gold rush town. It was a cinch Quinn wasn't going to assign her town duty, and technically she'd already put in eight hours today, so answering phones was above and beyond the call of duty. She was free, if she wanted to be.

Did she want to be free and footloose? She thought it over, and decided no.

Gathering the stack of boring cardboard folders, she pried the bottom file drawer open with her toe. She was about to dump the whole mess in when she saw the square steel box, a holder for five by seven file cards, shoved in the very back of the drawer.

Idly curious, she laid the files on the floor and pulled out the box, opening the lid and flicking the neat cards so she could see their headings.

Hand-printed in ink at the top of each card was a single name and age, then a list of physical characteristics, as well as notations that seemed random scribbled beneath.

Puzzled, she wandered over to the table and, starting with the *A* cards, she read a few carefully.

"Amy S.," the first card read. "36, blonde, face like a fallen angel, had a kid and put it up for adoption. Followed Billy C. up here, and stayed when he left for Yellowknife. Hooker now, poor kid."

"Anselm P.," the next card read. "66, shady past, immigrant from Germany, WW2? Soldier, probably. Leg injury, can't hold liquor, lives with Gerty. Bad actor when drinking."

Fascinated, Chris skipped back and forth, cross-referencing with strange information. There was a thumbnail sketch of each person mentioned. There were facts, assumptions, bits of physical detail, each card drawing some sort of picture of the name used. Sometimes, information had been penciled in at some later date, and some of the entries made her smile.

"Margie F., postmistress, 32," one of the *M* entries said in ink. "Cross-eyed older husband, Brian F." Farther down the card was scrawled in pencil, "M. pregnant. Town thinks definitely not her husband's." Still farther was the gleeful addition, in ink again, "Cross-eyed kid. Brian's definitely."

Chris read on and on, mystified. In the *P*'s, a sudden shock of recognition jolted her, and she read the card over and over.

"Cpt. Parker J. 66 yrs old." The next words sent a shiver through Chris. "Fugitive, outstanding twenty-year U.S.-wide warrant, abduction of son, Cole. Custody legally awarded to wealthy grandparents, Hawaii, upon death of wife."

The bearded face of the man she'd met her first

day in Dawson flashed in front of Chris's eyes, and she sat frozen, staring at the innocuous little card. It hadn't really occurred to her until that moment that the cards were written about real people, but now she deliberately searched for the first names of several acquaintances she'd met that week.

They were all there, filed by first name, descriptions easily recognizable.

She stared down at the steel box in horror, and then jumped up, raced to Quinn's office and snatched a handwritten report from his desk.

Heart hammering, she compared the writing to the tiny, cramped words on several cards. The style was identical. These cards had definitely been written by Quinn.

She flipped through them, trying to guess how many there were, concluding at last that there must be cards on half the town. At last she located the one on Parker Jameson again and reread it.

Feeling cold and sick and horribly fearful, she slowly replaced all the cards, closed the lid on the box and put them back in their hiding place. For reasons she couldn't begin to fathom, Quinn kept notes on his friends.

Why?

Worse, much worse, was the knowledge that if the information on one card was accurate, then Quinn was turning a blind eye to an outstanding warrant. Captain Parker Jameson, wanted for abducting a child. Nausea tilted her stomach as her police training suggested the most logical reasons for Quinn's actions.

Was Quinn blackmailing Jameson, being paid off for keeping quiet?

Was Jameson blackmailing Quinn?

If so, how could they sit so companionably over lunch at Nancy's Café?

Chris's anger and confusion accelerated with each supposition, because she didn't want to believe the worst.

She wondered why she desperately wanted him to have logical answers for her queries, reasons that explained why he kept those cards, why he did nothing about Parker Jameson.

Unwillingly, she admitted to herself that she liked Quinn despite the things he did that made her furious with him. There was a strength about him she admired, some hazy reflection in him of an ideal she'd always searched for in the men she met.

Certainly not perfection. Chris grimaced at the thought.

Quinn would never qualify as a very perfect gentle knight in shining armor, but then perfection didn't appeal to her anyway.

He did have a wicked, quirky sense of humor, strength of character, an odd air of vulnerability at times. A rough kindness. Even his comments on those damnable cards were unfailingly kind.

And she'd believed until now that he was honest.

When she was a teenager bored with school, she'd instigated intricate pranks that involved her sister and brother, delighted her schoolmates and nearly drove her teachers insane. After one particularly disruptive episode, her father was called to a meeting with the principal.

"Has Christine told you the absolute truth about everything she's done?" Paul Johnstone asked after listening to complaints about his younger daughter for more than half an hour.

"Well, yes, she has, but that's not the point," the pompous administrator huffed.

"It is to me," Chris's father had said ever so gently, before standing up and heading for the door. "Punish her fairly; she's more than earned it. But I care only that she was honest. 'Man is his own star,'" Paul quoted. His daughter, sitting in disgrace at the back of the room, had thought her heart would burst with pride for her father as he continued, "'That soul that can be honest is the only perfect man.'"

It was a measure she used for the rest of her life when judging anyone.

The question was, where was Quinn now on that yardstick?

CHAPTER THREE

FRIDAY NIGHT WAS HECTIC. Chris relayed dozens of calls and messages to Quinn over the radio, and once he brought two quarrelsome and extremely drunk men into the police office and locked them in the cells. There certainly wasn't a single chance to have a conversation with him.

The drunks argued noisily far into the night. Twice Chris pulled on her robe in exasperation and sternly ordered them to be quiet, but her words didn't have much effect. She was still awake when the patrol car finally drove into the garage in the early hours of Saturday morning.

"You two pack it up in there, or I'll come in and rattle your cage for you properly," Quinn ordered sternly as he passed the cells. "I'm tired, and there's someone trying to sleep down the hall. If you wake either of us up you'll answer to me. Understood?"

There was sudden respectful silence, and Chris listened to his weary footsteps continue down the hall and eventually go up the stairs to his bedroom. She'd planned a hundred different conversational gambits in her head, but 3:00 a.m. was no time to confront him, daylight or not. She went to sleep instead, and managed to sleep straight through her alarm. It was almost ten before she hurried through the kitchen door.

The scribbled note on the counter said:

Released our guests, have taken them out for breakfast. Figured you needed the sleep—that was a noisy night. Please start on statistics, use most recent as guide, mop out cells and fill in man-hour forms.

Q

How did he always manage to make her want to throttle him in righteous outrage while feeling touched at his kindness? Chris wondered as she filled a bowl with cereal and fixed a pot of coffee.

She knew he was undoubtedly buying those two reprobates breakfast out of his own pocket, and it was thoughtful of him to let her sleep in. Then, he promptly proceeded to wreck everything by suggesting that she struggle with the lousy statistics, mop out the awful mess those two drunks had undoubtedly left in the cells, and—the absolutely final straw as far as she was concerned—he actually expected her to fill in man-hour sheets for him.

The egotistical, overbearing oaf! She slammed her bowl down on the table and sent cornflakes and milk spraying all over, barely aware that she was muttering out loud.

"For crying out loud, Quinn, how the heck am I supposed to know what you do with your time? You sure as blazes never let me ride with you and find out."

And he sure didn't waste any time talking with her either.

She swiped viciously at the mess with the dishcloth and poured herself a huge mug of coffee. The single advantage in not having him around at breakfast was being able to make drinkable coffee, she mused morosely.

Well, today was the end of Quinn's disappearing act. Today, she decided with grim determination, he was going to have a long conversation with her about every single question she needed an answer for.

One way, or the other.

Chris decided to tackle the dirtiest chore first. She had a bucket of hot water full of strong disinfectant and the business end of a huge mop inside the first cell half an hour later, when the door from the office opened and Quinn appeared.

"Morning, Constable," he greeted her cheerfully. "I forgot to tell you that the magistrate, Sir Martin Braithwaite, is coming by before noon to sign the summonses for next week's court."

Sir Martin Braithwaite?

"Corporal Quinn," Chris said forcefully, "there's several matters I absolutely must talk with you—"

The telephone shrilled, and Chris was certain a look of relief flashed across his face.

"I'll get it. You carry on," he announced magnanimously, and disappeared into the outer office.

Chris swore steadily for several minutes, punctuating the pithy language with vicious sweeps of the mop. Undoubtedly, it would be an "urgent" summons, and he'd be gone the rest of the day unless she came up with a plan during the next three seconds.

She tried to force herself to calm down and think clearly, and then she heard his deep voice say, "That's fine, Dez. I'll have Ms Constable come by and pick it up for me, as soon as she's finished some office duties."

Chris's temper exploded at the exact moment a plan of action popped into her head.

She set the mop down and hurried to the outer office, where Quinn was lounging at a desk. Hastily, he started to get up, reaching for the car keys he'd dropped beside the phone.

Acting quickly, before he could get away, Chris said with just the right touch of panic in her voice, "Corporal, I think you'd better come back here and have a look at this." She knew exactly how to make her blue eyes appear big and innocent, her expression frightened and helpless, and Quinn all but leaped to follow her.

"What's the problem, Chris?"

His tone was full of such genuine, warm concern, and the unconscious use of her first name affected her strangely. She might have relented at that moment, except for that overheard conversation.

Ms Constable. Office duties, all right.

"It's absolutely horrible, just look in here," she said in a slightly quavery tone as she led the way into the far corner of the cell she'd just been cleaning and motioned at an invisible something on the floor. Quinn followed like a lamb, and in another instant, Chris had slipped outside and slammed the steel door firmly with Quinn inside.

He straightened up slowly from where he'd bent to peer at whatever it was that had frightened her, and she watched with satisfaction as comprehension dawned.

"What the... Just what the hell do you think you're doing, Constable?"

In two strides, he was holding the bars as if he would bend them, and Chris prudently moved back so that there was no chance of his long arms reaching her. She walked into his office and retrieved a chair, set it six feet from the cell, then sat comfortably down.

I'd better look and sound a lot braver than I feel, she decided after glancing at the thunderously furious expression on his face. She ventured one direct look into his eyes, and shuddered involuntarily.

The eye of a basilisk—wasn't that the serpent that could kill you with a look? Well, that image suited Quinn at this moment.

"Have you come unglued, Constable Johnstone? You get over here and unlock this door."

Each word was separate, and laden with menace.

Chris lifted one long, trousered leg leisurely over the other, folded her arms across her chest and shook her head firmly.

"Constable Johnstone," she said thoughtfully, testing the sound of the words. "That's a big improvement over Ms Constable." She couldn't tell whether the flush on his features was a trace of embarrassment at the truth of her statement, or a whole lot of rage. She'd bet on the latter. Well, in for a penny... "Why, Corporal Quinn, I'll bet that in about an hour you'll even agree that mopping up filth from those cells isn't exactly office duty, and after that, there's a chance you'll concede there seems to be a note of inequality around here concerning who does what."

Quinn stood absolutely still, glaring at her, but Chris could see his chest heaving up and down with fury.

"This is ridiculous. If you wanted to discuss your duties here with me, all you had to do was..."

"What, Corporal? Catch you and then hold you

down so you'd listen? I've tried to do just that for days, and you avoid me like the plague."

"Unlock this door, and we'll discuss anything you like."

"We'll talk with the door locked, and then later we'll negotiate your release."

His voice was low and his tone deadly. "I'll have you in orderly room in front of the officer commanding for this, Constable."

The anger and frustration, the sense of injustice and, worst of all, the terrible suspicion about him that had been building steadily in her exploded.

"How dare you threaten me with orderly room?" She leaped to her feet, overturning the chair and ignoring it. Stomping into the other room, she tore open the file drawer and snatched up the steel storage box, flew back to the cells and, holding it with both hands just out of his reach, shook it viciously at him.

"What about these, Quinn? What about all these cards about everybody in town? Maybe Staff would be fascinated by the quaint comments on these. Like the one about your friend, Captain Jameson, and the outstanding warrant on him."

Quinn became very still, but his piercing black eyes still met hers squarely.

"Those cards are both personal and private. You had no right to read them." His tone was icy cold.

"They were in the file cabinet, Corporal. The file cabinet happens to be RCMP property, and you distinctly told me to redo all the old files. Don't you remember? Now," Chris continued mutinously, setting the box on the floor between them, righting the overturned chair and sitting down again, "I feel you owe me an explanation." She was shaking badly, and she did her best to hide it, folding her hands in her lap.

An entire range of emotions had been coursing through Quinn as he stared at the incredible blue-eyed female glaring at him through the bars. He felt incredulous anger, but his sense of humor forced him to see the funny side of being locked up by his own constable. He had a grudging admiration for the slender, deceptively fragile woman who'd dared to do such an outrageous thing and who'd refused to be intimidated by his best bullying tactics.

And then, when she unexpectedly produced that damned card file, he'd been acutely embarrassed before being overwhelmed by a terrible shyness.

In order to explain, Quinn was going to have to reveal a part of himself hardly another living soul knew, and he wondered for a fleeting moment whether it would be easier to just stay in the cell and let her do whatever she had to with him.

Her silver-blue eyes never flinched. She went on staring at him, and he struggled with years of protective silence about his most private dreams. Desperately, he procrastinated.

"The magistrate will be here soon, Constable. What happens then?"

She shrugged. "I'll tell him I wrestled you in there and then locked you up. These cronies of yours are all so macho, they'll live for weeks on a wonderful joke like that." She pointed down at the steel box. "The cards, Corporal. I need to hear about the cards."

He could feel the dull red flush creeping up his neck and face, and he couldn't stop it. His knuckles tightened around steel, and his throat tightened around the coppery stale taste of fear.

"You're trying to look inside my head, goddamn it," he said finally, in absolute exasperation.

Chris didn't respond, but his choice of words intrigued her.

Despairingly, he plunged into an explanation.

"Sure, I wrote those cards about the people around here. People are the only thing that matter when it's all said and done, Constable. Those cards, they're just personalities I've collected, some unusual, some ordinary. Patterns, you might say." He stumbled over his next words, frowning. "I've, I, ah, I want to—" he hesitated, forcing the words out "—to write someday, and so I collect things, facts and feelings that set one human apart from another. That's all that stuff is, private little notes to myself. I'd almost forgotten I even left the cards there—nobody but me ever goes in that old file section anyway."

She watched as Quinn struggled, and sympathy and a new tenderness for him welled up inside of her. She wanted to believe him, this big, endearing, awkward man who was telling her, incredibly, that he wanted to write books. Every fiber of her being yearned to believe him, but there was always that cautious, skeptical training she'd absorbed.

"That sounds great, Corporal, but what about Parker Jameson?" she prodded. "There's an outstanding warrant on him, it says so in there."

He recognized the cool, impartial neutrality in her tone for the professionalism it was, and the police officer in him applauded her, even as his irritation grew. He knew exactly what she suspected, that there had to be some fraud connected with that unfortunate piece of trivia on the blasted card. That was exactly what he would have thought, in her circumstances.

True anxiety gripped him now. More important than his own pride was his friend's safety, and there was no other way out than to tell her the whole truth. And he didn't know her well enough to anticipate her reaction. Would she go strictly by the book, have Parker... She couldn't. He'd just have to convince her, make her see the way things were. Old Parker couldn't be made to suffer just because he, Quinn, was a careless, daydreaming fool.

"Parker married a girl in Hawaii years ago, daughter of a wealthy sugar baron," he began with a weary sigh. "He was in the air force, stationed there after the war, and her folks were none too happy with the match. Parker was nobody, you see, no money or connections, but he loved her something fierce, still does in fact. He carries her picture around in his wallet, he'll likely show you when he gets to know you better. Anyhow, they had a son, Cole." Quinn sounded almost curt. "And Parker's wife died with some flu or other when the kid was six, almost killed him as well. Afterward, Parker had nothing to stay over there for, wanted to come home to Canada. But her family balked at him taking Cole, hired fancy lawyers and eventually got custody of the kid awarded to them. Now, that boy was all the guy had left. So Parker got a friend to fly him and his son out one night, quiet, with little more than the shirts on their backs, and they came here to Dawson. Parker had nothing, he started his tour business out of sheer guts and determination, made sure Cole got an education. Nice guy, Cole Jameson. He's a doctor now, an orthopedic surgeon in Vancouver, absolutely adores his old man. So what should I do, Constable? Arrest him and Cole both, have them deported to face charges more than twenty years old? What the hell would that prove?"

There was a long silence. Chris swallowed and drew in a deep, shaky breath.

"I totally agree with you," she said softly. "I'd forget the whole thing, too, if it were me." She could feel the tears in her throat. She wanted to reach across and kiss him, her relief was so great. She felt immensely touched by the story, absolutely convinced that what Quinn was doing was exactly what she'd have chosen to do under the same circumstances.

He cleared his throat, relieved, and the tension gradually ebbed out of him. She was a good man, this one. It was going to be fine.

"Okay, Constable, now that we've settled that, unlock the door, would you?" he asked softly.

Chris came down from her emotional high with a crash, and he watched in disbelief as the softness on her face and in her beautiful blue eyes faded as if it had never been. Grim determination hardened her features all over again.

"Hold it, Corporal. There's a few more things we're going to talk about first. Like the fact that I trained to be a policeperson, not a janitor or a typist or an errand girl. I don't mind doing my fair share of office work, or washing cars or cells, but boy, you've never heard of the human rights code, Corporal. It stipulates equal pay for equal work, and I want my fair share of the real police work in this town. You can forget about making my life so miserable I'll pack up and leave, too, because you're beating a dead horse. I never quit." She delivered the last three words with absolute certainty.

"Are you trying to tell me how to run my detachment, Constable?" His temper flared, and behind the bars, Quinn tensed all over again in preparation for battle. What was it with this impossible woman, anyhow?

"I'm telling you I want a fair share in helping you run it, and no more snide remarks about my sex, either."

They both heard the chugging of an old car as it pulled up in front of the station, the clunk and growl as the motor died and then the loud slam of a car door.

"That's the magistrate, Constable."

"I'm sure it is, Corporal." Chris had to admire his coolness. He'd be a good partner to have in a tight spot.

She'd be a fine partner when the chips were down. She didn't blink or move or seem the least bit pressured, Quinn observed.

The moment of decision had come, and it was painful for him. He choked out the words.

"Okay, Constable Johnstone, I concede. Equal work, no more joking around. Now unlock this cage."

Should she demand to have the promises in writing? The front door of the station opened and closed, and an accented voice bellowed, "Quinn, old boy, are you there?"

Prudently, she decided not to push him any further. She had the cell door open before Sir Martin came through the door, but only just. By the look on Quinn's face as he brushed past her, it was a stroke of luck the magistrate was present.

Her corporal looked capable of unnatural acts, but

all he said was, "This is our magistrate, Sir Martin Braithwaite, Constable. Martin, this is my new right-hand man, Constable Chris Johnstone."

She took the fat little hand the rotund magistrate offered, smiled widely and hoped like hell she really had won the war.

CHAPTER FOUR

SHE HADN'T WON the war. And the following week proved that the battle was only partially fought, after all.

Chris felt her spirits soar early Monday, when Quinn handed over the keys to the cruiser and laconically ordered, "You follow up on this one, Constable. There's some sort of disturbance at this address— it's on the street that runs behind that little grocery store. Go see what's going on."

Using Quinn's sketchy directions, Chris pulled the cruiser into a narrow lane a few minutes later and marched smartly up to the door of the ramshackle house she thought was the right one.

Children and dogs seemed to be spilling out of doors and windows in neighboring yards.

"It's the cops," one redheaded urchin hollered in glee, and a small crowd collected at the gate to watch. Chris hoped she wasn't walking into a domestic dispute—she knew from past experience such scenes could be dangerous to the officer attending. Her heart hammered faster than normal as she knocked firmly and waited.

"Constable Johnstone, RCMP," Chris identified herself as the door opened, and the extraordinarily fat woman in the doorway gaped at her in disbelief, then peered over Chris's shoulder at the marked cruiser.

"But you're a female. Where's Quinn? He's the cop I talked with before." Keen disappointment was evident from the petulant set of the brightly lipsticked mouth.

"I'm the new constable," Chris said firmly. "Are you—" she paused and checked the name scribbled on her small notebook "—Mrs. Archibald Martinson?"

"Jennie Martinson, yeah. I never knew we had a woman for a policeman around here," Mrs. Martinson said suspiciously, staring up and down Chris's uniform pants and jacket. Jennie was wearing an A-line dress with huge poppies printed on it, and it billowed and flowed each time she moved.

"Don't seem right, somehow, a woman Mountie. You are a Mountie, ain't ya? What'd you say your name was again?"

"Constable Johnstone. The force has had female members for at least ten years, Mrs. Martinson."

Chris felt relieved to see that there wasn't any sign of a fight going on. In fact, there was no sign of anything going on, unless one counted the noise of the television, blaring a soap opera at them. Mrs. Martinson stood staring uncertainly for so long that Chris finally said briskly, "Now, what seems to be the problem?"

Quinn hadn't mentioned the purpose of her call exactly, and Chris now wished she'd taken more time to find out. The throng of children outside the gate was balanced by several more crowding around the large woman's legs inside the house.

"You better come in, I guess."

Chris followed her into a cluttered kitchen, and

took the chair indicated. She opened her notebook and waited patiently as the children were shooed away.

"It's the laundry again, see," Jennie finally said in hushed tones.

"The laundry?" Chris held her pencil poised above her pad, mystified.

"Yeah. My unmentionables, to be exact. I hang them out on the line, and when I go to take them back in, they're gone. It's happened three times already. Lost most of my underwear, past three weeks. And you know, in a town this small you can't just march out and buy new ones that easy," Jennie confided in an aggrieved tone. "The Mercantile don't always have my size, to say nothing of the expense. My man's getting right fed up, says he'll shoot the pervert what's doing it if he catches him, and then where'll we be? Besides, there's all these kids around, and some—" she hissed the words "—some sex nut like that loose in the town, who knows what might happen? I mean, what's Dawson coming to when a decent woman can't hang out her dainties without losing them? Decent men don't go round noticing underwear, you take my Archie now…"

Chris found herself listening to a discourse on what soon turned into thinly veiled complaints from Jennie about Archie's lack of interest in sexual matters. She was beginning to understand why Quinn had so generously let her have the call.

"Did you report this before?" she inquired when Jennie paused for a breath. Chris already knew full well what the answer would be.

Of course, Jennie nodded. "Sure, I reported it. Quinn came the other two times, said he'd keep an eye on the street. I told him exactly what went missing, too, he wrote it all down. D'you want a description? There were two pairs of panties, the elastic was going a bit in the yellow ones...."

For the next half hour, Chris recorded stolen pink, blue and white panties, reinforced bras and one lavender nightgown. She left after suggesting Jennie use the Laundromat instead of the clothesline for the next few weeks.

Chris confronted Quinn later that day. "About this stolen underwear file. Have you had other complaints about this sort of thing, or only this one?"

When he responded, the mischief was unmistakable in his eyes. "This is the first honest-to-God underwear deviate Dawson's had since I came here, and so far, Jennie Martinson's the only victim. Interesting case, huh?" he queried. "Delicate as well. Did she get into poor old Archie's problems with his libido? You're right, y'know, Chris. There's a hell of a lot of police work that really benefits from a woman's touch."

In the next few days, Quinn sent her out to follow up two reports of barking dogs, one of a lost child, found asleep under an upturned wheelbarrow, and a complaint from an old woman who insisted the devil was trying to rape her. All interesting, delicate matters that called for a woman's touch, Chris concluded in disgust.

Quinn, meanwhile, chose to look after two fist-fights, one all-out brawl, one report of arson at a deserted mine and a report of theft of equipment—all entailing some degree of excitement and even some traveling.

All the dull stuff.

Another week passed, and apart from the nuisance

calls Quinn allowed her to handle, Chris found herself still doing mostly typing and filing in an effort to keep busy.

One morning Maisie had gone on one of her frequent, vague "errands," Quinn was out on a call, and Chris was alone in the office when the door swung open to admit a tall, lithe young woman with an astonishing mass of copper-colored hair swirling around her angular face. She stormed up to the counter, angry color marking her pale skin like crimson flags. But Chris was quick to note that for all her flaming hair, the woman didn't have as many freckles as Chris herself did.

Sometimes it didn't seem there was any justice at all.

"Somebody's gone and trashed my car while I was working," the woman sputtered, banging a furious fist on the wooden counter. "I was parked at Diamond Tooth Gertie's, where I always park, and somebody rammed right into the front of it and didn't even stop. They smashed the radiator, and I need that car to get to work and home again, and Elmer at the garage says it's going to be at least a week until it's fixed up, he's got to order parts, you know Elmer, and what am I going to do for transportation in the meantime?" She paused and craned her neck, looking past Chris.

"Where's Quinn, anyway? I want to file a report and charge the guy who did it with hit and run and get him pitched in jail the minute Quinn catches him."

While the volatile woman caught her breath, Chris found the proper forms, and then went through the litany of introducing herself as Quinn's new constable. Some of the anger in the snapping green eyes faded to interest.

"You're the first female RCMP officer we've had up here. Do you find it any problem, being a woman lawman?"

Chris considered the question, and answered as truthfully as tact allowed.

"In larger centers women in law enforcement are commonplace by now, but it takes a while for people in these smaller towns to get used to me, I think. The whole tradition of the RCMP was pretty macho."

The redhead nodded. "Still is, especially up here. For instance, I wouldn't think Quinn would take too easily to having a woman as a partner," she commented astutely. "He doesn't exactly subscribe to *Ms.* magazine."

Chris couldn't help grinning wryly at that observation.

"My name's Liz Morrison, by the way." The buoyant woman reached a hand across the counter in a forthright manner for Chris to shake. "I have a homestead about ten miles out of town, up toward Forty Mile, which is why I'm so enraged about my car. I work at Gertie's as a dance hall girl during the summer, and I have to be able to drive back and forth at odd hours to feed my animals."

Chris was fascinated at meeting one of the glamorous women who worked at the popular gambling establishment. "I've walked into Diamond Tooth Gertie's once or twice, but I've never stayed for a show. Do you wear a costume and sing?"

Liz grimaced. "Net stockings, garters, satin petticoats, the whole regalia. As long as you've got legs your voice isn't much of an issue. Barbra Streisand doesn't have to worry about me, put it that way. Pays well, though; that's why I do it. I can make as much in a summer as I make all winter teaching school, and that place of mine eats money."

Chris was finding Liz more interesting with each fresh disclosure.

"You're also a teacher?"

"Yup, grades three and four at the elementary level. I clean up my act and wear my hair in a bun come September." She crossed her eyes comically and flashed a winsome grin. "The contrast adds color to my life, and helps pay the mortgage."

Chris glanced down at the long, slender hands on the counter. They were well shaped, but hard work had left rough skin and calluses, and the nails were cut short. There were no wedding rings.

Liz was more direct. "You married?" she inquired forthrightly, and when Chris shook her head, Liz said companionably, "Me either. I was, years ago, but he was killed in a plane crash."

"That's too bad," Chris said sympathetically, but Liz just shrugged.

"I was only twenty when it happened, and I'm thirty-four now, so it seems as if he was part of another life. It was a teenage marriage that was doomed to fall apart sooner or later. We had nothing much in common, now when I think about it."

Maisie came back just then, and greeted Liz like an old friend, as did Quinn when he arrived ten minutes later. It crossed Chris's mind when Liz greeted him with easy familiarity that perhaps there was something more than friendship between the pair. That caused a curious feeling in Chris's stomach, but

Quinn's actions a moment later ruled the possibility out. Obviously, he and Liz were just casual friends.

"Liz needs a ride home, Constable." He'd been careful to address her properly since that memorable Saturday in the cells, and usually there was remote coolness in his tone. Sometimes Chris had the crazy feeling she'd actually prefer the teasing warmth that used to accompany the maddening "Ms Constable." It had been a lot more fun in many ways.

"Why don't you take the cruiser and drive her?" he suggested magnanimously. "It's time you started getting acquainted with some of the back roads around here. Never know when there'll be a call out that way."

She felt like saying sarcastically, "Many barking dogs out toward Forty Mile, Corporal?" but restrained herself just in time. After all, the trip was a welcome break in routine for her, and she found the prospect of getting to know Liz better an exciting one. So far, she hadn't made any close friends, except, of course, for Maisie. And Maisie, much as Chris liked her, was more of a clucking mother figure than a soul mate.

Liz put all the voltage of her grin into action. "Thanks, Quinn. Hey, is it asking too much for Chris to wait an hour and a half while I do the chores, and then give me a ride back in? I have to be back at work by five, and I'll see about renting or loaning a car for tomorrow. But today, I'm up against it."

Quinn nodded. "Sure, there's no hurry. Take your time, girls."

They both glared at him but a queer sense of relief shot through Chris as she saw how unaffected he seemed to be by Liz's very potent female charm.

But then, why should she care what arrangements Quinn had for romance in Dawson?

They got in the cruiser, and Chris drove to the service station nearby. She filled it with gas, checked the oil, carefully washed off the dusty windshield and, motioning Liz out for a moment, she conscientiously vacuumed off the seats and the floor with the machine the garage provided.

When they backed smoothly out, and Chris drove carefully along the route out of town that Liz indicated, the redheaded woman remarked, "Wow, this poor old car must wonder what's happening, having you treat it so well. Quinn drives it as if half the demons in hell are chasing him."

It was unprofessional to talk about her corporal behind his back, so Chris didn't comment, although privately she heartily agreed. Quinn's driving set her teeth on edge, and she'd learned that he seldom filled the gas tank until it sat below empty. Instead, she inquired casually, "How long have you lived in Dawson, Liz?"

"I moved up here when Jake and I were married, lived here two years until he was killed, left long enough to get my teaching certificate and came back. So how long is that, twelve years in all? Where are you from, Chris?"

At Liz's direction, Chris was driving along a gravel road that wound along beside a rushing stream. She was enjoying the bright day and the novelty of talking with another young woman, and liking Liz more all the time.

"I grew up in the southern interior of B.C., near a little town called Summerland. Since I joined the Force, I've been posted to Namu, Burns Lake and

Terrace, and then I worked undercover for several years in various Canadian cities.''

"What were you doing undercover?"

The innocent query brought back images that had all but disappeared these past weeks. Chris grimaced. "For the last few months, I was pretending to be the lady friend of a small-time mobster."

"Did you have to go to bed with him?" the forthright Liz asked avidly, green eyes wide with curiosity.

Chris found she could laugh about the situation now, although a few months ago it hadn't been at all amusing. She shook her head vehemently and shuddered at the thought of bedding Louis Andollini.

"By the time he got that chummy, the case was nearly over, and I invented a social disease to put him off. But I had a few bad moments, all right. Luckily, I talk convincingly and move very fast."

Liz laughed. "Same ploy I use on two-hundred-pound prospectors at Gertie's who decide I'm the only one for them," she said easily. "Mind you, if only one of them was an intelligent, handsome, thoughtful, dashing prospector, I might not protest much at all, but I've practically given up hope of that ever happening. I've seen all those qualities in prospectors, but never all in the same guy."

"Would you like to marry again?" It was easy to talk with Liz, even about intimate subjects like this. She made it easy, with her air of warmth and easy friendliness.

Liz tipped her head to the side, considering.

"I've wondered about that a lot. I like living alone, but I miss sharing things with someone, things like long walks, crazy ideas, springtime, newborn lambs. Making love on Sunday mornings. And of course, there's all the not-so-hot things like mortgages, head colds and killing chickens. It'd be nice to find a partner for all those, but I'm pretty eccentric," she admitted matter-of-factly, "and that puts a lot of guys off. However, I'm also quite passionate, and that turns quite a few on, so who knows? Maybe I'll find Mr. Right after all, tucked away among the roulette tables. How about you, you want marriage and two point five children?"

Chris shook her head. "Not at the moment. Someday, for sure, but right now I like my job, I like being single, moving around, taking different assignments."

"How long have you been in Dawson?" Liz asked.

"Three weeks now." It seemed as if it had been a lot longer than that, somehow.

"And you've never been to Gertie's? My stars, woman, you're missing out on all the local color."

Chris thought of Jennie Martinson's underwear and wanted to argue, but she was tempted when Liz suggested, "Why not come down and have dinner with me on my break, and then catch the late show? I'll put my whole heart into my rendition of the cancan for you, I promise. I make up in enthusiasm whatever I lack in technique. Oh, turn off here, this is my place." She indicated a winding track off the gravel road, leading to a snug log A-frame house with several outbuildings nearby. A pen held a goat, and several chickens scratched inside a wire enclosure.

Chris drew up in the yard, and followed Liz into the deliciously cool interior of the house.

"Sit down, be comfortable, and I'll make some tea." Liz gestured at a chintz-covered sofa and several inviting easy chairs covered in dramatic primary colors that corresponded to the various flowers of the sofa pattern. The main floor consisted of one large open area, including the kitchen with its wood cook-stove. The area shared a brick chimney with a conical fireplace that stood in the living-room area. Books spilled out of brick-and-board bookshelves and lay stacked carelessly on tables and chairs, and plants flourished everywhere. A round staircase led up to a loft and Chris stared around enviously, comparing the setting here with her ghastly green room at the police office.

"What a wonderful house. I've lived in barracks so long I'd give anything to have a house of my own, but that's one drawback of the RCMP. You move a lot, so houses aren't practical."

Liz was setting a kettle to boil on a small gas stove.

"I built this with my own two hands and a touch of help from several burly college students, and it's taken me five years to get the money to get it this far, so it's pretty special to me. But there's still a lot of things to finish. And of course, I haven't got electricity out here, so it's still rather primitive by most standards. I hope to be able to get the power hooked up before another winter comes, though."

Chris could only imagine what it would be like to live here in the darkness of the long arctic winter, with only lanterns for light and wood stoves for heating. Liz had to have an amazing pioneer spirit to attempt—and succeed—at this sort of life-style.

They chatted over tea, and Chris went along when her new friend fed and watered her chickens, the goat and also several sheep.

"Milk, cheese, eggs and wool," Liz said succinctly, indicating the menagerie. "They supply a lot of my basic needs, plus a petting zoo when I want to bring my class out here to see a real farm in action.''

By the time Chris dropped Liz off back in town at Diamond Tooth Gertie's, the two equally independent women had decided they liked each other immensely.

''See you Friday night about eight, don't forget now.'' Liz closed the door of the car and disappeared with a cheerful wave through the back door of Gertie's, and Chris drove thoughtfully back to the office.

She'd made a friend, and it felt wonderful.

Quinn steadily refused all her offers to do her share of night patrol, so Chris was free Friday. Deciding what to wear to a gambling dance hall was a problem, and she spent a fair amount of time after her shower inspecting the rather meager civvy wardrobe her trunk had provided. She'd sent off to her sister Ariel most of the flashy outfits she'd acquired for undercover work. The slinky dresses were a lot better suited to Ariel's flamboyant personality than to her own, Chris had reasoned, and she'd guessed that the nightlife of Vancouver might provide a lot more opportunities for wearing such outfits than Dawson ever would. The times she'd peered in the door of Diamond Tooth Gertie's, jeans had seemed to be the order of the day, but tonight there was dancing, Liz had said. And, with the constant sunshine, it was decidedly hot. So what to wear?

Chris finally settled on a halter-neck tank top in a deep shade of pink that bared her arms and shoulders and skimmed across her collarbone, and a circle skirt whose white background sported abstract patterns of the same pink, as well as bright purple and red and green. She added flat pink strappy sandals to deliciously cool bare legs, and hooked a pair of dangling white shell earrings into her pierced ears.

Her chocolate-brown hair was hopelessly curly, which was the reason she wore it cropped so short. She finger-combed it now, fluffing the curls up, and then put on a little blue eyeliner and a good dose of pink lipstick.

She crossed her eyes at the invisible, harping critic who always stood just behind her left shoulder at times like this, urging her into nervous sessions with colored pencils and dots of hopeful cover for her freckles. *Dummy up,* she warned the critic now. *What you see is what you get.*

She was walking out the door, swinging her purse, when Quinn pulled into the driveway, spraying gravel in his usual fashion. He got out slowly, unable to take his eyes off his constable.

"Evening, Corporal Quinn," she said softly, giving him a half smile and hurrying off down the path. Why did she always feel that prickly sense of excitement around him, anyway? She held her shoulders high, knowing his eyes were on her, and warmth crept over her, warmth that had little to do with the sunshine.

"Evening, uh, Constable," he responded automatically, a moment too late, forgetting to shut the car door as he watched the folds of her silky skirt swish around her enticing bottom, noting how her long, bare legs tapered down to narrow ankles.

She hadn't had a bra on under that pink thing on top, either.

Quinn put both fists on the roof of the cruiser and laid his head on his arms in utter frustration. He could pretend to ignore most of her, most of the time, given proper warning, but he hadn't seen her in a skirt before tonight and naturally it had caught him off guard. He hadn't been prepared, for pete's sake, just driving innocently back here to have a quick sandwich on a Friday night.

A man couldn't relax in his own quarters with her around. It was subtle torture the force was inflicting on him.

There'd been the morning he'd come downstairs and glanced out the kitchen window to find his constable pegging out wisps of lacy pastel froth next to his own work shirts on the clothesline. How the hell could any red-blooded male not imagine right away what those miniscule panties and ridiculous scraps of bras must look like on the person hanging them out? There were even two of those one-piece rigs Gladys had had to show him how to undo once.

Teddies, Gladys had called them that night, and killed herself laughing because he couldn't figure out how or where the contrary thing unfastened....

His constable had one of those teddies the color of strawberry jam and another like strong coffee with milk in it, made of slippery stuff that his rough hands would catch on for sure....

And now there was always that hint of her light, sweet perfume hanging around the place, and the yellow tablecloth on the table in the kitchen, and plants springing up in windows. And she whistled sometimes when she was preoccupied, not even knowing she was doing it, pursing her mouth provocatively, and of course he thought about kissing it when she did that, what red-blooded man wouldn't?

He was only human, how could he not imagine her lying asleep in the bedroom right underneath his own, on these hot, bright nights when even a sheet was too much covering? He'd lost a lot of sleep since she'd arrived, and he knew without even going over there that Gladys, skilled though she was at her job, wasn't going to help him sleep any better as long as this constable was around.

A new thought struck him and he got back into the cruiser, forgetting all about his sandwich.

Where the hell was she going all dressed up like that, anyway? He had a right to know where she was, after all. He might run into a situation where he needed her before the night was over. Or—and this seemed far more likely when he thought about it— she might run into a situation where she needed him before the night was over.

WALKING INTO GERTIE'S alone was an experience for Chris, because it seemed that every single male in the room—and there was definitely a majority of males— turned and had a good long look at her before they went back to whatever they'd been doing.

She was used to being stared at when she was in uniform, but out of it, at times like this, her self-confidence slipped a bit.

She'd entered the small foyer, walked past the ticket booths that sold chips for gambling and hesitated at the doorway of the main room. Gertie's was large, with a bar, a small dance floor and a stage with red velvet curtains, but most of the space was taken up by poker tables to her right, roulette wheels on her left and blackjack tables down the middle of the long room.

The only legal gambling establishment in Canada was doing a roaring business tonight.

"Hey, Chris, over here," Liz called, and with a

feeling of relief, Chris located her friend, who was sitting at a table on the far side of the room.

Liz was wearing her costume, and Chris stared openly. The period-style dance hall dress she wore was a dazzling shade of sapphire-green satin, nearly the color of her eyes, with a low-cut corset-style bodice laced down the front to a narrow waistline and a full ruffled skirt that spilled out around the chair she was sitting on. The mane of copper hair was caught up in a high chignon secured at the crown with an ornamental comb, and curls escaped over ears and forehead. Makeup softened Liz's strong, attractive features into dramatic beauty.

"You're a knockout," Chris complimented feelingly, and Liz actually blushed with pleasure, although she replied deprecatingly, "It's a mirage. You know the saying, 'A little bit of powder and a little bit of paint, can make any lady look like what she ain't.'"

Chris laughed, and began to relax as Liz ordered her a drink and they decided what to have from the menu. As they ate, Liz gave her an affectionate but irreverent rundown on most of the people in the room.

"They call that sweet ole guy over there Windy Ike. If he ever gets started talking there's no stopping him, but his stories are wonderful if you've got time to listen. The lady dealing at the blackjack table is Susie. She owns a pile of real estate around here, and rumor has it she packs a Derringer in her garter, but I've never seen her pull it. The waitress, Martie, she was a stockbroker in New York. Came up here for a holiday and never went back. Happens to lots of people, there's something about the Yukon that gets in your blood. And oh yeah, the dark-haired rather soulful hunk heading this way is the actor the town hires each summer to portray Robert Service.''

"I've seen him doing his shows outside of Service's cabin. He's really very impressive,'' Chris murmured as a tall and extraordinarily handsome man, perhaps twenty-eight or thirty, strolled over and stopped beside the table, giving both women a charming smile and a deep, courtly bow. He, too, wore clothing reminiscent of the past century, a close-fitting dark suit and a pristine white shirt with a high, tight collar and a string tie. His fine dark hair fell over his forehead in almost studied disarray, and he actually looked like the pictures Chris had seen of the famous northern poet, although he lacked the fragility of the real Service.

"Christine Johnstone, may I present Dawson's own poet laureate, Robert Service? Also known as John Jason Prentiss, and familiarly known as Jack.''

"Delighted to meet you.'' His voice was deep and very pleasing. His eyes were blue, and they sparkled wickedly as he snagged a chair from a nearby table and straddled it. "You a visitor to Dawson, Christine?''

"Call me Chris,'' she corrected. "And no, I'm not a tourist. I'm living here in Dawson.''

Jack's eyebrows lifted questioningly. "How come we've never met? I thought I knew all the beautiful women in town. Liz is holding out on me, keeping such a charming friend a secret.''

"Besides playing Robert Service for the summer season, Jack's ambition is to be cast as Cyrano,'' Liz commented dryly, but the suave actor waved a negligent hand at her, his attention still on Chris.

"Haven't got the nose for it,'' he said. "Are you

working in Dawson, Chris? Because if you're looking for a job, there's a space open here at Gertie's in the chorus line, isn't there, Liz? Didn't Diana leave when she got married? You'd be a smashing chorus girl, Chris.''

"There sure is, and she would, but I don't think the people Chris works for want her moonlighting as a hoofer. She's Dawson's new RCMP constable,'' Liz announced with proprietary pride. ''Damn,'' she added resignedly. ''Gertie's waving at me, I've got to go. We're on in a few minutes. Order another drink, Chris, I already told Martie it's on me. See ya later.'' She was off in a rustling flurry of emerald satin.

Jack was staring at Chris with unabashed curiosity.

"You're actually in the RCMP? Whatever made you decide to go into police work?'' he queried, sounding amazed.

"And you're actually an actor? Whatever made you decide to be an actor?'' Chris responded with a grin, imitating his tone exactly. Jack looked nonplussed for only an instant, and then he tossed his head back and laughed heartily.

"Touché. One's no more amazing than the other, is it? Okay, I'll go first. I'm thirty-four, divorced for three years, and I'm not really an actor at all. I teach English literature at Simon Fraser University in Vancouver, and I've always admired Service's work and wanted to visit the North. Taking this job for the summer was simply an effort to break a dull mold I'd fallen into.''

"I've seen you from a distance, doing your shows over at Robert Service's cabin,'' Chris confessed. ''You're extremely good,'' she complimented sincerely.

Jack was openly pleased by her praise. "That's music to my ears. I'm afraid I didn't notice you. There's usually quite a crowd and I have to keep my mind on what I'm doing. Come closer next time and I'll quote a selection just for you. I do two readings a day, at ten and again at one in the afternoon. But I try to stay in character and in costume most of the time. There's always some sweet old lady who gets it in her befuddled brain that I am actually the great bard himself. I love it, the whole charisma of the thing."

He gazed fondly around for a moment, and then shook his head wonderingly. "I'm having more fun than I thought possible. Dawson's an incredible place." His eyes returned admiringly to Chris. "After all, where else can you find police constables who make you want to be taken into custody?" He gave her a mock leer, and twirled invisible mustaches, and Chris laughed.

For all his nonsense, she liked him. She'd learned that there was a certain percentage of men who harbored a deep resentment of women in what they considered male roles, such as policing, and always, they were men who were insecure to begin with.

Jack didn't seem like that. There was no sly undertone to his good-natured flirting. If she were to hazard a guess, she'd say he was a man who truly liked women, and who liked being around them.

And what about Quinn, her traitorous thoughts prodded. What category was he in? Were his chauvinistic attitudes actually resentment, or did he, too, like women?

Pay attention, Chris, she admonished herself. Are you going to let your boss ruin your first big evening out, when he's not even around? How did thoughts of Quinn manage to keep popping into her brain anyway? And why did his presence make her every nerve come alive, while this pleasant man beside her simply made her feel comfortable?

The honky-tonk pianist played a lively rhythm, and Liz and three other dancers did a fast, high-stepping version of the cancan, swinging their skirts high to reveal provocative black net stockings and flowered garters on long, curvaceous legs. The audience was loudly appreciative, clapping and whistling and cat-calling as the girls finished three numbers in a row and then disappeared behind the stage curtains.

The music changed to a slow romantic ballad, and one of the troupe sang a torch song in a low, throaty voice. Several couples headed for the small dance floor. Jack got to his feet and made his courtly little bow.

"Dance, Chris?"

"I'd love to." She did love to dance, and lately there'd been few enough occasions for it. Jack's style was excellent, light and smooth and certain without being ostentatious. Chris found herself having a wonderful time as one waltz followed another, and they'd danced through three sets when at last the pianist took a break.

Chris thought she caught a glimpse of Quinn walking swiftly toward the exit just as she sat down. He probably checked the premises several times over the course of a Friday or Saturday night. She wondered bitterly if he would ever trust her enough to let her do town duty and check on places like Gertie's. Probably not, she decided. Barking dogs and missing underwear were liable to be her assignments for her entire posting in Dawson. It was a depressing notion, and once again she did her best to thrust Quinn out of her mind. He had a disquieting habit of popping into her head uninvited.

Jack ordered drinks and Chris had beer mixed with ginger ale. Liz, who was on her break, introduced Chris to the other dancers and patrons. Soon a group of male admirers was milling around the women's table, vying for the honor of buying drinks and being introduced to Chris, who seemed to be the only stranger in the crowd.

"Hey, it's Ms Constable," a male voice greeted her. "Hi again, Ms Constable."

Chris turned to find Jim Murphy, the taxidriver she'd met at Nancy's Café, standing in the throng, and she sighed in resignation.

There it was again, Quinn's moniker, Ms Constable.

There didn't seem much chance of avoiding the label the insufferable man had landed on her. Several people overheard Jim, and within five minutes, he'd used the title so often twenty more people had latched on to it.

"Dance, Ms Constable?" Jack purred with a teasing gleam in his eyes.

Chris opened her mouth to object, and closed it again. It was no use. She might as well get used to being Ms Constable for her entire stay in Dawson.

"Thanks, Mr. Service," she murmured, and this time she didn't see Quinn at all when he entered the room. She had her eyes closed, swaying happily in Jack's arms to the music.

Quinn saw her. She was the only person he really did see, floating in Jack Prentiss's embrace like some exotic flower in her pink and white outfit.

Quinn knew Prentiss, he'd even had a few beers with him one night. Jack was an intelligent, good-looking, personable bachelor, and there wasn't a single reason for Quinn to develop such a sudden dislike for the man.

Dislike wasn't quite what Quinn was feeling anyhow. Watching Chris smile up into Jack's face, seeing his arm firmly around her waist, Quinn wanted nothing more than a chance to put his fist squarely in the other man's mouth.

He was jealous, and he didn't want to be.

He stalked out of Gertie's before he made a total ass of himself, but when the brawl broke out in one of the other bars later that night, Quinn waded into the writhing mass of bodies and fists with eager vehemence.

He picked up a fist in the eye and another in the ribs before he had the place quiet again, but in his mind the well-placed punches he managed to land were all intended for Jack Prentiss, and the massive prospector who'd instigated the whole thing thought twice about objecting when Quinn hauled him off to jail for the night.

Chris was home by one-thirty. Jack and Jim Murphy had both gallantly walked her the short distance to the detachment, and the sun was just sinking below the horizon when she left them at the door of the police office. They'd laughed about one thing or another all the way from Gertie's.

Feeling wonderful, she strolled down the hall to her quarters, whistling one of the dance tunes under her breath. Loud snores and the smell of secondhand whiskey were coming from the cell block, but the rest of the building was quiet, and Chris detoured into the kitchen for a glass of milk.

Quinn sat slouched at the kitchen table, one eye badly discolored and all but swollen shut.

"Heavens, Quinn, what happened? Just look at your eye."

Chris hurried over beside him. He had a nasty cut on his chin, and he swiped at it now and then with a grimy, blood-spattered cloth that must originally have been a handkerchief.

"Free-for-all down at Billy Boy's Tavern," he said tersely.

Chris hurried over to the fridge and extracted a bag of frozen peas from the freezer compartment. She took two clean tea towels out of a drawer and soaked one with cold water, wrapped the other around the peas and came over close to Quinn. She put the towel-wrapped bag gently on his eye and tenderly blotted at his chin with the wet cloth, her full bottom lip caught between her teeth in tender sympathy.

Her full, braless breasts were right under his nose, and he could smell her—light traces of perfume, a whiff of cigarette smoke clinging to her from Gertie's, mixed with the natural heady scent of warm fragrant woman. His body's reaction was instantaneous, and if she glanced down at him...

He brushed her hands away roughly, letting the peas fall strategically into his lap.

"I don't need a first-aid man around here, thanks anyway," he snarled, and the gut-wrenching jealousy she'd inspired in him made him cantankerous. "I need a six-foot brawny young male who'd be right there with me when things like this happen, backing me up instead of making a spectacle of themselves in the local watering hole,'' he complained grumpily.

''Making a spectacle—I don't believe you said that.'' The bubbly high spirits of Chris's evening were gone like smoke. She had an almost uncontrollable urge to land him a good one in the other eye, but instead she whirled around with a choked, angry exclamation on her lips and marched to the door leading to her quarters. She turned and glared before going through.

''As for backup, well tough on you, Corporal. You've got me, like it or not, and until you start treating me like a partner, you can just get your whole face rearranged for all I care. You richly deserve it, you miserable, old…grump.''

The window above the table vibrated with the slam she gave the door. Quinn winced and mouthed several uninhibited responses as her footsteps pounded down the hall, and then he snatched up the icy peas and put them back on his eye for a while. They were certainly cold. His head was throbbing now, but at least the peas had done the trick on other parts of his anatomy.

An unwilled grin spread slowly across his features. She had one hell of a temper. She looked flushed and beautiful and just the slightest bit cross-eyed when she lost it like that. And her freckles turned darker.

Another thought struck him, and the grin widened. From the looks of her when she first came in, it didn't seem to him as if Jackie boy had even kissed her good-night. If he had, it was one hell of a chaste kiss. She'd look a lot more hot and bothered and rumpled if he, Quinn, had kissed her, for instance.

That realization made him feel a whole lot better,

and he popped the top on a beer and drank it down before he remembered he was still on patrol for what remained of Dawson's Friday night.

CHAPTER FIVE

CHRIS WAS SITTING eating cold cereal at the table the next morning when Quinn entered the kitchen for breakfast. He sneaked a glance at her, and figured, correctly, that she was still raging mad at him. She glared at him with ice in her eyes and then tilted her chin aggressively without saying a word.

Hastily, he decided retreat was the best strategy, considering the way he felt this morning. His eye was good and sore, to say nothing of his ribs.

"Have to see a guy," he muttered vaguely and headed right on through the room. "I'm leaving the patrol car here. I'll have my portable radio with me. You can handle whatever comes in." *She wants to play cop, so let her go ahead,* he thought mutinously. He'd had his fill last night. Damn town had gone berserk there for a few hours.

Besides, there wouldn't be any calls to speak of anyhow until after noon on Saturday, when Dawson got over Friday night and geared itself up again for more of the same.

"I'll be back in a couple of hours. And oh yeah, release the prisoner in the cells, no charges, he's just in to sober up."

He'd head over to Nancy's and have breakfast; the walk would do him good. He'd see if maybe Parker was still there, lingering over coffee. It would be a relief to talk to somebody rational for a change.

Chris sent a smoldering glare his way, but Quinn was already gone.

She released the cell's visitor, who informed her chattily that his name was Clarence Goodhalk and that the big sucker who ran this place sure packed a mean right hook.

Afterward, she washed the patrol car and vacuumed it out, leaving the door open so she could hear the calls from the radio. There weren't any for the first hour. Then a call came from a man who lived in a trailer over by the river. Someone had gone into his deep freeze the night before and stolen half a freezerful of meat, right off his porch, and what was the RCMP going to do about it?

"I'll be over to take a look," Chris responded. It was just the sort of call Quinn would approve of her taking, she thought resignedly.

Half an hour later, she'd finished writing up a detailed report of the theft of moose meat and she was driving slowly back to the office, reveling in the fresh breeze blowing off the river and the almost cloudless sky overhead.

A car suddenly rounded the corner of the highway leading into town and came toward her—an older model, green Ford station wagon.

Chris sat up straighter in the seat and reached to turn her siren on. The damn fool was going so fast, he was almost out of control, yawing madly from side to side on the highway. She could see the shadowy form of the driver, but it was impossible to tell if there were others in the car.

Before she could put on the revolving red light on

the roof of her car or hit the siren switch, the station wagon went careering across the road, down the embankment, and without slowing at all plunged straight into the murky depths of the Yukon River. The nose of the car disappeared, and only a small sliver of the trunk was left visible.

Heart hammering and breath coming fast, Chris screeched to a stop on the embankment. For what seemed an interminable time she watched for someone to pop to the surface of the fast-moving river as she radioed Quinn.

"Bravo One, Alpha One." She made a determined effort to control the urgency in her voice.

Quinn was finishing his fourth cup of coffee and half listening to Parker go on about the tourists when the portable he'd casually placed on the table crackled to life.

The second appeal Chris made brought Quinn's deep voice over the radio.

"Alpha One. What's up?"

"Car with occupant is over the bank and in the river on second curve south of town on highway." Chris's eyes were glued to the river, but there were only widening ripples where the car had disappeared.

"Driver hasn't surfaced." He would drown unless he got out soon.

Quinn swore and she made up her mind as to what she would do.

"I'm going down after him."

Chris leaped from the cruiser and, standing by the open door she swiftly removed her Sam Browne, tossing it on the seat. With the small knife on her key ring she cut the laces of her ankle boots, then kicked them off and doffed her slacks and hat.

With only her regulation navy socks to protect her feet, she scrambled down the rocky embankment until she reached the water's edge.

There she forced herself to slow down, to inhale and exhale deep yoga-style breaths until she felt in control before she jumped into the bone-chilling icy coldness of the river.

"...going down after him...."

Quinn exploded into action. In seconds, he'd commandeered Jim's taxicab and its driver, and within ten minutes they had screeched to a halt on the highway directly behind the cruiser. Its whooper was on, the fireball on the roof revolving a red warning. The door was wide open, and on the seat and floor he could see Chris's clothes and shoes.

A shudder of dread went through him, and he turned to stare at the rapidly flowing river and the smidgen of trunk showing above the water. There was no sign of his constable. Quinn had no way of knowing how long she'd been down.

"Jim, there's a piece of towline in the trunk of the cruiser. Attach a rope to the bumper bracket and throw the end down the bank. Use the radio to call for the ambulance."

He tossed his hat and his own Sam Browne beside Chris's, and without a second's hesitation, he was down the steep bank.

At the bottom, he used the same key technique she had used on the laces of his boots, and he was about to step out of his pants when two heads bobbed to the surface near the submerged car.

"Thank God," he muttered feelingly.

Quinn had a healthy respect for many things. Not fear, just a wise caution. There was only one situation he feared with a deep and reasonless horror, one circumstance that brought him out of nightmares sweating and crying out with terror.

Quinn was a poor swimmer at best. He was afraid of diving into water, particularly water that was fast-flowing and deep. Like this. He was fully prepared to do it, but the experience had the feeling for him of one of his worst nightmares about to come true.

WHEN CHRIS DIVED, the shock of the icy water had all but paralyzed her. It was murky gray, and the current tore at her arms and legs, dragging her downstream. She fought her way to the car, and if she'd been even a few more feet away, she might have missed it altogether.

Dimly, she could make out the driver's unconscious form, see his long dark hair fallen forward over his face, his body slumped across the steering wheel. There was no water inside the car, which meant the pressure holding the doors shut would be formidable.

Chris braced her feet against the car's side, took hold of the door nearest the surface and heaved. It resisted, and desperation gave her superhuman strength for an instant...until it gave.

The river gushed inside the car and huge bubbles of air escaped, the force nearly tearing Chris's grasp from the doorframe. It took all her fortitude to allow the milliseconds to pass that would allow the car's interior to fill with water so she could grab for the floating figure inside and try to wrench him up and out, using the water's buoyancy to help her.

He was slender but tall, ungainly and immovable.

She was short of air.

An involuntary clenching of her chest, like a hic-cup, signaled oxygen starvation.

She grabbed his shirt and his long hair, tore at him with the last of her strength, and his body floated upward and out the door, in what seemed like slow motion to her.

The hiccuping in her chest was almost unbearable.

Kicking and struggling with the inert body she held, Chris shot to the surface.

Light. Air.

Black spots danced in her eyes.

Blow out, draw in. The pain in her chest became agony before it eased.

Ecstasy.

There was still eighteen feet between her and the riverbank.

With leaden arms, Chris elevated the helpless body she held, arms around his neck, resting his back on the length of her front. She cupped his chin in her palm, keeping his head on her upper chest and swimming on her back, using the last remnants of her strength, as she frog-kicked for the bank.

Rocks scraped her shoulders, but she struggled, ut-tering great gasping sobs of exertion, in an effort to pull him out of the water. But he was too heavy— she was going to lose him to the current.

All this, for nothing.

Suddenly, strong arms reached around her and heaved them both up and onto the rocky shore.

"Easy, Constable, got ya both, easy now…"

Chris collapsed on the rocky ground, gasping and shuddering.

Quinn, handling the unconscious man as if he weighed no more than a child, flipped him over on his side, placed a knee in his diaphragm and gave him a smart rap between the shoulder blades. Water and bile poured out the slack mouth, and Quinn gave a grunt of satisfaction. He flipped the man on his back, stuck a thumb in his mouth and pulled the jaw down. Pinching the nose shut, he blew into the open mouth.

Chris watched, hardly breathing herself.

Nothing.

But with the next attempt, the body convulsed, and again Quinn breathed strongly into the man's lungs. There was another convulsion, and the man drew a shallow gasping breath on his own, missed one, then drew another.

"Toss down blankets and that rope," Quinn bellowed, and Jim plus the crowd that had gathered up on the highway hurried to oblige.

Chris was shaking uncontrollably, but she managed to clumsily assist as Quinn rolled a blanket roughly around the unconscious figure. Above, half a dozen cars had stopped and men slid down the bank, anxious to help. They lifted the limp body up to the highway and into the ambulance. One of the observers was from the local paper. He had a camera, and he was rapidly taking shots of everything that happened.

Quinn swiftly turned his attention to Chris.

"Let's get you wrapped up in this blanket, Constable."

Water dripped from her matted hair down her face and off the tip of her nose. Her long eyelashes were clumped together, her lips were blue-rimmed and her teeth chattered.

"I c-couldn't get the d-door o-open on the car...."

"Never mind that now, you got him out. I don't know how the hell you managed, but you did."

The sopping-wet, long-tailed police shirt clung to her every curve, and frivolous blue lace panties showed below its hem. One of her long brown legs had an incongruous wet black sock hanging from its foot, and the other was bare. He saw her rose-painted toenails, and a tender knife of agony twisted inside him.

She was fragile, and female, and unutterably lovely.

She might easily have died down there.

"Throw that rope back down here and make it snappy," he shouted angrily, bundling her up efficiently in a cocoon of scratchy gray blanket, tugging off her single sock and tossing it carelessly away. He scooped her up and over one shoulder with one graceful motion into the traditional fireman's carry.

"Don't...I...c-c-can..." She struggled to protest feebly, but there was no contest.

"Shut up, Chris." He grasped the rope and easily scrambled them both up the bank, unceremoniously stuffing her into the front passenger seat of the cruiser. The ambulance had already left, but a large crowd of onlookers gaped curiously at them, and a flashbulb went off twice before Quinn got her inside far enough to slam the door.

The motor roared to life, and with an agonizing squeal from the tires, Quinn had the car turned and then they were speeding into Dawson.

"You're going to the medical clinic; we'll get Doc Chambers to check you out," he advised, hunching forward over the steering wheel and taking corners like a race track driver.

"Don't, please, Quinn. I hate doctors poking at me," she begged, turning to him in alarm and doing her best to control the shaking that seemed to have taken possession of her body. "I'm fine, honest. All I need is a cup of coffee or something and a hot shower. D'you think that guy'll live?"

"Of course he'll live, the goddamned fool. He had enough alcohol in him for insulation. It's you I'm concerned about—you're shivering like a soaked puppy."

He turned and scrutinized her carefully. Chris glanced at the road rushing past the window and clutched the edges of the seat. He hadn't slowed down one bit while his attention was on her, and she thought wildly that if she didn't die of pneumonia, she was probably going to end her life in a car crash any moment.

"Please, Quinn, slow down and just take me home. I'm warmer already. I'm not shivering, see?" she pleaded, holding out an arm and then retracting it abruptly when the blanket fell open to reveal her naked legs.

The disclosure didn't go unnoticed. Even with one eye half swollen shut, he'd taken it all in before his head turned stiffly forward. The intensity of that quick glance made Chris feel warmer, despite her blue lips.

"I'm not going to any medical clinic to see any strange doctor dressed this way either, so you might as well take me home," she declared rebelliously. "I won't go. I have hardly any clothes on!"

He rolled his eyes and shook his head. He didn't need reminding of her state of undress.

"Women," he growled, as he made another hair-raising U-turn and drove for the police office, screeching to a halt in the driveway and ordering sternly, "Don't you move, I'm coming around for you."

This time, at least, he gathered her into his arms instead of throwing her over his shoulder like a sack of potatoes, and she didn't object at all. Quinn's arms were reassuringly strong, and the peculiar feeling of warmth he always stirred in her spread through her entire body, banishing more of the river's chill.

"Why are you shuffling like that? I can walk now if I'm too heavy," Chris said as he fumbled the door open and made his way down the hallway, still stubbornly carrying her.

"I'm shuffling because I cut my damned shoelaces back there, and you're not too heavy at all, so shut up and stop wriggling. I thought I was going to have to dive into that river after you," he said, and she felt the involuntary shudder that traveled through his huge frame.

Quinn wrestled with the door to her room, cursed and finally managed to open it, before striding in and dumping her rather abruptly on her bed. He was doing his polite best to keep his eyes averted.

Parts of her kept poking out of the blamed blanket and seriously affecting parts of him, and it was an effort to keep this whole thing businesslike. It was difficult, looking at those wispy blue panties and those long incredibly slender legs.

He went into her bathroom and turned the shower on, adjusting the water as hot as he dared.

"Can you make it in there on your own?" he demanded when he turned back into the bedroom.

Half of him prayed she'd say no.

"Of course I can," Chris insisted, with a slight catch in her voice. She was wickedly tempted to say no and see what happened.

"Then I'll go in the kitchen and make you hot rum.

If you get...weak...or anything, holler," he instructed, and then he beat a hasty, shoe-slopping retreat down the hall, realizing for the first time that maybe he should head for the showers himself.

There was the accident victim's vomit sprayed all over his pants, and he was wet up to the thighs from hauling her out of the river. Muddy as well. And these shoes... He listened for a moment. She was still in the shower and everything seemed fine.

With a sigh of regret, he headed upstairs.

Fifteen minutes later, she came into the kitchen, moving a trifle shakily, wrapped in a blue terry robe zipped safely to the neck. Quinn was in clean uniform pants, obviously fresh from the shower. He was also wearing a white T-shirt, and his bare feet were showing under his pant cuffs. He was pouring boiling water into two glasses already more than half full of amber liquid, and he gave her a frown as she lurched a little on her way to the table.

"Warmer now?" he inquired, spooning great gobs of honey into the glasses and giving them a small squeeze from a plastic lemon.

She nodded, and he followed her over to the table with the glasses balanced carefully in his huge hands.

Chris curled onto the chair with her feet under her, and he took the other chair, holding his glass up solemnly in a tribute.

"You did one hell of a good job at that river today, Constable Johnstone," he complimented her solemnly.

She felt as if a balloon was inflating in her chest, about to explode. It was the first compliment he'd ever given her about her work, and she was bursting with pride and happiness.

"You'd have done exactly the same, Quinn," she said modestly. "Things like that are all supposed to be part of the job, aren't they?"

To her surprise, he shook his head.

"I can take on ten drunken men or walk fifty miles in a blizzard, but I'm a dud at swimming. In fact, I hate the water, always have," he confessed. "I hyperventilate or something, the swimming instructor at Depot used to say. How did you manage to stay under as long as you did today?"

She sipped at her strong rum, grateful for the warmth as it spiraled down into her stomach. That water had been liquid ice, and she never wanted to feel that cold again.

"I grew up beside a lake. My sister and brother and I learned to swim before we could walk. My mother had all these theories about babies being natural swimmers." Chris hesitated, wondering how much she could tell him without fear of ridicule. Her parents' Eastern philosophies often brought reactions of disbelief from the uninitiated. Quinn was looking at her with an expression of intense interest, however, so she went on, "Then Mom and Dad taught us yoga breathing and breath control when we were young, the ability to go into semitrance where your body uses very little oxygen. Shane and Ariel—" At his questioning look, she added, "My brother and sister. We used to have contests in the lake, pretending we were Houdini and seeing who could stay down the longest."

They'd also frightened summer visitors half out of their wits by faking drowning when things got dull. Ariel especially had perfected a wonderful dead act, rolling her eyes until only the whites showed, breathing so lightly it was impossible to detect…but Chris didn't know if Quinn was quite ready for that bit of memorabilia just now.

"That's what I used today, yoga breathing, but I've never been in water quite that cold before, and it didn't work as well as usual."

"It worked just fine," Quinn said with feeling. "The stupid young fool would have died for sure if I'd gone down. He can be damn thankful you were there instead of me."

She raised her glass and drank, but the glow spreading through her middle was due less to the rum then to pleasure at his generous compliment.

"Thank you, Quinn," she said softly. He met her eyes for long moments, and a current of hot, bright awareness passed from one to the other, surprising and alarming them both with its intensity.

Chris drained her glass, and Quinn drained his.

"I should…"

"It's time to…"

They both paused, disconcerted, and he got hastily to his feet.

"I have to get back in uniform and out on the road. We'll have to do an M.V. accident file on this business, but leave that for now and take it easy for the afternoon, Constable. That's an order."

"Yes, sir," she said meekly, and he gave her a suspicious look.

"I'd tell a male constable the same damn thing after a session like that."

Chris grinned.

"You're getting far too sensitive about this whole gender thing, Corporal," she said sweetly. "You'll never catch me arguing myself into doing reports when my boss says I don't have to." She yawned suddenly. "In fact, I think I'll take a nap. How much rum did you put in that glass, anyhow, Quinn?" she asked suspiciously when she got unsteadily to her feet.

He didn't answer, but he came over and gripped her arms from behind firmly, intending only to march her to her room before she fell over.

Instead, she turned sinuously in his embrace. Her face was suddenly upturned below his own, as she looked at him with a slight frown knotting the pale skin between her winged eyebrows.

"Why did..." she started to say, but the air raced from her lungs and she forgot the rest when his head dipped and his lips met hers.

She could feel the heat of Quinn's body against her, the insistent swelling that telegraphed his need through her terry robe. He smelled of the green soap he used, and his heart was hammering alarmingly against her breasts.

Chris tasted his surprisingly gentle lips and his seeking tongue, drank in the growing tempestuous passion of his kiss, overwhelmed by the maleness and strength of him. A tickling warmth gushed through her abdomen, making her knees weak.

Chris tried never to lie to herself, and she didn't now.

She wanted him, all of him. Now.

She hungered to feel Quinn touching her, loving her with the same searing passion his kiss held.

She flowed into him, signaling with every movement of her lips and tongue, every sinuous movement of the naked body beneath her robe, that she wanted him.

And he suddenly tore away from her, his rasping breathing loud in the quiet room. He cursed viciously under his breath, and marched her to her room, following close behind her. Chris's heart hammered, wondering if he'd follow her to the bed...but without another word, he stopped abruptly at her door, watched until she half collapsed on the bed's edge, then stepped outside and closed the door firmly.

She could hear his hasty footsteps going back down the hall.

So that was that. Feeling icy cold again, and abandoned, she drew in a shaky breath and pressed her fingers to her lips. The kiss was everything her imagination had conceived.

More. Quinn was the dark stranger in her dreams, the fantasy lover she longed for and never quite managed to capture.

Her face crumpled, and she wanted to cry like a child.

Get hold of yourself, Christine Johnstone.

The rum had gone to her head. It had lowered her inhibitions and trapped her in an emotional storm.

Chris lay down on the bed and snuggled her head into the soft pillow she'd bought to replace the overstuffed foam one the force had issued.

She fantasized calling for Quinn and asking him if he wanted to lie down with her for a while.

Just to make sure she stayed warm, of course.

Now this, my girl, she lectured herself sternly, *is a very dangerous side effect of alcohol.* Funny it had never happened to her before now.... She slid down the tunnel to sleep with the taste of Quinn on her lips.

She woke enough to stagger to the bathroom later. Her clock read 10:20 p.m. She'd slept all afternoon and into the evening, yet she could hardly drag herself out of bed. The muscles in her arms and legs hurt as if she'd been in a fight, and her chest ached with every breath. Groggy and sore, Chris lurched straight back to bed and collapsed again into sleep.

A sustained tapping on her door woke her next. This time her clock read 3:45, and she was sure it said a.m. It was broad daylight, but by now she was getting accustomed to the "land of the midnight sun."

Straightening her twisted terry robe and running her fingers through what had to be a disastrous mess of a hairdo, Chris opened the door a sliver and peered out.

Quinn stood there, a case of beer under one arm and a bottle of white wine and a water glass clutched in his hands.

He had an abashed, half-shy look on his face, and his black wavy hair hung down carelessly over his forehead. The bruised skin around his puffy eye was starting to turn lavender and green.

"Yes, umm, good night, uh, morning. Hi, Quinn," she stammered, and all she could think of was the way his arms had felt holding her, and how rumpled she must look. Was there sleep in her eyes? At least the soreness in her muscles was nearly gone.

He shifted from one foot to the other.

"I happened to be going by, Constable...."

Chris blinked. *Happened to be going by?*

"And I wondered if maybe I could buy you a drink. If you weren't busy or anything."

Was he making a serious pass this time? Her heart leaped, and then reason took over.

Quinn was probably simply redefining their boundaries, making a typically masculine effort to reinstate their working relationship as constable and corporal.

Having a drink together this way in barracks had been a ritual among the recruits, a way of apologizing for misunderstanding.

The import of Quinn's invitation struck her slowly. He was coming to her, on her territory, with what constituted a peace offering. It was what might be labeled a symbolic gesture, and matted hair and aching heart or not, she'd better make the best of it.

"That would be, that is, well, yes, I'd enjoy that very much. Come in." Chris opened the door and he stepped through, setting the beer and wine on the small table she'd placed under the window.

"Sit down, make yourself comfortable...." Gad, she sounded like a Sunday school teacher with the minister in for tea.

"Excuse me just a minute," she babbled, grabbing some clothes off the only chair and dashing into the bathroom.

She ran cold water in the basin and feverishly splashed her face until all the traces of sleep were gone. Her hair was flat all down one side, and she dipped her wide-toothed comb in the basin and doused the unruly curls until they sprang back to life. Then she doffed the robe and pulled on her jeans and a pink sweatshirt, took a deep breath and made her entrance.

Quinn was lounging on the wooden chair, tilting it back precariously. He brought the legs down with a bang and sprang up when she came in.

She looked quite beautiful in the pink sweatshirt and washed-out jeans, and her freckles made her look about fourteen.

"Want a beer, or a glass of wine?"

"Wine, please."

Chris moved over to her bed, straightening it self-consciously as he uncorked the bottle and poured a glass nearly to the brim.

He popped the top on a beer, handed her the wine and sat down again, leaning back and resting one booted ankle on the other knee. Quinn was still half in uniform, the way she was becoming accustomed to seeing him, and as always, he seemed to dwarf the chair he sat on.

"My apologies, Chris," he blurted all of a sudden, and she didn't have to ask what he meant. She looked down studiously into her glass.

"You're a very beautiful woman, and it's hard for me to remember you're also a member," he finished softly.

She dared to sneak an upward glance, and he gave her a rueful, lopsided grin.

"Peace?" he queried, holding his glass aloft.

"Peace," she repeated, wishing fiercely he'd stop being such a darned gentleman and just kiss her again.

But it was obvious he was a man of honor. And one of the cardinal rules Depot instilled in women recruits was the danger of becoming involved with a fellow officer.

Before meeting Quinn, the rule had made perfect sense to Chris.

Silence hung in the air between them, and threatened to go on endlessly.

"Town quieted down?" she finally asked. She took a sip of her wine. It was nice, not too dry, not too sweet.

"Yeah. We've got a couple of guests out there in

the cells, but they're right out of it." He scrutinized her. "You okay after your swim?"

She grinned ruefully. "I feel as if I wrestled a grizzly or two, but apart from aching muscles, I'm fine. Did you hear if the man in the car…lived?"

"He's fine. I went over to the clinic after I brought you home. Doc says he'll be right as rain in a day or two. Guy's name is Stefanik Rabowski, Russian immigrant, twenty-three years old, no fixed address, says he worked as a gas station attendant but lost his job last week. Blood alcohol reading of point one four."

Chris whistled. "It's a wonder he could even drive."

Quinn agreed. "Couldn't get much other information out of him—he's pretty weak and sick."

They were quiet for a while and it was a comfortable quiet this time, as they sat sipping their drinks. Quinn ended the quiet by gesturing at the family photo on her dresser.

"That the sister and brother you mentioned?"

Chris nodded. She reached over and retrieved the picture, holding it out to Quinn, pointing out each sibling as she spoke.

"This is Ariel; she's the oldest, thirty-three. She's a psychologist. She works with kids with learning disorders in Vancouver. This is Shane; he's thirty-one. He researches parapsychological phenomena at an institute in Virginia Beach. This is my mother, Rosemary, and my dad, Paul. They live in Summerland, in B.C."

Quinn noted the affection in her tone as she spoke of her family, and the tenderness of her expression.

"Fine-looking family. What are they all like?" he asked curiously, studying the photo.

Chris giggled. "Weird. Mom and Dad were hippies before anyone coined the word, and they accidentally became wealthy because they started making and selling natural jams and jellies from organically grown fruits just when people started wanting that sort of thing. Mom meditates in their orchard every morning, and she insists that's why the crop is always excellent. Dad's a fine businessman, but he's also a student of Eastern philosophies and yoga. We three offspring weren't at all what they expected, poor dears. They taught us to meditate almost before we could walk, instructed us in techniques that made learning easy and surrounded us with books on every subject. Instead of the quiet, high-minded brood they'd envisioned, we were known locally as those Terrible Johnstone Kids. Teachers drew lots to see who'd have to take us, and we were big on elaborate practical jokes. Ariel looks like an angel, so we used her as our front man. Shane's incredibly strong and agile, so he did the practical stuff—ropes and fences and all that."

"And you were the brains of the gang." It was more statement than question. He remembered quite clearly being locked up in his own cell block by this blue-eyed terror.

She assumed an exaggerated innocence, and made a "who, me?" gesture with her hands. "The thing is, we had a marvelous childhood, full of love and laughter. I miss my family, that's one part of this job that's rough. I don't get home half as often as I'd like."

"But basically, you enjoy being a Mountie?"

"I love it," she said emphatically. "Times like today make it seem the best job in the world."

He looked at her to see if she was joking, and he

had to laugh out loud in incredulous amazement at her earnest conviction. "You're a little bent, you know that, Johnstone? Jumping into rivers in the Arctic isn't what most people would class as a good time."

"It may be my one chance in life to be a hero," she insisted staunchly. Then she said, "What about you, Quinn? You've done it longer than I have, you must have the same feeling, that this is a great way to make a living."

He took a long sip of his beer and shrugged. "I enjoy the people. I haven't any illusions about the job or the organization," he stated flatly. He hesitated, giving her a measuring look. "When I joined the force, I was like most recruits, ideals ten miles high." His tone was tinged with sarcasm. "I was going to ride out on my horse wearing scratchy red serge and defend the honor of my country." He raised an eyebrow enigmatically and took another swallow. "I got over that soon enough. Now, I give them a good day's work for my paycheck, but my soul's my own."

Chris frowned at him, leaning her elbows on her knees. His cynicism disturbed her deeply.

"What happened to change you, Quinn?" She needed to know for she wanted to understand him.

Usually he passed off the old affair with an offhand comment about being in the wrong place at a bad time. It was essentially the truth, but now, for some reason, he was about to go into detail for her, tell her the way it had really happened, and that surprised him. Why was it important that she know the true story? he wondered.

The answer was disturbing—he wanted her to think

well of him. He wanted there to be total honesty between them

He opened his mouth to begin when the intensity
on her face stopped him. She wasn't being idly curious, or making conversation. Her eyes were troubled
and confused, and the vulnerability she showed frightened him.

She could be hurt badly, because she still had all
those high-minded dreams. She still believed the fairy
tale, the myth that good and evil were separate forces
in the world instead of one huge, smoggy gray area,
that it was her duty, her job, her birthright, to keep
them separate.

My God, she finds the whole thing fun.

It made Quinn intolerably sad, and it made him feel
ancient and hopelessly jaded to look into her eyes and
see those shiny dreams.

"I've heard rumors, Quinn," she prompted him
hesitantly when he didn't reply, "about some government inquiry where you were called on to testify. Was
that it?"

There'd been a cover-up order on information
about a high government official involved in an investigation Quinn was part of, and instead of denying
any knowledge of the matter as he was expected to
do, he'd done the unforgivable. He'd told the absolute
truth on the witness stand, baldly and openly disclos-
ing the bureaucratic bungling that had cost the government a great deal of money, and almost lost a good
man's life in the bargain. The money hadn't mattered
to him at all, but remaining silent, becoming part of
a cover-up for political reasons, wasn't part of his
makeup.

Quinn was fully aware of what his testimony meant

to his career, to any chance for advancement. He'd left the plainclothes section under a cloud and been relegated back to three shifts, and then finally banished to small towns in out-of-the-way places. After the first raging anger and the disillusionment passed, his eventual fate actually suited him just fine.

Careerwise, his was a holding pattern—so many years to put in before he could be legitimately pensioned off and forgotten.

He suspected it was just the opposite for Chris. She was one of the new breed, the fresh crop of computer-trained, psychology-oriented, modern-day enforcement officers whose training was a vastly updated version of the ten rough months he'd spent in Depot. She was ambitious, eager for promotion, a career woman. Ironically though, her ideals were the identical ones he'd had nineteen years before.

Don't shoot her down, Quinn, a small voice warned.

Don't spell out the way it was for you; she doesn't need to hear all that slime. Maybe she'll get by unscathed; who knows?

"Quinn?" she persisted. "What really happened to you?"

"Nothing as dramatic as whatever you've heard," he lied blithely. "A big case came along and I screwed up, it happens to a lot of young policemen when they get an expense account and a fancy car to drive around in. They start drinking and partying too much, and the job doesn't get done. So one day they transfer you back into uniform and send you to Dawson." Chris didn't seem convinced, so he added thoughtfully, "I've got no great ambitions about being commissioner, and you were right, I enjoy my work. Guys like me are a dime a dozen in the RCMP. You know that.''

Chris knew nothing of the kind. As far as she knew, Quinn was an original, but she decided not to say so.

He forced a light, teasing note into his voice to distract her. ''We're confirmed bachelors, we like to scrap a little, drink a few beers, wear out the tires on a car the government provides for us, keep order in some little town like this. Hell, it's even been rumored we're chauvinist bastards, although you and I both know there's no truth to that.''

His self-deprecating grin was wickedly alluring, and she laughed and forgot to pursue the original question, just as he'd intended.

''You're slowly improving at this chauvinist business,'' she conceded. ''But you've got a way to go yet.''

''I've been unfair to you, Chris,'' he stated, catching her by surprise. ''That's changing, as of today. Far as I'm concerned, you proved yourself a fine policem—'' he caught her look and swiftly changed his terminology ''—policewoman today in that river. From here on in, we're partners.''

Pleasure made her warm, and she didn't know how to answer. The disconcerting awareness was between them again instantly, and she fiddled with her glass for a second while he reached across and placed the picture of her family carefully on the dresser again.

''Interesting people, Chris. I'd like to meet them someday.''

She'd like that too, she decided. Then she asked curiously, ''What about your family, do you get home often? Where did you grow up, Quinn? Do you have brothers and sisters?''

He thought of the barren, joyless pattern of his childhood and a mirthless grin came and went behind his mustache.

"No home left to go to, it was sold after Pop died. I was an only child, my folks were old when I was born, eking out a living on a dirt farm in northern Saskatchewan. Mom died when I was three, my father four years ago after a long illness. He believed in hard work and plenty of discipline, church twice every Sunday. He was a tough old man, fanatically religious, and we didn't get along too well." Not at all, if the truth were told. "I always suspected he wanted me to be a minister. He was disappointed when I joined the force."

"So were my parents," Chris admitted with a sympathetic smile. How awful for Quinn, not to have the warmth of a family like hers behind him.

She was fascinated and touched by the personal details Quinn was sharing with her. "Mom and Dad are pacifists. They marched in every peace rally going in the seventies. They were horrified when the RCMP did the regulation security check on me. They felt it was a breach of personal freedom and a personal insult."

He laughed heartily and opened another beer.

"More wine?" He made a motion to fill her glass.

"No thanks. I hardly ever have more than a glass." *And not usually a water glass, either.*

His black eyes twinkled at her. "You mean I can't ply you with liquor and…" He drew out the rest and she felt herself blushing furiously, unable to meet his eyes. How could he joke this way, so soon after…

He relented. "…get you to breach the Official Secrets Act?"

Her eyes met his teasingly warm gaze. Teasing was just his way of smoothing over the awkwardness between them.

"One of us has to be awake enough to answer the phone tomorrow, Quinn," she responded pertly. "Answer the phone today," she corrected, glancing at the clock. Amazingly enough, more than two hours had passed since he'd arrived. It was 6:00 a.m. "It's Sunday, though, so it'll probably be quiet."

Impulsively, he set down the beer and stood up. "In that case, let's take advantage of the peace and quiet and go out for Sunday morning breakfast. Have you been over to the Klondike Hotel for their prospectors flapjacks?"

Chris shook her head, and her eyes danced. Things were happening fast, and she was having trouble keeping up, but she liked it.

"Then get your shoes on, Constable, and let's be off. Those flapjacks are worth getting up for."

"But you haven't been to bed yet," she objected weakly.

"I don't mind if you don't," he said earnestly, and they were both laughing as they hurried out of the building and up the sun-dappled street.

CHAPTER SIX

"AS OF TODAY, you're going to be my partner,"
Quinn had promised, and during the next weeks, he
made good that promise. At last, he shared the work
of the detachment equally with Chris, generously
teaching her his particular methods of small-town policing.

She was treated as a hero when the surprisingly
clear picture of her wrapped in the gray blanket, all
huge eyes and damp curls, appeared in the local paper
along with the dramatic account of Stefan Rabowski's
rescue.

A copy of that edition was sent by a Dawson resident to a friend in Montreal, whose husband was an
editor on the *Gazette*.

He obtained the right to publish the photo of the
pretty officer, along with the story, filling in a troublesome blank spot on his second page, and quite unknown to Chris, she stared out for a day at a large
reading audience miles away from Dawson.

The news librarian in the city's central library dutifully clipped the article, dated it and filed it away
under the heading, RCMP.

Chris was oblivious to all that. One sun-filled July
day slid into the next, and just when the constant sunshine was becoming commonplace, she noticed that
darkness was beginning to return to the land. First,

there was less than an hour each night when the sun disappeared and dusk fell, but rapidly the hours of darkness increased.

Almost before she realized it, July had become August, nights again held periods of darkness; the midnight sun was gone for another year, and she'd been in Dawson two full months.

For Chris, the busy days and nights were exhilarating, working with Quinn. He gave her the opportunity to work on her own, but he also included her in his investigations or inquiries if he thought she'd find them interesting.

Quinn's method of policing was unique in her experience. He had an effective way of involving the townspeople in the investigations he conducted without ever flaunting his authority or causing a backlash of resentment.

He did it mostly by conversation.

He took time to get to know the people of Dawson, he sat with them over coffee or lunch and talked about anything they cared to discuss. He walked the town and dropped in on shopkeepers until they viewed him as a friend. He remembered the names of their children and the fact that someone's grandmother in Seattle had had a heart attack. As far as was feasible, he discussed with them the cases he and Chris handled, the problems they encountered, and he gratefully accepted advice even though he often didn't use it.

On the surface it might have seemed he was wasting time. In actuality, he was turning half of Dawson into his deputies, involving them in the policing of their town. The facts he gathered gave him an uncanny sense of what was going on around him. He knew who was a resident and who was visiting, who was drinking too much, who was acting out of character, who was having a clandestine relationship with whom. And when he needed information, he knew exactly whom to approach.

He introduced Chris to Dawson as his trusted partner, and slowly she too became privy to Quinn's information grapevine. He generously shared with her all the accumulated knowledge he'd amassed over the years, and she was often amazed at his subtle understanding of people and their motives.

One thing remained unchanged, however. She'd started out as Ms Constable, and Ms Constable she remained to the residents of Dawson.

Chris found that she didn't mind in the least. The title even seemed to convey a rough affection on the part of the townspeople.

The professional part of their job went along fine. It was her private life that became increasingly difficult.

They lived in the same building, they often ate together, they wrangled in friendly fashion over the chores of cooking and cleaning, and the intimate awareness of each other as man and woman grew with every passing hour.

Quinn would wake in the night, his body hard and pulsing with urgent need of her, and he'd lie and curse the day the force had posted her to Dawson.

He didn't label his feelings as love or anything like it. He didn't analyze the sense of joy there was in being around her. He was afraid to name the protective sense of companionship he felt, the wonder of having someone to share the comic side of what could often be a tragic job. Communication was easy between him and Chris, as subtle as an exchanged glance, or as rowdy as a belly laugh over some ridiculous occurrence. They had the same sense of humor, the same appreciation of human foible and sensitivity to human pain.

But love?

Quinn had more or less grown up without it. He'd had sexual relationships over the years, had grown fond of certain women and hated leaving them when he was transferred.

But he'd never experienced the special bittersweet mixture of longing and fascination, familiarity and strangeness that Chris stirred in him.

He avoided labeling the emotions he felt for his constable.

He was too honest, however, not to name the reactions she stirred in his body. The wrenching physical need for her was becoming an obsession, and he felt embarrassingly like a randy teenager when his erection sprang inconveniently to life at odd moments of the day, instigated by something as inane as watching her bending to find the soap under the sink, or wriggling her way onto the seat in the car beside him, or even giving him a certain look from those bluer than blue eyes of hers.

He'd kissed her only once, and yet he fantasized about ways to pleasure her body with his own in the most intimate manner.

"Long time no see," Gladys had remarked with a wistful grin when they met on the street one morning, and Quinn could only nod and shrug. He didn't fully understand it, but the comfortable, blowsy sex he'd shared with Gladys was no longer appealing; in fact, it repelled him now.

He'd never imagined he'd be driven half-mad lusting over a fellow officer, and when he could, he did his gentleman's best to overcome, overlook and ignore the situation.

He was colossally unsuccessful.

THERE WAS A LULL in the town's tourist business the third week of August, with a corresponding drop in calls for the police office. The season was changing; the air already smelled of autumn, and the trees were blazing orange and yellow and crimson.

Over breakfast one particularly fine morning, Quinn took a long look at Chris, admiring the short curls molded to her head from her recent shower, her shining freckled face smiling happily at him over the breakfast table. The months ahead would be long and dark and intimate, alone with her. Dangerous.

The best thing he could do was spend as much time as possible away from her, he concluded. She was simply driving him totally nuts, looking like that, wearing those tight jeans and an abbreviated shirt that revealed the way her taut flesh curved into the waistband of her pants.

He opened his mouth and heard himself suggesting the two of them play hooky for the day.

"There's a friend of mine I'd like you to meet," he said impetuously. "Maisie's in, she can field the calls, and we'll take along a portable so if something desperate happens, we can be back in a couple of hours," Quinn reasoned aloud. "We'll use my plane. I want to visit Abe before the bad weather sets in anyway, and that can happen anytime in September up here."

"I didn't even know you had a plane," Chris said

excitedly. "And who's Abe?" She hurriedly stacked the dishes and put them in the sink, running hot water over them and throwing Quinn a dish towel. "Where does he live that we have to fly to see him?"

He was familiar with her rapid-fire questions when something excited her, and he patiently answered them one at a time.

"Abe's a guy I've known since I came to Dawson. He does some prospecting out along the Yukon. As for the plane, I bought a vintage Aronka Chieftain two years ago from an old guy I figured was a high-grader, but I don't get much chance to fly it."

"A high-grader?" Chris looked blank.

"Somebody who finds out from the government agent's office where a rich claim's been staked and then flies in to it before it's worked and skims off the high-grade ore, takes out three or four hundred pounds in his airplane. I figured Johnny Smiley'd been doing it for years, and I got hot on his trail when I was new up here. Wily old devil decided to take his poke and retire to Arizona while he was still ahead. He had a sense of humor, so he sold me his plane for a good price when he left. It's a collector's dream, a vintage floatplane. I keep it down in an old fishing shed. There aren't exactly a lot of airfields to land on in the Yukon, so most small planes are on floats. That way, you can use the river." Quinn reluctantly wiped the dishes as she washed. "How come we can't just let these drip? I never dried dishes before you came along and took over the kitchen," he complained plaintively.

"You never washed dishes either. Maisie told me you used to use every last dish in the house and then get poor old Slocum Charlie to come in and wade through the mess.''

"Well, the old guy needed the job. You're doing an honest reprobate out of his whiskey, washing up this way.''

Having to brush past Chris to get to the cupboard was infinitely preferable to having Slocum Charlie around, Quinn decided, prolonging the contact as much as he dared and stoically suffering the predictable reaction in his groin.

"So tell me more about this Abe person,'' she persisted, ignoring the pleasurable and disturbing feelings his nearness aroused in her.

She knew perfectly well that Quinn wanted her sexually, and apart from any intellectual input, her own body responded to him alarmingly.

In the daytime, she told herself stoutly that it was just a good thing she was mature and adult, so that she could rationalize the sensual electricity and tell herself it was just a normal reaction to living with a handsome, virile man.

At night, she remembered that single kiss.

But he hadn't made any effort to follow it up.

Which was a little disappointing, considering how he affected her senses. And a blind man could tell she affected him, as well. You'd think he'd try, at least. So she could spell out why a sexual relationship was a bad idea.

"Abraham Schultz lives up the river all summer. He keeps a cabin here in town, and if the winter gets too bad he moves in. He's an interesting guy, Abe. I think you'd like him. I check up on him every now and then, take him up some fresh vegetables and things.''

Within an hour, they were down at the float house where Quinn's plane was kept. He was a competent pilot, and soon the small two-seater craft was airborne.

Quinn followed the path of the silver-gray river, pointing out to Chris areas that had been small cities during the gold rush, and were now ramshackle collections of crumbled cabins and overgrown clearings, little more than dots on the rough landscape below. From the air, the terrain was a wonderfully colorful palette of deep green, fawn brown, orange and red and gold, snow-topped sawtooth mountains, stunted forests and tundra colored by autumn's paintbrush.

Chris had flown to Dawson that first day via Whitehorse, and she'd been astonished at the vast emptiness of the country from the air. Today again, it struck her how isolated the town of Dawson really was. They followed the river for many miles, and except for a rare cabin or two, there was no sign of man below. There were lakes and rivers and sky, spectacular and unspoiled, stretching as far as the eye could see, and it made her feel tiny and insignificant to be soaring along in the fragile man-made aircraft. What must it be like here when everything was buried in white silence and sun was gone for months?

The long northern night.

A thrill of anticipation swept over Chris and she glanced at Quinn, dark glasses hiding his eyes as he bent forward to peer down at some inscrutable landmark.

Would things change between them when winter arrived? Would he relax the superhuman control she sensed he imposed on himself and become her lover during that long dark time?

She shivered.

"Cold?" he called above the sound of the motor. "We're nearly there, take a look out your side window. That's Abe's cabin below, just where the river bends."

Quinn landed smoothly on the water and threw a rope to a tall stooped man who was waiting on the riverbank. Chris helped toss Abe the bundles of fresh fruit, vegetables and coffee that Quinn had loaded for him in Dawson, and she and Quinn made the short leap to shore.

Abe Schultz was about fifty, with gaunt aristocratic features and a lush silver beard and thinning hair. He had gentle, sad gray eyes surrounded by smile wrinkles, and his face was a mass of weather-beaten lines.

"Greetings, and welcome," he said, and he and Quinn shook hands and pounded each other's shoulders in the way men have of showing pleasure with one another.

Quinn introduced Chris, explaining who she was, and Abe shook her hand warmly, then studied her and planted an impetuous kiss on her cheek.

"Never thought I'd want to do that to a law officer," he quipped before leading the way to his rough log cabin.

It was compact and tiny, one all-purpose snug room, almost buried by the willows growing in profusion along the riverbank. At Abe's invitation, they sat on a bench outside the cabin door, and Quinn produced the forty ounces of good whiskey he'd brought for his friend—he'd told Chris it was called a "jar" in these parts.

Abe hurried into the tiny cabin, brought out three enamel cups and poured them each drinks so strong that the first swallow nearly strangled Chris. She choked, her eyes teared and when she got her breath back, she found both men grinning widely at her.

"She's a good policeman, but she's not much of a boozer," Quinn explained apologetically.

"That's a shame, Quinn. It's a serious drawback in a partner, but she improves the landscape so much I vote we just overlook her weaknesses when it comes to good whiskey," Abe teased.

Chris unceremoniously dumped the rest of her drink into Quinn's mug, wondering if she'd be able to fly the plane home, should it become necessary.

The two men talked easily, about Abe's gold panning and people they both knew in Dawson. Chris leaned back against the weather-worn logs of the cabin, closed her eyes and turned her face up to the sun, listening to their voices and the rushing noise of the nearby river in a contented haze of warmth and peace.

And curiosity. Abe wasn't the eccentric prospector she'd been anticipating, and she was curious about his cultured voice and sophisticated vocabulary. He seemed strangely out of place in this wilderness, as if he'd be more at home in a suit and tie than the rather grubby jeans and sweatshirt he was wearing.

She helped him later when he made them a simple dinner. There was barely room for two in the tiny cabin's interior, so Quinn graciously offered to sit outside and do nothing while they cooked.

Inside, Chris looked around curiously at the simple furnishings, the haphazard stacks of books. Her eyes rested on the framed photo of a beautiful woman on the makeshift table beside the bed. Abe noticed her interest and said with a peculiar note of tenderness in his voice, "That's my wife, Beverly. She lives in Vancouver."

Before Chris could comment, he added quickly, "You'll be staying in Dawson over the winter, Chris?"

Obviously, Abe didn't want to talk about his wife. He shoved another log into the already blazing firebox of the small flat-topped stove.

Chris drew her gaze away from the studied perfection of the sophisticated woman in the photograph, and swallowed the questions she'd like to ask.

"Yes. I'm looking forward to it. I can't imagine what it's like to have that many months of darkness."

He gave her his kindly smile and she wondered what had given his voice that touching undertone of sadness. "It's almost like hibernation. Many people find it intolerable, and head south after the first month. You can't blame them, the Arctic's not suitable for everyone. It can be a harsh land."

"But many people stay and seem to love it," she said. "You must, and I know Quinn does. How long have you been north, Abe?"

"Twelve years now. I'm fifty-four. I drifted up here for a summer when I was forty-two, not expecting much. I'd stopped expecting anything, as a matter of fact, at that stage in my life." He was putting fresh fish coated in cornmeal to fry in a black iron pan. "I was drinking too much, thinking too much. Entirely self-absorbed. And there was something about this country that forced me out of that state, forced me to look around. When I did, I found extraordinary innocence and peace in this land and the people who live here." A musing look accompanied the words, and he turned the fish neatly with a spatula. "Beauty.

Balm for the battered soul. I resigned my position that autumn and here I stayed. I've tried to return to so-called civilization several times, but I always come back. The Yukon has become a security blanket of sorts for me.''

Chris was emptying tinned beans into a battered saucepan.

''What kind of work did you do?''

''I was professor of English literature at the University of British Columbia. But that was part of another lifetime. You'll find most of us up here divide life into before and after, Chris.''

She glanced over at him, about to ask why he'd chosen this kind of life over an academic career he must have worked hard to attain, but she sensed a gentle reticence in his choice of words.

This was after, and perhaps he preferred not to talk about before.

Chris tactfully refrained from asking more questions, although she wanted to in the worst way. Abe began talking about the long winter and the breakup of the ice in the Yukon River—an event that heralded summer's arrival.

''Everybody in town makes a bet on the exact date when the ice will go, and it makes a sound like cannon fire when it begins to disintegrate. The entire population of the town races to the riverbank in the wildest state of excitement, regardless of whether it's day or night, and a madly festive atmosphere prevails,'' he explained in his scholarly fashion. ''It's an event, when the ice goes. You'll never forget it once you experience it, Chris.''

He studied the pots and pans and nodded with satisfaction. "Dinner's ready. Would you carry out that coffeepot and the beans, if you please?"

A cool breeze from the river wafted over them as they ate, and a marmot begged for a share of the food. Kingfishers flew back and forth from the river, scrounging bits.

"A brown bear comes down to fish now and then. He passes quite close to the cabin," Abe announced calmly. Chris found herself glancing nervously over her shoulder. She could live quite nicely without meeting a brown bear. Quinn noticed the gesture and gave her a huge wink, and the ever present electricity between them passed back and forth like a living current for a moment.

The dinner conversation would have been suitable for a much more sophisticated setting.

They discussed the North Warning System, a billion-dollar project designed to replace the antiquated DEW Line, and the impact the increased traffic and construction work would have on the Arctic. Quinn and Abe agreed that a sudden influx of workers could be devastating, to wildlife and humans both.

That led to a heated discussion of the native ecology, and on certain viewpoints they disagreed heartily. Chris marveled at both men's knowledge of and understanding for the northern land, and at one point Abe became quite carried away with fervor. He leaped to his feet passionately and shook his fists at the sky, and she suddenly saw a younger, different man inside the gentle professor.

Then she happened to glance from him to Quinn, and found that Quinn wasn't really paying attention to Abe's rhetoric at all.

He was staring at her with an intensity of passion

and need and longing in his eyes, and it was long moments before Abe's words again penetrated her awareness.

"Very few people want to come north and actually settle," he was summing up. "They come with their cameras and try to get a picture of an Eskimo or a team of huskies, but they really know very little about the Arctic or its people, except for smatterings of Robert Service or Jack London from high school days. Those visions are beautiful, but they're outdated now."

The men had another drink together, and to Chris there seemed to be a kind of magic in the warm sunlit twilight. The warmth of deep friendship between these very different men touched her. The ever present sound of the river underscored the gentle evening noises all around, and when Abe began quoting poetry in a soft voice, it seemed only a natural continuation of the lulling twilight.

Men of the High North, the wild sky is blazing:
Islands of opal float on silver seas;

He quoted the entire poem, and when the last word faded, Quinn's deep and resonant tones began a different, lighter ode.

There was Claw-fingered Kitty and Windy Ike
Living the life of shame....

Between them, the two men rollicked and hammed their way through the ballads of the North, and Chris laughed and wept and clapped.

They were beautiful, and wild, and she loved both of them.

But it was Quinn she wanted.

When they finally wound down, there was silence for a while, and then Abe said reflectively, "What this land needs is a modern literary voice, telling things the way they really are." Then he demanded suddenly, "What's become of that novel you talked about writing once, Quinn? In my opinion, nobody's better equipped than you to write about the North."

Chris saw the dull red of embarrassment creep up the V of Quinn's open-necked shirt.

"We'd had a few too many drinks that night, Abe," he mumbled. "I'm not a writer; I'm a cop."

But the way he protested indicated which he'd rather be. Chris thought of the files he'd collected, his ability to draw people out of themselves and tell him about their lives.

"You should try, Quinn. What've you got to lose?" she asked impulsively.

He looked at her for long moments, his black gaze inscrutable. Abe watched the two of them, his eyes moving from one to the other and seeming to see below the surface of each, assessing what was between them and what wasn't.

"Dreams," Quinn finally said softly. "I've got all my dreams to lose." Chris's heart wrenched with tenderness as she glimpsed the vulnerability he kept hidden. "Be a hell of a note to try and write and then find out I'm a total failure at something I've dreamed of doing all my life."

"Well, it would be a heck of a lot better than never trying at all," she suggested.

Quinn groaned. "Sometimes you wear me down,

Constable. This woman's motto is Never Give Up," he said, turning to Abe. Then he related how Chris had locked him in the cells, making Abe laugh heartily at his tale, and also diverting the conversation from the potentially awkward subject of writing.

"Speaking of cells, Constable," he said, glancing down at the watch on his arm for the first time all afternoon, "we'd better get back to town and see who Maisie's locked up in our absence."

They got to their feet reluctantly.

"Abe, thanks," Quinn said. A warning note came into his voice. "See you don't stay here too long after freeze-up, friend. I'll be expecting to share a jug with you back in Dawson."

"I'll come down when I'm good and ready." Abe took Quinn's extended hand and gripped it hard for a moment. "Good sledding, partner," he said softly. Then he turned his attention to Chris.

"This is a hardheaded, stubborn cuss of an ugly man, this partner of yours," he quipped. "But he's one of the finest all the same. See you take care of him for me, will you, Chris?"

She had the strangest feeling that Abe knew all about the unbearable sexual tension and the concealed feelings between her and Quinn.

Chris waved from the plane as the solitary figure below grew smaller and smaller, finally becoming lost in the vastness of the landscape as Quinn spiraled the plane up and tracked the riverbed back toward Dawson.

Chris was bursting with questions about Abe.

"He's a wonderful man, Quinn. Why would an educated man like that want to live such a lonely life?" she called above the motor noise.

"There's a lot of different ways of being lonely," Quinn replied, adjusting knobs and checking dials. "Abe doesn't talk much about it, but he suffered through a tragedy years ago. He was a respected educator, married to a sophisticated lady, had a five-year-old son and a near-perfect life. There was a car accident one night. Abe was driving. It wasn't his fault, a truck rammed into the back of the car. Anyway, his son died as a result. He blamed himself. He started drinking heavily, took a leave of absence from his job. Apparently when he first came north, he was well on the way to becoming an alcoholic. He and his wife separated, although far as I know they never did divorce. Well, for some reason Abe found peace in the North, and he stopped drinking so hard, but he never felt he could make it if he went back to his old life again. Loves his wife, though. He tried to get her to come up here with him once, four years ago, but she'd made a life of her own in the city and it didn't work out."

Chris stared out at the brilliant blue of the sky, tears making her vision blur. It was a tragic story, and she understood so much more about the solitary man they'd left behind in the clearing.

"But if he has problems with liquor, Quinn, should you take him a bottle the way you just did?" She frowned over at him, thinking how rugged and impossibly sexy he looked in his jeans and short-sleeved blue shirt. His hair was curling down over his collar the way it always did, and his forearms were matted sensuously. How often, riding beside him like this, she had to stop herself from reaching out and touching that hair, testing it for softness and texture....

He made an impatient gesture.

"I'm nobody's conscience, Chris. It would insult Abe, me not sharing a drink with him. Anyway, he only drinks to forget, and if it helps, what harm is there in it? His wife sure as hell isn't around to be bothered about him drinking too much."

"Did you ever meet her? Abe's wife, Beverly? I saw her picture back in the cabin. What was she like?"

"Yeah, I met her the summer she was up. She was sleek, well-groomed, expensively dressed. Delicate. Not suited at all for life in Dawson, that's for sure. She stayed for a while, and as soon as winter came, she hightailed it back to the south coast." He frowned behind his dark glasses. "Abe went on a rampage for a while after that. He fought and drank his way through every bar in Dawson. But then all the fight seemed to go out of him and he started spending more and more time up there in the bush alone. He worries me more now than he did when he was drinking."

They flew along in the twilight, cocooned by the noise of the motor, and it was several moments before Quinn added abruptly, "I think sometimes he doesn't have much of a life force left in him. I've seen it happen to strong men when they love hard and lose the people they care for. Parker Jameson, for instance. He lives for that boy of his, but part of him died with his wife back in Hawaii, and he's told me right out he won't be sorry to die himself. I get the feeling it's the same with Abe."

Chris was quiet, thinking over what he'd said. Then she raised her voice and asked the question that had been on the tip of her tongue for weeks now.

"Have, uh, have you ever been in love, Quinn?"

He gave her a quick, surprised glance and studiously returned to fiddling with knobs and buttons.

"Nope, I don't think I have," he lied.

"Never?" Her tone was incredulous. "How could a good-looking man like you get to your age without falling in love? Is that another thing you're afraid to try, Quinn, like writing?"

The words were out before she could stop it, and she knew by the way his hands tightened on the plane's controls that she'd made him angry with her quick tongue, but he kept his voice level and sounded reasonable.

"Fear has nothing to do with it. Moving around the way we do in the force doesn't exactly promote long-term relationships; you know that. There've been women I cared for, sure, but I never seemed to get around to marrying any, so I guess that means I couldn't have been in love with them, doesn't it? How about you, Chris?" He turned the tables on her neatly, and then realized it was something he'd wanted to ask her for weeks. "You been in love? Married?"

"In love, yes," she admitted. "Or at least I figured it was love at the time. His name was Reid Baxter, and he was the reason I got interested in joining the RCMP. He was a member, and when he quit to become a lawyer, it dawned on me it was his job that fascinated me more than his personality. So we split, and I joined the force, no hard feelings. That's as close as I've come to getting married."

Quinn hated Baxter with sudden jealous zeal, and the next thought came and went before he could control it.

Chris was his, damn it!

Dawson was below them, and he was grateful for

the concentrated effort required to land his plane. He didn't want to hear one more word about her former lovers, and he didn't want to examine his own emotions, either.

He banked hard and dropped them to the river so quickly Chris gasped and grabbed the arm of her seat, her eyes wide with alarm.

It was childish of him, but he figured it sure as hell drove all thoughts of Reid Baxter smack out of her head.

It was past eight when they got back to the office. A double page of handwritten foolscap with Maisie's particular brand of messages scrawled over it was waiting for them.

11:00 a.m. Mrs. Jennie Martinson says some perverts still taking her underwear off the clothesline, wants to talk to the nice lady policeman.

Maisie had added several exclamation points and underlined the word *nice*.

12:43 Liz Morrison dropped by to see you, Chris. Says to pop by Gertie's tonight if you get a chance. Norman and I saw her over there last night with a sexy new guy. Bet that's what she wants to tell you about, she had a real gleam in her eye.

12:52 That Staff Sergeant Billings with the whiny voice called from Whitehorse, he wants a pile of files I couldn't find. Said he'd call back at 3:00, but I said nobody would be here anyhow so not to bother. He'll phone first thing tomorrow morning.

Here, the word *first* was heavily underlined, and Quinn, reading over Chris's shoulder, muttered a pithy expletive.

"Billings'll rout us out of bed at four-thirty tomorrow morning to give me a lecture, so be prepared when the phone rings," he told Chris dolefully. "He's ex-British army, and he believes in spit and polish and punctuality and early rising, all that crap." A note of satisfaction entered Quinn's voice. "He'll be having a proper fit tonight, knowing we left the detachment unmanned for a whole day. Maybe I'll save him the trouble and return his call tonight before I go to bed, around midnight. He retires at eight-thirty, if I remember right."

They read the next message, and now it was Chris's turn to groan.

1:48 That loony-tune you hauled out of the river, Stefanik Rabowski? Well, he came by again with a whole bunch of fish he caught for you, Chris. I put them in the fridge and he hung around trying to get me to say when you'd be back. Says he'll come by to see you tomorrow after work. At least, I think that's what he said, he needs an interpreter. Lucky you.

Stefanik Rabowski had fully recovered and had decided with all the passion of his Russian nature that he was in love with Chris for saving him. He was now driving her insane by proposing marriage every second day.

When he was released from the hospital he'd appeared at the office with a huge bouquet of flowers that both Chris and Quinn suspected must have been stolen from gardens in the vicinity. He presented them with a sweeping bow and made an impassioned if hopelessly mangled thank-you-for-my-life speech in some version of Russian English. Chris had been touched.

Even Quinn felt sympathetic to the intense young man, and he found him a temporary job at the garage down the street, for which Stefanik was humbly grateful, although he didn't fall in love with Quinn for it.

Chris fervently wished he would.

"What am I going to do about this Stefanik?" Chris moaned now. "He follows me when I'm on patrol, popping up and offering to punch people for me, and he hangs around here, and he keeps trying to give me things, and he keeps on proposing at the most inopportune times. I wish Maisie hadn't taken the damn fish—it just encourages him. I can't handle a lovesick Russian staring at me soulfully every time I turn around."

Oddly enough, Quinn was not at all concerned about Stefanik's attentions to Chris. He'd talked to Stefan at length, getting at least half of what the guy said, and discreetly asked about him around town. The young Russian worked hard, drank too much and was generally well liked, although no one could understand him too well. There was nothing sinister at all about Stefan, and Quinn recognized the boy's adulation of Chris as a form of puppy love.

In fact, Quinn felt that having a six-foot impassioned Russian bodyguard around as backup when Chris was patrolling the town alone wasn't a bad idea at all.

Although his concerns in that area were a lot fewer since the night he'd arrived at a brawl just in time to watch his diminutive constable throw a headlock on an obnoxiously drunken miner a foot taller and a hundred pounds heavier than herself, heave him to the ground, and handcuff him as fast and efficiently as Quinn could have.

Chris could handle herself in a brawl. More often than not, though, she was able to defuse an ugly situation using her wits and her quick tongue instead of brute force, and Quinn admired her for that as well.

She was a damn good policewoman.

He just found himself wondering a little wistfully at times if there was anything she couldn't handle...besides Stefanik Rabowski, of course.

He turned the paper over to see what Maisie had written on the back of it, his arm grazing Chris's. Her skin was soft and smooth against his bare arm, and every nerve ending tingled with the contact.

Was she soft and smooth like that all over?

He wrestled his mind back to the messages.

2:15 Quinn, Parker Jameson phoned for you, said it was important and he'd be at his house all evening if you could stop by when you get back. Going home now, Norman's back from Whitehorse. Happy landings you two. M

"What do you suppose Maisie sees in Norman Bickle? He's nice, but he's so totally unexciting. And he's half her size," Chris mused.

"Maybe he's good in bed," Quinn said innocently, and Chris found herself blushing.

How many times had she imagined what Quinn was like in bed?

"Why is it men relate everything to sex?" she asked and Quinn shrugged.

"It's either sex or food with us," he went on blithely. "Right now you're in luck; it's food with me," he lied. "Let's have some sandwiches, and then if you'll do early patrol, I'll see what Parker's up to and take over about ten," Quinn suggested.

"Great, you make them while I have a shower and put my uniform on."

There was a lot to be said for the good old days when women were barefoot, submissive and pregnant in the kitchen and men went off to the coal mines, Quinn decided, as he buttered bread and slapped on thick slices of meat and cheese, pressing down hard on each so they'd flatten enough to fit in a mouth. Chris's mouth.

He hated the sandwiches he made. Chris was lots better at it, if he could only get her to do it.

Probably even in the good old days women like Chris were out marching in the streets and getting themselves thrown in the slammer over the right to vote or some such nonsense. Women like her hadn't ever been submissive, at any time in history. They were ambitious, energetic, fast-mouthed, bossy, opinionated, passionate....

Wonderful in bed.

He smashed the next sandwich down so hard all the stuffing popped out the sides and the bread looked ironed.

It was past nine when Chris at last had a chance to stop in to see Liz. They'd deepened their friendship over the past weeks, occasionally having lunch together or stealing a few moments of conversation at Gertie's when Liz was on her break.

"You're absolutely gorgeous," Chris said, taking in the royal-blue satin costume Liz was wearing, with its trappings of lace and ribbon.

"So are you, and that's going some in that outfit. I never get used to seeing you in uniform, wearing a holster and a gun," Liz said. She drew Chris over to a deserted table and called to Martie to bring them each a ginger ale.

Liz's green eyes were shining, and her angular face looked soft and slightly flushed.

"Listen, I have to talk to you. I've met this man. Tell me quick, Chris, do you believe in love at first sight?"

Chris sipped the soft drink and considered the question. She certainly believed in something at first sight, after meeting Quinn. Electricity, sexual desire, attraction. But love?

She threw caution to the winds. "Probably," she said. "Who've you fallen for so fast? Is he in here now?" She craned her neck around trying to spot any unfamiliar and gorgeous men.

"He'll be here in ten minutes; can you wait? Oh, damn, I've got to go, there's the music starting for our number. Don't go away now, I want you to meet Mario."

Mario Anselmo was definitely enough to turn any woman's head, Chris admitted to herself when Liz brought him proudly over to the table during her next break. He was six feet tall, muscularly slender, deeply tanned, with crisp wavy dark brown hair and a well-trimmed beard and mustache—both showing interesting patches of white. He had only the faintest trace of a charming Italian accent, and his gray silk suit was molded to his lean frame in a way only masterly tailoring could accomplish. A discreet charcoal scarf, also silk, was tucked into his breast pocket, and his finely woven shirt was pristine white.

He looked wealthy, sexy, foreign and dangerous. Chris didn't trust him.

There was something disturbing about his eyes, Chris concluded warily, as she smiled at him and shook hands. He didn't seem at all fazed that Liz had a police officer as a friend, though. Or maybe he was an exceptionally good actor.

"What brings you to Dawson, Mario?" she asked, as soon as the introductions were over.

"I'm here on business. My firm is based in the U.S. but we travel worldwide," he replied in his smooth, charming voice, smiling openly and revealing nothing.

Chris was about to delve further into Mario's business affairs when Quinn strode into the room and came straight over to their table. His gaze flickered over Liz, paused briefly and settled on Chris.

"Chris, we've got an emergency," he said quietly. "Let's go."

CHAPTER SEVEN

"WHAT IS IT, Quinn?"

Chris raced after him, jumping into the cruiser as the motor roared to life. Gravel spun under their wheels as he swung out of the parking lot.

"A guy from that trailer park outside of town saw me walking over here and stopped to tell me he figures somebody's being murdered in one of the trailers. He says the people are new Canadians, don't speak much English and just moved in. There's lots of screaming and hollering going on in a foreign language, he says. Maybe it's a domestic dispute."

Chris fervently hoped not as the car sped along the bumpy gravel road that led to the small trailer community. Domestic disputes were her least favorite calls.

It wasn't difficult to find the right place. Just as Quinn's informant had said, the screaming and yelling made the small, beat-up trailer easy to locate.

Cautiously, they climbed the rickety wooden steps and banged on the door.

"RCMP," Quinn hollered above the din inside.

The narrow door was flung open wide, and a crazed-looking dark man with terror-stricken eyes took one look at them and beckoned them inside, folding his hands over his heart in obvious relief at their presence.

"Poleece, to come, yess, yess, oh, please, thank you," he repeated over and over. His small stature gave him a boyish appearance, but Chris guessed him to be in his early twenties.

Quinn cautiously looked past him into the small kitchen, but there was no one else there.

Moaning, and then the muffled scream of someone in pain started again from the back of the trailer. Quinn carefully ushered the visibly shaking man ahead of him through the sliding wooden door separating the two areas. The man was eager to oblige, clutching Quinn's tunic sleeve in an effort to make him hurry.

On a double bed against the back wall a young woman lay, her legs outspread and her pregnant stomach contracting in the throes of birth. She wore an old-fashioned white nightgown, long sleeved and buttoned to the neck. Its bottom was hiked up around her straining thighs.

She was in the midst of a contraction when Quinn came through the door. Chris was several feet behind him, and she heard the woman's voice subside and then a string of rapid, half-sobbing words came pouring out as the contraction ended. Her husband gestured at Quinn and Chris and broke into rapid-fire sentences, obviously assuring her that help had arrived.

Then another contraction gripped her, and the high-pitched wailing began all over again. She threshed her head from side to side and tore at the bedclothes, and her huge stomach flattened alarmingly. Her arms and legs were childishly slender in contrast to her middle. She looked about eighteen.

"Quinn, my God, I think she's having a baby."

Chris gasped. She felt cold drops of perspiration pop out on her forehead.

Quinn was already stripping off his jacket and unfastening his Sam Browne. He unloaded the revolver and tossed everything on a chair.

"I think you're right," he agreed dryly. "Her water's broken. It looks like it's too late to move her, so I guess we'll have to play midwife, eh, partner?"

Chris's eyes were riveted to the bed, focused on the writhing figure and the dark pool of blood now coming from the straining vaginal opening. The room smelled of sweat and fecal matter, and Chris could feel her own blood curdling in a hot, sick knot in the pit of her stomach.

"You had training at this in your northern survival course or whatever they're calling it nowadays, didn't you, Chris?"

Quinn was on one knee beside the bed, holding the little woman's hand tenderly in his own, reassuring her before Chris could answer. He was watching the second hand on his watch. As soon as the contraction ended, he gave the fragile mother-to-be a huge grin.

"You just relax now and don't be scared anymore, honey. My partner and I have done this lots of times. Heck, we're old hands at helping babies get born...."

The expectant mother's face contorted and her wailing drowned out Quinn's calm tones as another contraction began. Quinn kept right on talking, uttering low, reassuring words Chris couldn't make out, letting the woman pull on one of his hands with both of hers.

He waited through the contraction, and when it was over he said, "Good, you're doing just great. They're coming every two minutes. What's your name,

honey? If we're going to do this together, I oughta
know your name, don't you think? I'm Quinn, this is
my partner, Chris.'' He repeated the names, pointing
at his chest and at Chris, and the woman gasped,
''Marisa.''

The man, hovering in the corner of the room, nodded and said in a trembling voice, ''I am José, José
Condura.'' Then he promptly burst into tears and buried his face in his hands.

''Chris, see if you can calm Daddy down, get him
out of here, tell him to boil some water or something.
We're going to need lots of towels and sheets and a
basin of warm water with some sort of antiseptic in
it so I can wash up, and we should try and clean her
off a little.''

Chris gently took José's arm and began to usher
him out, grateful beyond measure that she was being
excused from the room.

''Also, make sure the heat is turned up,'' Quinn
added. ''We need it to be good and warm in here.
Use the radio in the patrol car to call the telephone
office. They'll get hold of Doc Chambers for us. Better hurry up—I don't think we have much time.''

Chris swallowed hard. ''José, come help me
please,'' she ordered weakly, moving back along the
narrow passage into the kitchen and drawing a deep
breath into her lungs to try and calm herself. She patted José clumsily on the back, doing her best to
soothe him as well.

''José, we need lots of boiling water.''

What the hell did you do with boiling water around
babies? She didn't know, but Chris somehow got him
started filling pots and kettles anyway and putting
them on the tiny three-burner propane stove. She

raced outside to the cruiser and put in a fervently urgent plea for a doctor, and hurried back inside.

"Towels, sheets, washcloths?" She waved a dish towel and José understood, directing her to the cupboard where the linen was stored. José was much calmer now, his faith and trust in the officers evident each time he looked at Chris for reassurance.

Chris wasn't calm at all. Her hands shook uncontrollably as she snatched sheets and towels—all immaculately clean—and hurried back into the bedroom, dumping the load on the chair. She found the miniscule bathroom and ran warm water in a basin, adding disinfectant from the medicine chest.

She happened to glance into the small mirror over the sink. Her face was utterly drained of color, the freckles standing out like drops of coffee on her nose and cheeks. Sweat rolled down her forehead, and her eyes looked glassy and just as terrified as José's had been when they arrived.

Get hold of yourself, Johnstone, she warned silently through gritted teeth. But the reprimand had no effect. All she could think was, *Why me? Why this? I can't do it, I'll mess it up for sure.*

Blood. There was going to be lots of blood.

She couldn't stand the sight of blood. It made her sick and dizzy and light-headed, and that poor little woman in there was relying on her.

Gripping the edge of the sink, Chris struggled for control.

Marisa was relying on them both, she reminded herself, and a tiny bit of her panic began to ease. Quinn was in charge, he was in there now being wonderfully reassuring, and it would turn out fine. Marisa and the baby would be safe.

Even if his partner disgraced herself, the way she was pretty sure she was going to. The way she had once before.

Chris had stood with the other members taking the northern survival training, gowned and masked, watching a doctor deliver one baby after the next in the maternity ward of a large Edmonton hospital. She'd been trying to memorize the rapid-fire instructions the obstetrician gave, fighting off the nausea and panic she felt and praying she'd never, never have to deliver a baby herself.

Undeniably, birth was a miracle. Watching the tiny forms slide out and hearing their first cries had been awe-inspiring. But there'd also been quantities of blood, and finally Chris had simply fainted.

Twice, to the chagrin of her instructor, who brought her around and sent her right back into battle both times, only to have her do the same thing once more. And now, with no doctor, no sterile surroundings, and Quinn counting on her...

"Please, God, don't let there be blood," she begged pathetically. "Please help us to get Marisa's baby born safely, with...no...blood."

"Chris, hurry up, we need you in here."

She picked up the basin and went bravely in to Quinn. Never had she been more grateful for the presence of a strong, take-charge man than she was at this moment.

He'd been kneeling uncomfortably on the bed, with Marisa huddled back near the wall, and his thick hair was sticking to his forehead with sweat. He'd rolled his sleeves up, and his powerful forearms were bare. He'd never looked more masculine, or more competent, and Chris knew that had she been Marisa, having this man helping her would take away the panic.

Nothing dared go wrong with Quinn directing.

"Let's get her closer to the edge, Chris, where it's easier to reach her. Easy, brave lady, we're just going to slide you over here, see, like this. Good for you…"

Working swiftly, they moved Marisa between one contraction and the next so that she was closer to the edge of the bed. Next they removed the soiled linen from beneath her and hastily unrolled a fresh sheet, then layered towels under her. The tiny woman was visibly calmer than she'd been just after their arrival, even though the pains were almost continuous now. She looked touchingly fragile, and she kept a hand on Quinn's arm during the whole procedure, her huge dark eyes never leaving his face.

"You want a pillow behind you, Marisa? Help prop her up a little with these, Chris.…"

Despite the knot in her stomach and the irrepressible nausea threatening her again, Chris was also aware of his closeness, of the enforced intimacy of the room, of the power and gentle strength Quinn exuded, and she was once more humbly grateful he was there.

They no sooner had Marisa settled than another contraction began. Quinn positioned Marisa so that her hands were holding on to her thighs, and his nonstop monologue held a note of excitement from the end of the bed.

"Marisa, I can see your baby's head now, he's got a full head of hair, lovely dark hair just like his mommy. You work good and hard with the next…"

Marisa's eyes grew wide, and a low, grinding,

groaning noise came from her throat as the contraction began, grew, peaked and ebbed.

"That's it, wonderful. His head's born." There was a note of awe and elation in Quinn's voice.

Chris was supporting Marisa's legs and she saw the wet dark head resting facedown in Quinn's palm. She looked, and then she shut her eyes to avoid seeing the trickle of new blood.

"Sideways," Quinn was muttering with a break in his deep voice. "Let's help these shoulders turn, he's got to come out sideways...."

The tiny bones in the baby's shoulders felt like bird's wings under his desperate fingers. *Don't let me do any harm,* he prayed earnestly. As if in answer, the half-born child turned easily under his hand, perfectly positioned now.

The next pain began, one small shoulder appeared, Marisa arched in a bow, and in a rush of fluid the small pale body slid forcefully from the birth opening and into Quinn's hands.

"It's a girl," Quinn announced, and Marisa collapsed, sobbing quietly. Chris tried to draw air in and failed. Her chest felt constricted, the air in the room too thick to breathe. Quinn checked the baby's nose and mouth, wiping off mucus, waiting....

Why didn't she cry? She had to cry.

Quinn and Chris, eyes riveted on the minute form Quinn cradled, held their own breaths a long heartbeat until...

The healthy gasping wail was quaveringly loud in the sudden stillness of the room. They watched thankfully as the baby's body turned healthy pink with each new indrawn breath. She cried with increasing volume, sounding more and more enraged at the indignities she suffered. Her face was screwed tightly into a comical grimace, her ridiculously small arms flailed and she kicked against Quinn's shirtfront. He stared down at her in wonder, cradling her in both huge hands, a rush of thankfulness filling his heart.

"You give 'em hell, peanut," he whispered to her, and he glanced triumphantly at Chris, humbled by the overwhelming emotion flooding his chest. Chris was crying silently, tears flowing unheeded down her pale cheeks.

Quinn felt tears filling his own eyes, and he had to clear his throat gruffly before he could say, "You've got a beautiful little daughter, Marisa. Look."

Quinn held the slippery infant another moment before he carefully laid her facedown on her mother's stomach, the round dark head resting on her mother's breasts, the umbilical cord still part of Marisa.

Chris felt the room whirling around her. Quantities of blood stained the fresh towels on the bed. She concentrated hard on gently patting the moisture from Marisa's forehead and straightening the sheets as much as she could, ignoring the sick dizziness.

"You okay, partner?" Quinn breathed quietly, anxious about the extreme pallor on Chris's face, but deciding it was just the heat and the high excitement of the moment.

He was holding the thick cord carefully between his thumb and forefinger, waiting until its pulsing ebbed and finally stopped.

"Chris, could you hurry up and find me some nylon cord, something to use to tic this with? And you might tell José he has a new daughter."

Chris fled into the other room, brushing past José, who was standing flattened to the wall in the hallway, his eyes almost bulging from their sockets as he gaped at the sight of his wife, smiling beatifically now, cradling the minute form of his naked new daughter.

Chris leaned weakly against the cupboard for a few blessed seconds as the whirling in her head ebbed. Then she yanked open drawer after drawer, muttering "cord, cord, cord," as if she were demented, finally locating a neatly rolled ball of parcel string with a length of stronger cord wrapped around it.

There were scissors in the drawer as well, and she dropped them into the sink and doused them with some of the gallons of water now steaming on the stove. And then she faltered.

She had to go back into that bedroom. With the blood. She glanced longingly over at the door leading outside. She had an overwhelming urge to walk out the door of the trailer and disappear.

The only thing that stopped her, the only thing that had kept her from falling apart during this whole ordeal, was Quinn. He was a rock, a confident, quiet giant in the tiny space of the bedroom, who somehow managed to make everything seem natural and easy. She decided shakily that she'd never admired anyone the way she admired Quinn right now.

On trembling legs she walked back into the bedroom and watched as stoically as she could as he set about cutting the umbilical cord.

"We can leave lots of space between the end of the cord and baby's tummy. Doc Chambers will do it again nice and neat anyhow."

With a frown of concentration on his perspiring face, Quinn firmly tied off the cord about six inches from the baby's navel, and tied it again a few inches from that.

How could those huge hands be so gentle, so adroit at the delicate task? The very thought of severing the baby from its mother made Chris shudder with terror. It was so…final.

He was brave.

He used the scissors confidently between the two knots, and then folded the end attached to the baby and tied it off once more, a security measure Chris remembered from her own training.

Emotions in turmoil, Chris gently spread a fresh towel over the squirming baby to keep her warm, smiling weakly down into the beaming face of the new mother, and nodding at the soft flow of words from Marisa, who was obviously expressing thanks.

I'm not doing badly, Chris congratulated herself. But where did Quinn find the strength to keep going on and on like this?

The tiny room was growing warmer and warmer, the inevitable odors becoming more pronounced all the time.

"They said the baby's weight on the mother's abdomen should be enough to expel the placenta," Quinn was saying a trifle worriedly. "Go get me a basin to hold it, would you, please, Chris?"

Another blessed few moments alone in which to get hold of herself, run icy water over her wrists, time to try and subdue the quaking in her stomach, the whirling clouds in her head. Where in heaven's name was the doctor? Surely he'd had time to get here by now.

All too soon, she was back in the bedroom again. She walked through the door to hand him the basin she'd found. Then she took one look at what Quinn was doing, and the dizzy weakness she'd been fighting all along overcame her.

He held the round mass of bloody placenta in both hands like a trophy, examining it closely. It looked like a pie-shaped piece of bloody liver.

"I think it's all here. What d'you think, Chris?" He held it out for her to examine. "We'll save it for the doc."

He glanced up just in time to see his constable's eyes roll back in her head. The basin slid to the floor, and she followed it down in a crumpled heap.

"IT'S THE SIGHT OF BLOOD. I've never been able to stand the sight and smell of blood," she confessed miserably a few hours later. "I failed you, and poor Marisa, if she'd ended up with only me there tonight..."

Chris shuddered at the thought.

"God, Quinn, I'm so sorry. I was useless, or the next thing to it. I felt humiliated, having the doctor tend me as well as Marisa."

They'd come home, had showers, changed their stained and sweaty clothing, and they were now sitting companionably in the kitchen. Quinn made her hot, strong tea and insisted that she drink a glass of brandy with it.

He was looking at her with the most peculiar expression in his black eyes, kind and tender, and... Chris scowled.

He couldn't possibly be pleased with a partner who fainted on him, could he?

He traced the lines of his thick mustache thoughtfully with thumb and forefinger, and there was a mes-

merizing appeal in the way his narrow lips were outlined and emphasized by the soft dark hair.

"You know what I like best about people, Chris?"
His deep tones were thoughtful.

She watched him, not knowing what to expect. One
thick eyebrow was arched, and he was half smiling
at her.

"I like their weaknesses, the things about them that
make them just as human as me." He was studying
her face as if he'd never seen it before, feature by
separate feature, and that all too familiar warm awareness made Chris shift her eyes nervously away. She
had the feeling his eyes left burn marks where they
touched her skin.

"You had me worried there for a while, Christine
Johnstone. The whole time you've been here in Dawson you've done everything close to perfect, never
once showing me you were scared or uncertain." He
leaned forward, deliberately reaching for the hand she
rested beside her teacup on the table. His large, strong
fingers closed around it, swallowing it, his rough palm
abrasive against her soft skin. She stared down at the
dusky hairs on the broad wrist and the back of his
hand and wondered how this simple hand-to-hand
touching could create such turmoil in her pulse and
her breathing.

"That day you pulled Stefanik from the river, remember?" he asked darkly. "I felt then just like
you're feeling now, inadequate, more than a little
foolish, angry with myself. Ashamed, embarrassed.
It's hard to admit we all have an Achilles' heel. I
guess it's nature's lesson in humility when we start
getting too big for our breeches."

She brought her other hand hesitantly to where

their folded fingers made a knot on the table, shyly tracing his fingers one by one with a forefinger. She heard his breath catch unevenly, saw the banked fire the simple action stirred in those velvet dark eyes.

There was dangerous electricity coursing through him tonight, a wild exhilaration he'd felt ever since the safe birth of the baby, earlier.

Coupled with that was a welter of feelings for the woman across from him. She looked small and almost fragile in the harshness of the fluorescent light, and her full bottom lip quivered now and then. She had on the fluffy blue robe he was so familiar with by now, the zipper pulled modestly to the nape of her slender neck. He watched a pulse beat there, fast and shallow, and he longed to put his lips against it, to feel the patter of her heart beneath the sensitive tip of his tongue.

He told himself it was only tenderness and compassion he felt for Chris…until she'd fainted.

He'd moved swiftly in that small room tonight and caught her in his arms just before she hit the floor. Her face was drawn and bloodless, and she'd felt soft and malleable as he scooped her up and carried her to the sofa in the front of the trailer.

She'd scared him badly, lying there so white and still.

He'd had to fight his panic at the thought of losing her.

When she began to come out of it, he'd brushed away the tears that trickled helplessly down her cheeks while she was still too weak to control them, cradling her head in the palm of his hand just the way he'd cradled the baby's head not much earlier.

"Easy, honey," he'd said gently, and the tenderness he felt made him tremble.

"I'm going to be sick," she whispered in desperate shame then, and he scurried her to the cramped bathroom just in time, holding her patiently from behind while she retched into the bowl.

He found a bottle of mouthwash, and she rinsed and spit, looking like a little girl about to burst into uncontrollable tears at any moment.

Quinn took her back into the kitchen, depositing her in a heap on the sofa, deathly pale and visibly trembling, and he'd tucked an afghan firmly up under her chin.

José was kneeling beside his wife in the bedroom, pouring out long, musical paeans to Marisa and their daughter, and Quinn decided that what all of them needed was a bracing drink of something or other.

Quinn had been trying to find tea bags to go with the gallons and gallons of boiling water when Doc Chambers bustled in, his balding head shining in the light, his rotund figure moving easily in spite of its extra pounds.

"Sorry I'm late," he apologized blithely. "Seems to be the night for babies. Mrs. Lalonde just had hers; that's what kept me."

He pronounced himself delighted with the delivery and the healthy baby girl, took Chris's pulse and said reassuringly, "Half of the medical students in my class fainted at one time or the next, Constable. Nature's inclined to be messy when it comes to birth, but she gets the job done all the same. You both did a commendable job."

Amid an outpouring of thanks in fractured English

from José, and a beatific smile and soft words from his wife, they had finally been able to leave.

Now, Chris gazed at Quinn across the table. She was acutely aware of him, of the feel of his hand, gentle and yet electrifying on her own, the strong lines of his face, the contrary lock of midnight hair tumbled over his forehead.

His chest, with its mat of dark curls, was outlined by the thin T-shirt he'd pulled on after his shower. He was virile, and yet touchingly vulnerable.

She's seen his tears when he'd held the newborn baby.

Quinn was strong, but capable of being incredibly gentle. She remembered vividly the way the fragile child had looked, cradled in his hands, the potent contrast of thick, hair-matted forearms against transparent baby skin, and the thought sent a shudder of desire pulsing through her body.

The healthy dose of brandy he'd insisted she drink was making a warm fire spread slowly through her, making the nerve endings in her fingers sensitive to every stroking motion his hand made over hers.

"Chris." The strained huskiness in his voice made her look up at him questioningly.

His black gaze was stormy, and a frown brought the bushy eyebrows together over his high-arched nose.

"When you first came here, I had a lot of doubts about having you as a partner. I concocted a stack of reasons why it wouldn't work, and you showed me it would. But there was something we never got around to discussing openly."

Her stomach tensed, and the hand covering hers tightened spasmodically, almost crushing her fingers.

"From the moment you stepped off that plane," he ground out passionately, "I've been telling myself that when two police officers work together, there's no way they can get involved as male and female. They can't allow it to happen." He used his free hand, balled into a fist, to bang the tabletop for emphasis on key words, and the spoon beside his cup jumped with each blow.

Chris, too, jumped a little with each forceful thump, feeling as if he was crushing her fragile dreams.

"No fraternizing between the members: I'll bet the force tells you that in one of their new psych courses, don't they?" he asked, relentlessly.

Chris managed to nod.

Quinn nodded his own head in frowning confirmation. "Yeah, I figured they'd have to, men and women working together in isolated places like this one. Well, for once they're a hundred percent right about something. I made up my own mind about it in the beginning, soon as I first laid eyes on you. We're hired to do a job, to work together. For us to get involved is utter madness. It could be detrimental to the detachment, it might ruin the good working relationship we've built up, it could probably land us both in orderly room for all I know. Chris, I can't let myself fall for you. It just absolutely can't happen."

Chris stared at him and felt like screaming with frustration and disappointment. But she nodded agreement, because what he was saying was no more than the truth.

He resolutely drew his hand away from hers, and she felt bereft and cold and horribly alone as he got slowly to his feet and took several steps around the table, his granite gaze holding her blue eyes captive.

The harsh bass tones of his voice suddenly smoothed to velvet, and then he was standing over her, his dark head silhouetted against the light as she stared up at him, confused.

"I don't like it, Chris, not one damned bit. But that's the way it has to be." He sighed, the sound deep and weary, and then he reached out to touch her hair lingeringly, longingly. With a smothered oath, he snatched his hand away and hurried out of the room. She heard him taking the stairs two at a time, as if he didn't dare slow down.

When she finally went to bed, it took Chris a long time to reach the peaceful, meditative level that led to sleep. It might be easier to accept Quinn's words if she were a person who believed implicitly in rules, she thought petulantly as she tossed this way and that, her long cotton nightgown binding around her hips and legs. The problem was, she'd lived most of her life bending, testing and breaking iron-clad dictums if they came between her and what she knew to be right for herself.

At last she forced herself to review what he'd said, word by word. She considered the entire situation carefully, rejected Quinn's reasoning and the sober rules of the RCMP in favor of what her own heart told her, and then it became easier to find the peaceful place inside herself and rest there. In the floating moments before sleep, the scene came, just as it always did.

Strong arms encircled her. The dream lover who was Quinn embraced her. His lips closed over hers, firm and familiar and dear. He was the other half of herself, and they were spinning together, down the dark pathways into sleep...when the door to her room opened suddenly, and she snapped awake to the sound of Quinn's deep, nearly desperate voice in the semi-darkness.

"Chris, wake up." He walked toward the bed, urgency in his tone. "You know what they say about the best-laid plans of mice and men? Well, I've been lying up there, tossing and turning, arguing with myself, and all the high-minded resolutions in the world can't change what I feel about you. Chris, Christine, I...want...you."

He caught her upper arms and half lifted her from the pillow, the low growl of his voice almost feral with intensity and passion.

"It happened the very first instant I laid eyes on you. It would take a saint or a eunuch to go on denying it, and God knows, I'm neither one." The final words were whispered close to her ear as he sank to his knees beside her narrow bed.

"Chris, I need you with every fiber of my being. I want you so much I'm sick with it. I'd do anything to have you, I'd go out and hunt dragons if you asked me to."

He pressed his face into her hair, and his hot breath felt like fire on her tender skin.

"I have to have you, that's all there is to it." His arms crushed her to him, and she melted, boneless and breathless in his embrace, feeling as though she'd finally found home.

His hard mouth with its soft tickling mustache closed over hers in a kiss that threatened to devour her, and a low groan came from his throat. He kissed her feverishly again and again, inclining his head so his lips fit hers exactly, tasting her tongue and the tender inner flesh of her lips, running the palms of his hands feverishly over her back. The cocoon of blankets impeded him, and he thrust them away, finally rising lithely to his feet and lifting her up easily to fit against him, until the stinging core of her body in its flimsy blue gown rested against the surging hardness of his erection.

His breathing was fast and shallow, his words uneven. "Forgive me, Chris. Here I am, waking you up, telling you everything I feel, everything I want, without giving you a chance to say a thing."

Her voice was a thready whisper, and he had to incline his head so he could hear. She felt small, incredibly voluptuous, molded to him.

"I can't hear you, love, tell me again," he begged desperately.

Still shyly, but a bit louder this time, she whispered, "Your bed, or mine? Mine is awfully narrow."

The next instant, Quinn had slid an arm under her knees, and they were down the hall, through the dimly lit kitchen, heading for the stairwell. Arms clasped around his neck, Chris protested, "Put me down, let me walk up, Quinn, you'll wreck your back, trying to carry me up those stairs."

He was already on the fourth step. "Every female constable by the name of Chris must be carried upstairs and ravished once in her life by a corporal named Quinn. Didn't you read that in your constables manual?" he replied, panting only a little as he took five steps, then six.

"Quinn, that's blasphemy. Besides, if you keep this up, you won't have any energy left for the ravishing part," she argued, unable to stop laughing now as he made a great production out of struggling up the last three steps, making her squeal and threatening to drop her. He reached the top at last and pretended to stagger slightly and gasp for breath.

"Oh, my back," he moaned. "How much do you weigh, anyhow? No more flapjacks for you; you weigh a ton."

By now she couldn't have stood even if he had put her down. She was weak with laughing, and breathless at the thought of what was about to happen. The door to his bedroom was open, and he maneuvered them through and then kicked it shut with his foot. There was a loud bang, and the sound echoed in the night.

His room was in total darkness, but Quinn moved confidently and deposited her in the middle of his rumpled bed, depositing her tenderly, his hands loath to leave her body for even an instant.

Chris's remaining laughter died in her throat, and she felt the bed sink as he took his place beside her.

CHAPTER EIGHT

QUINN PROPPED HIMSELF on an elbow and reached over to flick on a small bedside light.

"I need to see what I'm doing; do you mind having the light on?" he asked huskily, and she gave her head a single, negative shake.

She wanted to see him, too.

He lowered his head until their lips met. His were softly exploring, caressing and stroking back and forth, the tip of his tongue leisurely investigating the corners of her mouth, delicately meeting her own in a tentative search that left her wanting more.

He was still balancing above her, memorizing her with his eyes, not touching any part of her except with his lips.

Chris reached up and touched his shoulders curiously, finding the muscles marble-hard beneath the cotton T-shirt. She slid her hands down the firm biceps, then back up to touch the tips of his ears, the tendons in his neck, to brush across his chest.

"I've longed to touch you like this," she confessed, threading her fingers into the clean softness of his thick, wavy hair, letting herself trace the craggy lines of his nose and forehead, shivering at the stubbly feel of his cheeks beneath her fingertips.

He closed his eyes, and when her fingers came close to his mouth he turned his head and lasciviously drew first one forefinger, then each of her fingers in turn into his mouth, sucking them slow and hard and suggestively, making her catch her breath as spiraling sensation traveled instantly to her breasts, making the nipples harden into tight knots, making heat gather in her loins. His lips went to the pulse at her wrist, and his tongue throbbed there in rhythm with her pounding heart.

He looked down at her and there was fire in his eyes, banked and smoldering with passion.

"I'm going to savor every single inch of you tonight." His voice thrilled her with its deliberate intensity. "I've waited too long for this to rush one single moment." He gathered the hem of her long gown and pulled it up inch by slow inch, tantalizing both himself and her, uncovering Chris as if unwrapping a treasure beyond price. Lips and tongue paid homage to each new bit of skin.

But Quinn's passion was too intense, his need too great to delay for long. One plump and rounded breast emerged and then the other, flushed nipples knotted and eager for his lips, and a low, agonized groan wrenched its way out of his throat.

In one long, not quite steady motion he drew the gown quickly up and over her head, and Chris's amber-toned body lay nude against his white sheets.

"How absolutely beautiful you are," he whispered. He used both hands as well as his hungry hot mouth, palms curving to sculpt her form, beginning high on her chest and sliding both hands slowly, sensuously, down her body. She felt a shudder ripple over her, and watched its echo reverberate through him as he made slow, thorough contact with taut breasts, narrow rib cage, small waist, flat belly. He paused there, dipping his head and circling her navel with his lips, mustache tickling the sensitive skin and sensation bringing every nerve ending to quivering life. His mouth traveled lower, down to the place where tight, thick curls formed a neat dark triangle on her abdomen.

"Quinn." Chris's voice sounded breathless and husky. She reached out and held his head between her hands, stopping the course he was intent on following.

"Not me alone," she said shakily. "I want you naked with me." She sat up, and her unsteady hands reached for the T-shirt he wore, tugging it out of his pants and clumsily pulling it up and over his head. She caught her breath at the furry expanse of chest.

With only a slight pause, she fumbled with the buckle of his pants. Impatiently, Quinn got to his feet and in one fluid motion, stripped off his pants. His erection strained at the bonds of his blue jockey shorts, and in another simple motion, they were off and he was magnificently bare for her eyes to devour.

"You're beautiful, too," she said shakily.

The same soft fur he had on his chest was liberally sprinkled all over his body, dark and mysterious and enticing. He was a big man, a male who could seem overwhelmingly powerful at times, well formed but larger than life.

To Chris, he was the fulfillment of every dark and passion-filled dream she'd ever had, and she silently extended her arms to entice him back to the bed.

"I need you, Quinn. Please come to me," she whispered, and then he was beside her, skin pressed to naked skin, roughness and softness melding and limbs moving, hard and soft and large and small, each of them unable to get close enough to the other, to savor the differences igniting the inferno burning inside them.

In all her dreams, Chris had never imagined lovemaking like this, passion bordering on frenzy, both soul and body consumed by the desire to become one with Quinn.

There was deep loneliness in him, and she longed to banish it, to fill the empty spaces in his heart and in his life.

He, in turn, felt as though he must brand her with his mark, make this trembling woman forever his with every way of loving he knew or could imagine. Broken phrases and soft words of praise for her beauty came from his heart, and he kissed and caressed her until she strained upward for his touch, begging for more and for less as his hands prepared the way and his lips relentlessly discovered all the hidden places that had filled his dreams for endless weeks.

Unable to bear the aching in her moist center any longer, she reached wordlessly for the hard burning part of him she craved and guided it inside.

He was utterly still for an instant, savoring the joy of the moment, the thick, clogging delirium of being inside her soft core. Then her feminine muscles tugged rhythmically, and he gasped and struggled for control, for time in which to bring her to the place of ecstasy.

He was on top of her, his weight half smothering her; he was in her, and yet he could never be near enough for Chris.

There would never be days or weeks or years enough in a lifetime for loving such as this.

He lunged, and her slender long legs slid sinuously

up, past his hard buttocks, around his waist in a clasp beyond her control, an instinctive need to lock him within her.

Their magically elusive destination came closer as he lunged again and again, his body sending out waves of heat, perspiration and love's secretions making every touching part of them slippery against the other's fevered skin.

A scream caught and held in her throat, and she was sure she'd die if he failed to penetrate her one last time.

"Please, now..." she begged with the last of her breath, and in an endless moment the world exploded, first for her, and when her inner quaking reached its crescendo, for Quinn as well.

Everything she was shattered and melted and re-formed into rapture, and into love for Quinn.

Everything Quinn had mistaken for this act in the past fell away, and like one reborn, he perceived the unlimited reaches of what love might be.

They cradled each other, sated and full of peace, his head resting on her breasts, and after a long dreamy time they fitted their bodies together like two spoons and fell asleep.

WHEN THE PHONE RANG, they were still asleep, Quinn's arm pinning Chris protectively against him in the narrow bed. It took several shrill rings before they stirred, and Quinn reluctantly unfolded himself from the warm cocoon they occupied to fumble for the receiver.

He came fully awake to the peevish tones of Staff Sergeant Billings. Quinn cursed roundly under his breath.

"Got you out of bed, did I, Corporal?" Billings sounded smugly pleased.

"Not at all, I'm up already. Good morning." Quinn hastily sat up and swung his legs out of bed to make the claim as close to truth as possible, squinting at the clock on the bed table and dragging a corner of the sheet to cover himself with.

Six forty-five.

"Been up an hour already," he lied heartily, twisting to tuck the blanket closer around Chris's bare shoulder. Her eyes were still firmly closed.

Billings sounded slightly let down, and that pleased Quinn.

"That replacement vehicle for the jeep is here in Whitehorse now. We'll get it up to you before the snow flies," Billings related.

Quinn made the proper responses. His shoulders were freezing.

"We've arranged a prosecutor for the Patterson case. Tell the magistrate he'll be arriving the morning of the twenty-third."

"Fine, Staff, I'll do that." These were urgent matters, all right, Quinn thought sarcastically. Definitely things that couldn't wait till a decent hour. Billings went on at length about the files Maisie had mentioned, throwing in a pointed remark about the detachment being unmanned all the previous day.

Quinn's mind began to wander as Billings veered from that subject and began to discourse on the weather. Quinn turned so he could look at Chris's lovely face silhouetted against the white bed linen.

Incredibly vivid details of their lovemaking made his body react urgently. Her eyes opened, and she gave him a sleepy feline smile before snuggling deeper into the covers.

"How're you making out with Chris?"

Billing's query was sharp and abrupt, and Quinn came out of his reverie as though he'd been doused with cold water.

"Uhh, making out, Staff?" Even to his own ears, Quinn's voice sounded strangled and guilty. "Well, we're, uhh, we seem to be making out quite well, actually."

"Glad to hear it, Corporal. Keep up the good work," Billings ordered heartily.

Quinn cleared his throat, sure he was choking.

"Yes, sir, I certainly intend to."

Billings hung up soon after that, and Quinn replaced the receiver, blew out his pent-up breath and slid beneath the covers again for another few stolen minutes, warming his hands before he dared put them on Chris's wonderfully warm body.

"Was that Staff Billings?" she inquired sleepily, moving his roving hand into a more interesting place.

"Yeah." Quinn concentrated on fitting growing parts of his body into intriguing recesses in hers.

"What did he want, those files Maisie couldn't find?"

"Yeah." His body was growing warm at an alarming rate, and she'd turned over and stretched like a sleepy kitten, making wonderful opportunities available to his fevered touch.

"He also asked about our sex life," he said as casually as he could manage.

She froze. "He what?"

"He asked how you and I were making out, and I

told him the truth. I said we were making out really well."

She giggled, and her warm breath tickled his neck.

"Seriously though, Chris, we will have to be really careful about gossip. Dawson has the best moccasin telegraph around...." His warning dwindled into a rumble of pleasure. She nibbled gently under his jaw and then outlined his ear with a wet tongue, her hand testing the reaction much farther down his form and lingering, well satisfied with what she discovered.

"Well, then, Corporal, we'll just have to go on acting as if we can barely stand the sight of each other, won't we?" she suggested in a sultry whisper.

BREAKFAST, MUCH LATER that morning, was wonderful.

Quinn made his special bacon and eggs—Chris had learned that that was about the extent of his culinary skills—and the detachment phones were quiet for once.

They talked about José and Marisa and their new daughter, both of them still feeling awed by the birth.

"Exactly how many babies have you delivered?" Chris asked as they lingered over their coffee. Chris had learned to warm milk and mix it with Quinn's vile brew to keep from burning out the lining of her stomach.

"This was only my second try at it. The other one was sad, she was a young Indian girl who was waitressing at Gertie's. Nobody even knew she was pregnant, poor kid. Stomach flat as a pancake. Had the baby in her hotel room, and I got there before Doc Chambers." He raised an enigmatic eyebrow. "She didn't make a sound, no screams, nothing. The only noise in there was me fervently praying out loud. I was pretty nervous, almost as bad as José was last night.''

"Poor José. His wife in labor, and me nearly hysterical,'' Chris said morosely.

"I talked to José a bit before we left last night,'' Quinn said thoughtfully. "He doesn't have a job. He and Marisa came up here only a week ago. Somebody told him they needed a baker in Dawson. I suspect they're pretty hard up. Olaffson, the old Swede who owns the only bakery here in town, told José he doesn't need any help.''

"Olaffson should think again. His bread is fine, but he could sure use some variety and imagination. I asked him once if he ever makes bagels or croissants, and he looked at me as if I was suggesting something indecent,'' Chris remarked.

"He was probably hoping desperately that you were, the old lecher,'' Quinn said, giving her a knowing look. Her face was flushed, and there was a heaviness about her long-lashed blue eyes that hinted at sensuous fulfillment. Any male more than ten and less than ninety-three would feel aroused by her at this moment.

Quinn felt wildly lecherous himself, and not for the first time that morning, he wished they were back upstairs in his room.

"I think I'll drop by and have a chat with Olaffson,'' Quinn decided. Olaffson owed him a favor, and he had a feeling he was about to collect on it—that is, if José could make these bagels and croissants Chris wanted. If not, he'd simply have to learn in a hell of a hurry.

A more serious matter came to Quinn's mind.

"Remember that message Maisie left yesterday about Parker wanting to see me?" Quinn asked suddenly, and Chris nodded, wondering over Quinn's serious expression. "Well, the old guy's pretty upset. There's a dude in town asking questions about him, and Parker's certain it's about that old abduction warrant. He doesn't care much if they catch him after all this time, but he's convinced the scandal would hurt Cole's career. Parker devoted his life to raising Cole. His son means everything to him."

Chris frowned at Quinn. "It seems unlikely to me that anybody would care about the case after all this time. And Cole's an adult. You said he was a well-established surgeon. Would it hurt him in any way?" Chris asked.

"Pretty unlikely, but you'd never convince Parker of that. He's naturally a touch paranoid over the whole thing. The part that puzzles me is there must be a limitation of action on such a charge, which would fall short of twenty years. So what's this Anselmo guy doing digging up stuff about Parker anyhow?"

Chris gasped. "Anselmo? Mario Anselmo?" She was horrified. "Quinn, my gosh, that's the guy Liz's fallen head over heels for, the guy she wanted me to meet last night. He was the suave man in the gray suit sitting with us when you came in to Gertie's. He told me he was here on business, that he worked for some firm in the U.S." An awful suspicion began to form in her mind.

"He…he couldn't be some creep trying to blackmail poor old Parker, could he? Or even worse, blackmail Parker's son, Cole Jameson? If Cole's a surgeon, he must make plenty of money." Another, even more disturbing suspicion came to mind. "He wouldn't be just using Liz in order to get information about Parker and Cole, would he? She's lived here for years, so she knows both of them really well." Chris was distressed by the suggestion. Liz had waited so long to fall in love again. If Anselmo was only using her—Chris could imagine how bitter and disillusioned such a deception would make any woman feel, especially a woman as independent and proud as Liz.

Quinn nodded somberly. "He could easily be using her for a cover. Anselmo would need an excuse for hanging around Dawson all this time, and a passionate romance is a good one. I think I'll try to get a line on this Anselmo on the computer, see what we can dig up about him."

Both of them felt deeply disturbed at this new turn of events, and when Chris, smartly uniformed, came into the police office half an hour later, Quinn was hunched over the terminal.

He glanced up and she felt his eyes on her like a caress.

"You look better in that uniform than any constable I've ever seen," he remarked gruffly, and for a silent, charged moment they shared the delight of being lovers. Then, with an effort, they became police officers once more, with jobs to do.

"I'm going over to get a statement from Mrs. Martinson about this new report on theft of her underwear," Chris explained with a sigh. "This case puzzles me, Quinn. I checked back, and these complaints started coming in about six months ago. At first, there was only the Martinson case, but there've been two other complaints in the past few weeks, and I went and talked to the other women. They're both just as…plump as Jennie, and the thefts come in spurts. The guy seems to steal like crazy for two weeks and then forget it for a month, then start all over again. It's a regular pattern.''

Quinn felt a little more sympathetic toward the unfortunate underwear bandit than he had before Chris arrived and took over the troublesome file. For one thing, he was humbly grateful it was her file now and not his. He'd dreaded having to talk at length with any more women about the color and shape of their underwear.

Also, he'd had a few deviant fancies himself, watching Chris's dainty garments dry on the line outside the kitchen window, and he felt a little sorry for the crazed individual who crept around stealing women's panties.

''He's some sort of harmless sexual deviant, poor devil,'' Quinn said absently, his eyes on the information flashing across the screen. He read it and sat back in disgust.

''This is useless. There's not a scrap of information about our friend Anselmo on this damn computer,'' Quinn complained. ''I'm going to give airport special squad a try and see what they come up with. It's a long shot at best.''

As she drove to Jennie Martinson's, Chris felt anxiety build within her for Liz. She remembered the vivacious woman telling her about her life the first day Chris had met her, and the wistful longing in her friend's face when she'd spoken of falling in love again someday.

Now, it looked very much as if the ''gorgeous'' man to whom Liz had finally given her heart was something less than honest.

Was he also a criminal?

For Liz's sake, Chris fervently hoped not. But the situation didn't look too hopeful, she admitted, as she pulled up in front of the Martinsons' dilapidated house.

Jennie's husband, a miner who resembled a certain simian wrestler Chris had seen on television once or twice, was home this morning, and he made it crystal clear he was not amused by the underwear thefts. The simpering Jennie went through details of purple and hot-pink and scarlet and blue, trimmed with black or cream, while her Archie described graphically what he intended to do to the hapless thief if ever he caught him. Chris suppressed a shudder at some of Archie's threats and found herself hoping the thief was a good runner.

"Because my Jennie's a fine figger of a woman, I've gotta pay extra fer her lin...ga...rey," Archie growled in his raspy voice. "This bloody pervert's costing me a fortune, and I'm gonna take it out of his hide if I catch him in the act." With a massive arm protectively around the blushing and obviously cherished Jennie, Chris left, promising that she and Quinn would try to patrol the area as often as they could.

She reread the file once she was in the car, and was struck by the modest descriptions of Jennie's first sets of "lin...ga...rey" compared with what she'd just reported stolen.

No doubt about it, Jennie had obviously gone from discreet white and pale pink, elastic uncertain and no lace, to frothy though outsize concoctions straight from the pages of Frederick's catalogue. And her marital relations seemed to have improved drastically.

Well, Chris concluded, there was certainly no law

against replacing plain with fancy. And from the way Archie had looked at his wife back there, Chris suspected the new knickers might have made the difference in the Martinsons' flagging sex life. Jennie certainly sounded happier than she had the last time Chris had interviewed her.

Nice, but it didn't help Chris catch the thief.

THAT WEEK PASSED QUICKLY for Chris, the days packed full with the work of the detachment, the lengthening nights spent in Quinn's arms, sleeping a bare minimum and making love to excess.

In a small detachment like Dawson, one of them had to be constantly on call, so either Quinn or Chris was on town patrol from early evening until the small hours of the morning. When at last the town was quiet, the working partner hurried home to wake the one who slept with kisses and caresses, and they spent what was left of each night making love.

Their need for each other was insatiable, and each passionate joining created a new desire, hotter and more urgent than the last.

"You two oughta put in for overtime. You both look like the wrath o' God," Maisie commented one morning, and then studied them both with speculative interest when Chris blushed to the roots of her hair and Quinn hurriedly escaped into his office.

The final weekend in August marked a transition period in Dawson, as if the town were packing away summer's trappings in a trunk for the winter. The small tourist shops closed up tight, as did many of the other businesses.

People Chris had considered residents of the town were leaving to spend the colder months in warmer climes, and among the hardy souls who remained, there was an air of fellowship, of brave souls girding for hard times.

Chris experienced a sense of belonging now she hadn't completely felt before. She was staying in the North, and as she went about her work, she felt a keen anticipation for the long dark season just beginning.

With a lover like Quinn, who wouldn't welcome nights that were months long?

It was late Saturday afternoon of the long weekend when Liz came breezing into the office and, at Quinn's direction, hurried down the hall and into the kitchen to find Chris. They hadn't met since the night Liz introduced Mario Anselmo, and Chris felt both uneasy and ridiculously guilty for her unfounded suspicions as Liz sat down at the table to share a pot of tea.

Quinn had been totally unsuccessful in finding out anything at all about Anselmo, although he was still trying. Anselmo had now discreetly inquired about Parker all over town, not realizing that everyone he asked would casually end up mentioning the fact to Quinn.

Parker had closed down his tour business a week early this year, and Chris had been shocked to see how drawn and tired the old man had looked when he dropped by the office to have coffee with Quinn one afternoon.

"Constable, honey, what's wrong with Parker?" Maisie had demanded later in shocked tones. "I swear, the old dear looks just like death warmed over," she stated in her forthright way.

Chris privately agreed. Parker Jameson had aged ten years in only a few short weeks, and the heartiness and pithy humor that had been so much a part of his personality were now entirely missing.

And ironically enough, Chris reminded herself as Liz stirred honey into her steaming tea, it was all the fault of a man who'd made the woman across the table look ten years younger than her age. There was a glowing softness to the attractive redhead that hadn't been there before, and Chris felt helplessly angry over the situation her friend was unwittingly involved in.

"I dropped by to see if you could come out to my place and have a nice gabby lunch with me tomorrow, Chris. I start teaching again on Tuesday. I'm finished at Gertie's as of last night, and I figure we should celebrate the metamorphosis from dance hall to classroom. Can you come?"

"I'll check with Quinn. It should be fine." Chris hesitated briefly, a faint hope stirring. Maybe Anselmo had taken off for parts unknown. Maybe she was mistaken about Liz's feelings for him.

"What about your friend Mario, Liz? How come you're not celebrating with him?" Chris asked baldly.

Liz blushed crimson, and a tender softness veiled her green eyes at the mention of Anselmo. In that instant Chris's heart sank. It took one woman madly in love to recognize the symptoms in another, and Liz was definitely in love.

"Mario had to fly to Los Angeles on business for three days. He'll be back next Tuesday. I just dropped him off at the airport; that's why I want you to come over tomorrow, so you can listen to me babble on and on about him." Her eyes shone like emeralds. "Chris, I can't believe my luck, I can't believe I'd ever meet a man like Mario up here. He's everything I ever dreamed about.''

Feeling like the worst kind of traitor, Chris smiled weakly and mumbled something inane. After all, what evidence did she and Quinn have that Mario was anything other than Liz thought him to be? The man had no criminal record. And there was no way to explain what their suspicions were without revealing Parker's secret.

The whole damn thing was a miserable mess.

It got to be more of a mess when she told Quinn about Liz's invitation later that night.

''That's a great way to find out more about Anselmo,'' Quinn said immediately. ''Try to lead Liz on a bit, get her talking about him if you can. Don't be obvious, but find out where he says he's from, what cover he's using, everything Liz will reveal without getting her suspicious. You don't have to get too personal, of course.''

Chris gaped at him.

In the first place, Quinn didn't seem to have the faintest idea what women talked about among themselves, and she quickly decided not to enlighten him.

In the second place, did he actually believe she was going to pump a friend for information that would eventually break that friend's heart? About this, she was extremely vocal, and a heated argument resulted, the first they'd had since they became lovers.

''It's your duty as a police officer, and Liz will probably be grateful when she finds out what kind of guy she's mixed up with,'' Quinn stated baldly.

''Police officer, hell. Once in a while I'm off duty, and this is one of those times. And Liz, *grateful*? She's more liable to despise me for not being honest when she finds out. Besides, what if we're totally wrong about this? We don't have one shred of real evidence that Anselmo is up to anything. All we've got is conjecture. I refuse to pry and probe and report what a good friend tells me in confidence, Quinn, and that's that,'' she raged. ''You'll just have to find out some other way, because Liz would never forgive me if I did that to her.''

''I'm not asking you to do anything wrong. I just want to find out about this man. And speaking of friends, what about Parker?'' he raged back, eyes narrowed at her in anger. ''Parker's my friend, and this slimy Italian—'' he used an expletive that made Chris wince ''—is driving Parker into an early grave with worry. It's all he talks about. I want to nail this Anselmo or whatever his name really is. I want to see him squirm the way he's making Parker squirm.''

Chris did too, but not at the expense of a friendship she valued. The whole thing was giving her a headache.

''Well, I won't repeat to you what Liz tells me about him, and that's final. She loves him. It would mean betraying a friendship. You'll just have to find out what you want to know some other way,'' she insisted, and Quinn swore viciously.

They slept apart that night, for the first time in a week.

Instead of being a pleasant afternoon, the hours spent with Liz the next day in her cozy house made Chris feel like a spy. The most innocent and natural questions and comments took on a sinister aspect. Chris tried valiantly to change the subject several times, but like all women starry-eyed with love, Liz always returned the conversation to Mario Anselmo.

They shared the fluffy omelet and biscuits Liz had prepared, and then carried their cups of tea to the overstuffed chairs in front of the blazing fireplace. The day was chilly and overcast, and the fire enclosed the cheerful room in a warm and intimate way.

Liz had been listing Mario's virtues ever since she served the salad.

"He grew up on this small villa outside Milan, his mother still lives there as well as his three sisters and their families," she was explaining now. "Mario was married a long time ago, but his wife died and they had no children, so he buried himself for years in his work."

Hating herself, Chris said, "I didn't have time that night we met to find out just what he really does, Liz."

"He works for a large insurance firm. I'm not exactly certain what the job entails, because he's said it's pretty confidential. Besides, Mario's looking for a new direction in his life just now."

I'll just bet he is. Inside her head, Chris could hear a small, cynical voice making comments on the innocently damaging things Liz was revealing.

"Does he like it here in Dawson?" Chris hated herself for probing, but she couldn't resist.

"He loves it. He's read all about the gold rush, and he spends hours talking to people like Windy Ike over at Gertie's, and old prospectors that come into town for a few days."

Poor Parker. This guy was probably an underworld expert at blackmail.

Liz curled her feet up under her and stared dreamily into the fire, and the blaze made her hair into a flaming halo.

"I feel as if I'm living in a fairy tale, Chris. Mario is so romantic, so…caring with me. Nobody's ever spoiled me the way he does. He treats me like a Dresden doll, me, with my chapped hands and knotty muscles from building this house."

"Has, umm, has he said anything about staying up here? I just, well, I'd feel so awful if you ended up getting hurt. I mean, you haven't known him very long at all."

Liz smiled fondly. "You're worried that he's going to walk off and leave me, you mean? It won't happen, Chris. I'm thirty-four, and I've had casual affairs before. This one's different, Mario's different. We read the same books and like the same music. We don't need to go anywhere to have a good time, just sit here and talk. Oh, Chris, we're so in love. I never dreamed I'd fall in love like a teenager again, and I have. I even sound like one, self-centered and going on about my man. Gad, I must be boring you silly. Forgive me, tell me what's happening in your life, how you're doing with Quinn. I saw the piece in the paper about that guy you saved from drowning, the whole town's still talking about it.…"

They chatted for another hour before Chris had to leave, and as she waved back Liz was standing alone in the yard of the isolated farm. Chris ached for Liz and her bright dreams, but she was afraid there was no way to avoid the inevitable. Liz was going to be hurt, and there was nothing Chris could do to avert it.

She drove back to town through the eerie dusk, puzzling over why love seemed to bring nothing but sorrow to so many people.

Abe Schultz had loved deeply and lost his child and his wife and his will to live.

The mess Parker Jameson was in this minute had started with love for a beautiful Hawaiian woman.

As a result of that tragic love, Liz was now having her serene life turned upside down by an Italian crook she herself loved.

Chris glanced in the rearview mirror at her own thoughtful blue eyes, and saw the question she'd never dared ask herself in the few short days since she and Quinn had become lovers.

What would their destiny hold?

Quinn said he adored her, he lavished praise and attention on every inch of her body, he held her as if loath to ever let her go, but he hadn't once said that he loved her.

Perhaps that was the reason she'd never admitted her own love for him, although she was certain of it.

Well, it was early days for such proclamations, Chris told herself stoutly. They'd be together all winter, so there was time for their relationship to grow—providing they didn't spend too much time arguing and being angry the way they had yesterday, and too little time making love, the way they had last night.

Chris steered absently up a hill, lost in her reflections, and when she reached the top and glanced at the sky, her foot hit the brake and the car skidded to a stop in the gravel.

She'd heard descriptions of the Northern Lights, read technical jargon on what atmospheric conditions caused them, but nothing could have prepared her for the experience itself.

Ahead of her the night sky was hung with a shimmering curtain of incandescent radiance—primrose and silver, amber and violet, opal and gold, throbbing, pulsing color that quivered and waved and streamed its way across the polar sky. It was a passionate, silent, overwhelming spectacle that made her feel sad and awed, wild and lonely all at the same time, filled with recognition of one of nature's mysteries. The sight literally sent shivers down her spine.

Slowly, she started the car again.

Wasn't love one of nature's mysteries as well, just as unpredictable and overwhelming as these banners of color. Maybe she ought to stop trying to analyze love, and simply appreciate it the way nature forced appreciation for the aurora.

Perhaps she'd stop at the grocery and pick up the fixings for spaghetti. Quinn loved her spaghetti, and she could tell him his suspicions about Anselmo were well-founded without revealing any details or breaking her trust with Liz.

Maybe she'd better throw in a homemade chocolate cake as well, and the two of them could try to figure out what to do about Parker and Liz and Anselmo.

Before bedtime.

CHAPTER NINE

LATE TUESDAY, Parker Jameson received a phone call from his son Cole, in Vancouver. When Cole hung up, an agitated Parker immediately called Quinn, his usually booming voice a thin whisper of anxiety.

Dr. Cole Jameson had told his father he was arriving in Dawson as soon as he could cancel his office appointments and book a flight, probably on Thursday afternoon. It seemed he'd had a visit from a man named Mario Anselmo, and there were important matters he needed to talk over with Parker right away. And no, they weren't things he cared to discuss over the phone.

"It's the uncertainty of it, Quinn, of not knowing exactly what this Anselmo's up to. It's near killing me," Parker confessed. "I'd like to take a gun after this Anselmo, and just…" Quinn did his best to calm the old man, but Parker was near hysteria. Couldn't Quinn figure out a way to get Anselmo out in the open so Parker knew what he was up against before Cole arrived?

Quinn and Chris talked it over half the night, and the plan they finally decided on was, Chris liked to think, brilliant, simple and forthright.

She was honest enough to admit the entire thing was also Quinn's idea.

"Let's arrange to get the principal players in this

charade into my office in the morning and find out exactly what's going on by simply asking direct questions," he suggested. "Liz told you Anselmo was due back Tuesday. That's today. I'll phone him at the hotel and tell him to get his ass over here first thing in the morning. That may make him decide to leave town in a hurry, but he also may try to brazen it out. One way or the other, we'll get a feeling for what the hell is going down."

"Can I tell Liz to come, too?" Chris inquired, without much hope, and as she'd expected he would, Quinn flatly refused.

"Parker believes our Italian friend is prying into his life. That's not exactly a criminal matter, but I'll stretch the rules a bit on it. Affairs of the heart are definitely not a police matter unless the lovers become violent. There's absolutely no reason to include Liz, it's an invasion of Parker's privacy."

Chris felt Liz had a right to know what was going on too, and she opened her mouth to argue, but after a moment's reflection, she realized he was right. Damnation, why did Quinn have to be right so often? It was infuriating.

As far as violence and matters of the heart were concerned, there was liable to be plenty of cause for involvement in the near future. Liz might have a temper to match that red hair.

At ten the next morning they arrived, an impeccably tailored Mario Anselmo, and a bedraggled Parker Jameson. Parker was a shadow of the robust man Chris had met when she first arrived in Dawson. As well as looking unkempt, Parker now looked as if he hadn't slept in days, and Chris was shocked at the change in his appearance and manner. Quinn ushered them both into his office.

"Constable, honey, should I bring you all coffee?" Maisie said in an eager whisper when Chris came out for another chair. Maisie had watched the two men file in and she was obviously consumed with curiosity about what was going on.

"No, thanks anyhow, Maisie," Chris replied. She did her best to appear calm, but she could feel animosity and anger building against Anselmo as she carried a spare chair into the cramped office and firmly shut the door. He'd actually held out his hand to greet poor old Parker a few moments before, and it seemed the action of a cold and callous man. You didn't shake hands with someone you were bent on destroying, Chris thought righteously. Parker had glared balefully at the younger man and ignored the extended hand, and Chris had silently applauded him.

Quinn, seated behind his littered desk, turned eyes of cold black granite on Anselmo as soon as Chris sat down.

"Mr. Anselmo, I've asked you to come here this morning and I want you to level with us before somebody around here takes against you. With the exception of yourself, we have no secrets in this room. Mr. Jameson feels you've been making intensive inquiries about him the entire time you've been in Dawson, and yesterday he learned you were also in contact with his son in Vancouver. Why, Anselmo?"

Chris was watching Mario closely, and she had to reluctantly admire his composure. One long, elegant leg was crossed over the other, brown-socked ankle on brown-suited knee, and the strikingly handsome bearded face betrayed absolutely nothing of what he was thinking or feeling.

Parker's agitated breathing sounded loud in the room, and as the silence stretched Chris began feeling she was in the presence of the irresistible force—Quinn—and the immovable object—Anselmo. Regardless of what Anselmo's game was, he was a brave man to confront Quinn so impassively. Chris hoped Quinn never leveled that particular, narrow-eyed icy glare on her.

Quinn's voice was lethal.

"An explanation, Anselmo, or we sit here the rest of the day."

"Could this conversation perhaps be delayed one more day, until Mr. Jameson's son is present?" Anselmo asked quietly.

Parker shook his head, a near-desperate look on his flushed face. "I want to know, right now, just what the hell is going on. What right did you have to go and see Cole, anyway?" he demanded fiercely, clutching the arms of his chair with both white-knuckled hands and leaning toward Anselmo as if he would leap at him any moment.

A small frown came and went on Mario's handsome features, and Chris thought she detected warmth in the dark brown eyes.

"It's unfortunate I've had to cause you any distress, Mr. Jameson. You understand, however, I have a job to do. Let me first explain exactly who I am." He reached into the inside breast pocket of his suit jacket and extracted a leather folder, opened it and handed a business card from inside to Parker. Parker looked at it uncomprehendingly and handed it to Quinn.

"As you can see, I work for a company known as Invicta International. I was not being entirely dishonest when I said I was an insurance investigator." He turned the voltage of his smile on Chris for a moment, and she silently sympathized with Liz. Whatever else he was, Mario was one hunk of a man.

"Invicta is a private investigation firm. We specialize in insurance work," he explained. "At the moment, I'm retained by the Hawaiian law firm of Tanaka and Company, with the purpose of locating the heir to a rather large estate."

Parker slumped in his chair at the mention of Hawaii, and Mario glanced from Parker over to Quinn. "Finding Mr. Jameson wasn't exactly the easiest job I've ever undertaken. The trail was pretty cold."

Now Parker's face was chalk-white, and Chris felt like putting her arms around him and patting his back when he cleared his throat and said with pathetic bravado, "Well, you got me, so now what're you going to do to me?"

Anselmo frowned and looked slightly confused.

"Do to you, Mr. Jameson?" His expression changed and he said offhandedly, "Oh, that old abduction warrant, of course. Why, in relation to that, nothing whatsoever. All the concerned parties are now deceased, you see. Your former father-in-law died eleven years ago, and last January, his wife died as well, after years of ill health. The estate was left entirely to their grandson, Cole Jameson, and that is what posed a problem. In order to locate him, I had to find you first, Mr. Jameson. You were the key to locating your son. Because of the amount of the inheritance, there was a need for extreme caution. I had to be absolutely certain I had the right individual before revealing my purpose. I apologize if my inquiries have caused you any embarrassment, but I'm sure you understand now why there was need for circumspection." A wry grin came and went behind his trim mustache. "I'm afraid I had no idea how protective the residents of Dawson are about any information regarding one of their own."

Parker, who'd seemed dazed up till now, suddenly showed animation as Anselmo's words sank in. He sat up straighter.

"You're telling me that Cole's going to get a chunk of money from that sugar estate my in-laws owned?"

Anselmo smiled widely and nodded with obvious satisfaction.

"He certainly is. A very substantial amount, I might add."

Parker leaped to his feet, startling everyone. There was a fierce scowl on his bearded face and his chin tilted aggressively toward Anselmo.

"Well, you go back there and tell those fancy lawyers that Cole doesn't need or want their stinking money," he bellowed at the top of his considerable lungs. "It never brought my in-laws a moment's happiness. It was because of that money they figured I wasn't good enough for their daughter. They never saw how much we loved each other, how happy we were together. Love didn't matter to those people, only money did. Damnation, if I hadn't gotten Cole out of there when I did, them and their money would have ruined the kid." Parker's face was crimson and he was visibly shaking as he wagged a finger an inch under Mario's nose. "He's a doctor, my boy. Him and I both worked hard to get him an education, we never took any handouts from anyone, and we're not starting now. You go tell 'em that from me, you hear?''

With that, Parker stomped to the office door and swung it open so fast he nearly knocked Maisie flying. She'd obviously been caught hovering outside the door, listening to the whole confrontation. Instead of being embarrassed, she drew herself up to her plump height, shoved her oversize glasses up her nose and said loudly, ''You tell 'em, Parker. Money's the root of all evil, I always say.''

Parker stormed past her without a word, and they heard the outer door slam behind him. Maisie gave the room a cheery grin and a nod, and said chattily to Chris, ''Constable, honey, I was just coming to tell you Mr. Rabowski's here again. He said Corporal Quinn talked to him about becoming an auxiliary, told him to come by and fill out some papers.''

Quinn had discussed the plan with Chris, but darn Stefan anyhow for choosing this moment to appear. Chris hated to leave now. With Parker gone, she intended to ask Mario point-blank what his intentions were concerning Liz. Had he simply used her friend as a cover and a source of information? Chris was determined to find out.

Quinn probably suspected as much, because there was thinly disguised relief on his face as he explained blandly, ''Those forms, Chris. They're necessary if we're going to make Rabowski an auxiliary. Try and explain to him as you go along what the questions are and what they mean.'' He nodded in dismissal, graciously excusing her and getting up to hold the door and then shutting it with a pointed glare at Maisie when Chris reluctantly exited.

Stefan sprang up when Chris appeared, his black hair slicked down wetly and his flannel shirt buttoned tightly around his muscular neck.

Stefan was like a happy, affectionate puppy dog when he was around Chris. Her impatience faded when his strong, carefully shaved face split into a wide grin. He was always so good-natured…as long as he stayed off the booze. Drinking turned Stefan into the same heedless madman he'd been the day he drove off the road and into the river.

"Hullo, Constable Christine Johnstone."

Stefan was probably the only person in town who called her by her full, proper name. "Iss not beeyootiful day, yes?"

Chris glanced outside. It was gray and dreary.

"Hi, Stefan. You're right, it's not a beautiful day, it's supposed to snow, of all things. Come over here to the counter and we'll fill out these forms."

The process took more than an hour. There were requisitions for uniforms, requests for security clearance, forms for medical coverage. Fortunately, Quinn had already done a quiet investigation and found that Stefan was a legal, landed immigrant. Stefan was bursting with pride at the thought of becoming an auxiliary policeman, and Chris had a suspicion that soon his adoration of her would be transferred healthily to love for his volunteer work.

She fervently hoped so. She kept pointedly reminding him that he had a much better chance of being accepted eventually as a recruit in the RCMP if he remained single, and his proposals to her had tapered off considerably.

As she helped Stefan, the murmur of conversation came steadily, if unintelligibly, from the direction of

Quinn's office, and twice the sound of hearty male laughter surprised Chris. It seemed Mario Anselmo and Quinn had stopped glaring at each other and decided to become friends. *If that isn't just like men,* she fumed. Let them find out they were on the same side of the fence and they instantly formed an old boys' club. What did it matter if Liz ended up getting her heart broken?

Chris and Stefan were just finishing the last form when Quinn's office door opened and the two men came out, relaxed smiles on both their faces. Quinn shook Mario's hand firmly, and Mario walked over and took Chris's hand in both of his, his charm very much in evidence.

"It's been an interesting morning, Chris. The RCMP is fortunate to have such a beautiful woman in its ranks."

Quinn looked much less friendly all of a sudden, and Stefan was positively bristling with anger when Mario strolled out of the building.

When she finally got rid of Stefan, Chris couldn't help saying to Quinn, "Well, you and our Italian friend certainly hit if off. I'm afraid I still don't entirely trust him. Did he happen to mention whether or not he planned to have a little talk with Liz about who he really is?"

Quinn gave her a quelling glance, looking pointedly over at Maisie, but Maisie said brightly, "That's okay, I heard everything that was going on, Corporal. Don't worry about me. Boy, that Italian guy's some smoothie, huh? He could park his shoes under my bed any time he wanted."

Quinn gave Maisie a long, silent stare, and Maisie colored and started typing feverishly.

"We'll be having lunch back in the kitchen if we're needed," he said sternly, and Chris followed him down the hallway.

She rounded the corner and let out a squeak of surprise when he caught her in his arms and kissed her nearly breathless.

"What was that for?" she said, sighing as he reluctantly released her. They'd agreed to keep their private feelings under control during their working hours, and till now Quinn had been scrupulous about their deal.

He frowned at her, loving the sparkle his kisses had brought to her bright sapphire eyes, the sudden rosy flush high on her cheeks.

"That was just in case you had any fantasies about Anselmo's shoes, the way Maisie has," he growled. "I saw the way he looked at you."

"For heaven's sake, Quinn, he was only being polite," she chided, but privately she thought it did him some good to be a little jealous. They began making lunch at the counter.

"Did he mention Liz at all?" she prodded, and Quinn looked up from buttering slices of bread, an expression of mock horror on his face.

"You don't really think I'd reveal the confidence of a friend, do you?"

Chris recognized her own lines being parroted back to her and had the grace to flush before she pressured him.

"C'mon, you sure didn't think he was any friend three hours ago. Tell me what you talked about, what you think about him. I need to know if he's just fooling around with Liz or if he's serious. He wasn't entirely honest with her, you know." She was opening a tin of tuna and mixing in mayonnaise and chopped onions.

"I think he's honest enough, but what does one man know about another's intentions when it comes to women? Men don't reveal their feelings in that area even to their best friends, never mind to someone they've only just met." Quinn spread matched slices heavily with butter and slapped filling between them, making Chris wince when he pressed the top slice down with heavy-handed zeal.

"I'd guess he's a brilliant investigator," Quinn went on, "probably one of the best. He started out with the Italian Federal Police, was seconded to Interpol, worked for them nine years and then resigned to go with Invicta International." Quinn felt quite proud of what he'd learned in such a short conversation. He slapped the sandwiches on a plate, and she carried them over to the table.

"He's forty-six, born in July. He grew up on a villa outside Milan, he has three sisters, he's a widower with no children and he's romantic. He's thinking of changing his life-style to something much simpler in the near future, or at least that's what he says, and what Liz believes," Chris related calmly, and Quinn's eyebrows rose to his hairline.

"Police forces should have a policy of hiring only women in their Investigations branch," he mused. "How the hell did you find all that out so quickly?"

"From Liz. Women talk about the important things when they're together."

"Hmm." Quinn chewed his sandwich and wondered a trifle uneasily just what fascinating details Liz had learned about him in the course of conversation.

"Nothing. She doesn't even know yet that we're

lovers," Chris said with a mischievous grin, surprising him so he stopped in midbite to stare at her.

"How did you..."

"Easy. Sometimes I can read your mind."

"You have no idea how comforting knowing that is to me," he said weakly.

She wrinkled her nose at him and blew him a kiss.

CHRIS DIDN'T HEAR from Liz at all that day or the next, and she worried about her friend. She tried several times to contact her, but Liz was never available. It was one thing to fall in love with an insurance man. It was quite another to find out you'd been a source of information for a high-profile private eye.

It had begun to snow by the weekend, and the gentle white flakes fell steadily for two days and a night, covering the town in a white and silent mantle.

Quinn announced that Cole Jameson had arrived on Friday, and that he and Parker were having heated discussions about the inheritance. Parker was adamant about Cole refusing it, and Cole felt all the money should go to his father.

Mario Anselmo left abruptly on Tuesday's flight to Whitehorse, and Chris drove carefully over the icy roads to the school on Wednesday afternoon to see if Liz wanted to come for tea after classes and fill her in on what the heck was going on.

Liz came hurrying over to the patrol car, wrapped in a fur-lined parka the same green as her eyes. Today, though, her eyes didn't have their usual vivacious shine, and she looked pale and drawn.

"Tea sounds great. Got any brandy?" she inquired. She was unnaturally quiet as they drove together to the office.

She stayed quiet while Chris made them each a cup of tea and sliced and spread cream cheese on the fresh bagels Quinn had proudly presented her with that morning.

"These are scrumptious. I didn't know the bakery made anything like this," Liz commented, spreading jam on one.

"They didn't before. They hired a new baker. Remember the baby girl Quinn and I delivered? Well, these bagels are gifts from the new father. He's working at the place now. Every morning this week, José Condura's sent over a batch of something scrumptious. If he doesn't quit it, I'm going to need to join Weight Watchers before Christmas. And guess what they've named that poor little girl?" Chris paused for dramatic effect. "Quintina Christina Marisa Condura, after Quinn and me and the mother."

"Hope the kid turns out to be a good speller. What does Quinn think of having a baby named after him?" Liz asked, with a strained facsimile of her usual wide smile.

"He's bursting with pride. He's already got two snapshots of the baby on his desk," Chris confessed. She didn't add that she and Quinn had spent two hilarious hours at the local store, blowing a large portion of their respective checks on baby gifts for Quintina. He'd leaned toward stuffed teddy bears and fluffy pink dresses. They'd both settled on disposable diapers, but Chris had also fallen for and bought miniscule pink and white lacy pajamas, tiny leotards and a pair of the smallest running shoes she'd ever seen. They found an excuse now to drop by the Conduras' trailer at least every second day and hold the sweet-smelling baby.

Liz smiled valiantly, took a sip of her tea and suddenly burst into stormy tears.

"I...I had a miscarriage once, when I was m-marr...married," she choked out, rummaging in her purse for tissues.

Chris put down her own cup and hurried over to put a comforting arm around her friend.

"Gosh, Liz, I had no idea, I'd never have gone on about the baby if I'd known," she apologized.

Liz found a tissue and blew her nose hard.

"Don't be silly; it's not that at all. That happened years ago. Oh, Chris, everything makes me cry these days. You must know Mario's left town," she said wearily. "We had a terrible fight, and of course you know the whole story by now, Mario told me he'd talked to you and Quinn. He wasn't what he said, he was here looking for Parker, and I realized why he'd been talking to everybody at Gertie's. I just felt terribly used, like some kind of stupid traitor, and the worst part is I...still...love...him." The final words were a wail of misery, and Chris went for the box of tissues on the cupboard.

"He kept saying it was his job, that he hadn't really lied to me about anything, but he didn't tell me the whole truth either. So now I don't know what to believe about the rest of the things he said, about...about l-loving me. I lost my temper, and he kept insisting that I simply pack and go away with him to Los Angeles, he kept saying he'd prove how much he loved me, but he had to get back because of some emergency or another, and he got in a towering rage when I wouldn't go. And then he had to leave before I calmed down enough to talk, because with the snow there might not have been another plane out of here for a week.''

It was just about what Chris had imagined would occur, and her heart ached for Liz.

"So now what are you going to do?" she queried softly when Liz had calmed down and they each had fresh, hot cups of tea.

Liz shrugged despondently.

"Dig in for the winter and nurse my wounds, I guess. One thing being older does for you is teach you that nobody really dies of a broken heart. You just lose all your friends, boring them with the details." She made a valiant effort at a smile and a change of subject. "Now show me that bilious green room of yours and let's see if we can figure out what color would make it pleasantly unisex."

Chris had asked Liz to help her redecorate weeks before, and as she led the way past the cells and to the single person's quarters, she realized guiltily that the room's color had stopped being an annoyance: Chris hardly slept down there anymore.

Her nights were spent upstairs. In Quinn's arms, the walls could be purple with blue spots and she wouldn't notice.

Liz followed her into the bedroom, and after the first glance she shuddered dramatically.

"Quinn actually chose this shade? That man has to be color-blind. Now what we can do is this...."

"...AND LIZ SAYS for sure you're color-blind, painting the rooms that green. Whatever made you do it, Quinn?"

It was 2:00 a.m., and Chris had been on town patrol all evening. When the snow increased about midnight, and the streets of Dawson had begun to resemble a deserted movie set between scenes, she'd dropped Stefan at his boardinghouse and hurried home to Quinn.

He'd been hunched over the kitchen table as he was so often these evenings, working on the outline of his novel, and the way his dark eyes lighted when she came in warmed her heart.

Wickedly, she'd also warmed her icy hands on the furred and heated skin of his belly and chest, worming her way unexpectedly under his shirt and making him wince and threaten delicious punishment.

They'd showered together, and together soared to some wild place inhabited only by them. Mindlessly, consumed with each other, they tormented and teased and explored, and then fulfilled the appetite each aroused skillfully in the other, until at last they were sated and at peace.

"Cuddle me," Chris always demanded after their lovemaking, wriggling as close to him as she could get. Then, flush against her lover's damp body, she talked on and on in a sleepy monotone, confiding all that the day had held, her thoughts and doubts and triumphs and defeats. Quinn would know the instant her breathing changed and sleep stole over her.

She wasn't sleeping now, and he murmured in mock outrage, "That's slander. I'm not color-blind at all." He held her close and secure against him. "I just never thought walls mattered much until you came along and reeducated me. Besides, Gordon down at the hardware had that paint on sale."

Her soft giggle was a palpable thing, with his arm across her breasts locking her to him.

The more he was with Chris, the more he found

himself forced to notice things that he'd never given much thought to before.

There were the small things, like paint and table-cloths and plants.

He'd grown up in a womanless house, taught to be neat but totally ignorant of the subtle womanly touches that made a difference to how a man felt about the space he lived in. When he joined the force, one set of billeted quarters followed the next, and he kept each dreary room in the exact order he'd been taught in training, never adding much in the way of personal possessions.

This room where they lay now was a good example. It was still basically the way all the others had been. His Stetson and boots were on the shelf over the bed, his rifle suspended on hooks underneath, his red serge dress uniform hung on a hook behind the rifle. Against the foot of the bed was his traveling trunk.

Even here, however, Chris was leaving her mark. Her hairbrush and a bottle of pink moisture cream sat on his dresser, a lacy peignoir hung rakishly on the doorknob, her wispy panties and bra lay strewn on the carpet where he'd tossed them earlier.

But she hadn't made any real changes up here as yet, not the way she had in the rest of their living quarters.

At first, Chris's colorful posters and plants, the addition of cheerful yellow curtains at the kitchen windows, the general female clutter she strewed everywhere while insisting at the same time that the kitchen utensils be kept hospital clean—these things bothered him. He understood only his own way of keeping house. He'd never had things around simply because they were pleasing to the senses.

Gradually, he found the color and texture she added to their living area made it more comfortable, although he never got used to washing up while there were still clean dishes available. But he found himself noticing when a plant grew a new leaf, enjoying the splash of color the gay throw and several yellow and blue pillows made on the old sofa. In his rare leisure time, he basked in the warmth and coziness of surroundings that had been utilitarian, dreary and gray.

Even his diet changed because of her. He ate at home much more often than he ever had before, trying foods he'd never thought of trying, simply because she made them.

Salads, he mused, as her body relinquished its last bit of awareness and her breathing assumed the deep and even rhythm of sleep. He'd never bothered going to all that trouble, but Chris was big on salads. And muffins. She made muffins a lot.

Those were the small changes. It was the larger ones, the ones inside of Quinn, that were far more disturbing to him.

He was an excessively private man, a person who'd mastered the art of drawing others into revealing themselves while he listened and said little.

Chris wouldn't stand for that. She prodded and poked and asked questions, and he forgot he didn't like talking about himself.

First he'd told her about his years of policing, then about his lonely childhood, and finally, haltingly, he'd told her about his dreams, the books he longed to write, the characters he'd created in his mind. And she kept at him until he'd actually made a beginning of the novel, until he'd developed an outline of a plot. For the first time he was daring to try to write his people down, to make them come alive on paper the way they were in his head.

All because of Chris.

She'd wriggled herself under his skin in a manner no one, male or female, had ever managed to do before, and lying here quietly with her sleeping in his arms, Quinn was frightened.

He wasn't sure—what did he have to compare this with?—but he suspected he was falling in love with her.

He corrected that as the arm pillowing her curly head slowly went numb.

In the daytime, he only suspected he loved her.

In the dark of night, holding her like this while she slept, inhaling the fragrance of her, aware of the incredible softness of the body pressed so trustingly against his own, he knew beyond any shadow of doubt that he loved her.

Physically, his unending need for her amazed him. He'd always been a lusty man, but with Chris his body seemed insatiable.

She'd also taught him other ways of needing.

She made him laugh, and she made him so angry at times he felt like strangling her, but she also had ways of making him proud or protective or joyful.

When he was a young man, he'd dreamed of finding a woman like Chris. Somewhere along the way, he'd stopped dreaming, and ironically, now that he was no longer young, she'd found him, and Quinn was afraid.

He was afraid of hurting her, and he was afraid of losing her.

In his experience, the things a man cared most about in life were the very things fate chose to take away.

He was a burned-out small-town cop, he told himself, and Dawson or some forgotten town like it was as far as he would go in the RCMP.

She was a starry-eyed ambitious career officer, marking time in Dawson until bigger things came along, and all the love in the world didn't make up for the lure of ambition and success to someone like Chris.

Sooner or later, their two paths would prove incompatible, because he would be a detriment to her progress through the RCMP ranks. He understood the rules.

But tonight, and last night, and the one before that, he'd kept on shoving those fears out of his mind, because he'd have sold what was left of his soul to the highest bidder for one more night spent loving her, one more day spent arguing with her, one more hour drying dishes for her in the kitchen with her plants and posters and tablecloths.

Chris Johnstone, I love you, he whispered despairingly, soundlessly, into her sweet-smelling hair, and she stirred and burrowed deeper into his embrace.

Outside the window, the snow came drifting down and the arctic darkness took a firmer grasp on the land.

CHAPTER TEN

WINTER BROUGHT increasing periods of sunless twilight, but Chris found it also brought peace to the detachment. There was more leisure time for her and for Quinn. Instead of enforcing the law, they seemed instead to be in partnership with the other year-round residents of Dawson, battling the rigors of the environment as a team.

As the days shortened, and weeks passed, the weather became a force to be reckoned with.

In September, there were still flashbacks of warmer weather, but by October the snow cover was deep, and it was definitely winter. By November, stars shone dazzlingly bright well into late morning and appeared again by early afternoon. The sun was visible for three hours, and then two, and then gradually less and less as the year wound down.

Chris, expecting a sort of imprisonment from winter, found herself surprised and delighted at the wealth of things there were to do outdoors. As long as there wasn't a blizzard blowing, she and Quinn spent part of each day outside.

Quinn taught her to snowshoe and cross-country ski.

He taught her to operate one of the two snowmobiles belonging to the detachment, and within two hours she could whip it along a trail as well as he could.

"It's not natural for a woman to be so mechanical," he grumbled.

"Don't pout, you're getting really good in the kitchen," Chris soothed.

Snowmobiling soon became her favorite outdoor pastime. The feeling of skimming along at top speed, wind tearing at her parka and white world flying past like a speeded-up movie entranced her.

Winter deepened, and Chris was shiveringly appalled at how cold it could be.

At first the average temperature was a chilly eight to twenty below. In November, it began to drop frequently to thirty, occasionally to forty and, twice to fifty degrees below zero.

Fifty below, Chris decided in disgust, was ludicrous.

The heating system in the detachment building lost the struggle to maintain comfortable warmth, and Chris's fingers and toes were cold all the time. People stayed home except for urgent errands. Schools closed down, and the town hibernated.

Clothing became a major issue, and for the first time in her life, Chris found herself craving fatty foods.

Getting dressed for work in the morning, she had always started with a feminine layer of silky lingerie to offset the tailored unisex look of her uniform. She'd slide into pale peach or blue satin panties and bra, or a slithery one-piece teddy, and then she'd cover the frothy underwear demurely with khaki shirts and navy-blue trousers.

The contrast never failed to drive Quinn quite wild when he undressed her.

Now, however, dressing and undressing became a time-consuming affair, and although the lingerie next to her body was still pastel-shaded and delicate, Chris found herself adding—and Quinn doggedly removing—layer after layer of clothing.

Indoors, she wore long cotton underwear, a police shirt, wool whipcord trousers, wool socks, issue oxfords and, topping all that off, a thick wool cardigan.

If she was going out, Chris substituted heavier wool underwear, a second pair of double-thick knee-high wool socks, an eiderdown vest, and then one of two specially designed issue parkas. One was quite ordinary, warm and anything but exciting, designed for everyday wear.

She fell in love with the other the instant she received it.

It was a native-made trail parka for traveling, a one-piece over-the-head pull-on garment of white feltlike material inside a navy waterproof and windproof covering, with wolverine fur trim around the hood and cuffs. The garment reached low on her thighs, and to Chris's delight, a decorative border of brightly colored native fabric art was added several inches above the bottom hem. She pulled on felt booties, and then tucked her pant bottoms into mukluks, caribou-skin moccasin bottoms with a calf-high canvas top lined in eiderdown, cross-tied around the ankles and calves with thick leather thongs. Bright red wool pom-poms on the ends of the thongs bounced cheerfully with every step.

On her hands, she wore gray wool mitts inside another pair made of leather. On her head was the traditional RCMP blackish-brown muskrat fur hat with earflaps that folded down.

To Chris, this outfit was romantic and terribly exotic, and she adored it.

"If only I had a dog team, I'd feel like a member of an expedition heading for the Pole," she told Quinn longingly, the first time she got on all of the ensemble in the proper order.

Quinn studied her, a wide grin on his face and a fond twinkle in his eye as he admired the way the soft fur framed her piquant features.

"You look a little plump," he teased, leering wickedly at her rotund outline. Then he insisted on taking her picture so she could send copies to her family.

"I'll borrow a dog team one day soon and you can learn firsthand why almost everybody prefers snow machines," he promised.

He did, early one morning late in November. In a high state of excitement, Chris hurried into her trail costume and outside to view the five-dog team and the picturesque carryall Quinn had borrowed for the day.

It was a scene straight out of a movie. The dogs were huskies, smaller than she'd thought they'd be, but beautiful animals, barking and snapping at one another in their traces, obviously eager to be off down the trail.

Enormous and darkly handsome in his native parka, with frost beginning to form on the edges of his mustache, Quinn looked like every photo ever taken of the northern Mountie.

"Why would anyone prefer the noise and gas fumes of a snow machine over a beautiful dog team like this?" Chris asked virtuously as she helped

Quinn straighten the carryall and the traces. She was going to ride in the carryall for the first little while, and Quinn would balance on the runners behind. Then she would get the chance to drive the team, he promised.

"You're not really going to use that whip, are you?" she demanded anxiously. "These dogs are so sweet."

Actually, several of them looked downright vicious, but Chris felt full of generosity toward the brave, strong animals.

Quinn gave her a knowing look and laughed. "I'm going to, but you don't have to," he assured her, and she silently vowed that she certainly wouldn't. Men and women had such vastly different methods of handling things.

"Muuush, you huskies," he roared at the team for her benefit. And, in a welter of flying snow and barking dogs, they were off, the animals pulling with a vengeance and the carryall gliding smoothly along the snowy path out of town.

Chris felt as if she was part of an illustration on a Christmas card.

They'd hardly gone five hundred yards, however, when several of the dogs slowed and then squatted, one after another, obeying nature's call. The others didn't seem aware of what was going on, and pulled the carryall right through the mess.

Quinn stopped, and Chris got off.

"If this stuff freezes, it gets too hard to pull," he explained. They cleaned the runners.

"Do they always do this?" Chris asked, wrinkling her nose in disgust.

"Always," Quinn said shortly.

"Somebody should tell them to go before they leave home."

When they were ready to begin again, the intricate network of traces was hopelessly tangled, and it took a good ten minutes to straighten them out. The dogs snarled and barked and fought through the procedure, and Quinn whacked them with his whip before they'd behave enough to pull again.

Chris bit her lip and forgave him. The dogs were really being naughty, and she felt a bit out of sorts with them herself.

On the trail once more, she noticed one of the dogs looking back at Quinn every few seconds, and thought how cute he looked, when Quinn suddenly landed the animal a crack across his backside with the whip.

Chris was outraged.

"Why'd you hit that nice friendly one?" she roared at him.

"Watch him closely," Quinn ordered, and when she did, Chris could see that the dog wasn't really pulling at all. He was cleverly pretending, and gauging Quinn's reactions.

When they were finally out of sight of Dawson, Quinn slowed the team and handed it over to Chris. She pointedly refused the whip.

"Muuush," she roared, and three of the dogs yawned and sat down. Two others instantly started a fight that took Quinn and Chris five minutes to break up.

The traces were hopelessly tangled.

The dogs wouldn't run in a straight line when she did finally get them started. She silently accepted the whip when Quinn handed it to her, and after nearly taking her eye out with the thing, she quickly learned how to use it.

For the next hour, they jerked along in fits and starts, and every second of the time, Chris worked.

If one dog wasn't slacking, another was. The animals were diabolically clever at guessing how much they could get away with before she noticed. It was impossible to guess whether they were actually as tired as they acted, or just putting her on.

By the time she stopped so they could eat the lunch she'd packed, she was fed up to the teeth with driving dogs. She handed the whole mess back to Quinn after lunch, and found she had to run alongside the carryall if they were going to reach Dawson before Christmas. When she tried to ride, they slowed to a pathetic snail's pace and panted and grunted unbearably.

When they arrived back in Dawson three endless hours later, she felt like embracing the shiny snow machine in the garage and feeding the despicable sled dogs a good dose of arsenic.

Quinn had never enjoyed a day so much or laughed as hard in his entire time in the Arctic. At Chris's insistence, he explained the reason for the problems they'd encountered.

"In the days when dogs were the only method of travel, sled dogs were accustomed to working hard, existing on a meager ration of one frozen fish a day on the trail. Today, they're a novelty. There's still a few good working teams around, but basically the dogs are like spoiled children these days. They just aren't used enough to toughen to the work, and they don't like it."

Neither did Chris. The dog fiasco made her endlessly grateful for snow machines, and as often as she could, she pulled on her trail parka and mounted her mechanical steed.

It became a ritual to ride the creekbed trail out every Saturday afternoon to visit Liz. Chris had long ago confided in Liz about her relationship with Quinn, and the two women spent delicious hours discussing men and clothes, and men and decorating, and men and life.

On a particularly gray Saturday afternoon, the two of them sat comfortably close to the blazing fireplace in Liz's open living area, mugs of hot apple cider redolent with cinnamon making the entire room smell delightful.

"I've got to head back pretty soon. Quinn has a fit if I'm later than five or six," Chris said reluctantly, glancing at her watch.

"Take some of this fruit when you go," Liz insisted, gesturing at the latest huge box of fresh California oranges, grapefruit and avocado that Mario had air-freighted to her the previous week. "He must think I'm going to get scurvy. Heck, maybe I am. My skin's starting to break out from all this luxury, anyway."

"Mario must have the air express people believing in miracles," Chris commented, admiring the latest showy bouquet of fresh flowers that also arrived from Los Angeles every week like clockwork. Liz was being courted royally, with a steady stream of phone calls, telegrams, flowers, fruit and perfume. "This stuff costs a small fortune to ship all the way up here."

A small, satisfied grin flitted across Liz's face. "I know. It's absolutely sinful, and I love it. Every woman should be spoiled like this once in a lifetime.

I always figured I'd lost out on romance somewhere along the way.''

"Things are okay between Mario and you, then?''

Liz hesitated, and then nodded slowly. "I hope they will be. Everything happened so quickly for us, there wasn't time to stop and think. He says now that this was the last place he ever expected to meet someone he cared about, and I'd certainly given up hoping a guy like him would walk into Gertie's and fall for me. We were both off balance. Even though we're miles apart right now, having time to write long letters and do a lot of thinking is good for both of us. I'm going out to be with him for Christmas holidays, and then he'll come up here in the spring. If we still feel the same way about each other, we'll get married next summer.''

Chris was delighted for Liz, but a feeling of anxious foreboding washed over her when she compared Liz's love affair with hers and Quinn's. She and her own seemed to exist only in the present, and nothing was ever discussed about a future. She explained this to Liz. "I try and pretend spring won't ever come,'' she admitted slowly. "I'm pretty certain the force will transfer me out of the Arctic before a year is up.''

The trial and the Andollini threats were becoming a dim memory to Chris. She hardly thought anymore about the reasons for her being sent to Dawson, except for the annoyance of still having to communicate with her family through Ottawa. And now, she shuddered at the thought of being separated from Quinn.

"Then what? Will you and Quinn be transferred together if you decide to get married?'' Liz asked.

Chris frowned, an expression of frustration on her windburned features. "We've never talked about any of that. I've tried to get him to open up, to say what he plans, but he gets this closed look on his face and just clams up on me. The truth is, I'm scared to push it. He's so damned stubborn at times.''

"Have you even told him that you love him?" Liz asked softly.

Chris blushed crimson. "Only when we're in the middle of making love. I've never sat him down in the middle of the day and actually discussed it.''

"Well, maybe you ought to. I realize now that there were things I should have asked Mario straight out instead of being so damned polite. If I had, we might have avoided a lot of problems.''

Chris left soon afterward, and as the snow machine bounced and thumped over the rough silver terrain, she pondered Liz's advice.

It was only late afternoon, but the moon was up, and it cast a blue glow. The whine of the motor filled her ears. If she turned the machine off, there would be utter silence for the seconds it took her ears to adjust, and then the eerie far-off howl of wolves and the snapping of ice freezing more firmly beneath her would sound loudly in her ears.

At times like this, she often thought of Abe, of how he'd tried to explain the fascination of the North. There was the loneliness, but at the same time Chris often had a feeling of kinship with nature she'd never experienced before.

When she was nearing Dawson, she saw a dark form racing toward her on another snow machine, and when she was closer, she saw that it was Quinn.

"I was getting worried about you. The wind's rising,'' he called gruffly above the motor noise.

Before falling in love with Quinn, if a male had

acted as if she needed to be taken care of, Chris would have told him in no uncertain terms just how capable she was of taking care of herself.

Quinn's concern made her go soft and tender inside.

Liz was right. She had to tell him how she felt about him.

She needed to hear how he felt about her.

So over a late supper, she did.

She waited until he was finished eating, and when he tilted his chair comfortably back on its rungs and peeled one of the fat oranges Liz had insisted on giving Chris, she drew in a deep breath and said firmly, "Quinn, there's something we need to talk about."

He raised an eyebrow and gave her his affectionate smile. Her nose was red from the wind, and her freckles stood out intriguingly. He popped an orange segment in his mouth and savored the tangy flavor.

"I hope Liz doesn't wear down and fly off to L.A. too soon," he stated. "These are the best oranges I've tasted in years." He swallowed and took another piece. "Talk away, I'm listening."

"You know I'm in love with you, Quinn." She breathed the words, holding his gaze with her own, and his chair hit the floor with a jolt. He dropped the rest of the orange as if he'd been burned, and his expression of stunned disbelief annoyed her as seconds ticked by without a word.

"For heaven's sake, Quinn, you don't have to look so shocked. We've been making love all this time. I just feel we should talk about our relationship out of bed for once, figure out what direction it's going. The winter won't last forever. I'll probably be transferred come spring, I want to know what your plans are."

He ought to have known this was coming.

He had known, but he'd never quite figured out what he'd say when it did.

He looked at her, noting the anxious uncertainty bravely hiding behind the bland expression, and agonized remorse twisted his gut, freezing the lump of food he'd just eaten into an indigestible block.

Chris, a silent voice inside him cried, *what have I done to you?* But he knew the answer, had known it all along.

He simply hadn't been able to make himself face it.

He'd made the worst possible mistake by loving her, by encouraging her to love him. He'd mess up her life if he allowed it to continue, mess up all the ambitious dreams she had for her career.

He tried to get air into his lungs, and then he did the only thing he could think of doing.

He blatantly lied to her, hating himself with every syllable that he uttered.

"Are you asking me what my intentions are, Chris? Hell, I never thought you modern women equated sex and marriage," he grated out brutally, and he had to look away from the shocked hurt in her blue eyes.

"Sex? Sex? Is that all…"

He couldn't let her continue.

"See, Chris," he interrupted, "I thought you understood that I'm not the marrying kind, not a one-woman sort of man. Up here, hell, lots of people shack up for the winter, it's part of being bushed, but there's no point in making it out to be more than what it really is. I like you fine, you know that, but…"

"Shack up for the winter?" The horrified disbelief

in her voice made him feel physically ill. "Is that all I am to you, just a shack-up for the winter, Quinn?"

He swallowed painfully. "Of course not, I just used that to illustrate…"

Her face was red with anger and hurt, her wide eyes stormy and beginning to cloud with tears.

"Don't bother explaining, I get the message. I just never considered myself as a glorified hot water bottle before. It takes a little getting used to." Her voice was trembling, but she refused to fall apart in front of him. Besides, there was something he wasn't admitting, it showed when he met her eyes like that and then looked quickly away.

Chris, God, don't look like that, you're ripping my soul to pieces.

He's lying. I remember that psychologist telling us to watch the pupils of a person's eyes to tell if they're lying or not, and he's lying to me. Why? I know he loves me, every ounce of intuition tells me so. But why doesn't he want to?

She loves me, and I want her so much this is killing me. And if I tell her I do, she'll never give up, never accept the facts. But love isn't enough, it won't be enough when the chance for promotion comes along and she doesn't get it because she's my wife, when a posting she wants goes to somebody else, when she gets passed over time and time again just because she's married to me.… It won't work, and she'll end up hating me. Leaving. She's ambitious, she can't help that, or change it.

Suddenly, they were both on their feet, stormy blue eyes seeking shuttered black, until at last she said flatly, "I don't believe you, Quinn. I know damn well you're in love with me, there's some other reason for what you're doing, and I'm not letting you get away with this garbage, so there." Chris began snatching dishes from the table and stomping across to dump them in the sink.

"I'm simply going to wear you down, Quinn," she warned. "You're not getting out of this that easily. I've got all winter to make you tell me the truth. We're alone here most of the time, so you'll give in by spring."

He gaped at her, and then he roared, "What the hell is it with you, woman? I tell you point-blank what the score is, and all you can say is you don't believe me. What in blazes am I to do to prove it to you, move another woman into my bed?"

Her eyes spit angry sparks. "Go ahead. She'll hit the snowbank three seconds after you try it."

Now his face was as fiery red as hers. "You have to be the most contrary, infuriating, bullheaded female I've ever had the misfortune to meet." He swung toward the stairwell, fist balled at his sides, but the sound of her carefully controlled voice followed him.

"Don't forget determined, Quinn. I'm very determined, you know. And oh, yeah, I cooked tonight, and I have to pick up Stefan for town patrol in half an hour, so it's up to you to wash these dishes," she said sweetly. Then she left the room, ignoring the stream of foul language issuing from the kitchen.

By the time Chris shut the door to her room and collapsed shakily on her bed, he still hadn't used the same curse twice.

Alone, however, her show of bravado vanished and her face screwed into a tearful knot. She pounded her knees with her fists, and as the hot tears rolled down her nose, stinging her chapped skin and soaking into the layers of clothing on her chest, she moaned, "He has to love me, he has to, he has to."

After a few minutes of misery, she sniffed loudly and straightened up, then washed her face and hands at the bathroom sink and tugged off a few of her outer layers, replacing them with her uniform.

Inside her head, she could hear the quiet, confident tones of her mother and the advice Rosemary had always given her headstrong brood of children when their lives weren't going the way they wanted.

"Each of us creates our own reality every day of our lives. All we need to do is visualize whatever it is we want or need, and as long as it's a good desire and we do it confidently enough and often enough, seeing it clearly in our mind's eye from inception to final completion, it will be ours. The law of positive visualization is absolute."

Chris wanted commitment from Quinn. She wanted him as her life's partner. She wanted his life, his ring on her finger, and eventually his children.

She blew her nose, buttoned the final button on her shirt, tucked undershirt, underwear, sweater and top shirt into her trousers, and sat down a bit stiffly on her bed.

I hope you're right, Mom.

Taking a deep breath, Chris closed her eyes and relaxed, then envisioned a mental movie screen a foot in front of her. On it, in brilliant color, she drew wonderful X-rated winter scenes of herself and Quinn in bed, reluctantly moving ahead to a scene of springtime, of Quinn down on one knee proposing to her, of them both in red serge under an arch of crossed lances being married in the summer, and then—she cautiously allowed several years to elapse here—Chris envisioned herself kissing two adorable children goodbye as she went off to work in a staff sergeant's uniform.

Slowly, she allowed the blissful scene to fade. With a satisfied feeling of having done all she could to manipulate fate, she opened her eyes, hauled on her everyday parka and went off to work humming quietly to herself.

Quinn heard her warming up the patrol car in the heated garage, and as soon as she'd backed out and driven off, he headed for the phone in his office. He found Billings's home number and dialed, glancing at his watch.

Ten-fifteen. Past Staff's bedtime.

Well, hauling Billings out of bed didn't bother him one bit.

The cranky, sleep-filled voice that eventually barked into the other end of the receiver illustrated he was correct.

"Quinn here." He had no patience for the usual sparring and he broke into Billings's muttering abruptly, his voice sounding strained even to his own ears.

"Look here, Staff," Quinn began, "that female constable you sent me. She, uh—" Quinn found it necessary to clear his throat "—she isn't working out after all. No fault of hers, you understand, it's just that I'm too old and set in my ways to start changing at this late date."

Every word was an effort. He could see Chris's face in his mind's eye, the betrayed and vulnerable expression in her eyes.

Quinn's stomach cramped painfully, and sweat

broke out on his forehead despite the icy drafts wafting through the building from the increasing wind outside. He shut his eyes, and continued.

"It's difficult in a small detachment working one on one. It would be easier on her if she were posted to a larger place...."

An exclamation of disgust from the receiver made him pause, and Billings snapped, "We appreciate that on a two-man detachment it can be hard with one male, one female, Quinn. We're not totally unaware of your situation up there, you know," he stated pompously. There was a slight pause, and a martyred sigh came over the crackling wire, as if Billings had come to a decision.

"Quinn, what I'm about to tell you is on a strictly need-to-know basis, which is why you weren't told earlier."

Billings paused for effect, and lowered his voice to a confidential level. "Constable Johnstone was deliberately posted to Dawson in an effort to hide her whereabouts for a year or so. You know she was working undercover on that car theft thing, the Andollini case. Well, that was only the tip of the iceberg. She and the other operatives on that investigation uncovered a cesspool of armed robbery, drug dealing, loan-sharking and prostitution, and the evidence they provided was enough to put two of the kingpins, Louis and Frank Andollini, away for a good long stretch." Billings sounded smugly satisfied, as if the investigation had been his personal triumph.

"However," he added after a moment, and now his tone was ominous. "However, Quinn, one of the brothers wasn't convicted, although we know he was just as guilty as the other two. Angelo Andollini is a

free man, and a bitter, vindictive one. There were
strong indications from the underworld that he
planned to retaliate against Johnstone and the others
who worked on that case.''

There was a trace of concern in Billings's tone
now.

''Apparently this wouldn't be the first time the Andollini family has arranged to get rid of witnesses or
to seek revenge. We feel they were successful a few
years back and two of our best young people died.
Therefore, the deputy in charge of ops in Ottawa has
directed that we take maximum precautions in order
to ensure the safety of Constable Johnstone. As you
know, it's almost impossible to do security on a person in a big city, so getting her out of circulation was
the best solution. And really, old boy, what better
isolation can you find than Rory Borealis land?''

Billings's scratchy cackle grated in Quinn's ear.

''So basically,'' Billings summed up briskly, ''it's
out of my control, and I'd say you've got her for
better or worse till next summer. Now, Quinn, that's
the full story, so upward and on, and let's see if we
can avoid any more calls in the middle of the night.''
His tone made it an order. ''Agreed, Corporal?''

Quinn replaced the receiver as if it were breakable,
and a shudder ran from his boots up to the roots of
his hair. His heart was racing and he felt as if he
couldn't get a deep breath into his lungs. He forced
himself to go over what he'd just learned as logically
as possible.

Because of his own knowledge of undercover operations, he didn't question the fact that Billings
hadn't told him all the facts about Chris earlier. He
knew that under rules and regulations, classified ma-

terial in undercover operations was relayed strictly on a need-to-know basis, and until now, he hadn't needed to know.

But unreasonable rage consumed him with the next thought, and he leaped to his feet, sending his chair crashing to the floor.

Chris's life could be in danger.

What the hell were those idiots doing down in O Division, letting her get in that deep, letting a woman like Chris do their undercover work for them?

After a moment, honesty forced him to admit that no one on earth controlled Chris except Chris herself.

Quinn knew the lady he loved, and the knowledge had mostly been gathered the hard way. He'd learned that no one could force her to do something she didn't want to do, or stop her from doing something she decided on.

He'd seen her in tight spots, admired the avid determination that drove her, marveled at the combination of deceptive physical fragility, that peculiar air of innocence combined with incredible mental toughness.

He also knew how vulnerable she was, how feminine, under that tough facade.

He yanked his office door open and began to pace up and down the hallway.

It took a while, but finally he admitted reluctantly that if he were choosing an undercover operative to infiltrate an operation like the Andollinis', he'd have blessed the day Chris came along. She must have been perfect for the job.

It was his love for her that got in the way of his reason.

At least she wasn't in danger here in Dawson, he

consoled himself. Billings was right about Dawson being absolutely safe, especially in the middle of winter. This was Quinn's turf, and he knew what was going on in his town. At the moment, he personally knew every single resident by name and occupation.

The next thought sent him striding into the kitchen, and he yanked open a cupboard and found the bottle of Scotch he kept there. He poured an ounce into a water glass and then added a judicious three inches more and downed half the dose at one swallow.

"You've got her for better or worse till next summer," Billings had said. Hours and days and weeks and months alone in this building with her.

"I'll wear you down," Chris had warned, and he groaned aloud. He didn't for an instant doubt her ability to do that very thing.

He couldn't send her away, and he doubted he could keep on lying the way he had tonight.

She hadn't believed him anyway.

The liquor burned its way down his gullet.

What in God's name was he going to do to keep his hands off her and his love hidden from her for that long, apart from getting and staying dead drunk till spring breakup?

He frowned down at the whiskey bottle. His body was reacting to the generous slug of alcohol, and he thought fleetingly of Abe Schultz. Abe had tried the whiskey route, and it wasn't any solution.

Abe still hadn't moved into his winter quarters in Dawson, either, Quinn pondered. He'd sent Quinn a note with another prospector early in October, saying that he'd be down in November.

It was now the end of November and Abe hadn't

shown up yet, which was typical of Abe but worrying to Quinn.

Maybe the thing to do was get out of here for a couple of days or a week, travel upriver and check on Abe, Quinn considered.

The idea began to have merit.

It would give him time to think, and Chris could handle the detachment easily with Stefan's help. There wasn't a damn thing happening anyhow.

As soon as he'd made the decision, Quinn began the task of packing for the trip. He knew without trying that sleep was impossible, alone in the bed upstairs. The flannel bed sheets held Chris's delicate aroma, the silent reminder of how it felt to hold her, love her, sleep with her locked in his embrace.

He forced himself not to think of her, not to think of the years of his life he'd be without her. He tried to empty his mind of any reminder of her by concentrating on the book he was trying to write instead.

He bundled all his notes and the first few chapters of his novel in a waterproof bag and tucked it into his pack.

When Chris came back shortly after midnight, the wind had died down and the moon rode high and white in the starry sky.

Quinn was all ready to leave.

CHAPTER ELEVEN

"WHERE ARE YOU GOING?"

Chris was stunned to find Quinn dressed for travel, with a small cargo sled packed with extra fuel, sleeping bags, food and a perma stove.

He explained to her about checking on Abe, aware the whole time that it sounded like a flimsy excuse to avoid her.

Chris thought so, too, and in typical Chris fashion she told him so.

"You're just running away from me," she accused furiously after he'd briefed her on everything she needed to know about running the detachment in his absence.

"Damned right I am," he agreed, with a deep sigh.

"Well, I think that's a cowardly thing to do," she snapped. Quinn did his best to ignore her stony glances and accusing glares as he pulled on his trail parka and went out to the garage.

He started the snowmobile, and she ran to the door in time to see him disappear into the darkness.

It was terrible for her to stand and watch the machine's small taillight fade into the gloom.

He didn't even glance back at her or wave. She slammed the door viciously on her way back in, shivering and halfway between a temper tantrum and an orgy of weeping.

Why did she have to fall for such an impossible man? How could he just turn his back and drive away from her like that?

Wasn't she irresistible?

Maybe he didn't love her after all.

IT TOOK QUINN most of the next four hours to reach Abe's cabin, and he was less than a mile away, following the river, when he spotted the frozen body in the snow.

He knew before he rolled the figure over and looked into the peaceful face that it was Abe.

CHRIS WAS OUT on a call when Quinn got back to Dawson late the next afternoon with his grisly burden on the sled behind him.

She pulled into the driveway in the cruiser, got out to open the overhead door to the garage, and felt her heart soar when she spotted the snowmobile abandoned in the middle of the cement floor.

Quinn was home already. He'd reconsidered, he was feeling badly about leaving her that way, he...

She dashed through the door, and stopped short. He was standing in the outer office waiting for her, and Maisie was sobbing loudly into a lace handkerchief.

"Quinn? Maisie? What's the matter, what's wrong?"

He still wore the heavy wool pants and thick checked shirt he'd had on when he left, but something terrible showed in his face. His dark eyes were brooding, red-rimmed and bloodshot, and he seemed not to really see her standing before him.

"I found Abe Schultz dead a mile downriver from

his cabin. I brought his body in,'' he finally said abruptly.

"Abe dead? But what...what happened to him?'' Chris gasped.

"Suicide.'' Quinn said the world softly. "He chose to deliberately freeze to death. He went out walking, no parka or mukluks. There was a note in the cabin for me, along with a letter for his wife. Doc Chambers will do an autopsy when the body thaws.''

Chris knew without asking that either she or Quinn would have to attend that procedure. Without hesitating, she said quietly, "I'll take care of that, Quinn.''

He seemed about to object, and then his shoulders slumped. It was a measure of how much he'd accepted her as his working partner when he said wearily, "I'd appreciate it if you could, Chris.''

"Of course.'' It was the last thing in the world she felt like doing.

But it was one thing she was able to do for the man she loved.

It was also the last thing she could ever do for Abe.

"I've already phoned Beverly Schultz in Vancouver. She's coming up to take him home for burial as soon as she can get a flight out, probably tomorrow sometime. Could you meet her and make the rest of the arrangements?''

Chris nodded dumbly, and he went on in that flat, tonelessly polite voice, "I'll do the sudden-death report. Doc will decide as to an inquest or inquiry. Once that's concluded I'll be heading out again.''

Chris wanted to scream at him in protest.

"I've decided to take part of my annual leave,'' he explained as if it were the most ordinary thing in the world.

"Including traveling time, I'll be gone four weeks," he went on, and at last he met her anguished gaze, but there was no recognition in his look.

"You'll be in charge while I'm gone. I've already cleared it with Billings—my leave forms are in the mail." His glance went through her, past her, to some dark spot on the wall behind.

"That's about it, Constable. Maisie, I'll be here in my office for the next few hours if you need me."

He turned on his heel and shut the office door behind him.

"It's terrible, just terrible, poor old Abe..." Maisie sniffled, and Chris stood immobile, trying to absorb all that had changed. Pain and shock mingled as she shrugged out of her parka and tugged off her boots, and with the rising emotions came an aching need for comfort in Quinn's arms.

She'd only met the gentle Abe once, and still she felt bereft at losing him.

How must Quinn feel? He'd suffered the shock of finding his friend's body, he was obviously hurting badly, and yet he didn't seem to know how to reach out to her for support.

She took several quick steps toward the office door, intent on trying to share his grief and pain, and then she stopped uncertainly, and her confidence ebbed.

What if he didn't want her sympathy? He hadn't been very friendly a minute ago.

But Maisie was here listening, that had to be the reason.

Hadn't he said he was leaving again, as fast as he could? For four weeks. He was running away again.

Four weeks. Her heart sank at the thought. The past two days without him had been as bleak as any she'd ever spent, and now he'd be gone a whole month, right through Christmas and New Year's and... She swallowed the lump in her throat. How could he go away and leave her for so long, after all they'd shared?

He'd been cold and aloof and totally impersonal with her just now, making it perfectly plain he wanted only a business relationship.

She'd seen him impatient with her in the past, or exasperated, or furious. She could deal with him in any of those moods. But this Quinn, this stranger with the tight, narrowly drawn mouth, the remote eyes, the expressionless voice—what could she say to him?

Maybe he just needed to be alone.

Doubts, once admitted into her consciousness, began to take over.

Maybe, for the first time, her intuition was wrong and Quinn really meant what he said when he insisted he didn't love her.

She walked quietly past his closed door, down the hallway and into her own room before she started to cry.

Quinn stood waiting, listening, fighting the harsh, spare tears that dripped from his eyes, the sobs he choked down with every painful breath. If she came through that door now, he'd never have the strength to let her go again. But she didn't come.

THE AUTOPSY HELD the following morning confirmed that Abe had died of exposure. Hard as she tried, Chris was unable to summon the necessary degree of mental dissociation during the clinical proceedings, and by the time it was over she felt bruised and inwardly battered with the strain of appearing professionally unmoved.

The body on the table was Abe. He'd been a unique and beautiful human being, and his voluntary death seemed so senseless to Chris.

A copy of Abe's crumpled note was stapled to the autopsy report. Chris read it when she was at last alone, able to allow the pent-up tears to roll freely down her cheeks. She could hear Abe's cultured, mellow voice in every line of the Service poem.

"Quinn, old friend," the note began:

We talked of sullen nights by moon dogs haunted,
Of bird and beast and tree, of rod and gun;
Of boat and tent, of hunting trip enchanted,
Beneath the wonder of the midnight sun;
Of bloody-footed dogs that gnawed the traces,
Of poisoned seas, wind lashed and winter locked,
The ice gray dawn was pale upon our faces,
Yet still we filled the cups and still we talked.

Underneath the quote he'd scrawled,

Those conversations with you were the Northern Lights that lit my life up here, but man's only real immortality is in the written word. So write, Quinn. WRITE. For me, and for yourself. Good sledding, pardner. Abe.

The temperature dropped a quick ten degrees before noon that endless day, and Chris felt as if her very soul was turning to ice as she drove cautiously, resentfully, over slippery roads to the airport to meet Beverly Schultz.

The cold had brought clear skies, and in the northeast the liquid curtains of the aurora borealis shifted and flowed and billowed, mysterious rainbows of color across the sky, changing from rich purple and green and blue to shades of amber and turquoise. Any other day the spectacle would have humbled and thrilled Chris with its ethereal beauty.

Not today. Today she was oblivious to nature, angry at the harshness of a land where a man could freeze to death as easily as Abe had...a land that allowed him to do it.

Most of all, Chris didn't want to meet Abe's grieving wife or try to be consoling and kind. She felt drained and bone-tired and dreadfully alone. She wanted to go somewhere by herself and cry out loud like a child.

Quinn had described Beverly Schultz that day in the plane, and Chris remembered what he'd said as she watched the tiny figure climb gingerly down the steps of the small aircraft, wrapped from head to toe in a rich muskrat coat with a hood that almost obscured her face, high-fashion boots covering her dainty feet.

"Sleek, well-groomed, expensively dressed," Quinn had said. "Delicate."

This woman was all those things. Chris hurried over, introduced herself and escorted Abe's widow to the cruiser, struggling to find the appropriate words to comfort her.

Mrs. Schultz tossed back the dramatic hood on the fur coat to reveal a small-boned face. She had deeply etched lines around her eyes and mouth that even the cleverest of makeup didn't hide, but apart from those reminders she seemed absolutely devoid of emotion.

"Why, how dramatic, I've never seen the borealis before," she commented, as if this were a pleasant social occasion. She peered out through a thawed patch on the windshield at the spectacular show. "They're quite breathtaking, aren't they?"

"...conversations with you were the Northern Lights that lit my life...."

Chris felt a sob rise in her throat. There hadn't been enough time in the hours since the autopsy to overcome the anger and sad frustration that welled up at the memory of Abe and the dreadfully lonely way he'd died. The presence of this composed widow without a trace of tears marring her expensive mascara suddenly infuriated Chris. Where was the warmth, the love Abe had obviously needed? Where were the tears at losing him?

All of Chris's own emotional turmoil channeled itself into intense dislike for the cool, composed woman beside her.

How could you let a beautiful man like Abe live out his life alone, Beverly Schultz? Chris wanted to ask. Quinn said Abe loved you passionately. Is a good man's love so easy for you to ignore?

Couldn't you have banished whatever demons haunted him?

How can you bear the thought that he died the way he did?

"I rather expected Corporal Quinn to be here," Mrs. Schultz suddenly remarked in her low cultured voice, and Chris recited the message she'd rehearsed, stumbling only once in her delivery.

"Corporal Quinn isn't in Dawson at the moment.

He's away on annual leave. I'll be happy to assist you in any way possible.''

Quinn had been gone exactly an hour and forty minutes, Chris calculated miserably, checking her watch. He'd driven off in the same fashion he had twenty-four hours before, on a snow machine with a well-stocked sled behind. Chris had felt as if she were trapped in a recurring nightmare, watching him leave for the second time, and Maisie's presence had again made any private conversation impossible.

She was quite sure Quinn had planned it that way.

''You're not going back up to Abe Schultz's cabin, Corporal?'' Maisie had demanded in shocked disbelief when he announced his destination.

Chris was just as shocked as Maisie.

He gave them a sickly parody of his usual grin. ''Abe won't mind, and you can tell Mrs. Schultz I'll package and send her all his personal belongings. I'll be down in about a month.''

That was all. The women could only stand helplessly and watch as he tore off upriver as if all the demons in hell were after him.

There must have been a way to stop him.

But was there any way to stop Quinn from a course he'd decided upon? Chris doubted it.

''Did you have a good flight?'' she inquired politely of Mrs. Schultz, aware that the silence had become uncomfortable.

''Rather bumpy,'' the cultured voice responded. She shivered dramatically. ''This bitter cold is shocking to my system after rainy Vancouver.''

''I'm sure it must be.'' It seemed obvious that the cold bothered her much more than Abe's death had.

How could they be discussing the weather as if it

were the most important thing on their minds, when Abe was lying…

"I'm sorry about your husband," Chris managed to say at last. "I only met him once, and I liked him very much."

Mrs. Schultz made no response beyond a spare nod of acknowledgment, as if accepting a compliment on her hairdo.

Unfeeling bitch, Chris concluded.

"You're staying at the El Dorado?" Chris asked as she guided the car competently away from the airport and back toward Dawson.

A small, brittle laugh came from the figure beside her.

"I seem to remember there wasn't much choice about accommodation up here. Isn't the El Dorado the only motel that stays open past October?"

"Just about," Chris confirmed, suddenly feeling defensive about Dawson.

Is that why you left him here alone, because the hotels weren't up to your standards?

During the short drive, Chris swiftly filled in the information Mrs. Schultz required, and when they arrived at the motel she helped carry the monogrammed bags into the room, then dutifully handed over the official documents and the sealed envelope Abe had left for his wife.

Mrs. Schultz took them in leather-gloved fingers and dropped them into her stylish bag with hardly more than a glance. Chris wondered if they'd even get read.

"Thank you, Constable, you've been very kind," Mrs. Schultz said politely. Then, as if dismissing Chris, she peeled her fingers free from the leather gloves, one by one. "I'll be leaving Dawson as soon as possible—that is, if it doesn't storm badly and trap me here for days."

She glanced around the modest room and shuddered, unfastening the lush coat and letting it slip from her shoulders to reveal a trim figure inside black wool jersey, with a discreet string of pearls at the neckline. She was the perfectly outfitted widow.

Chris turned toward the door, placing a card on the small table just inside it. "This is the number of the detachment. Call if there's anything you want to know or need help with."

She hoped there wouldn't be. Mrs. Schultz was a cold fish, in her opinion. She couldn't for the life of her link the woman with what she remembered of Abe.

Chris escaped outside and the icy air seemed refreshing.

Two days passed before she heard from Mrs. Schultz again. Chris was in the office with Maisie, doing her dogged best to bury herself in work, but in two days there'd been exactly one call. Things were so quiet she'd finally resorted to typing reports for Maisie in a desperate effort to stay busy. All she could think of was Quinn, miles away and alone in the dark days and nights with only Abe's memory for company.

That, and the painful knowledge that the man she loved would rather be in that lonely cabin than here with her. It was enough to drive her mad if she let it.

"Dawson RCMP, may I help you?" Maisie listened to the caller, and in her syrupy telephone voice said sweetly, "One moment, please." She gestured to Chris to take the call.

It was Beverly Schultz.

"Constable Johnstone, I'm flying out in the morning, weather permitting, and I wondered…" There was the slightest note of hesitancy in the low voice. "There are several things I need to discuss with you. I thought perhaps we could deal with them in a civilized fashion, over dinner tonight? At seven. The dining room here is quite pleasant, actually."

Chris was caught off guard. She absolutely didn't relish the idea of dinner with the woman, but she had offered assistance. And she couldn't, in all conscience, plead a busy schedule.

She heard herself reluctantly agreeing.

The dining room at the motel was nearly empty when she arrived, with two tables occupied. One held four local businessmen, all of whom greeted Chris with friendly waves. Across the room, another table was occupied by Mrs. Schultz, who was dressed in a smart gray suit with a petal-pink blouse and gold jewelry. She didn't wave.

Chris was wearing her uniform, because technically she was on duty. The disparity in their outfits seemed to illustrate to Chris how little she and the elegant Mrs. Schultz had in common. They might easily be from different planets, Chris concluded dismally. It was going to be a difficult dinner.

"Please, call me Beverly," Mrs. Schultz said unexpectedly when Chris greeted her and sat down. "And perhaps we could dispense with the 'Constable' as well?" she suggested with a smile that didn't reach her eyes.

Chris nodded agreement, musing that first names didn't ensure intimacy in this case.

The next half hour was filled with ordering food

and discussing the questions Beverly had about certain necessary forms and regulations concerning Abe's death. By the time they'd reached dessert, an awkward silence had fallen between them.

Chris pointedly glanced at her watch and drained her coffee cup. She was about to thank Beverly and make her escape when the other woman suddenly said, "You mentioned the day I arrived that you'd met my husband."

Chris noticed that the beringed hand holding the coffee cup was trembling slightly, and she glanced across the table in surprise. Till now, Beverly had deliberately avoided any personal reference to Abe, and her composure had been absolute. Why the sudden switch?

Chris said cautiously, "Yes, I did meet him. Corporal Quinn and I flew up to his cabin late in the summer and we spent the day."

Beverly toyed with her spoon, not looking at Chris. "I know this is an imposition, but...would you mind telling me about that day, Chris?" She made a small, helpless gesture with her hand. "You see, my husband wrote me many letters while he lived here, and I spent a few months in Dawson with him once, but I really know very little of his life here. I've realized over the past several days that I find it hard to visualize him in this setting."

She lifted her chin and met Chris's eyes, and for the first time, there was feeling there, a welter of confusion and pain, and need, as if a screen had been moved aside for a moment. "I'm sorry to put you on the spot like this, but I don't know who else to ask except for Corporal Quinn. Even if I did... You see, I don't understand, myself, quite what it is I need to hear about…about Abe.'' Her hands fluttered nervously across the cloth, straightening it. ''Ours was an unusual marriage. We lived apart for many years. Memories begin to blur with time. Because you're a woman, I thought perhaps… I'm not doing a good job of this, am I?''

What did Beverly want from her? Chris wondered resentfully. Memories of hours she hadn't cared enough to share with Abe, a snapshot of her husband taken with someone else's camera?

And yet, the woman obviously needed reassurance of some sort. Because of that, she seemed more human, even a little vulnerable, and Chris's dislike lessened a tiny bit.

Feeling inadequate, but also feeling the first measure of warmth and sympathy for Beverly, Chris gave the other woman what she could.

She did her best to recreate that long summer day when she'd met Abe. She spoke haltingly at first, but soon the scene was clear again in her mind's eye— Abe's cabin, the meal the three of them had shared, the palpable warmth between Abe and Quinn. Soon her words flowed easily.

''They both got a little wild as the day progressed, not on whiskey, but on words. They got into heated arguments about everything under the sun, and once Abe got to his feet and shook his fists at the sky when Quinn wouldn't agree with him,'' she recalled with a smile.

Beverly's lips also tilted ruefully. ''Abe was always like that, always passionate. It was a part of him I never understood. It frightened me.''

Imagine being frightened by passion, Chris thought sadly, thinking of herself and Quinn. It wasn't

Quinn's passion that frightened Chris, that was certain. It was this awful, cold withdrawal of his, this removal of himself to a place where Chris couldn't follow. She'd never dreamed he could be like that, she just didn't understand him. How could he be so cold to her, so unresponsive, when she'd been so open about revealing her love?

Beverly was waiting through the silence patiently.

"Abe told us incredible stories that afternoon about prospectors he'd met, and he quoted Robert Service, and then he and Quinn got into a competition, each of them reciting a verse and the other picking it up." Chris could almost feel the exuberant energy again that there'd been that day beside the river, the sense of peace and contentment.

"Abe was happy, Beverly; I'm sure of that. I don't know the reasons for his suicide—" Chris spoke the word deliberately, wanting honesty between herself and Abe's widow.

Abe had been open and honest, guileless, and it seemed a sacrilege to be less than honest about his memory.

Beverly winced at the word, but she didn't look away, and Chris felt grudging respect for her courage. She tried to remember what she and Abe had talked about. "I know he said he loved the North. I remember he told me he'd found peace and innocence here in the Arctic. 'Balm for the soul,' I think he called it."

Tears shone in Beverly's eyes, but she didn't allow them to fall. "Abe and his dramatics, his incredible idealism, his need for perfection," she said with a catch in her throat. "He couldn't settle ever for half of anything." She gave a little shrug, and spoke more to herself than to Chris. "It was the reason we couldn't live together. I never believed I could live up to whatever his expectations of me were, you see. The only way I knew how to deal with emotion was to withdraw, take a step back and remove myself from it. From him. It was a thing I'd learned in my childhood, in order to survive." Her eyes clouded at some dark memory, and all at once Chris could see the utter loneliness in Beverly's soul as she continued thoughtfully, "Abe pursued, I retreated." A sad ghost of regret came and went in her smile, and she finished softly, "At some point, he gave up. Now, his retreat is absolute, and I wish it might have been otherwise for us. I wish I'd been able to be different, because I did love him, in my fashion." She drew herself upright in her chair, and Chris could see her drawing steely control over her emotions once more. When she spoke again, the vulnerability was gone. Her face and voice were once again composed and utterly reserved.

"I'm grateful to you, Chris, because you've made me see him clearly again."

Chris felt like weeping for the tragedy of it all, for this rigid woman, for the warm man who'd been Abe Schultz—but there was also something else in Beverly's words, some message Chris was only beginning to sense.

Some of the things Beverly said reminded her uncomfortably of herself and Quinn. Like a bell sounding in her mind, she imagined herself silently accusing Quinn: You're running away for me. You're a coward.

Pursuit.

His weary response: Damned right I am.

Retreat.

Did Quinn, too, have to step back from emotions in order to deal with them? And was he unable to live up to what he thought her expectations were?

Was she like Abe in her relentless pursuit?

Chris had a nagging feeling there was a lesson here to learn. She felt she could understand Quinn's actions a little more after tonight, and she no longer felt as if she and Beverly were from different planets.

They were both women, and in their separate ways they both loved, and agonized because of it. They just went about it in diverse ways.

They companionably sipped the fresh coffee the waitress brought. When Chris left shortly afterward to cruise the silent streets of what she now thought of as her town as well as Quinn's, she knew that by remembering Abe the way she had tonight, the worst of the pain and horror she'd felt at his death was eased, as well as some of the bitterness and anger she'd felt at Quinn's leaving.

Her aching need for him hadn't eased, however. That simply grew stronger each moment he was away. And unlike Abe, Chris would never give up.

Fervently, she prayed that Quinn would find a measure of peace in the lonely cabin by the river, and she sent silent waves of love floating across the miles to him, borne by the endless silver dance of the lights in the polar sky.

MILES UPRIVER, Quinn sat watching the spectacular show through the single tiny window in Abe's cabin. On the rough table in front of him was a half-filled bottle of whiskey and a glass. The top half of the liquid in the bottle was inside of him, and it might as well have been water for all the good it was doing.

He was absolutely clearheaded, and about as miserable as he'd ever been in his entire life, and that was going some. He'd had some stinking rotten days in the past, but today was the winner.

All around him were physical reminders of Abe. Inside his head were incessant memories of Chris.

He loved them both, yet both were lost to him.

He was physically exhausted, and he couldn't sleep.

He should be hungry, but he couldn't eat.

He eyed the notebook he'd tossed on the table.

Write, Abe had instructed.

There wasn't a single other thing to do to ease the awful pain in his heart, so he picked up the pen and began.

CHAPTER TWELVE

"MERRY CHRISTMAS, Ms Constable." The words came out in a puff of white, as if they were packaged for the festive season by the icy air of Dawson's streets.

Chris smiled and returned the cheery greeting for the fourteenth time that morning, but with each repetition it became more difficult to sound enthusiastic.

The truth was, she felt abandoned. By Quinn, who was still gone, and even by Liz, who'd left to spend the holiday with Mario.

Early that morning she'd driven Liz to catch the plane out, and her friend had been almost hysterical with excitement and nervousness.

"Chris, does this suit look too dressed up? Maybe I should've left my hair down. Oh, Chris, I feel as if I don't really know him anymore. What if there's nothing left to talk about? And I've been up here so long I feel bushed. His friends will figure I'm weird."

It was difficult to watch Liz wave goodbye as she finally mounted the boarding stairs. It would have been nice to have just one someone she cared for around at Christmas, Chris thought morosely. She was feeling miserably sorry for herself.

She'd learned when she was fresh out of training that Christmas and New Year's were work days, busy ones that weren't particularly cheerful times for police

officers—the season invariably brought a rash of violent family fights and car accidents caused by the
drinking that accompanied the celebrations.

Would Dawson be any different? So far, the town
was quiet and exceptionally well behaved, wrapped
tightly in its mantle of permafrost and icicles. It was
December 23, and Quinn had been gone for three
weeks and two days. The entire holiday season would
be over before she could begin to expect him back.

Chris was doing her absolute best at taking good
care of Dawson in his absence, but her heart just
wasn't in it. She managed to keep up a facade of
cheerful efficiency for the townspeople, but she soon
found Stefan and Maisie weren't fooled at all by her
efforts. She missed Quinn more than she thought it
possible to miss anyone, and it showed.

"Constable honey, you ain't eatin' enough to keep
a fly alive these days. Come spring you'll take all
those clothes off and find out you disappeared over
winter," Maisie said fussily the week Quinn left. "No
use frettin' away over that man. You take it from me,
you give him time and he'll smarten up. He's just
stubborn as they come." She lifted her penciled eyebrows knowingly at Chris's expression. "Heck,
honey, you can't fool old Maisie that easy. I wasn't
born yesterday. I saw from the first how you two
spark on each other. Why, you and Corporal Quinn
are so in love a blind man couldn't help but see it;
the whole town knows what way the wind's blowin'
with you two. And we're all pullin' for the both of
you."

They'd been so cautious all along, careful to avoid
any hint of gossip, and it turned out the entire town
knew anyway.

I can't wait to tell Quinn, was Chris's automatic response—before she remembered.

Maisie was going briskly on with her lecture. "The path of true love never runs smooth, although it'll all turn out in the end, you take it from one who knows." She'd looked wistful for a moment. "Only wish that Norman Bickle would have had a touch of spark to him. I could never abide a man without any wickedness. Now Quinn, he sure ain't lackin' in that department, but Norman?" Maisie snorted indignantly. "Polite, churchgoin', and as dull as an old dishcloth."

Maisie had broken off the relationship with the diminutive salesman a few weeks before Christmas, and Chris couldn't help but feel sorry for Norman. He'd hung around the office with a hangdog expression for several days the last time he was in town, trying to make up with Maisie. But Maisie knew her own mind. When she was done, she stated firmly, she was done and that was final.

She opened a bakery bag now and plunked a fat croissant on a clean file folder, shoving it at Chris along with a cup of hot coffee.

"You eat this, honey. That nice José Condura just dropped 'em off, along with the biggest Christmas cake you ever saw. I swear if you deliver any more babies of his, my hips will go plumb out of control. I've put on twelve pounds with this baby." She wagged a finger. "Go on now, eat."

Stefan was less direct but just as concerned.

"Iss not happy time for you, Constable Christine Johnstone, yes?" he inquired gently. "If I can be of service, only to ask. Anything, only to ask. My life, it is yours." He did force a smile from Chris when he added ingenuously, "Also, Corporal Quinn, he tells me, Stefan Rabowski, he says, you are dead man if not take fine care of Constable Christine Johnstone in my absence, yes?''

Official notification had come through that Stefan's appointment as an auxiliary constable had been approved, and Chris was afraid Stefan would wear out his new uniforms the first week with the amount of pressing and brushing he lavished on them. The RCMP had no prouder auxiliary, and none more dedicated to his job than Stefan. Chris trusted and relied on him, and she was coaching him in English grammar so he could eventually apply as a regular recruit.

To her eternal relief, he'd finally stopped being a passionately frustrated suitor and become an affectionate younger brother instead.

Late that night, alone in the room Liz had helped her redecorate in cheerful tones of blue and yellow, Chris concentrated on Quinn with all her energy, as she tried to do every night, visualizing the happy, loving scenes she wanted to share with him.

The longer he was away, the harder it became to make the images come alive, and the more difficult it was for her to believe in the eventual reality of sharing a life with the man she loved.

Tonight, she missed him so much her body seemed to physically ache. In despair, she finally gave up on meditating and huddled under the down-filled comforter her parents had sent her for Christmas— via Ottawa, of course. She willed the creeping hours to pass until her lighted clock would confirm that another dark morning had arrived so that she could pile on her layers of underwear and her uniform and go back to work.

It would signal that she'd survived one more night without Quinn's arms around her.

It would be the morning of Christmas Eve.

Chris eventually fell into an uneasy, dream-filled sleep, and it was the telephone that woke her instead of the alarm.

"Merry Christmas, honey." Her father's resonant voice sounded clear despite the miles, and Chris clutched the telephone and shut her eyes tightly as her mother's sweet, quiet tones joined in the greetings.

"Merry Christmas, Chrissie." Only her family ever called her Chrissie. Christmas Eve had always been the Johnstones' special celebration, with gifts opened at midnight and a buffet feast spread out. It was like a miracle to hear their voices on this special morning.

In a scalding rush of homesickness, Chris imagined her mother on the bedroom extension, her small, lithe body perched atop the bed, beside the wall-size window that looked out over the lake. A moment later Ariel and Shane each took a turn at wishing her well.

Everyone was home for Christmas—everyone except her. Her heart wrenched in loneliness and longing.

"We got special permission from those bureaucrats in Ottawa to phone you directly just this once," her father announced after the first rush of words was over. "They've put the call through for us."

"Is all this high-security nonsense really necessary, Chrissie?" her brother Shane asked a shade anxiously. "If you need a bodyguard, just say the word and I'll put on my snowshoes and come up there."

Shane would, too, Chris thought.

"When will you be coming home, honey?" her mother wanted to know.

"In the summer," Chris promised firmly. Outside her window, the darkness was thick and still. Would summer ever come again?

"Any male specimens worth mentioning up there, any knights in furry armor?" Ariel demanded in her distinctive husky tone—as if Ariel needed any more admirers. Chris's older sister was the family beauty, but she showed no signs of settling down with one lucky man, much to Rosemary's chagrin. Rosemary, and Paul too, wanted grandchildren to spoil, and so far not one of their unlikely brood showed any signs of accommodating them.

"Only one worth mentioning," Chris heard herself telling her sister. "Only one knight, Ariel, and he's mine."

How could she sound so confident, and yet feel so insecure?

Distance evaporated for a time as they caught up on one another's lives. They all expressed concern for her and the restrictions the RCMP had imposed on them all. Chris assured them, as she always did, that the security measures were nothing but bureaucratic nonsense, but she'd be home for a whole month next summer, that she was having the time of her life in the Arctic, that she adored the gifts they'd sent weeks before via Ottawa—gifts she'd opened in a fit of homesickness late the night before.

"We love you," they chorused after a long but still all too brief time. When at last the receivers clicked and the line went dead, Chris hung up slowly and reminded herself ten times in succession that this was the life she'd chosen, that she loved her career, that winter in the Okanagan wasn't very warm either at times, that there was a lifetime of Christmases ahead to spend with her family.

Honesty demanded the bitter truth. It wasn't really her family she wanted anyway.

It was Quinn.

She thumped back down under her comforter, pulled the covers over her head and hollered as loud as she could, "Quinn, damn you, why don't you come back? I need you, Quinn, hear me? I need you." And then she cried.

QUINN MUST HAVE HEARD HER, because he pulled into the garage on his snow machine at three that afternoon.

Maisie had worked in the office for the morning while Chris was out on the road, and then she stayed on after her usual quitting time to help Chris decorate the small tree Stefan had cut for the detachment.

They fastened on the last bit of tinsel, and Chris placed the gifts she'd wrapped for Stefan and Maisie underneath. There was a hand-knitted sweater Chris had commissioned Jennie Martinson to make for Stefan, and a pair of dramatic earrings for Maisie as well as a generous bottle of the older woman's favorite musky perfume.

For Quinn, Chris had ordered a leather-bound, embossed set of the classics, with an additional matching volume of the poems of Robert Service way back in November from a Vancouver bookstore. That heavy package now joined the others under the tree despite the fact that Quinn wouldn't be around to open it.

Maisie arranged her own gaily wrapped packages and then, from the closet in his office, she added several more from Quinn. Two of them, clumsily wrapped and carefully labeled, said simply, Chris.

"When he left last time he asked me to give them out on Christmas." Maisie snorted in disgust and took a healthy gulp of her eggnog and rum. "Should'a made him stick around and do his own gift-giving," she remarked caustically.

Maisie spent half an hour trying to persuade Chris to come home with her and spend the evening with her rowdy, friendly group of cronies.

"There's no reason for you to work. There's not a thing doing in this burg, honey—that phone hardly rang all morning. Nobody's even gonna miss you here. We're having a rum and eggnog party and a singalong." Maisie was still talking when they both heard the garage doors open and the unmistakable sound of the snow machine as it drove in.

Quinn was back!

Maisie leaped up and began pulling on parka and mitts and boots with frenzied speed.

"That's the corporal back. I'm skedaddling so you two can be alone. Now you take my advice and just play it real casual, as if you never missed him one bit, you hear me, Constable honey? Here's a brush, run it through your hair, there, you look fine."

Maisie was dressed and out the front door of the office before Quinn came in, ducking his head through the doorway. He paused on the rug to stamp loose snow from his mukluks and to shove the furry hood of his trail parka back on his shoulders impatiently, revealing a roughly bearded, ravaged face with cheeks burned dark red from the wind and snow, and deep-sunken bloodshot eyes that swept the room hungrily and then came to rest on Chris.

Her heart was hammering and her hands were damp with nervous perspiration. She fervently wished that just this once Maisie had stayed around a little while.

Heavens, he looked like a stranger with that three-week growth of dark beard on his chin, she though inanely.

But Maisie was absolutely right about one thing, Chris determined.

The thing to do was pretend she hadn't missed this huge man one bit, to act as if she'd seen him only hours before, to not let on for one moment that he was affecting her like a double dose of an aphrodisiac right this minute.

"Hello, Quinn," she said evenly, proud of the control she was exerting on her vocal tone.

And then, inanely, she added, "Merry Christmas."

"Welcome home," she said, her voice quavering. Finally, without a scrap of dignity or reserve left in her, she catapulted herself across the room and into his arms, nearly knocking them both backward with the force of her body.

"Quinn, oh my God, Quinn, I missed you so, I needed you, I..."

His arms closed around her, crushing her against his parka. She could smell cold air and the tang of a wood fire, the good clean outdoor smell of Quinn, and she tipped her head back and looked up into his eyes with all the misery of the past weeks showing plainly in her face.

"Damn you, Quinn, don't you ever go and leave me like this again. I missed you something awful and don't you tell me again you don't love me, either. I can tell by the look on your face right now that you do, so don't bother lying.''

The whole long ride back across the frozen landscape, Quinn had rehearsed this meeting, planning the cool and casual way he'd greet her, the businesslike tone he'd use, the manner in which he'd keep her at arm's length.

He'd planned to stay at the cabin another full week, and then this morning he'd looked at his watch and noticed the date.

December 24. Christmas Eve. He'd pictured Chris, alone in Dawson, isolated from her family, rattling around in this drafty old building by herself, and he'd remembered all the Christmases he'd spent alone at one detachment or other, working while the rest of the world celebrated.

He couldn't leave her alone like that. He couldn't stand the thought of her being alone like that.

Carefully, he'd gathered up the impressive stack of scattered, scribbled pages that comprised his growing manuscript, and then he'd packed his few belongings, along with the box containing Abe's things. By the time he was ready to leave, he'd felt a sense of urgency that had sent him off down the trail with hardly a backward glance.

The cabin was only a one-room shelter in the wilderness, after all, and Abe wasn't there anymore. He'd begun to live instead between the pages of the more than half-completed book that was in Quinn's knapsack.

The woman in his arms was also in that book. She wasn't exactly Chris, but he had fictionalized the essence of her, the fervency of his feelings for her.

Quinn could feel the heat radiating from her body

even through all the clothes each of them was wearing, and he studied her face, the freckles and upturned nose and lovely, long-lashed eyes that were shining now with tears. The intensity of her need for him was reflected there. He marveled at her, at the wonderful, shining aliveness and impudence and indomitability of Chris that set her apart from any other woman he'd met.

"You're not going to say you don't love me, are you, Quinn?" she persisted in that direct, infuriating way she had, her chin set stubbornly even when her eyes revealed her uncertainty. He made a sound deep in his chest, as if something was breaking inside of him. His voice was hoarse, choked with surrender and what might have been hopelessness, because there wasn't a way in the world he could lie to her again.

"No, Chris." His chapped lips, half buried by the silky mustache, came slowly down until the features of his face blurred in her vision, and she caught her breath in wonderful expectation of his kiss.

"No, I'm not going to say I don't love you, ever again."

Her arms rose to encircle his neck, and his mouth was on hers, his breath sweet and tasting of fresh air, his lips both rough and sweet on her own, his beard not scratchy at all but soft and sensual against her skin. At the last moment, his control broke and his mouth ravaged hers with abandoned longing.

As his tongue slid into her mouth, his arms were so tight around her ribs she couldn't breathe. The ache in her empty woman's body shot from dull to intense in bare seconds, and Quinn's own need for her drove him almost out of control.

"Chris, my Christine, hold me...." He bent over

her, enveloping her in his embrace, sliding his hands down her back, cradling her rounded buttocks and then lifting her impatiently in a frustrated effort to fit her against his body.

"Too many clothes, your parka, take your parka off...." She gasped, and he released her reluctantly and grasped the bottom edge of the garment, hauling it over his head in one clean sweep, disarranging his wavy hair so that she had to reach up and smooth it out of his eyes.

He wore a thick navy sweater underneath, and in seconds it joined the parka on the floor. She caressed the soft flannel of his rumpled shirt, wishing it was his bare, softly matted chest instead. This was better, but still not bare enough. *Not nearly enough.*

She was once again in his arms, his hungry lips on her forehead, nibbling at her chin.

"This is all wrong, Chris," he choked out between kisses, "I swore I wouldn't, it's wrong for you to get mixed up with me...."

"Why not let me decide what's right and wrong for me?" she whispered almost incoherently, kissing his neck, rubbing her face on his beard. She fumbled with the buttons on his shirt and then nearly swore aloud when she got them undone only to encounter his thick underwear.

"I can't stand this, Quinn, all these damned clothes," she said in a fit of temper. "I want—" She stopped with a tiny sound of surprise and pleasure when he scooped her into his arms and strode down the hall, past the empty cells and into her bedroom, kicking the door shut behind them.

He dumped her on her back on the bed, his breathing hoarse and uneven, too aroused himself by now to go slowly. He knelt over her, thighs tight on either side of her hips, and with dogged determination he began removing her clothes, bending to ravage her mouth as layer followed layer.

Sweater, uniform shirt, long-sleeved cotton T-shirt. The top of her two-piece, waffle-padded blue long johns. Obediently, she raised her arms overhead again and again as one garment after another disappeared.

At last Quinn paused, slowed, and a growl of desire came from his throat as he uncovered her delicate lacy pink cotton camisole, whose thin fabric afforded a glimpse of full golden breasts. Her rosy nipples stood erect and eager, begging for his lips.

Chris caught her breath and arched upward helplessly as his hot mouth closed over one pulsing breast and then the other, wetting the flimsy fabric with his tongue. The shards of sensation shot downward as if the pleasure centers of her body were wired cleverly together.

A choking cry escaped her, and she tried to guide his head back down to her breasts when at last he pulled himself up again, away from her, to slip this one last confection up and over her rumpled curls.

"Please, Quinn."

But he was fumbling now with the belt on her slacks, undoing the buckle, then the zipper, sliding to his feet beside the bed as he tugged the confining slacks down over the narrow hips she tilted obligingly upward for him. The heavy whipcord caught on the tops of her shoes, and he impatiently pulled off one boot and then the other, peeling away her several pairs of socks as he did so.

He worked the trousers down her calves and finally tossed them in a heap on the carpet. He hooked his

thumbs under the waistband of her long blue underwear bottoms, and her scrap of pink bikini panties
went as well as he stripped them smoothly away. Finally, she lay naked for him.

His hand trembled as he caressed the V of soft dark
curls at the base of her flat belly, letting his fingers
slip to where he could discover the moist and welcoming velvety flesh.

She gasped, opening her thighs and moving against
the welcome pressure, and Quinn was painfully reminded of his own layers of constrictive clothing as
his body surged and swelled, full to bursting, threatening explosion with the power of his need for her.

''Easy, love, we're nearly there,'' he consoled her
with a break in his voice, and then, with a smothered
impatient exclamation he began the laborious process
of removing his own clothes, ingeniously bending forward, while his hands were busy with buttons and
buckles and elastic, to rub his whiskery cheek against
her flat belly. He uttered muffled words of praise and
love for her into the incredible beauty of her downy
skin as he trailed his tongue along her midriff and
down, down, until the heated, urgent spot at the junc-
ture of her legs became the target of mouth and
tongue and gentle lips.

She was driven mindless by her need, broken
phrases of appeal tumbling from her lips as he tan-
talized first one hidden place and then the next, and
Chris kept her eyes blissfully closed, concentrating on
the ecstatic agony of sensation he aroused in her with
his mouth and tongue. His burning, rapid breath was
tantalizing on her inner thighs, the tip of his tongue
unerringly finding the center of her need. He inflamed
her beyond bearing, until awareness and sensation be-

gan to meld into one soaring blur of color and heat and driving urgency, until she felt she could stand no more, and yet she would die if he stopped.

Her hands buried themselves in his hair in a wordless plea for help, and then the summit came and she journeyed into a silent sun-drenched place where she and Quinn were one.

The aftershocks faded and she looked up into his flushed face. His weather-beaten features gentled into an expression of such tenderness her heart soared.

"I love you, Christine," he said fiercely, and then his lips came softly down to hers again, and she tasted herself on his tongue as the world slowed. She felt the heavy weight of his erection pulsing against her lower belly, and opened herself to him, welcoming the first hard, endless thrust that filled her with re-awakening awareness.

The rhythm was all his at first, and she only followed. But then, taking her by surprise, Chris's body quickened and she began to take the lead, dancing just ahead of him, racing him along the path.

In the end he was a guttural cry ahead of her, and then their voices mingled as they found the trail together.

It was a long dreamy time later when she persuaded him to pull on some clothes and celebrate Christmas with her by opening the parcels under the little tree.

He opened the mitts from Maisie, the bottle of Scotch from Stefan, and then, as Chris watched with unbearable shyness, he tore the careful wrappings from the books she'd bought.

She could tell immediately that he was both touched and pleased. He caressed the leather covers with all the reverence of a man who loves books, and his smile was blazingly warm.

"Thanks, Chris. When I was a kid, all I ever wanted for Christmas was books, and—" he caressed the leather cover as if it were her skin "—all I ever got was clothing. My father didn't believe in buying books when you could borrow them from a library. He never understood how much I needed books of my own."

She glowed with the pleasure of giving, but only till Quinn handed her his gifts to her. She unwrapped them greedily, as gluttonous as any child on Christmas morning.

Inside the first package was a pair of exquisitely beaded ankle-high leather moccasins lined with rabbit fur, and she squealed with delight.

"No more cold feet," she almost sang when he took them from her and slipped them on. They were a perfect fit, and the rabbit lining and trim was toasty warm.

"Quinn, these are perfect. How did you know my size? They're handmade, aren't they? Who made them?"

He just smiled and handed her the second parcel. When she unwrapped it and opened the heavy box it contained, her mood sobered. She lifted the small soapstone carving.

An Inuit figure in a parka was holding on fiercely to a huge snow goose, trying to stop it from flying away. The human arms were wrapped around the bird, whose flapping wings were spread wide on either side. The bird struggled, and the human struggled equally, and only one could be victor.

The carving was beautiful, and it frightened Chris

with its message of inevitable tragedy, and its reminder of the harsh realities of this arctic land.

"Who made this, Quinn?" Tears smarted in her eyes.

"I know the carver well," Quinn said softly. "His name is Jimmy Aliuk. He drinks too much and ends up in jail pretty often. His mother, Josephine Aliuk, made the moccasins." He traced a finger over the carving.

"It's beautiful, but it's sad too, isn't it?" she asked quietly. "How can the man catch a goose like that with his bare hands?"

Quinn met her eyes, his gaze shuttered. "The snow goose tries to find a hollow in the snow to bed down in at night. In the spring, the snow is soft from the warmth of the sun, and overnight a crust forms. By morning, the bird is often frozen by his wings and his feet into the snow, and the Inuit race out and capture him before he can break free."

The tears glistened on Chris's long eyelashes. "Abe would have understood that story perfectly," she said, and Quinn nodded. "He did. He was the one who first told it to me."

Chris reached up and lifted a Christmas card from where it was balanced on the boughs of the small tree.

"Beverly Schultz sent me this."

The card was expensive and starkly simple, an abstract design of zigzag color across a silver background. Inside, Beverly had written in small, precise script: "This reminded me of the aurora. Call if you're ever in Vancouver, Chris. Sincerely, Beverly."

Quinn studied the message and remarked thoughtfully, "She's not exactly gushy, is she?"

The remark was such a classic understatement that

Chris began to giggle, and their mood was suddenly lightened. They made hot chocolate and ate huge slices of José's cake, and at two in the morning they finally went back to bed.

Wrapped in Chris's down quilt, they slept deeply, she in blissful contentment, he in uneasy exhaustion, knowing even in sleep that he'd broken his promise to himself by making love to her.

Some internal clock awoke Quinn when morning came, even though the room was just as dark and silent as it had been all night.

He lay quietly, reveling in the sensation of having Chris tucked tightly against him, her buttocks firmly wedged into his middle, and knowing that every new experience they shared together would simply make their parting more painful when the inevitable hour arrived.

He had to talk to her, he had to make her understand, before any more time went by.

He should never have made love to her last night.

That thought created a blackness inside of him that rivaled the darkness outside, and gently he disengaged himself from Chris, tucking the comforter closer around her lovely sleeping form, before he stole out of the room.

Chris awoke when he came back half an hour later. He was balancing two mugs of fragrant steaming coffee. He set the coffee down, but he didn't come close to the bed, and she held her arms out to him invitingly. He hesitated, tousled her short dark curls and drew back when she tried to pull him down for a kiss.

"Merry Christmas, sleepyhead," he said instead, moving away even more. "You want two eggs or three for breakfast?"

"Can't I have you for breakfast?" she mumbled sleepily, smiling up at him with innocent lechery. As she became more wide-awake, she noted with alarm the haunted expression in his eyes.

Chris struggled to a sitting position, and when he saw her shoulders were bare he uprooted the quilt and wrapped her more snugly in its cocoon.

"What's wrong now, Quinn?" she demanded impatiently, frowning up at him. She scrutinized him closely. "You've gone and shaved off your beard. It makes you look different. I liked it the way it was," she commented absently.

He cupped her chin then for an instant in one large hand, and smoothed his thumb longingly across the velvet of her cheek before he drew away again.

"We have to have a serious conversation, Chris. But not now. Tell me how many eggs you want, and we can talk after breakfast," he suggested, stalling. Chris shook her head vehemently.

"Now. I want to get it over with now. I know something's wrong, I can see that look on your face, and I want to know what's up right now."

With an awful sinking inside of him, Quinn wondered where to begin. He stared at her sleep-soft face, and he cursed the uniforms they'd both chosen to wear, everything those uniforms represented and the inevitability of changing what already was.

"Chris, what are your long-term goals? What do you want out of your life and your job?"

She wrinkled her nose endearingly. "You want to get into all that heavy stuff first thing on Christmas morning, when I'm barely awake yet?"

Chris was trying her best to tease him out of it, but the effort failed. He went on looking at her in that intense way, as if demanding an answer, and she sighed in resignation.

"You know what I want, Quinn. We've talked about it lots of times. I love my job, I want to go as far up in the ranks of the RCMP as it's possible to get on brains and ability. I want to be the first female commissioner. I've told you that, but if I can't then I'll be the next best thing." A suspicion formed in her mind and her blue eyes widened with comprehension.

"Quinn, that's it, you're worried that I wouldn't be a good wife to you, or want to have a family, because of my career and these ambitions. Oh, Quinn, that's just not true, lots of women balance their career and their children. I might not be conventional about those things, but I still want them...."

"Stop, Christine," he ordered, interrupting her torrent of words wearily. "Stop and really think about this. You're a career Mountie. You've already attracted notice at headquarters by completing what I understand was a brilliant undercover operation. You're in a holding pattern up here in Dawson, but it's very temporary. In fact, you'll likely be transferred out and up sometime next summer. You know that in order to win quick promotions, you have to be willing to go wherever the force sends you, take all the management courses available, be flexible and willing to do what it takes for advancement."

She nodded uncertainly. What he said was absolutely true.

"So what are you planning to do, Chris, take me along as a pet on this ride of yours?" he asked suddenly, startling her.

She gasped at the harsh and angry tone of his voice, and shook her head vehemently, but he went on.

"Chris, I'm not one of your new breed of police-men, you know that. I've been labeled a renegade, a maverick, and they leave me in this town because the force finds me impossible to deal with. I prefer it this way. I have no illusions about my career, no ambitions about promotion. I want to do what's left of my service and take my pension and live the rest of my life as a private citizen, probably in someplace like Dawson. I'm frozen into place as firmly—" he snatched up the carving she'd placed on her bedside table before they slept "—as thoroughly as this goose is frozen in the snow. Now can you imagine what it would do to your chances in the force to get hooked up with me? We're like this man, Chris, we're trapping something wild and free and beautiful, keeping it from flying. Have you thought about what would happen to us, to our relationship, with me feeling as if our love was holding you down? Or have you wondered how we'd run a marriage with me here and you in...in Calgary?"

"But..." She groped for words, for a way to deny what he was saying. "But Quinn, you're the best po-liceman I've ever met. I love you, sure, but I also admire you in a professional sense as well. I've learned more from you than I could have learned any-where about small-town policing, dealing with peo-ple. There's no reason for you to feel the way you do. Why, you could be anything, work anywhere...."

He got to his feet, ramming his hands in the pock-ets of his pants and towering over her.

"I could, couldn't I, Chris?" His voice was steely and cold. "I could clean up my act and write the officer's exam, I could meekly request a transfer to wherever they send you. You're forgetting that this is exactly the way I choose to live my life. Besides, how do you think I could sit back as your husband and see you accepting assignments that would put your life in danger the way this last one did? You'd have to compromise just as much as I would, and this is the exact conversation we'd have over and over as time passed. My reputation and my love for you would shoot you down over and over.'' His face was suddenly ravaged with loss. ''I thought we could avoid all this, that it hadn't gone too far between us to end it, but I was wrong. I love you. Don't you think I haven't tried to dream up a way out of this for us? Up there alone in Abe's cabin, I fantasized every single scene that might work, I tried to think of a possible way I could marry you without destroying both of us in the process.'' His shoulders slumped and he turned away from her, staring unseeingly at the bright curtains covering the window.

''But there isn't any way, Chris. And holding you in my arms, loving you like I did last night...'' Quinn's voice wavered, and he had to stop and clear his throat before he could go on. ''Christine, love, I can't do that over the next months and then watch you walk away when it's over. I'm just not tough enough for that. All I can hope to do with any dignity is to work with you on a strictly professional basis for the rest of your time here, giving us both a chance to recover if we can. In order to do that, I—'' again he had to clear his throat ''—I have to keep to myself, stay away from you, Chris, and I need your help with that.'' He gave her a self-deprecating imitation of a smile and gestured at the bed where they'd made such spectacular love. "I've no resistance to you at all, obviously. You burn with a flame that consumes me, and I just can't let that happen again between us, go on happening, it would destroy me when the time came I had to watch you go. For both of our sakes, I can't let it."

Chris felt helpless anger arise in her. She searched her mind desperately for some way to negate his words, his reasoning.

There was none. Every word he'd spoken had been the truth, and there wasn't any refuting his logic. In her usual passionate, impatient manner, she wanted to drag him down beside her, to use her body and her lips to keep him hers for every moment that was left to them, but she didn't.

She thought of Beverly, and she didn't.

"I never believed I could live up to whatever his expectations of me were," she'd said about Abe.

Chris had learned restraint. She'd learned that there were vastly different methods of dealing with love, and the loss of it.

Before she'd met Beverly Schultz, she wouldn't have really listened or accepted what Quinn said. It was because of Beverly she was now able to look up at him with her heart breaking in two and tears glimmering in her eyes and tell him she understood.

She did understand. There were vastly different ways of dealing with love, and with the loss of it.

For the first time in her experience, Chris couldn't for the life of her see any way around a problem, or wish it gone with the force of her will.

"Are you going to help me with this?" he demanded evenly.

"If it's what you really want," she finally said in

a stiff, uneven voice, "just—just a purely business arrangement between us from here on in, well—I'll do my best, Quinn."

"It's not what I want, Constable," he said harshly. "It's what damned well has to happen if we're going to get through the winter in the same house." He turned abruptly toward the door, not wanting to look at her one more time, sitting there vulnerable and tantalizing with bits of bare flesh showing, with her full mouth still slightly swollen from his kisses. Even the bedclothes still held the perfume of their loving trapped inside them.

"I'll give you a full report of everything that's gone on in the detachment as soon as I'm up and dressed," Chris offered, in some ridiculous facsimile of a professional tone.

If it was going to be all business, they might as well start immediately.

At least until she could think of a better plan.

CHAPTER THIRTEEN

THE HOLIDAY SEASON PASSED in a sort of limbo for Chris after that.

Just before midnight on New Year's Eve, there was a serious car accident on a downtown street, and the exact birth of the fresh year was marked only by twisted metal and cries of pain as Chris and Stefan and Quinn did their best to extricate a young man and his girlfriend from the wreckage.

There was that event, and a particularly wild party with its share of drunks and inevitable fistfights. All of them were up until five on New Year's morning.

On New Year's Day, while Chris was sleeping, a special television broadcast commemorated the bravery of Canadians during the past year, and because of the conscientious zeal of a librarian, and the thorough research of a young and eager reporter, a still shot of Chris, wrapped in a gray blanket after rescuing Stefan from the Yukon River, appeared briefly on television sets across eastern Canada.

Unfortunately, the television reception in Dawson was far too sketchy to pick up the broadcast.

It attracted a fair share of attention, however. A man lounging in front of his set in Montreal drinking beer suddenly sat up and peered closely at the screen.

Phone calls were made to and from the Niagara peninsula, and Dawson suddenly became the center of interest for Angelo Andollini and some of his friends.

TWO WEEKS INTO THE NEW YEAR, Chris and Stefan were paying routine visits to the hotel bars just after their supper break.

The few establishments that stayed open in the winter operated with half staff, and there were a dozen or so familiar diehard patrons drinking beer tonight in the El Dorado lounge, as well as three men sitting in a dimly lit corner, talking earnestly over a table littered with glasses. Chris gave them a fleeting, vaguely curious glance as she entered.

Two were salesmen whose routes brought them to Dawson fairly regularly. The third man was a stranger, and she watched him for only a second. It was unusual for strangers to come to Dawson in the wintertime.

The friendly greetings from the men at the bar drew her attention.

"Hey, Ms Constable, you seen Lefty around? His old lady was in looking for him a while ago."

"Hey, Ms Constable, you hear about Parker Jameson spending the holidays in Hawaii? Boy, some guys have all the luck."

The good-natured banter distracted her, so Chris didn't notice the way the man in the corner was staring at her until she turned toward the bar. In the mirror, she unexpectedly caught the steady dark gaze of the potbellied man sitting with the salesmen.

He didn't look away when she caught his eye.

His face was in shadow, and he had a shiny bald head with the barest fringe of hair around his ears. She could almost feel the bold intensity of his narrow eyes trained unsmilingly on her features. There was something about his unrelenting scrutiny that made Chris vaguely uncomfortable, and after a challenging moment, she turned away.

Stefan was aware of the man's interest as well. He deliberately moved so that he was between Chris and the stranger's table while she chatted with the bartender for a moment.

Assured that everything was quiet, Chris and Stefan pulled up their hoods and left, and the dark coldness of the street hit them like a fist after the warmth inside.

Stefan swore in Russian and growled, "That fat one back there with the bald head, you have seen before, Constable Christine? Iss not polite, the way he looks at you so long."

Chris frowned. For some reason, the man had seemed familiar...and yet not. She seldom forgot a face; it was one of the reasons she'd been good at undercover work. But the face in the bar didn't ring a bell at all. Although there was something....

The heartsick despair she'd been feeling since Christmas had made her habitually short-tempered and impatient.

Certainly she didn't need Stefan bristling like a guard dog just because some stranger stared at her.

"There's no law against looking, and I've told you before, I can take care of myself if necessary," she reminded Stefan huffily, and then felt mean when she saw the hurt on his eager young features.

"I'm sorry, Stefan," she apologized. "I'm just tired and grumpy. Look, there's not a thing doing, so c'mon, I'll buy you a hot chocolate at the café and we'll call it a night," she suggested contritely.

Strangely enough, the fat bald man appeared in her dreams several times over the next weeks, but the vague uneasiness the dreams created was more than overpowered by the nighttime agony of dreaming she was asleep in Quinn's arms and then waking up alone.

Early in February, Chris was sitting listlessly in the office, thumbing through an old batch of Wanted posters forgotten in a file, when one of them caught her attention.

A man was shown in classic full face and profile poses, but on a second sheet, he was pictured without what must obviously be a hairpiece. The contrast was astonishing.

Chris was sure she'd never seen this particular criminal before, but the difference in the visual identity between one picture and the other made something connect in her mind as if a piece of a jigsaw puzzle was fitting into a slot perfectly.

She shut her eyes and without effort visualized the face of the baldheaded man who'd studied her so intently in the bar that night with Stefan.

Carefully, fearfully, she added a luxuriously lush hairpiece to his features, and a pair of glasses, and the resulting image made her come out of her chair with a sharp exclamation of distress.

She'd just remembered where and when she'd seen the man before.

She told Quinn the whole story immediately.

"I only saw him once. It was just before the end of the undercover operation, and he came to a nightclub to arrange a deal with Louis Andollini. They went into a back room, and I didn't see him again. He was wearing a curly salt-and-pepper wig and a pair of horn-rimmed glasses, and I never suspected he was disguised. That's what fooled me that night I saw him here. He looked so different.''

Quinn kept an iron control over his reactions, but absolute horror grew inside of him as she calmly told the story.

"Do...d'you think he was sent up here to locate me?'' she asked. Quinn shook his head. It seemed ridiculously ironic to think that she might have been discovered here, in the winter isolation of Dawson.

"It was probably just bizarre coincidence,'' he reassured her. But after dinner he quizzed Stefan about the incident, and when the young man voiced his concern about the stranger's attention to Chris, Quinn knew it was more than probable that she could be in danger. It sounded as if she'd been recognized, all right, and once her identity was established, it wouldn't take the underworld long to move in, if that was their plan.

There was absolutely no way of knowing for sure, and the very idea of such danger to the woman he loved brought Quinn closer than he'd ever come to panic.

But he was a policeman, and his years of experience gave him an idea of what to do, an idea of what could be done.

He patiently and methodically set about finding out exactly who the bald man was and what his business had been in Dawson.

Through the clerk at the hotel, the bartender, the woman who cleaned the rooms and several others in Quinn's unofficial information network, he learned that the name the man had used was Duke Gregson, that he had been ostensibly scouting out Dawson as the possible site of a new gambling casino he and some invisible partners wanted to open. He'd announced loudly that he was giving up the idea because of the climate. He'd stayed three days and flown back to the outside, apparently never to return.

"There's no way of knowing if Gregson knew ahead of time you were here, and came to check on you, or whether he accidentally recognized you in the bar, or just thought you were a pretty cop," Quinn explained to Chris. "I've sent out inquiries on him. He's a small-time hood but he's never been convicted, and he actually does own a couple of gambling places, so his reasons for being here sound okay. I just don't know."

It was not knowing that drove Quinn nearly mad with frustration and fear, but he did his best to appear calm.

"All we can do to safeguard you is keep a close eye on every single stranger who comes to town over the next month or so. I'll take over late town patrol, and I want Stefan with you at all times when you're out. Also, make sure you've got a portable radio with you constantly. Is that clear?"

Chris nodded sullen agreement to the stern stipulations he made, knowing they were sensible. She stared into Quinn's frowning face, aching for one single personal note in this whole thing.

It was one thing to agree not to sleep with him. It was another to accept his acting this coolly logical and objective over a situation that couldn't help but frighten her a little.

More than a little, if she were honest.

It wouldn't hurt him to show he had blood in his veins instead of the ice that seemed to show in his eyes when he looked at her these days, would it? It wouldn't kill to reveal that there was feeling for her behind this polite and frozen restraint he chose to maintain, would it?

She gave him a petulant glare, and said, "Quinn, for heaven's sake, can't you..."

"That will be all, Constable." He wheeled around and stalked out of the room, leaving her wishing there was something handy to brain him with.

The actual truth was, he found both logic and objectivity difficult to sustain during the next few days. He succumbed to moments of absolute terror and panic, and cold sweat broke out on his body if he allowed his imagination full rein.

He phoned Staff Billings and told him exactly what was happening. There was a long, thoughtful pause before Billings said, "I think we're getting a little jumpy here, Quinn. Keep your finger on the pulse, of course, and let me know if anything breaks. I'll initiate some inquiries with our sources in the East."

Billings's calmness didn't rub off on Quinn at all.

He had to forcibly restrain his emotions. He urgently wanted to lock his constable up safely in the cells...or better yet, much better, handcuff her to his bed until he knew for certain what was going on, until he could figure out a foolproof way to protect her, until he could make sure beyond any shadow of a doubt that no harm would come to her. She was his very life, whether he let her see it or not.

And of course, he couldn't let her. She was a fellow officer, and he had to stand back and allow her to do her job.

But Quinn's subtle method of involving the citizens of Dawson in his police work allowed him to now do surveillance in many areas at once by simply talking as openly as possible with his friends.

Jim Murphy, who had been on the scene when Chris saved Stefan's life, was still driving taxi.

"Could you just keep me aware of what fares you pick up at the airport for the next month or so when the plane makes it in, Jim? I can't give you all the details right now but you know I'll clue you in as much as I can. Apparently, our little town has attracted the attention of the syndicates in the East, and people can come in and out of here sometimes without me knowing it. But you'd know, Jim. I need your help with this. Can I count on you?"

Like a clever general positioning his troops, Quinn contacted one person after the other. He used the same basic phrasing of a request for information with Al, the airport manager, with Slocum Charlie, who was working for the winter as night clerk at the El Dorado, with Martie, who was waiting tables and doing the rooms there and with Elmer who operated the service station.

For three weeks, only familiar faces arrived on the two flights, and the road from Whitehorse was all but closed by a new snowfall.

Quinn felt both frustrated and relieved. If something was going to happen, he wished it would happen soon, because the strain of waiting was beginning to tell on him. He looked haggard when he studied himself in his shaving mirror each morning, and since Christmas, he hadn't been sleeping well so his eyes were constantly bloodshot. The lines around them seemed to deepen every day.

Whatever Chris saw in him had nothing to with looks; that was certain.

But whatever it was didn't seem to be wearing off, for either of them. He knew instinctively that she was as bothered by him as he was by her. She did her job as efficiently as ever, and they went on sharing the mundane chores and the cooking. Only it grew harder every day to be friendly, impersonal and businesslike when all he wanted to do was barricade the door, take the phones off the hook and love her the way his body demanded.

He began staying away from their quarters as much as possible.

Tuesday, the fourth of March, he happened to be in the office when a call came from Jim Murphy.

"Don't know if you're still interested, but I drove three strangers into town off of this morning's flight from Whitehorse," the young man announced importantly. "Two men, maybe in their forties or fifties, and an older woman. They're all three at the El Dorado. I tried to get them chatting, but none of them said much except to complain about the weather."

Quinn's adrenaline surged, and he thanked Jim. Within half an hour, two other calls came in, and he gradually learned that the three newcomers didn't seem to know one another, that they were in separate rooms at the El Dorado, none adjoining, that the names on the register there listed the men as Bernie Evans, 210 Fifth Street East, Saskatoon, Saskatchewan, and Grant Mcfee, 1402 East 180th Street, Everett, Washington, and the woman as Sadie Price, Apt. 811, 1551 Cardero Street, Vancouver.

Quinn radioed for Chris, whisked her into his office and away from Maisie's curiously wagging ears, then filled her in on what was happening.

Chris paled and swallowed, but said nothing. Together, they quietly did their best to identify the visitors.

First of all, they checked out the men's names and the addresses they'd given on the police computer, using approximate ages and asking for a list of best possibles.

Chris watched in amazement as the computer gave a mechanical groan and began to spew out paper. It seemed there was a vast number of Evanses and Mcfees, but when at last Chris and Quinn had sorted through the printouts the answers were disappointing and inconclusive.

There were no records or warrants on the two most likely prospects the computer came up with. Which could mean a clever alias, or a legitimate reprieve for either or both.

Quinn and Chris were no further ahead than they had been two hours previously.

"You stay right here in the office until I figure out what's going on," Quinn ordered Chris in a no-nonsense tone.

"But Corporal, that could take days," Chris wailed, and Quinn suddenly and irrationally lost his temper.

"I still happen to be in charge here, and by God, you do what I say," he thundered, slamming the door as he left.

Maisie gave Chris a delighted grin.

"Well, Constable honey, at least he's still alive and kicking. I was starting to worry about him lately, with that stiff-upper-lip stuff. I sure wish you two would get your act together, it's nerve-racking with both of you acting so polite. Everybody's asking me what's wrong between you two."

Quinn flooded the motor twice on the cruiser before he could get it out of the garage, and he had to walk past the hotel twice before he was calm enough to go in and have a quiet conversation with Slocum Charlie and Martie.

"I'd like a record of any phone calls these guys receive or make, Charlie. Martie, I want you to hang on to the garbage in their wastebaskets for me, and get me a water glass tomorrow morning from each of their rooms that they may have handled if you can." He showed her how to smuggle the glass out so that the prints would be preserved.

On his way out through the lobby, Quinn met a plump, motherly-looking woman with blue-rinsed hair and a friendly smile. She'd been chatting to the day clerk behind the registration desk, and she greeted Quinn cheerfully. "Good afternoon—" her eyes went to the chevrons on his shirt collar, and she finished triumphantly "—Corporal." She held out a well-manicured hand sporting several expensive rings. "I'm a free-lance writer. My name is Sadie Price. I'm researching a story for an airline magazine, and I just wondered if maybe you could answer some questions for me," she asked.

For the next fifteen minutes, Quinn patiently responded to gushingly phrased queries about unemployment in Dawson, interesting local characters, local arts and crafts and snippets of Dawson's colorful history.

When Quinn finally escaped her pudgy clutches, any lingering doubts he might have entertained about Sadie Price were entirely gone. She was obviously exactly what she appeared to be—a rather boring, nosy writer about to do yet another stock piece on the rowdy Yukon.

First thing the next morning, Quinn carefully lifted the prints from the water glasses Martie proudly produced and gave them to a truck driver he trusted who was heading for Whitehorse at noon that day, with instructions to deliver them to the RCMP offices, identification section. He enclosed a note for his friend there, Corporal Larry Campbell, asking that he phone Quinn the moment the prints were identified.

Chris raged at Quinn that evening when he categorically refused to allow her to do her evening shift.

"Stefan and I will do your patrols for the next few days. You stay right here," he ordered shortly.

"I'm a police officer exactly like you. I refuse to be imprisoned here like some helpless child," she howled at him.

Her hidden fears and her awful need for his arms around her made her anger escalate out of control. When Quinn refused to be baited or bullied, she stamped off to her chilly room and slammed the door so hard a glass fell into the sink in her bathroom.

Early the next morning Slocum Charlie dropped by the office, on his way home after his night of work at the hotel. Quinn had been unable to sleep more than a few hours, and he poured a mugful of his virulent coffee for Charlie in the kitchen. Chris was still asleep.

"That Mcfee, he drank in the bar till closing time. He had a snootful when he went off to his room. Evans now, he made a phone call out to Saskatoon about nine last night, talked maybe ten or twelve minutes." Charlie lifted the steaming mug of coffee to his toothless mouth and slurped, then grimaced.

"Kinda strong, ain't it? Got any cream, Quinn?"

While Quinn was rooting in the fridge, Charlie said thoughtfully, "That writer woman, now, in room 320? Well, she called Montreal last night, five after twelve. Didn't say much, about a three-minute call. She's a real pest, that one. Questions, questions all the time. Wants to know about the roads in this area, where do they go. Told her mostly nowhere, but she rented herself a truck anyway—a real snappy four-wheel-drive unit from Elmer down at the garage."

Elmer had already told Quinn that.

"Writers are all a little bit bent, Charlie," Quinn advised knowingly.

Charlie left, and Larry Campbell phoned.

The prints Quinn had sent were not on file.

Quinn relaxed a little. Maybe he'd been slightly paranoid over this whole thing. It was beginning to look as if Duke Gregson had only been admiring an exceptionally attractive woman when he'd ogled Chris.

When she appeared moments later, Quinn told her that it looked as if the whole incident had blown over, and she could work the day shift after all.

Chris met Sadie Price at Nancy's Café when she stopped there for lunch at noon. The older woman introduced herself, then wasted half of Chris's lunchtime asking questions about what it was like to be a female RCMP officer, what Chris found to do for recreation in the wintertime in Dawson, what trails were best for using a snowmobile.

Slocum Charlie arrived at the office right on schedule the next morning, and Quinn mused that it was lots easier to start Charlie on a routine than it was to stop him. He'd probably call by the police office every morning all winter now.

Quinn didn't have the heart to tell the eager old man that the investigation was over. He made them both bacon and eggs, then sat patiently and listened to Charlie's litany.

"Mcfee got pissed again. He's a real drinker all right. Evans hooked up with one of Gladys's new girls, hadn't come out of his room yet when I left this morning. Oh yeah, and that old lady in 320? She made a phone call again to Montreal right smack dab at 12:05, just like the night before. Same length of call, four minutes on the outside. She's a big spender, too. Robertson down at the hardware sold her a pair of high-powered binoculars yesterday—biggest sale he's made in weeks."

Quinn thought the conversation over for a long while after Charlie left, and later that morning he surreptitiously took the glass Martie had smuggled from Sadie Price's bathroom.

Feeling like a total fool, Quinn lifted the prints and drove them out to the airport to put them in the care of the pilot who was making that day's flight back to Whitehorse.

Larry was going to think he'd gone stir-crazy, lifting prints from frumpy, middle-aged ladies, Quinn reflected on his drive back from the airport. But those binoculars nagged at him. Why the hell would a writer need high-powered binoculars?

He drove slower than usual because the roads were icy. The weather wasn't bad-cold, but clear and still.

Good traveling weather.

There were more and more times these days when he longed to be back up at Abe's cabin, isolated by distance from the temptations that being around Chris presented.

He rubbed a gloved hand wearily across his face.

Chris would be back at the office right now, sullenly doing the monthly returns and car accounts he'd given her to do. They were time-consuming enough to keep her busy the rest of the day.

At least he didn't have to hang around there the whole day again and watch her like a lovesick moose—the report from Whitehorse wouldn't come until late afternoon or even tomorrow, and Quinn fully expected no record of Sadie's prints, anyhow.

Parker Jameson had finally come home from Hawaii a couple of days ago. Impulsively, Quinn decided to drop by Parker's place and see how the trip had gone, wanting to hear about the inheritance and how Parker and Cole had made out.

There wasn't a single other thing that needed his attention, anyway. The town was quiet as a tomb. The only vehicle on the road, other than his own, was that silver four-wheel-drive rental, with Sadie Price hunched over the wheel, driving excruciatingly slowly down the street ahead of him. He passed her finally, and she waved cheerfully through the small area of unfrosted window.

Quinn waved back, feeling sheepish when he thought about sending her pudgy fingerprints away that morning.

Back at the office, Maisie was reading a paperback romance. Chris was cursing under her breath as she struggled with the tedious forms Quinn had given her to complete, noting kilometers traveled, gas and oil consumed, repairs.

Boring, boring, boring, she recited, privately.

These long dark days were finally getting to her. The winter solstice in December still hadn't produced much in the way of increased daylight. No wonder animals hibernated, Chris thought with a huge yawn.

The phone rang, and Chris heard Maisie say, "She's right here. It's for you, honey."

The caller was Liz, and Chris said eagerly into the receiver, "I've meant to phone you. Are you feeling better?"

Liz had had a severe cold and flu after her trip at Christmas, and she still didn't sound like her usual buoyant self. "I'm okay, I guess," she said. "It's teachers' professional day today, so I'm off. Think you can come up and have dinner with me? I really need to talk to you, and this damn weather's been so bad lately...."

Chris glanced down at the infernal forms. It made absolutely no difference whether they were finished today or tomorrow, and she hadn't had a real day off in weeks.

Besides, after the past few days of virtual imprisonment, she was suffering from cabin fever. She longed to get out on her snowmobile and tear along through the icy air, leaving the heavy weight in the pit of her stomach behind in the thrill of snowmobiling along the trail. But she knew that Quinn would object if she asked his permission to go see Liz.

"I want you to lie low just another couple of days," he'd ordered brusquely just that morning. "I'm almost positive there's nothing to worry about, but staying in the office a bit longer won't hurt."

It did hurt, though. Maisie was driving Chris nuts with useless advice about romance, and she was eager to talk with Liz. Surely she and Liz could come up with a new angle on this roadblock she'd encountered with Quinn, as well as the reservations Liz was experiencing about Mario after her trip. Chris knew the visit hadn't gone well, but hadn't seen Liz long enough to sort out why.

Chris hesitated for a moment and then made up her mind. She was a free agent, after all. Quinn hadn't actually ordered her to stay at the detachment, he'd only suggested.

"I don't see why not, I'll get dressed and be on the trail in half an hour," Chris promised impulsively.

Maybe Liz could help her with the problems of her relationship with Quinn. If creative visualization had the power Chris had always thought it did, there were certainly no signs yet of the happy ending she'd created for the two of them. In fact, the whole future of their relationship was looking totally dismal.

The more Chris pondered the problems of career versus romance, the more the situation seemed as impossible to her as Quinn had insisted.

As usual, Maisie had just unabashedly listened to Chris's conversation.

"Goin' out the trail to Forty Mile, huh? Want me to get the corporal on the portable for you?" she asked.

Chris shook her head emphatically. She didn't need Quinn forbidding her to go out in that dogmatic manner of his.

"Don't bother him, Maisie. I'll just write him a note telling him where I'll be. You can give the message to him when he comes in," she said breezily.

Maisie shrugged and returned to her novel. "Suit yourself, honey. Just leave it on the desk. I'm just getting to the steamy part of this book."

Chris did, and then dashed off to her room and began the laborious process of dressing for the trail. A short while later, she was ready. She checked the pockets of her navy parka for mitts and toque, and called a cheery goodbye to Maisie.

In the garage, she opened the overhead double doors and grunted as she wheeled out the snowmobile.

She let the motor warm for several minutes, enjoying the anticipation of the ride up the frozen creekbed to Liz's place. The road was deserted on either side of the detachment except for the silver truck that writer woman had rented from the garage.

It passed slowly, and Sadie Price waved.

Chris waved back and then gunned the small machine down the road and out of town.

PARKER HAD COME BACK from his stint in Hawaii with a sunburned face and a more moderate attitude toward Cole's inheritance.

"The boy has some scheme for opening a medical clinic over there, so part of the money goes back into the economy and benefits the people who worked so blamed hard to make my wife's parents wealthy in the first place," Parker was explaining to Quinn over apple pie and coffee at Nancy's Café. "I've got no argument with that." Parker took a huge bite of his dessert, a satisfied look on his face. "Truth is, I'm proud of that boy of mine. Didn't let it go to his head at all, becoming an instant millionaire. I used to spend a lot of sleepless nights when he was growing up, wondering if the day might come when Cole would hold it against me, taking him away from what would have been a hell of a sight easier life than the one he and I had here in Dawson. We both had to struggle and pinch pennies to see him through medical school. But know what he said to me?''

Parker waited for Quinn's ''What's that, Parker?''

''He said, 'Pop, you never appreciate a thing unless you have to work hard to get it. Besides, you and I were happy, and that's something money can't buy.' Now ain't that a fine thing to say?''

''It's nothing more than the truth, Parker. You're a fine father to Cole.''

Parker's weathered features crinkled into a self-conscious smile as Quinn's portable radio crackled to life on the table.

''Corporal, there's an urgent phone call from Whitehorse. The guy is actually holding on till you get back here. Better hustle your tail,'' Maisie suggested irreverently.

What the hell has Staff Billings got his shirt in a knot over now?

Quinn tossed down some money and hurried out.

Driving a bit faster than was safe on Dawson's icy streets, he was halfway back to the office when he glimpsed a silver-colored rental truck heading out of town at a good speed.

Crazy city woman was going to end up in a snowbank, going that fast. He'd pull her over if it weren't for that call, Quinn thought.

He should scare her a little and give her a ticket. Teach her some respect for Dawson's roads. Deciding he was in too much of a hurry to stop, Quinn went on.

Back at the office, he pulled off his mitts and, still wearing his parka, picked up the receiver Maisie indicated.

It wasn't Billings at all. It was Larry, from Ident.

"Those prints you sent up this morning, Quinn. Things are slow here so I photo-faxed them to Ottawa right away. Listen to this," he said, and the note of excitement in his voice was clearly discernible.

"The thumbprint's the only one that gave enough characteristics, and we have a possible ident." Larry paused for effect, and Quinn felt his hand freeze over the receiver. His stomach began to drop as Larry cleared his throat and read, "Mildred Jean Evans, FPS number 731301A, alias Mary Jane Ewing, alias Gertrude Davenport, alias Sadie Price. Flagged, caution: violent. Excellent marksman, known to be long-time associate of Carl Schroeder, well-known hit man on Eastern Seaboard, now doing time at Stony Mountain pen. Although never convicted, she's been investigated on several occasions as hit woman for syndicates working out of Buffalo, New York."

Quinn's entire body seemed to be turning to lead. He was unaware of Maisie's concern as the color drained from his face, and his eyes widened with horror.

Larry's voice continued companionably. "If this is your girl, Quinn, she'll be white female, five-five, one-fifty pounds, forty-three years old, fading blond hair, plump, no marks, scars or tattoos apart from appendix scar, lower right abdomen."

Quinn didn't recognize his own voice. He could see that figure of Sadie Price behind the wheel of that silver truck, and he cursed his own blind chauvinism. *Never thought of a woman hit man, did you, Quinn?* some internal voice taunted.

Where had she been heading when he last saw her?

"Thanks, Larry. That's her, all right. Gotta go."

Maisie studied him curiously.

"Maisie, where's Chris?" Quinn demanded harshly, before the receiver even hit the cradle. "Get her in here right now."

Maisie stared at him over her glasses and slowly shook her head. "Can't do that, Corporal. She's not here, she left on the snowmobile half an hour ago. She wrote you a note," Maisie said as she leisurely fumbled through the messy pile beside her and extracted the folded sheet of paper. "Here it is, but I know where she's headed. I heard her tell Liz Morrison she'd be out that way. Hey, you okay, Corporal? You don't look so hot," the older woman finished with concern.

Everything inside of Quinn twisted, contracting painfully.

Chris was on the snowmobile. The creek trail she'd have taken paralleled the road in places. At this time of year, there wouldn't be any traffic.

Except for one silver-colored van.

Chris would be in no hurry, dawdling along enjoying the winter peace of the trail and the scant daylight of the afternoon. Price could park somewhere along the road—Quinn could imagine half a dozen likely spots—and that silver van would blend right into the landscape.

Then there was only watch, and wait.

It would be child's play for a marksman to pick off an unsuspecting figure in a navy parka, silhouetted against an all-white background.

At that moment, some part of Quinn became all policeman, and he took a precious second to review his options.

It was useless to try to catch Price in the cruiser.

Sadie had too much of a head start, and the same held true for the option of following Chris on the other snowmobile along the creekbed.

There was one other possible route, a tricky and dangerous shortcut known as Moses Harper's trap line. It eventually intersected the route Chris was following. Before it did, however, the path led up steep-sided hills and abruptly down again, over rough terrain that had accounted for several serious accidents among veteran snowmobilers in past winters.

If he was going to catch them—and God, he had to catch them—there was no other way.

Quinn felt as if he were moving in slow motion as he flung open the gun locker and snatched an issue .308 Winchester, loaded the clip and raced into the garage. He strapped the rifle to the side of the snowmobile and cursed like a madman at every small delay.

Moments later, he was roaring out of town.

Time and again he came heart-stoppingly close to disaster on the suicidal mission, and hours seemed to have elapsed by the time he reached the creek trail.

Had Chris passed? There were no tracks, and for the first time he felt a glimmer of hope.

Then he burst over a hillock and saw a silver truck far ahead in the gloom. It was parked inconspicuously by the side of the road, almost invisible in the early-afternoon dusk.

As Quinn came closer, he realized that the driver's side door was open, a figure leaning over the hood.

Instantly, he cut the power on his machine, and in the fraction of a second before he came to a full stop, an invisible fist hit his ribs and knocked him off the snowmobile, several feet backward into the snow. The machine turned sharply and the motor died.

It was only after the impact that the sound of the rifle exploded in his head, followed by spinning silence.

Dizzy sickness and a burning pain spread through him, and at the same time Quinn realized clearly what had happened.

Sadie Price had mistaken him for Chris. Their parkas were the same color.

Time expanded and then contracted for Quinn, and the silence became a buzzing inside his head.

He fought unconsciousness as the buzzing increased. Then he recognized the sound he heard dimly as the motor of a snowmobile, the whine of an approaching vehicle.

Chris was about to come over the hillock just behind him.

CHAPTER FOURTEEN

Chris.

Still behind him, just below the hill.

In another few moments, she'd be clearly visible to the marksman, who was still crouched by the side of the truck.

Quinn slowly turned his head to one side, waited for the dizziness to clear, orienting himself. His snowmobile was several feet away, on its side, and he could see the rifle rack from where he lay, nearly facedown in the snow.

He tried to pull breath into his lungs, but the intensity of pain in his chest made him gasp. He panted instead, clawed at the snow with both arms, hauling himself toward the machine, the rifle.... And the sound of Chris's motor grew louder and still louder in his ears.

Frantically, he braced on an elbow, clawed the rifle free, and the dizziness and burning agony nearly overcame him as he rolled to his back. He was holding the weapon.

Quinn fumbled with his mittens, drawing them off one after the other with his teeth. His fingers slid along the trigger guard, found the safety catch and released it.

Somehow, powered only by his will and his love for Chris, he heaved himself over and forced himself to his knees. He rested the rifle on the seat of the snowmobile, and again and again he had to fight to remain conscious as pain ripped through him.

Steadying the gun, focusing his blurred vision on the figure beside the van, he made himself breathe slowly out, hugged the rifle into his shoulder and, knowing he had only once chance, he squeezed the trigger.

The kick of the rifle sent white-hot agony through every nerve. Quinn never heard the explosion at all. He toppled into oblivion just as Chris soared over the top of the hill behind him.

In one confused glance, she saw the parked van in the distance, the snowmobile and the kneeling figure beside it wearing a navy-blue police-issue parka.

Instantly she cut the engine, and as the motor died, it took her a horrified instant to recognize the sound of a high-powered bullet ricocheting through tree branches just above and behind her. Almost simultaneously, she heard the crack of two rifle shots as they exploded through the stillness.

In the same frozen split second, the figure beside the van flew backward and sprawled, motionless, on the snow-covered road. Closer to Chris, Quinn slid slowly downward and lay just as motionless in the hard-packed snow of the trail.

The next half hour held frozen frames of action, and the blank clips in between Chris never did remember.

She knew Quinn was dead when she first knelt over him and saw the chest area of his parka slowly turning dark with the seep of blood from his wound. A long wail of agony escaped her.

But then she realized he was breathing, and she

went into frenzied action, using his mitten liners to create two pressure pads, sliding them in under his parka, fighting nausea and faintness when her hand encountered the warm, sticky gush of fluid pouring out both chest and back where the bullet had passed through his body.

Blood. Quinn's blood.

She anchored the pads tight with her scarf, cursing the weakness that flooded over her at the sight of so much blood.

Could anyone bleed this much and live?

She never remembered how she got his inert form onto her snowmobile and over to the silver van.

He came to for an instant when she was trying to move him.

"Chris," he breathed like a prayer, his voice thick. "Did...I...get...her? You...o...kay?"

Sadie Price was definitely dead, and Chris could feel only cold relief and satisfaction. "I'm fine. Don't talk, please, darling, don't try and talk," Chris all but sobbed. "You got her, yes, you saved my life, now please, Quinn, you've got to help me get you... Quinn."

She almost screamed the words at him, but his eyes glazed over and rolled slowly up, and his head dropped.

She forgot everything then except the monumental task of getting Quinn's limp body up and into the van. He outweighed her by at least a hundred pounds, and she was terrified of hurting him even more, tugging at him as she must in order to move him.

"Quinn, please, please wake up," she begged. "Don't you dare die on me. You've got to help me do this. I love you, how I love you, but I can't lift you by myself. Wake up and help me, just for a minute, you stubborn, miserable, bad-tempered wonderful man...."

Sobbing, begging, cajoling, she finally saw his eyelids flicker again. He slipped in and out of consciousness, and staggering, reeling beneath his weight, she used those instants of half awareness to bully him into helping her.

At last, at last he was in the van. She was faint and trembling uncontrollably. She'd taken her parka off and wrapped it around Quinn. He was more on the floor than the seat, but at least she was able to close the door.

She didn't remember starting the van or turning it, or even careering down the narrow road. She did have a clear picture of meeting Stefan in the cruiser halfway back to Dawson.

Stefan had been sent out along the road by the worried Maisie, and Chris paused only long enough to holler at him to radio Doc Chambers, to make certain help was waiting the instant she arrived in Dawson with Quinn. He was deeply unconscious now.

Doc Chambers was indeed waiting for them, and he quickly treated Quinn for blood loss and shock. However, Quinn obviously needed more sophisticated medical help than Dawson's small clinic could provide.

Chris radioed a panic call to Whitehorse, to Staff Billings, and by early evening, the police aircraft had come and gone, taking Quinn with it. He still hadn't regained consciousness.

Chris watched the plane lift into the blessedly clear, cold night, and she knew that all that mattered in the world to her was on board. She wanted to be on the flight too, at Quinn's side, more than she'd ever wanted anything before, and once again her job and his had prevented it.

"You okay, Constable?" Billings had demanded when she called for help. "You able to carry on, and all that?"

"Yes, yes...I'm all right, Staff." In fact, Chris had never been less all right. "I'm alive because... because Quinn..."

"Quite." Billings's voice had taken on a tone of brisk efficiency. "I understand our corporal pulled off a neat bit of work. Telex us the basic details immediately, giving us all the information available in keeping with operational instructions...."

His voice droned on, and she stayed behind and took charge of the millions of details, the reams of telexed requests and demands, the work of Dawson's detachment, knowing that there was no assurance at all that Quinn was going to live through the night. For the first time ever, she hated her job and the responsibility it carried.

Quinn had been so right. Their jobs would always come between them....

"How, how...is he?" she'd asked the young doctor from the flight's medical team, half running alongside the stretcher holding Quinn's limp body as they raced him into the plane along the garishly lit runway.

"Don't know yet. Doc Chambers says the bullet appears to have punctured his lung. He's lost a lot of blood. Can't tell with bullet wounds until you see what damage is done. We'll let you know as soon as we can."

There wasn't time to think at all over the next hours. Calls came and went to headquarters, questions were asked and answered, a ton of paper needed filling out. The small telex machine spit out information like a demented monster.

And still, no word came about Quinn.

In the early-morning hours, everything finally became quiet. Chris and Maisie and Stefan huddled in the detachment kitchen, making coffee that no one drank. Everyone was waiting for the phone to ring. The seconds seemed eternal.

When the call came, Chris snatched up the receiver.

"Staff Billings here." The high-pitched voice sounded ominous, and Chris felt her entire body begin to shake uncontrollably. She steeled herself for what she was about to hear.

"Corporal Quinn appears to be out of danger. His condition is critical, but they have him stabilized. The bullet punctured the lower lobe of the right lung. It didn't affect any other vital organs. The surgeon assures me that he was able to repair the lung."

It took an eternity for her to realize he wasn't saying that Quinn had died. When her frozen muscles relaxed enough, Chris turned to the fearful, expectant faces of Maisie and Stefan.

"He's come through the operation; he's stable," she managed to choke out, and Billings gave up trying to say any more until the happy cheers in the background subsided.

Chris was crying. The pent-up tears began to rain uncontrollably down her cheeks as she did her best to absorb the rest of Billings's message, but the words hardly made sense.

"We're sending Corporal Nelson from subdivision General Investigation Section up there first thing this morning to give you a hand tying up the reports."

Maisie, crying just as hard as Chris was by now, handed her a fistful of tissues, and Chris mopped at her eyes, unable to control the heaving sobs tearing out of her.

Billings was going right ahead regardless.

"We've already telexed the details east, and there's a good possibility that we can connect this Price woman with our friend Angelo Andollini. That would put him behind bars where he belongs, and you could relax and enjoy the mad social whirl of Dawson for the rest of the winter, Constable." His dry chuckle sounded a bit forced. "Actually, Corporal Nelson will only stay for a few days. Things are normally pretty quiet up there at this time of year. If you anticipate problems, we could always send somebody up from Whitehorse detachment to give you a hand?" Billings's voice rose questioningly, and he seemed to be waiting for some response.

Chris sniffed loudly in his ear, summoned up her pride in her ability as a police officer, and heard herself weakly reassuring him that there was no need, she was certain she could manage quite nicely with auxiliary member Rabowski's help, which of course was exactly what Billings wanted to hear.

This was Quinn's detachment, and she'd run it for him just the way he wanted it run, until he could come back and take over again.

But Chris's heart sank as she realized that being left in charge of Dawson would mean she couldn't even get away to visit Quinn in hospital.

She wanted so badly to see him, to touch him, to reassure herself that he really was alive, that he would get well.

She'd been so afraid he was going to die.

But he was alive. He was alive, and that was really all that mattered.

When the euphoria wore off, however, the doubts began.

Would he even want to see her, even if she could somehow wangle a trip to Whitehorse?

After all, it was her fault totally he'd been shot, her fault that he was going through any of this. Sadie Price had been sent after her.

Chris remembered clearly what he'd said about her undercover work.

"I couldn't sit back and watch you put your life in danger."

It wasn't her in the hospital right now. It was Quinn.

He'd nearly lost his life because of her. And that fact pointed out as nothing else could have how right he'd been about their chances for a life together.

During the days that followed, Chris doggedly worked with Corporal Nelson, preparing the inquest into the shooting of Sadie Price. There was a mountain of paperwork necessary, and all the time she worked a sense of black and awful desolation was growing in her.

Chris heaved a sigh of relief when the petulantly meticulous man pronounced the investigation complete on the third morning and caught the plane out at noon.

Maisie phoned the hospital in Whitehorse twice every day. On the fourth morning Quinn was finally moved out of intensive care. Maisie badgered the hospital staff into rolling him near a phone that evening, and she and Chris and Stefan each took turns sending good wishes.

Maisie and Stefan thoughtfully left Chris alone when her turn came, and her stomach was tied in knots with all the things she needed to say to him, all the things she needed to ask.

"Quinn, I…oh, God, Quinn, I'm so sorry for what happened, I'm so glad you…" Chris's voice trailed off, and she felt like biting her tongue. What had she been about to say, for heaven's sake? Glad you didn't die? *Just what every patient needs to hear.*

"…not your fault, you didn't even faint at the blood, although you were pretty green, I seem to remember…. I'm proud of you, Ms Constable." Quinn was trying to joke around but he sounded awful.

The thin, strained voice on the other end of the line didn't seem remotely like him.

Chris rubbed a fist across her eyes, wiping away the tears that insisted on raining down and dripping off her nose. She'd been like a leaky faucet for days, crying at the most inopportune times.

Now she felt worse than ever because she couldn't seem to link this thin, reedy voice with the Quinn she knew. He sounded disoriented when he asked her something about the detachment.

His words were slurring, an indication that he must still be incredibly weak. Chris asked him what things he needed her to package up and send him.

"My shaving kit, my bathrobe, the big manila envelope with my manuscript in it from the second drawer of my desk," he said in a near whisper, and she knew he wasn't going to be able to talk much longer. Chris opened her mouth to blurt out the things she needed so badly to tell him, and found she couldn't.

She was too emotional from the tumultuous bundle

of love and caring and guilt and remorse she'd packed around since the day he was shot, to say anything meaningful at all...like simply, "I love you with all my heart." Or, "I need you on any terms whatsoever."

"We're all thrilled that you're getting better," she managed to say, finally, and then the nurse came on and ended the call.

Disgusted with herself, Chris hung up the phone slowly and a feeling of utter hopelessness overwhelmed her.

She admitted for the first time the awful truth that had been staring her in the face since the accident.

There simply wasn't any chance for her and Quinn as long as they both worked for the RCMP. In spite of everything, because she was so stubbornly determined that it would all turn out fine, some part of her had gone on hoping.

It was silly and immature of her, she could see that now, to think some miracle would occur, and they'd end up in each other's arms with the blessing of the force, free to continue their careers. This shooting had proved how impossible it was for them to share any sort of normal life together, or even for them to be together as long as they were both in the force.

For the first time since the shooting, she took several hours off the following afternoon and drove out to visit Liz. She drove as fast as the road would allow past the spot where the shooting had occurred and kept her eyes riveted to the road. She was visibly trembling and badly shaken when she finally pulled into Liz's snow-packed driveway.

"You need a drink," her friend declared as soon

as she saw Chris's pale face, and poured them each a brandy.

"How's Quinn?"

Dully, Chris related the good news about his being out of intensive care.

"And how're you?" Liz demanded next.

"I'm fine," Chris said automatically, and then she set the brandy glass clumsily down on the floor, sloshing out the contents on the hooked rug under her chair. She grabbed for Liz's hand. "That's not true. I'm not fine at all, Liz. I'm coming apart inside. I've gone along believing that somehow things would work out for me and Quinn, despite all our problems, despite both of us being in the RCMP. Now, since the shooting, I realize there's no possibility of that happening. There's just no way we could ever make it work, there's no happy ending." One by one, she listed the reasons, the very things she'd been able to rationalize so well when Quinn had listed them to her. Liz listened patiently, not saying much. She gave Chris encouraging nods now and then.

Chris realized there was an almost hysterical note in her voice, but she didn't care about control or dignity or reserve. Liz was her friend, and it was so good to be able to talk about all the demons haunting her.

When Chris was finally finished, Liz was silent for a few moments. When she spoke, her voice was quiet and thoughtful. "There's always a way if you choose it, Chris. I finally realized that about me and Mario."

Liz explained that she'd come back from Los Angeles after Christmas, disillusioned and convinced that Mario's fast-lane type of life wasn't at all what she wanted, despite the fact that she loved him.

"His life is year-round sunshine, and noise, and

smog and all-night parties, and it drove me up the wall. I'm used to snow and silence and all-winter darkness. He says we could spend part of each year up here, but I worked so hard on my house, and my farm…this is where I live. I don't want to just visit. And I get the impression he feels the same about the coast. Anyway, we fought with a vengeance each time we discussed it. We're just total opposites. I'm Yukon, he's California.''

"But you love each other! Why can't each of you give a little, go and live in Minnesota or something? You can't give up a perfectly good romance because of geography,'' Chris exclaimed. It was so easy to see a solution to another's romance.

"I thought of that. But you know, when it came to making a decision about him and all the other parts of my life, I started to wonder if maybe it was the idea of romance I was in love with more than Mario himself. And much as it hurt my pride, I had to wonder too if the same wasn't true of him. Falling in love with a Yukon dance hall girl in green satin is both dramatic and exciting, and neither of us saw each other as we really were, as ordinary people, until I flew to Los Angeles.'' Liz looked both sad and resigned. "It's not just that, either,'' she went on. "The truth is, he told me more about his job and it scares me silly. Invicta International takes on jobs that are real James Bond stuff, and Mario thrives on exciting assignments that are often dangerous. I went through adjusting to widowhood once. I'd rather not do it again.''

Chris had no answer. She knew all about the effect dangerous jobs could have on a relationship.

Liz sighed and finished her brandy. "Anyway, I

told him everything, honestly, the day I left, and I had a feeling he was relieved.''

''I'm awfully sorry, Liz.'' What an ineffectual expression to mark the end of a dream.

''Well, we're a fine pair, you and I,'' Liz remarked ruefully. ''I'm over the worst of it by now, but I guess what I'm trying to tell you is that there's always a way to make these things work, if the sacrifice is worth it to you. It wasn't for me, but you should consider your own options, Chris. You could leave the RCMP, you know. That would solve the major problems between you and Quinn.''

Chris nodded miserably. She knew only too well what her choices were, but she hadn't dared confront them. Not yet.

Why did love have to involve so much personal agony and heartache? As she did so often, Chris thought of Abe, and of Beverly Schultz, and suddenly, she found herself telling Liz the couple's story.

''Beverly said she was afraid, that she couldn't live up to his expectations of her,'' Chris finished.

''That's what wrong with all of us, I guess,'' Liz summarized thoughtfully. ''We all figure that we have to be so much more than we are, just to have someone love us. Then we feel hurt because we want to be loved just the way we are, and we end up messing the whole thing up.''

For several days after her visit with Liz, Chris felt as if she was carrying on an impassioned debate with herself. Her body went automatically through the necessary tasks, and her brain went over and over the things Liz had said.

She could quit the force.

Even Quinn had once asked her whether she was

ready to give up her career for love of him, and she'd never once seriously considered it. Until now.

Was she capable of leaving the job that meant so much to her?

She certainly was willing at this very moment, but what kind of shrew would she become in five years down the line if she did?

To hell with worrying about five years from now. She loved him.

But what effect would it have on both of them, on her own personality, on the person Quinn loved? How much would she change?

For the best part of a week, Chris spent the most miserable period of her entire life making the decision to quit her job and be with him.

When the time came that she was absolutely certain of her decision, she called the hospital, eager to tell Quinn what she'd decided, what she was willing to sacrifice for her love for him.

The professional voice on the other end informed her that as a result of the collapsed lung, he had developed pneumonia in the past six hours and was once again on the critical list.

And no, even if Chris dropped everything and made the trip to Whitehorse, she wouldn't be allowed to even see him.

All her impassioned dreams shriveled to nothing again, and Chris lapsed back into the horrifying limbo of not knowing whether Quinn would even live.

She found the only lifeline she had to cling to during that time was her job. She was in uniform every waking hour, and she manufactured things that needed to be done until Maisie threatened to quit and even Stefan began to avoid her whenever possible.

She was a crazy, driven lady, but she understood as never before how much her work meant to her.

It was another week before the assurance finally came that once again, Quinn was only seriously ill.

Only.

Chris was drained, emotionally exhausted, and once again immensely relieved, but she knew with certainty now that she couldn't leave the RCMP, not even for Quinn, and she could hardly summon even regret for that decision.

The emotional seesaw of the past weeks now seemed to have numbed some vital part of her psyche. Everything was on hold. The only thing that mattered now was that Quinn continue to improve, continue to get well again.

Chris ran the Dawson detachment with a vengeance, and she treated each separate day as an entity, refusing to look into the future, making sure she was so exhausted at night that she wouldn't be able to think of the past.

She simply existed, did her work, and waited for Quinn.

ONE MORNING late in March, Quinn struggled to a sitting position for the second time that same morning and slid the rough copy of his book out of the manila envelope.

He'd just been through what constituted a shouting match with his doctors, and he'd lost. He still couldn't shout, of course; whispering was more his forte at the moment. But he'd put up a good fight all the same.

His lung was recovering nicely—the surgeon used some technical jargon about the operation he'd had—but Quinn decided it hadn't been that different from repairing a puncture and pumping up a car tire. Anyway, it had worked fine. The pneumonia had been a rotten trick, like kicking a man when he was already down, but for the past several days at least, he'd been feeling much better, and he'd told the doctors when they came by on rounds this morning that he was going home to Dawson.

He was feeling much better, and there were urgent matters he had to attend to.

They'd all but laughed at him.

"We happen to have a lot of time and effort invested in you, Quinn," the jovial doctor with the steely eyes told him. "You nearly died and messed up our good reputation, not once, but twice. That lung hasn't had time to properly heal, the pneumonia's left you vulnerable to other infections, and we're keeping you here if we have to tie you down to do it. In fact, your Staff Sergeant Billings has given us permission to handcuff you to the bed if necessary, so why not spare us the trouble? Make yourself comfortable, enjoy the scenery, the excellent food, the good conversation. You're our guest for at least another six weeks, like it or not," was the official verdict.

Afterward, Quinn had privately raged, but he'd also sweated and trembled and he'd had to lie down, cursing and furious at such embarrassing weakness, but aware that he wasn't as strong as he needed to be to get dressed, walk to the elevator and sign himself out as he'd planned.

He had it in his head that he absolutely had to see Chris.

During the hazy, pain-filled days after the shooting, Quinn had clung to the knowledge that Chris had escaped without injury, that he'd been able to protect her after all. That knowledge was somehow all he'd needed to endure whatever was happening to him.

Something had changed in Quinn during those days, however, something deep and basic, and it began to slowly take shape as his body rallied and began healing itself.

Coming close to death had made murky areas of his life suddenly seem crystal clear to him, and the most important one was his love for Chris.

How foolish, when life could be this short, to hold love at arm's length the way he'd been doing. He'd been afraid of love, because it was strange to him, but now he knew without a doubt that he couldn't allow Chris to walk out of his life. He was going to marry her, cherish her, live with and love her every single day left in their lives, any way he could.

And that decision forced him to face something else about himself.

In his chauvinistic way, he'd challenged Chris, asking her whether or not she could leave the force to be his wife.

He should have turned that question around, and honestly looked at what should have been obvious ever since the weeks he'd spent at Abe's cabin.

It was he who should leave the force, not Chris.

Without being consciously aware of it, Quinn had become a writer instead of a policeman. He wanted to finish the book he'd started, then go on to another and another, write down all the people and all the scenes he'd been storing inside his head for so long.

It was time for him to leave the RCMP, and when he did that, there would be no barriers left between him and Chris.

He worked it all out between bouts of respirators

and pain-filled nights and shots that sent him into some cottony, confused oblivion.

When he finally had their future perfectly clear in his mind, he wanted to jump out of the hospital bed and fly back to Dawson and propose to Chris on the spot.

Which was how he'd gotten in the argument with the doctors this morning, and lost. Well, there was always the telephone. It would be harder to say what he had to say without holding her in his arms, but he'd try his best.

The very pretty nurse with the red-gold curls bounced into his room.

"Morning, Corporal," she said warmly, wondering if he knew how much of an uproar he was creating among the female nursing staff. To the best of her knowledge, every last pantsuited one of them was in love with him—including the fifty-six-year-old supervisor, who still believed in chastity belts.

He was so dramatically handsome with that dark coloring against the white sheets, the dashing mustache above a chin that strong.

"Nice to have you feeling better." She glanced at the pages of scribbled words curiously. "Boy, that's a lot of paper. You writing a book or something?" she teased lightly.

"I'm trying to," Quinn admitted. Might as well get used to telling people what his job was.

"You wrote one before? What name do you write under?"

"This is my first crack at it," he said slowly.

"My cousin's husband writes a column for the Whitehorse paper. He's got a degree in English and he's taken lots of courses. He's written three mystery novels, but he only got one of them published,'' she commented, plumping the pillows at his back and straightening the spread. ''He says you don't make a whole lot on one book unless it's a bestseller. He's got a job at the bank. I could ask him the name of his editor if you want,'' she offered eagerly.

Insecurity swept over Quinn. What if his book never sold? He'd read enough to know that selling a first novel was no easy task, and what the hell did he really know about writing? He didn't have any degree, that was for sure.

What about money? He was fairly well off, but he hadn't saved nearly enough to be able to afford to live indefinitely without a paycheck. And his newly liberated attitudes about women didn't include having his wife support him.

How did you ask a women to marry you if you were a writer who'd never had a letter to the editor published, never mind a book?

He suddenly had misgivings about phoning Chris and blurting out a proposal. In fact, he was going about this all wrong.

He'd better talk to Billings, put in his letter of resignation, do this one step at a time.

He'd better finish this book and at least make an effort to sell it. It was going to take time, all of it.

''I'd appreciate you asking your brother-in-law about the editor,'' he told the red-haired nurse. ''Any chance you could find me a portable typewriter to use? I need to revise this thing and get it typed out properly before I can send it to anybody.''

''Sure,'' she said easily, delighted to be able to tell the other nurses that she and Corporal Quinn had a common interest. ''There's one downstairs nobody's using, I'll bring it up for you as long as you promise not to overdo it, and I'll talk to Jason tonight about the editor. What should I say your book's about?''

Chris thought of Abe, and Parker, and Stefan, of Maisie and Liz and, always, of Chris; people whose essence made up the characters on these scribbled pages, along with the Yukon setting.

"Oh, it's about heroes, and beautiful damsels, and love and adventure and courage. It's about the knights of the North,'' he said dramatically, wondering how you ever told anyone what something was about and managed to make it sound as if you weren't a raving lunatic.

"What's the title?'' she demanded, and he was about to say he didn't know when the title popped into his head.

"It's...I'm thinking of calling it *Northern Knights*,'' he said slowly, testing the sound of the words to see if they were right.

They were, and a pleased smile came and went beneath the mustache the pretty nurse found so attractive.

"Yup, that's it. *Northern Knights*.''

By evening, the stack of neatly typed pages on the bedside table had grown steadily, and over the next few days the nurses finally gave up trying to make Quinn turn out his bed light at a reasonable hour.

Staff Billings was so surprised by Quinn's letter of resignation that for once he couldn't find a single clever thing to say, and for several nights he even had trouble falling asleep at a reasonable hour.

The nurse's brother-in-law, Jason Armitage, surprisingly came by to meet Quinn, one writer to the other, and they got along so well that he offered to take the finished manuscript with him and hand it to his editor when he flew to Toronto in ten days' time for publicity on his own novel. If Quinn had it finished, of course.

Quinn drove the nursing staff nearly berserk by refusing to follow any of their rules during the next week, but he finished the book.

Then he lay back in bed and rested for half a day before he started the next one.

Maisie phoned Quinn at least twice or three times a week and each time she made certain Chris was around so that she could talk to him as well. As soon as Chris was on the line, Maisie would discreetly disappear until the call was completed.

Of course she listened in, and each time, she became more chagrined at the conversations the two officers had.

No one would have ever suspected there was more between them than a purely business relationship.

Chris talked about police work, and Quinn listened.

Quinn talked about the progress of his book, and Chris listened.

They both talked about the weather, and then after an awkward pause they each said goodbye and hung up.

Maisie thought the calls were the most sinful waste of government money she'd ever come up against, and she told Chris so in no uncertain terms.

Privately, Chris agreed.

"I WANT TO LET HIM KNOW that I love him, but there doesn't seem to be anywhere to go once I've said it. All the old problems are still the same, so I never say it," Chris said miserably to Liz one sunny day in April.

They were having a hurried lunch together at Nancy's Café. It was a weekday and Liz only had an hour before she had to return to her classroom. Chris had an appointment with the superintendent of an apartment building right after lunch.

Someone had left a large, locked trunk behind in one of the rooms, and never returned to reclaim it. The manager naturally wanted to rent the apartment again, and he'd phoned the detachment to see what should be done.

Liz glanced at her watch. "Don't expect any helpful advice from me about romance," she warned morosely. "Obviously, I'm a total failure when it comes to meaningful relationships."

She'd shown Chris a card from Mario. It was a tactful note that said it was wonderful to know you, I'll never forget you, I've met a girl who looks a lot like you, happiness always, and goodbye. So that was that.

"When's Quinn getting out of hospital? It seems he's been there forever," Liz asked, changing the subject. Neither of them had any constructive advice for the other and they both knew it, even though talking over their problems together was comforting.

"He's finally pinned them down to the first Friday in May," Chris replied.

"That's only three weeks from now. Why don't we plan a welcome-home party for him?" Liz asked impulsively.

Chris was nervous about seeing Quinn. She was terrified that she'd break down and say or do something humiliating. Suddenly, the idea of a little party with a few of his friends around to ease the pressure sounded just fine.

"Hey, I think that's a wonderful idea," Chris said enthusiastically. "We could have a little get-together over at the detachment...."

"We could have the school band, and meet him at the airport, and get the mayor to make a speech. Everybody figures Quinn's a local hero, we ought to tell him so."

"Uh, right," Chris agreed a little less fervently. She suddenly wasn't at all sure that Quinn would want a hero's welcome. In fact, she was absolutely certain he wouldn't.

"Maybe we'd better not..." she objected, but Liz had spotted Jim Murphy and Parker just coming in the door. She waved them both over, and seconds later, Quinn's homecoming party began to assume all the proportions of a visit from the prime minister.

By the time Liz left to go back to school, the whole thing was out of control, and half an hour later, when Chris walked dazedly out to the cruiser, a committee had been drawn up to organize the whole thing. Plans were already afoot to get the use of the community center, have a sit-down potluck dinner for several hundred people, with a welcome-home cake decorated with the RCMP crest. The cake would be made, of course, by José, and carried in by the dancers from Gertie's in full costume.

It was simply out of her hands, Chris concluded after she'd done her best to dampen the whole extravaganza.

She drove over to the apartment complex, wondering exactly when she'd finally accepted the fact that she and Quinn would part when her transfer came through that summer. Staff Billings had passed along the welcome news that enough evidence had been found in Sadie Price's effects to arrest Angelo Andollini and lay charges of conspiracy to commit murder. Billings was certain the charges would result in a long imprisonment.

Chris was out of danger at last. She'd decided to ask Billings to arrange a transfer for her in the next few weeks—any transfer as long as it was a long, long way from Dawson.

She'd never stop loving Quinn, but she wanted to be as far away from him as possible, as soon as possible.

A person could only stand so much.

"What name did the man use on your register?" she asked the fat super as he hurried her up to the modest room on the second floor where the trunk had been left and unlocked the door.

"Norman Bickle. He was a salesman for copier machines, but the company he worked for told me he'd quit. They don't know wherc he's gone."

"Norman Bickle?" Chris repeated in amazement. "A very short, meek little man with slicked-down black hair?" The superintendent nodded. "That's him. Wouldn't be much good in a brawl, but not a bad sort of guy. You know where he is?" he asked. "He owes me fifty-seven bucks for storage."

Chris hoped with all her heart that nothing bad had happened to Norman. Maybe he'd been so heartbroken over the breakup with Maisie that... She shuddered. Her imagination was running away with her.

"No, I haven't seen him in months," she replied. The man led the way into the rather dingy rooms, and hauled the large trunk out of the corner. Chris popped the lock with a flat bar.

She opened the lid, glanced at the contents and sank back on her heels in stupefaction.

Neatly folded inside the trunk were stacks and stacks of women's lingerie, bras, panties, nightgowns, pink, blue, beige, lavender and yellow slips. And when she lifted out a pair of panties, she shook her head, bemused.

They were immense. In fact, all the lingerie inside the trunk was at least size extra-large, and Chris was somehow certain that a fair amount of it belonged to Jennie Martinson.

Poor, meek little Norman Bickle was also Dawson's underwear bandit, the town's one honest-to-goodness certifiable sex pervert.

Norman Bickle, whom Maisie had accused of being as dull as an old dishcloth.

Why, there was a lot more naughtiness in Norman Bickle than Maisie had ever suspected! And was she going to be caught speechless for once when she found out. Maisie, who prided herself on knowing everything that went on in Dawson.

For the first time in weeks, Chris started to laugh.

CHAPTER FIFTEEN

TWO DAYS BEFORE he was discharged, Quinn received a phone call from Robert Anderson, a Toronto editor.

"We'd like to go to contract with you for *Northern Knights*," the man said in a professional-sounding voice. "We like the novel very much, and we're interested in anything else you might have written about the North. You've hit the crest of a trend. The Arctic is the interesting 'place of the moment,' and we believe your book will sell very well."

Quinn's ecstatic bellow after he hung up brought nurses and doctors running. They thought he was having some sort of relapse, but when he told them what had just occurred, they smuggled in a bottle of wine and helped him celebrate.

He hurried to the phone in the hall to call Chris with his news, but he replaced the receiver slowly before the call was completed. The full import of what was happening made his heart pound and the blood thunder through his veins with excitement and anticipation.

He'd be seeing her. In forty-eight hours, he could watch the excitement and pleasure play across those mobile, innocent features instead of imagining her reaction over the phone.

He remembered exactly what her mouth looked

like, full and slightly parted, waiting for his kiss, and he shuddered. His body reacted instantly. Well, he was a whole man again, no question at all about that.

There were no barriers now between him and Chris.

He was about to become a published writer, and he'd resigned from the RCMP, effective immediately.

He was free.

He could ask her to marry him.

How the hell did a man go about that? It wasn't something best done on the telephone, he knew that much, but he'd had absolutely no practice at proposing.

He wanted to get the damn thing right the first time, because he was only planning on doing it once.

Did men still get down on one knee to do it properly, or did that go out along with suits of armor?

He could only hope that when the time was right, the proper method would be instinctive.

THE EARLY-MORNING CALLS from Billings had become annoyingly familiar to Chris, and she was sipping her first cup of coffee at six-fifteen on May third when the phone rang.

"Morning, Staff," she said mischievously before he could announce himself in the usual ponderous manner.

She heard the sound of his dry chuckle. "Well, Constable Johnstone, it's nice to know there's one other early bird out after the proverbial worm, what? How are things up there in Rory Bory land this fine spring morning?"

Chris rolled her eyes heavenward. Billings was a little hard to take, especially today, when her nerves were stretched tight because Quinn was coming home.

The weather was cooperating unbelievably well for the time of year. She got to her feet and stretched the phone cord, pulling the yellow curtain aside a little. Just a week ago, it had been ten below and trying to snow, and now for three days it had been almost balmy.

Dawson residents had started doffing their old winter parkas and emerging, as if from a chrysalis, announcing that it was spring. They'd been making bets on the breakup of the river for weeks already, and the whole town seemed to vibrate with an undertone of high excitement.

"As you probably know, Corporal Quinn has been released from hospital here and will be arriving at Dawson by police plane at ten this morning. I've decided to pop on up there with him, Constable. Time I paid you northern folks a visit, what?"

Chris plunked herself down in her chair and scowled at the phone in silent consternation. The last thing she needed today of all days was a surprise inspection from Staff Billings.

Forcing what she could only hope was a measure of enthusiasm into her voice, she said weakly, "That's just fine, sir. We'll be pleased to have you."

As pleased as she would be to have a blizzard blow in.

Billings was hemming and hawing and clearing his throat, signs that Chris recognized were the prelude to some sort of announcement.

"This is in strictest confidence, Constable. It's not general knowledge quite yet, but you should be aware that our Corporal Quinn has retired from our noble force, effective immediately.''

Chris was incapable of speech for a moment. She felt blankly amazed, shaken by the announcement. She also felt as if Billings was talking about a total stranger.

Quinn, retired from the RCMP? Why, Quinn would never retire. He was Dawson's symbol of law and order, he was their hero, he was the unofficial mayor of the town, judging by the frightful extravaganza the entire place had arranged for his return today.

A measure of outraged betrayal mingled with surprise. How could he have done something this major without even hinting to her about it, after all they'd had between them?

After all that was still burning and hurting inside of her?

Confused and suddenly a little angry, she stammered, ''But, but I don't understand. What, why… why would he do such a thing, Staff?''

Staff Billings heaved a dramatic sigh.

''Ours is not to reason why, and all that. It saddens me to see one of our best give up the struggle, but his reasons are his own. Now, I did think that with a fine officer like Quinn, a few well-chosen words would be appropriate to commemorate the occasion, which is the real purpose of my visit today. I thought you might arrange to gather the office staff, and the auxiliary, and any significant friends, and I will make a short address in honor of the day, Constable. Very casual, of course.''

Oh, what the heck.

The entire town was turning out, and so far eight

people were scheduled to make some sort of speeches.

Why not Staff Billings?

Why not make it a proper military fiasco?

"That would be really nice, Staff, but there's something you ought to know about all this," Chris explained evenly. "Quinn's homecoming has turned into a civic ceremony here. The mayor will be present and several dignitaries. There's a large party scheduled to welcome him, and I'd like to suggest, Staff, that it might be appropriate if we wore red serge for the occasion."

There was a moment's pause while Billings considered this new state of affairs.

"Quite right, Constable. Quite right. I shall don the scarlet trappings, and you too. See you at ten, Constable Johnstone. Upward and on."

She hung up, trying to absorb what Staff had confided, but her thoughts were in chaos.

What was Quinn up to? He was driving her into emotional collapse, that's what he was doing. She felt as if her nerves were jumping out of her skin, and her hands shook. She folded them in her lap and took several deep breaths and allowed her head to slump to her chest. Slowly, using every ounce of her training and will, she sank into a meditative state, and she determinedly visualized a blank mental screen.

A tall, dark, handsome man was kneeling at her feet. She could see his mustache, his lips moving, hear his voice asking her to marry him.

The scene changed, and fellow officers in red serge held crossed swords to form an archway as she and her new husband came out of a church, and bells rang.

The scene changed, and she bent to kiss two small

cherubic faces as she went off, in uniform, to work. Their daddy stood at the door, waiting to kiss her.

Slowly, she returned from her inner self to the reality of the kitchen, but now she was calm and confident.

Her mother had always insisted that visualization worked, and after all, weren't mothers always right?

She showered, slipped into her sexiest wisp of scarlet chemise, donned her official uniform and dabbed perfume behind her ears.

She'd done absolutely everything she could. The rest was in the hands of God.

Chris had to organize volunteers to keep the boisterous crowd off the runway when at last the small silver plane circled and landed.

The ramp was secured, the mayor cleared his throat several times without covering the makeshift microphone, in nervous preparation for his welcoming speech.

The school band began to play, and Chris felt her stomach tighten and her heart begin to pound. Tiny droplets of sweat were already forming on her forehead from the combination of unfamiliar warm sunshine and the red serge jacket she wore.

The first figure to deplane wasn't Quinn, but Staff Billings, looking absolutely resplendent in scarlet. The sun actually reflected off of his highly polished boots, and he touched his hat in a form of salute at Chris as she stood stiffly at attention near the bottom of the ramp. Staff Billings's narrow, angular face was set in frozen formality beneath his Stetson.

But as he paused beside her, she was almost certain one of his hawklike blue eyes closed and opened again in a wink.

Quinn came next, and over the slightly discordant notes of the brass section of the band, a ragged cheer went up.

Chris hardly heard the noise. She was terrified for a few moments that she might faint and totally disgrace herself.

Her whole attention was focused on the tall, wide-shouldered figure ducking his head to clear the door at the top of the ramp. She watched as, a trifle awkwardly, Quinn came down the stairs, nearer and nearer to where she stood, the midnight eyes under their bushy brows searching out her own and his gaze never faltering as he descended the steps.

He'd lost weight, and the strong lines of his beloved face were thrown into bold relief.

Chris's face was tilted up to him, but the rest of her body was at stiff attention as he came unsteadily down the ramp.

He'd never seen her in red serge till now. She'd lost weight. She looked like a slender girl, dressed up in someone's uniform for a lark. Instead of a Stetson, she wore a smartly brimmed black hat with a gold band on its crown, and even the staid military cut of the narrow skirt couldn't hide the curves of her bottom, the long slender length of her legs.

Chris. My Chris…

He wore casual civvies—a pair of gray dress pants with an open-necked pale blue shirt, a smart tweed jacket over the top—and he was achingly familiar to her and yet strange at the same time.

Funny, she'd forgotten how big he was, the sheer overwhelming size of him. He was a massive man, towering over both her and Staff Billings as he reached the last step and paused just an arm's length away.

Chris tried to speak, and she had to clear her throat before she could.

"Welcome home, Corporal Quinn." Her damned voice wouldn't behave; it quavered alarmingly. She let her eyes feast on the sharply etched lines of his face, the way his razor had left his chiseled cheeks slightly raw looking above the bushwhacker's mustache, just as always. He'd always looked just that way in the mornings.

"Thank you, Constable Johnstone."

His voice seemed to have come from some spot deep in his chest, and it sounded gruff to him. Her freckles had faded over the winter, but her eyes seemed even bluer than he remembered, sapphire stars in that endearingly heart-shaped face. A renegade brown curl was sticking out from under the hat. He could hardly stop himself from bending and kissing her, but it seemed as if the whole damn town was looking on, as well as Billings.

He just might kiss her anyway. He wasn't bound by the rules of the RCMP any longer.

Quinn's eyes were sparkling now, as if she and he were sharing a private joke, but Chris didn't feel at all amused. The last time she'd seen him, his eyes had been closed and his face mushroom-white. He'd been lying on a stretcher unconscious, his blood all over her parka and her hands. There hadn't been a chance to even kiss him goodbye.... She shuddered, then tore her gaze away from him and nodded at the people watching.

"I think the mayor has a short speech he'd like to

deliver, if you'd just go over to that platform they've fixed up…''

Quinn had planned to propose to her during the first fifteen minutes, but he had to revise. There was a delay in the proceedings just then when Maisie broke away from the crowd and raced over to give him a hug and a huge, wet kiss, and then another.

In a frenzy of enthusiasm, she grabbed Staff Billings and kissed him, too, and the crowd cheered.

You had to hand it to Billings, he took it right in his stride. In fact, Quinn noticed Staff's eyes linger on the over-generous amount of bosom protruding from Maisie's tight satiny green dress.

Then Stefan nearly dislocated Quinn's arm shaking his hand, unabashed by the tears coursing down his dramatic Slavic face.

Quinn lost track of Chris for a few moments, and when he located her again she was seated sedately beside Staff Billings at one side of the platform. Quinn himself was firmly enthroned beside the impatient mayor at the other end.

The mayor's speech went on and on. People first listened attentively, then shuffled and sweated under the unseasonably warm sun, then removed parkas and even sweaters before he finally seemed to be winding down.

Quinn's heart leaped when the speech ended at last. The mayor had announced that everyone was going directly to the community center for a luncheon. Now, surely, there'd be time to talk to Chris on the drive over.…

He'd forgotten Staff Billings. Chris drove the cruiser, washed and polished and shining for occasion, Staff sat at attention beside her, with Maisie hitching a ride in the back seat. Quinn had the honor of riding with the mayor and his wife in their battered Ford station wagon.

When they arrived at the community center, there was a crush of people pressing around to shake Quinn's hand and welcome him back, and he felt overwhelmed by the rush of affection and regard being lavished upon him.

He was ensconced at the center of the head table, and the speeches began all over again. At least now everyone could have a drink or two or three while they lasted.

Staff Billings was getting impatient, because he couldn't very well make the touching and witty farewell speech he'd prepared for Quinn unless Quinn first announced his retirement.

Prodded by Billings, Quinn finally got reluctantly to his feet, and with eyes for no one except Chris, he announced that he was no longer Dawson's policeman, he was now just an ordinary citizen like anyone else.

It bothered him that Chris didn't look the slightest bit surprised or excited by his announcement. Her face was an impassive mask the whole time he talked.

Didn't she care?

The rest of Dawson certainly did. An uproar resulted, and when order was finally restored, Billings made his speech.

It was witty, complimentary, erudite…and lengthy.

When it finally ended, the food was served immediately—a magnificent sit-down dinner had been arranged by the women of the community. Quinn found himself lodged firmly between the mayor's wife and the star of the women's curling team, with Slocum Charlie and Parker across the table.

Chris seemed to be having a wonderful time laughing and sharing confidences with Maisie and Billings and Stefan, three tables away.

Quinn was losing both patience and courage at a rapid rate.

He'd been back in Dawson—he checked his watch—four hours and sixteen minutes, and he hadn't had one single instant alone with Chris.

Enough was enough.

Determinedly, he struggled away from the table, upsetting a wineglass and knocking two spoons to the floor. He began to inch his way along the wall toward her table.

Chris was aware of Quinn every single instant, of the way he bent his head attentively to listen to what the mayor's plump wife was saying, of the way he carefully scrunched his wide shoulders into the less than roomy space at the crowded table.

She saw him look over at her, and her hands clenched nervously on her wineglass when he got to his feet, eyes still on her, and began to make his way toward...

The explosion ripped through the room, sounding as if a charge of dynamite had been let off just outside the building, followed by grinding and crashing as though a giant were gnashing his teeth over Dawson.

At first Chris was too stunned to move, and by the time she was able to remember the list of rules to be followed for a bombing, her slightly tipsy Staff Sergeant identified the sound for her.

"At ease, Constable, it's just the ice going out on the river," he bellowed in her ear. His voice was barely audible above the screams and madcap hollering going on all around them, and the noise created by the chaotic pushing and shoving and racing for the door.

In six minutes, the hall was empty. Everyone went catapulting out the doors of the community center in a noisy boiling heap, off in a mad stampede to watch the Yukon River ice shift and heave and struggle in its springtime ritual, and to figure out who owed whom how much in the Yukon River sweepstakes.

Almost everyone left.

Staff Billings obligingly allowed the tide of bodies to flow around him, and then he sleepily sat back in his chair to enjoy the double whiskey he'd just been served before the exodus. The late nights were getting to him. It had been nine forty-five when he finally got to sleep last night.

He'd seen enough ice on enough rivers up here at the top of the world to last him a lifetime. Besides, he wanted to see what the dickens was going on down in the ranks between Quinn and Johnstone. He wasn't certain, but...it wasn't natural for a constable to cry as much as Johnstone had done these past weeks.

What was the force coming to? It wasn't natural for a constable to cry at all, he reminded himself sternly.

Marisa Condura was in the ladies' washroom nursing little Quintina Christina, and she naturally didn't allow anything like an explosion to interfere with such an important function. José stuck his head in the door and told her what was going on before he followed the crowd. Quintina smiled groggily up at her mother, and they settled in together to finish the meal.

"Constable Chris Johnstone, I presume?" Quinn

asked, as if no one else but the two of them existed. "Are you the one who arranged this party for me?"

Chris had watched Quinn coming purposefully toward her across the empty room, and she'd gotten to her feet and moved away from where she and Billings sat so she could meet him halfway, in a space between the deserted, littered tables, under the crepe paper streamers the high school girls had used for decoration.

She looked up into his face, the rugged, powerful face that would be part of every dream until the day she died, and she thought her heart would break with wanting him.

"Oh, Quinn," she whispered despairingly. "I didn't want to put you through all this, it just sort of got away on me. I wanted to have a chance to talk to you quietly, to..."

The hurt feelings she'd suffered earlier came to the fore, and unreasonable anger surged.

"Quinn, why couldn't you have told me you were thinking of retiring? I don't think it was fair of you to let me find out from Staff Billings. I know perfectly well how things stand between us, but the least you could have done was confide in me. Here I've been doing my level best to hold this detachment together for you, just so everything would be perfect when you took charge. It hasn't been easy. And now..."

She hadn't changed one bit.

She was still feisty, aggressive and adorable.

Difficult, headstrong and willful.

Life wasn't going to be easy with her, but he'd always liked a good scrap anyway.

He watched with delight as he saw the same righteous indignation he'd observed on her face hundreds of times before, and he remembered the day she'd locked him in his own cells.

He reached out and put one large palm over her mouth, stifling the flow of indignant words.

"I sold my book, Chris."

Her eyes grew wide and then filled with incredulous pleasure. She moved his hand away from her mouth impatiently.

"Oh, Quinn. Oh, that's just super. I'm so happy for you." Tears sparkled in her shiny eyes, and she said softly, "Abe would be so proud."

Quinn nodded, and they were quiet together, remembering the good times.

Then he said abruptly, "Staff Billings says you've requested a transfer. Any idea where?"

What did it matter? She shook her head, and the familiar sick feeling came over her when she thought of being somewhere Quinn wasn't.

"I've decided not to do any more undercover work," she said slowly. "It stopped being an exciting game to me, back there on that hill…when you…"

This time, he only placed a gentle finger on her lips to silence her.

"Good thing, because we'd have some royal battles over it if you tried," he said matter-of-factly. "Having an RCMP commissioner for a wife is one thing, but having an undercover agent…" He shook his head. "A man has to draw the line somewhere."

She was afraid to believe what she thought he was saying.

"Quinn, are you asking me, are you telling me, do you want me…"

"Don't you know a Mountie always gets her man?"

In the background, Staff Billings jerked awake for a moment, cleared his throat and said impatiently, "Come, come, Quinn, get on with it, man. Upward and on," but Chris and Quinn ignored him.

Slowly, amid the crumpled paper cups and giddy streamers, the cigarette butts and discarded napkins, Quinn sank to his knees, and formally proposed to the RCMP constable, who stood resplendent in her formal red serge.

She was crying again, but she accepted.

There's something for everyone...

Behind the
Red Doors

From favorite authors

Vicki Lewis Thompson

Stephanie Bond

Leslie Kelly

A fun and sexy collection about the romantic encounters
that take place at The Red Doors lingerie shop.

**Behind the Red Doors—
you'll never guess which one leads to love...**

Look for it in January 2003.

HARLEQUIN®
Makes any time special ®

A "Mother of the Year" contest brings
overwhelming response as thousands of women
vie for the luxurious grand prize....

Kate Hoffmann

Jacqueline Diamond

Jill Shalvis

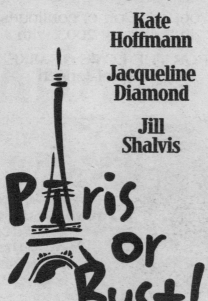

Paris or Bust!

A hilarious and romantic trio of new stories!

With a trip to Paris at stake, these women are
determined to win! But the laughs are many as three of
them discover that being finalists isn't the most
excitement they'll ever have.... Falling in love is!

Available in April 2003.

HARLEQUIN®
Makes any time special®

COOPER'S CORNER

Cooper's Corner continues in February 2003 with

FOR THE LOVE OF MIKE!
by Muriel Jensen

Check-in: The cozy Twin Oaks B and B—the perfect retreat for single dad Michael Flynn to kick back with his two young daughters...and their St. Bernard. Single mom Colleen O'Connor had the same idea for her and her two little boys...and their Siamese cat. Bad combination!

Checkout: Soon Mike and Colleen found themselves fighting...their attraction!

HARLEQUIN®
Makes any time special ®

Visit us at www.cooperscorner.com

CC-CNM